LOVE

TROUBLE

Love Trouble

NEW AND COLLECTED WORK

Veronica Geng

A Mariner Original

HOUGHTON MIFFLIN COMPANY
BOSTON NEW YORK
1999

Library of Congress Cataloging-in-Publication Data

Geng, Veronica.
Love trouble : new and collected work / Veronica Geng.
p. cm.
"A Mariner original."
ISBN 0-395-94557-7
1. United States — Social life and customs — 20th century — Fiction. 2. Humorous stories, American. 3. Satire, American. I. Title.
PS3557.E425L68 1999
813'.54—dc21 98-47177 CIP

Book design by Anne Chalmers
Typeface: Linotype-Hell Electra

Printed in the United States of America

QUM 10 9 8 7 6 5 4 3 2 1

Grateful acknowledgment to Frederick Barthelme for the drawings of failed neckties on pp. 49–50, and to Carlos Clarens for photo research. Photos on pp. 20—29 from Photothèque and Jerry Ohlinger's Movie Material Store, Inc.

"The Revised Dictionary of Slang and Uncontrollable English" was published in somewhat different form under the title "Prime Time Terms" in *The Eighties: A Look Back*, edited by Tony Hendra, Christopher Cerf, and Peter Elbling (Workman Publishing Company, Inc., New York). Copyright © 1979 United Multinationals, Inc.

"Macdonald" was originally published in slightly different form as the introduction to *Parodies: An Anthology from Chaucer to Beerbohm — And After* (Da Capo Press, New York). Copyright © 1985 Dwight Macdonald.

The lines from Howard Moss's poem "Remains" that appear in the journal entry for "A Lot in Common" are reprinted with the permission of Atheneum Publishers, an imprint of Macmillan Publishing Company, from *Notes from the Castle* by Howard Moss. Copyright © 1979 Howard Moss.

Some of these pieces originally appeared in *American Film, Gentleman's Quarterly, Harper's Magazine*, the *New Republic*, the *New York Review of Books*, the *New York Times Book Review*, *The New Yorker, Not the New York Times*, and *Soho News*.

Contents

Introduction by Ian Frazier xi

I PARTNERS (1984)

Report from Your Congressman 3
Lulu in Washington 8
My Mao 14
Ten Movies That Take Women Seriously 19
The Sixth Man 29
Partners 32
Buon Giorno, Big Shot 34
A Man Called José 36
Petticoat Power 39
What Makes Them Tick 45
More Mathematical Diversions 47
James at an Awkward Age 52
Teaching Poetry Writing to Singles 55
The Stylish New York Couples 60
Masterpiece Tearjerker 62
Serenade 67
Curb Carter Policy Discord Effort Threat 76
Kemp, Dent in Reagan Plans 77

The Reagan History of the United States 80
Pac Hits Fan 84
The Sacred Front 87
The Revised Dictionary of Slang and Uncontrollable English 102
Coming Apart at the Semes 105
Record Review 112
Indecent Indemnity 116
Now at West Egg 124
Supreme Court Roundup 126
Lobster Night 129
Pepys's Secret Diaries! 136

II LOVE TROUBLE IS MY BUSINESS (1988)

The New Thing 141
Tribute 146
Love Trouble Is My Business 149
Totaled 152
Secret Ballot 155
Our Side of the Story 159
Macdonald 164
For Immediate Release 168
Canine Château 174
The Buck Starts Here 180
Settling an Old Score 182
The Twi-Night Zone 193
Codicil 200
The 1985 Beaujolais Nouveaux: Ka-Boum! 203
Equal Time 207
Remorse 210
Mario Cabot's School Days 215

What Happened 219
Hands Up 224
More Unwelcome News 226
Poll 234
My and Ed's Peace Proposals 238
Pat Robertson's Catalogue Essay for a New Exhibition of Paintings by David Salle 240
A Lot in Common 244

III NEW STORIES (1987–1996)

Not an Endorsement 255
Man and His Watch 258
Summer Session 261
My Ideal 268
Nowhere to Run 272
Post-Euphoria 278
Salt of Life 281
Faculty Lounge Surveillance Tapes 287
The Cheese Stands Alone 290
Prime Suspects, U.S.A. 292
Testing, Testing . . . 295
Makes the Going Great 297
A Good Man Is Hard to Keep: The Correspondence of Flannery O'Connor and S. J. Perelman (*with Garrison Keillor*) 300
My Dream Team 304
La Cosa Noshtra 310

Editor's Note

The first two parts of this volume, "Partners" and "Love Trouble Is My Business," were originally published as books of the same titles in 1984 and 1988, respectively. The order of these stories is the author's own. The fifteen pieces of writing in Part III, "New Stories," are arranged here in chronological order and are collected for the first time. They originally appeared in *Harper's Magazine*, the *New Yorker*, the *New York Review of Books*, and the *New York Times Book Review*. We have not included the author's many significant reviews of movies and books. Thanks are owed to the Wylie Agency and to James Hamilton for their help in assembling *Love Trouble*.

PAT STRACHAN

Introduction

Veronica and I used to make fun of introductions like this. As she mentions on page 168, we used to trade dumb phrases we had culled from introductions to humor anthologies. We even kept lists of them. We kept all kinds of lists—of funny jobs, of overused comic key words like "schnauzer" and "rutabaga," of weird places in news stories where bodies had turned up ("in a crawlspace," "in a steamer trunk," "in a shallow open grave in Rambouillet forest near Paris")—but I seem to have lost the dumb-phrases-from-humor-anthologies list. The only phrase that survives is the one she remembers: "With tongue firmly planted in cheek." The excessive wryness of it still makes me shudder. So I proceed under a certain constraint here, afraid of falling into with-tongue-firmly-planted-etc. writing.

Also, I'm constrained by her (possibly strongly disapproving) voice in my head. Veronica not only wrote humor pieces; for years she edited them in the fiction department of the *New Yorker* magazine. She was the best editor of humor pieces I have ever worked with, and one of the best editors, period. She could take a shard of a humor piece and offhandedly sketch the missing remainder, leaving you, the writer, with the fun and easy job of filling it in and collecting a nice paycheck along the way. What she might think of something I write remains prominent in my judgment of it even today. I wrote humor pieces specifically for her to read, and when she didn't like them, as happened sometimes, I would be depressed for days and consider radical revisions of my entire life in order to make myself funny again.

She probably would not mind that I feel constrained here, though. As she also mentions, she liked the constrained voice, with its tentative sentences teetering above self-doubt. Her way of listening for the real intention below the words made her scary to talk to sometimes. The occasional long pauses she let fall before responding in a conversation inflamed my dread, as I waited for my disguise to be seen through and my bluff to be called. But she liked heedless sincerity, too—the blurted statement with all niceties of discourse thrown aside. I used to blurt things to her now and then. Once I blurted that I loved her, and she laughed at me, correctly; what I felt wasn't exactly love, but more a younger sibling's hero worship. Veronica wrote pieces of the highest literary ambition and complexity that were also so funny they could make you laugh out loud. The ability to do that is as remarkable as being able to hit a major-league curve ball, although statistically more rare.

Her writing came directly from her life, and these pieces taken together have the character of an autobiography. Her childhood is here, and her parents, her brother, her college, her early years in New York City, her enthusiasms, her friends, the later years on the *New Yorker*. She never set out to have such a largeness of scale in her work, however. She distrusted literary aspirations for the larger form and the grander theme, and avoided them. Having such aspirations myself, I once asked her why she didn't write a novel. She said, "Why does everybody tell me to write a novel? I don't *want* to write a novel! I like the pieces I'm writing now." Her devotion to the humorous piece of indeterminate, shortish length remained thorough and unwavering. She had a rent-controlled apartment on East 64th Street in Manhattan and few financial responsibilities, and didn't need the big book advances or screenplay payments that can lead you in over your head. Her focus of purpose had a lot to do with her skill at what is, after all, an epigrammatic genre. And this skill produced so many funny sentences that will last, such as "Her previous marriage ended in pharmaceuticals."

In her story "A Lot in Common," the narrator describes how, when she was a girl, she and her friend Marie used to go to the park and draw women in spike heels and seamed stockings. Once when we were talking about what we used to draw when we were kids, Veronica did that drawing for me. Repetition had apparently honed the image down to just a single foot in a high, spike-heeled shoe. I remember the careful three-dimensionality of the high heel, the square reinforced part of the stocking at the back, the straightness of the seam, the slightly blunted point of the toe. She drew this image with complete authority, precision, and style. Some kids draw a particular cartoon character over and over, or spaceships or cars or machine guns; Veronica drew that high-heeled shoe. Later she did another drawing for me that included the entire woman, not just the foot. But the foot alone was somehow better. The clarity and luminosity of this one detail suggested a limitless range of possibilities, a romantic sense of elusiveness beyond anything you could draw.

She had read everything, it seemed, and she also knew ballet, opera, painting, baseball, movies. (When George Balanchine was directing the New York City Ballet, for weeks at a time she went to the ballet every evening.) Some writers fear influence, and avoid reading certain books because they think that other voices might infect and overpower their own; Veronica welcomed it. Her writing is a party of influences, a rarefied mingling of all kinds of voices. Audible through much of her writing is the echo of Henry James, whose work she knew in her bones. But she could tune in voices from all over the literary map—voices of S. J. Perelman and William Faulkner and Alexander Zinoviev and Pauline Kael and Roland Barthes and Samuel Pepys and Donald Barthelme and many others. What really impressed me about Veronica was her ear for the sound of an official kind of American authority. Her father was a career Army officer in the quartermaster corps, and the family moved with him to different postings in Europe and the United States. Veronica absorbed the speech of confident Americans telling people what to do. She knew all of this voice's nuances, from its highest-flown bureaucratese to its most basic slang. (The phrase "mox-nix juice" is an example of the latter that I can't get out of my head, even though I still don't know what it means.) The overbearing American guy voice is perhaps the one Veronica knew best of all.

I see now that I was not as helpful a friend to Veronica as I might have been, and that in particular I underestimated or avoided thinking about the force of anger in her writing. She could be playful with the overbearing-guy voice, and she sometimes even celebrated it, as in the part about Lyndon Johnson in her story "Settling an Old Score." More often, though, she fiercely mocked it. Her contempt for it, and for other contemporary stupidities, was withering. Often her writing was the purest satire, in the sense that its preferred outcome would be for its object to fall down dead. In recent years, written humor has been pretty much domesticated to the 750-word piece on a magazine's back page—the "parting shot" school of humor, whose purpose is to leave the contented reader with a smile. Almost alone, Veronica kept alive a style of humor that is far more challenging and dangerous and uncongenial. Her writing stood in the path of certain steamrolling voices of power, and with a flick of a finger turned them upside down. She just understood better than the rest of us how coercive, how oppressive, such voices can be.

She was an unfailingly brave writer. She followed the idea that was in her head and never let extraneous circumstances deflect her from it or push her around. In the writing process itself she was enterprising, inventive, and persistent almost beyond belief. If she saw promise in a piece, she would pursue it for months, even years, until she finally got it to work. Nowadays there's a widespread and mistaken notion that the writer is a variety of high-level service employee providing text for one boss or another at the ringing of a phone; Veronica showed that a writer thrives only outside captivity and in the solitude of her own ideas.

Like artful stage machinery, the virtues Veronica brought to her writing remain invisible behind it. Most striking about her pieces still is how effortless and just-happened-upon they seem. The point of a humor piece, finally, is that it defy gravity, that it dance. One after the other, Veronica's pieces do. Whether she is one of the greatest humor writers ever, it may be too soon to say. Rereading her, I believe she is. "La Cosa Noshtra," the last piece she wrote and the last in this collection, has a voice as perfectly tuned, an erudition as fine, a sense of comedy as precise as in any humor piece I know. When I got to the end of it, my sadness that she is gone was overwhelmed by admiration for the work she left. I read her last paragraph, her last line, over and over in laughing wonderment. Then—and you might do this, too—I went back to page one and began again.

IAN FRAZIER

I

Partners
(1984)

Report from Your Congressman

Dear Constituent:

As the new year is evidently under way, I am completing a nearly striving-packed decade as your full-time Representative in Washington, D.C. I want you to know how firmly I have urged you to support me, and how deeply I appreciate the authority you have vested in me to exceed my authority. As your Representative, I played a cameo role in last year's Legislative Session, during which a substantial number of new laws were enacted under or near my sponsorship or with my vigorous opposition. Here are some highlights:

- toughened penalties against juveniles who escape from middle-income housing
- outlawed lethal incentives
- streamlined "Saturday Night Special" judicial-selection procedures
- mandated pending evaluation
- simulated energy

As your full-time Representative, I have been fully concerned with expanding my priority concerns. Here are some focal points:

- teenage grand juries
- turnstile preservation
- costly and inefficient urban coalitions
- "head shops" at consulates and missions to U.N.

- transportation bootlegging
- subhuman conditions in Off-Track Betting parlors
- no-fault gang warfare
- gene-splicing discounts for senior citizens
- fiasco control
- clearinghouse habitability
- ombudsman repatriation

UGLY PROBLEM

Until recent years, the ugly problem of absentee housing has been virtually ignored. Now a full-page report prepared by my staff shows that "ugly problem" is merely one of those sociological euphemisms.

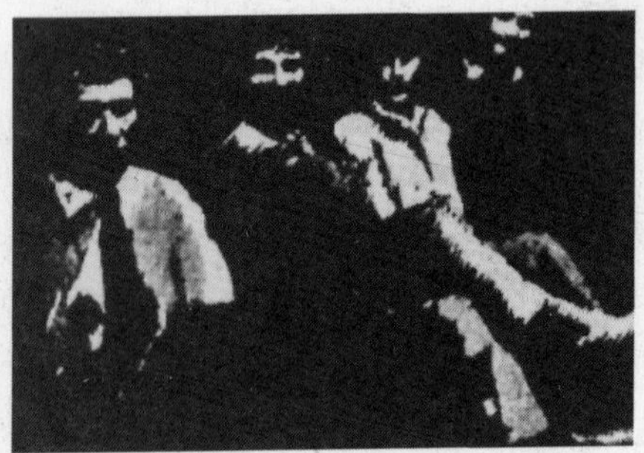

My full-time family has been a source of great strength to me during my years in the House. L. to r.: My family.

TRIGGER LEVELS OF UNEMPLOYMENT: ALBATROSS OR SAFETY NET?

Amid some unemployment, from men to women, such problems are offset by a situation that is serious but not critical, yet nonetheless stops short of complete success. Not only have unemployment figures belied employment but also employment has not prevented unemployment. It is imperative that we note that the battle seems to go on without end. Recent events would indicate that it does.

On December 3rd, I telephoned the Bureau des Élections in Paris to ask whether the French government intended to hold full, free, and democratic elections in the near future, as promised. Seated next to me are full-time executives of the Bell Telephone Company, which placed the long-distance call.

A SENSATIONAL PLACE

Individual efforts directed against the specter of federal takeover of private businesses *can* succeed. On December 15th, district resident John Occupant tasted victory when John's Restaurant opened to the public after a series of meetings with accountants and wholesalers from the area. On a full-time study of the location, I saw the fine comments which informed and articulate local spokespersons inscribed on photographs decorating the walls of this community project:

- Dear Johnny, You've been fabulous. Thank you for your hospitality.
- John's has the BEST Italian food!
- To Johnny, with love and appreciation.
- To John, Mucho aloha!
- John: And to think I weighed 90 pounds when I met you!
- To John: What a fun dinner. Kindest regards always.

TV APPEARANCE

On Sunday, December 23rd, I gave an interview on the NBC program *NewsNewsNews.* Following is a brief excerpt from the transcript ("A" is the voice of your Congressman):

Q: A lot of people are against it.
A: Well, I must say, Bill, particularly as a Congressman, people can be for or against a lot of things—
Q: Are you for or are you saying you're against it?
A: —and some of their reasons, you know, some of them have some merit.
Q: Now, what is your position?
A: Yeah, I mean, not only that but I want to emphasize repeatedly, Bill, that we frankly just don't have the answer, though, to that, as yet. And we wouldn't in Red China be able to have this full, free, and open discussion, by the way. And Bill, I want to congratulate you for asking me. The questions have been just brilliant.
Q: Well, it is certainly no secret that you have been a guest in our studio today.

EFFORT PAYS OFF

I am pleased to announce that U.S. Customs officials at JFK International Airport recently confiscated a quantity of Genoese bobbin lace concealed between the pages of a copy of *Childe Harold's Pilgrimage,* by George Gordon, Lord Byron.

QUESTIONNAIRE

This month's question relates to rumor dispelment. Which of the following strategies would you support?

- ❑ fire into the air
- ❑ fire over the heads of the crowd
- ❑ fire in the neighborhood of the core group

- ❑ bomb only those using legibly written or typed provocative remarks
- ❑ pump five bullets into the rumor itself

LATIN AMERICA

Earlier this month I visited the southern cone of Latin America, where I enjoyed touring the Avalanche of Smut. I also renewed contact with the many fine full-time Latin American contacts I maintain through an unofficial instrumentality in corporate form. While we cannot expect to find a complete solution at the federal level, I was heartened by the response from a Chilean general. Under my questioning, he admitted, "You see, there are no guns here. We are throwing them all into the desert."

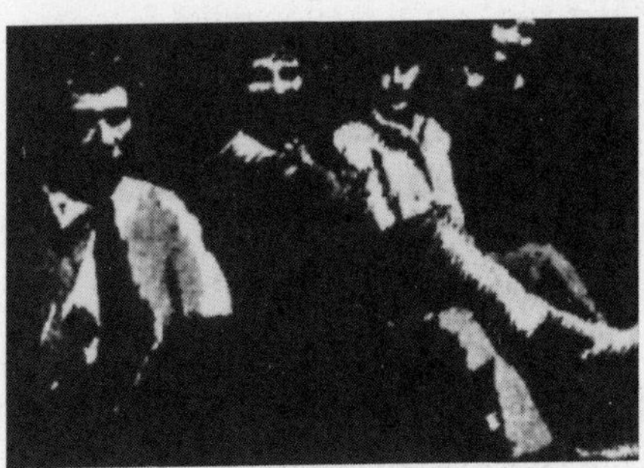

In a spontaneous gesture, I visited my personal family in the hospital.

THE UPCOMING ELECTION

Whoever my opponents will be, their records as legislators and as persons who were active during the Nixon Administration will raise questions. There is already a growing and, I believe, dangerous tendency. A lack of leadership is no substitute for inaction. That's why I challenged all of my opponents *last* year—in head-to-head debate, singlehandedly.

What kinds of things worry you? Probably the same things that worry me. Hopes. Dreams. Major thrusts. The night after I first took the oath of office, nine years ago, I dreamed that someone suggested I go somewhere or buy some tickets to something. By now, I have learned how to meet tough positions head on. That's why I want full-time to continue to serve you in the House of Representatives. There is much more to be said. Please vote for me so that I can say it.

RECYCLED ON PRINTED PAPER

Lulu in Washington

> And so I have remained, in cruel pursuit of truth and excellence, an inhumane executioner of the bogus, an abomination to all but those few people who have overcome their aversion to truth in order to free whatever is good in them.
>
> —Louise Brooks, *Lulu in Hollywood*

One evening in January 1929, while I was reading a book at supper in the expensive Park Avenue apartment of an ugly, vulgar banker, I received an urgent cablegram from J. Edgar Hoover, asking me to appear in a clandestine film of a sex party among government officials. The offer I did not consider unusual. I had never truckled to convention, having learned early to face the fact that I would always be disgusted by a society which had a social mentality. Nor had I any idea that other actors submitted to the enslavement of performing, like monkeys, with a public in mind. Due to a mere accident of birth, which at the time I took no notice of, I was erotically irresistible to both men and women, but false humility was a gift I had been denied. I never knew how to suppress my scorn for actors who, sheeplike, could awaken lust only in that mooing, ravenous herd which must buy its sensations with nickels obediently shelled out at the box office. The pistol of my talent I fired straight at my own heart. And so, when the banker cautioned me that my eagerness to abandon Broadway and Hollywood for Mr. Hoover's private venture might be a self-delusion, I could only reflect how little he had bothered to learn about me as I lay reading in his bedroom every night.

I had always been abnormally truthful, though it never occurred to me to be vain about it. My integrity, like my sexual beauty, came so naturally that I was quite mystified by the attention it drew if I happened to mention it. Thus it was that the banker's presumption in questioning my self-knowledge, which I specialized in, I saw through as a pathetically ill-disguised alibi for keeping me in New York as his private property to flatter his ego. I left for Washington, packing only his first editions. Having often told him he was too stupid to appreciate them, I could not be so sanctimonious as to leave them in his possession.

Half a century later, a Southern boy who came to my hotel room canvassing for Jimmy Carter was shocked when I gave him a few sense impressions of what Washington had been like between the wars. Seeing him then adjust his clothing in a nervous, puritanical way, and unwilling to be taken for one of those women who like to seduce young men with lying promises of pleasure, I laid out some facts in a cold, joyless manner. At the Adlon-on-the-Potomac, the hotel where I stayed in Washington in 1929, the coffee shop was headquarters for the local pimps, readily identifiable by their loose-leaf "briefing books." Tramps dabbled their aching feet in the big Reflecting Pool, while just across the gardens Constitution Hall offered, for a price, a choice of buxom or flat-chested Daughters of the American Revolution. Round and round the Ellipse strolled lobbyists whose black leather shoes advertised sadomasochism. Farther east, off Capitol Hill, Supreme Court clerks who to my knowledge had never opened a book held sixteenth-century-death-cult orgies at the Folger Shakespeare Library. Literally a slave market was the so-called Senate, where one day from the Visitors' Gallery I saw a peroxide-blond lesbian German tourist auctioned off, by a Senator from California, to a constituent from Paramount Pictures. (I was the only person not startled with disbelief when I realized, years later, that the buyer had been Paramount's young director Josef von Sternberg. His "discovery" of the woman, in 1930, in Germany, as "Marlene

Dietrich," was the fraud I had known must be at the bottom of her curious stardom, which was so baffling.)

These hypocrites, along with certain respectable citizens of the type who hated me and spent their weekends in the National Gallery pretending to ogle the culturally acceptable repression of second-rate quattrocento madonnas, were quite predictably outraged when a leak to the press, which I never had anything to do with, confronted *tout* Washington with an all too accurate image of itself in the title of our film, *D.C. Sex Party*.

The tragedy of a girl too unflinchingly honest to aspire to anything more than passive amorality: our theme was no less than that of Sophocles' *Antigone* and Ziegfeld's *Weimar Golddiggers of 1922*. Only the dull brains of carrion-mongering "columnists," who, being illiterate, disliked me, could have conceived the rumor that *D.C. Sex Party* was a crude, hasty improvisation designed merely to give J. Edgar Hoover embarrassing footage with which to blackmail his enemies in the Administration. On the contrary, the Director, as Hoover was called by the entire cast and crew, had for years contemplated the material of *D.C. Sex Party*, turning over and over in his mind its disturbing scenes of a woman's erotic degradation at the hands of influential men until each image burned with an unbearable clarity that sought discharge on film.

The great paradox of the Director's genius was that having so little worldly experience, he had acquired by compensation an uncanny power for obsessive focus on some humbly observed fact. His method was to force the fact's banal sterility into cruel bloom, releasing the clean aroma of the awful truth. This I learned the very first day of shooting, when the lesbian character called Dolly Madison was supposed to pursue me, in the "Cabinet" scene, through a *Caligari*-like maze of vertiginously angled and teetering FBI fingerprint files. Unaware then that the Director had not married, I took one look at the foul, clumsy harridan cast as Dolly and at once concluded that she was his wife. After all, this sort of nepotism was universal practice in Hollywood, and why else would he have chosen her when he could have used Garbo, Dietrich, Lillian Gish, or any of the other butch types who were by that time desperate for work, their inexplicable popularity having been mercilessly sabotaged by the studios?

Just before the first take, the Director led me aside and whispered shyly, "Look, Loo-loo, just do whatever it is they say you—you know—do." I was astonished. Hollywood directors gave an actor reactions to fake and floor marks to hit, as if from a printed list; preened themselves on artistic ideals which remained inscrutable and stole the shirt off one's back. I called them the Chinese Laundrymen. So suddenly awarded my freedom by the Director, I instinctively drew on the full energy of my natural indifference, and unerringly played the whole "pursuit" slumped against a cabinet labeled "D—Dillinger."

But the Director I had underestimated. Dolly, taken aback at my failure to put up any resistance, which in a single stroke had undercut her most effective scene, glanced briefly past me to make sure the camera was still rolling (it was) and then throttled me. Writhing frantically under those huge, hairy hands, I met "her" gaze and realized I was looking into the eyes of Secretary of State Henry Stimson in a dress. Whereupon I, in a rage at having been duped—I, who asked, and gave, nothing but the truth!—stripped his fingers from my throat and violently forced them again and again onto a nearby ink pad and fingerprint form. And so it was that the Director not only furthered his grand design but liberated in me a dynamism I had always secretly known I possessed.

Stimson, who ever after detested me, quit the picture in a huff, so I suggested that the Director replace him with Humphrey Bogart, who at the time happened to be working just a few blocks away as a hustler at Union Station. Despite Humphrey's loathing for me, I was the first to claim that he had once been the greatest dramatic actor of an otherwise pitiful bunch. His limits, though, were keenly exposed when he appeared with someone like Bojangles Robinson or Fred Astaire, who easily blew him off the screen with their almost musical quality. Sadly, Humphrey's work had turned to rubbish after I lost interest in him. However, certain that he had retained his talent for cross-dressing, I longed to see him in marabou-trimmed mules in the scene where Dolly was to discover me with my head in the lap of the

Congressional page. Decades later, D. W. Griffith disagreed with me, saying that alongside me Bogart "would have looked too phony," and I had to concede that audiences always felt he was in some sense playing a part. Anyway, the economy-minded Director omitted the remainder of Dolly's role and went on to shoot the "Cabinet" sequence, in which, slashed with jagged shadows prefiguring my murder by the head of the General Accounting Office, I permitted my flesh to receive the fingerprints of Commerce, Labor, Navy, War, and Treasury.

Off the set, the Director stringently curtailed my behavior. That I was told to keep early hours, however, did not dissuade me from slipping out of my room one evening. After the first hard week of work, I longed for a promenade down Pennsylvania Avenue to investigate the nightclubs around the Marine Barracks in a flimsy concoction of silk threads and sequins which had cost a friend of mine five thousand dollars. The coast was clear, but going down the hotel stairs I found my path blocked by the Director, whose sixth sense could penetrate the very walls. On the spot he gruffly telephoned the wardrobe mistress: "Get Loo-loo three of the suits." The next day, all my own beautiful dresses were taken away and replaced with white Arrow shirts, black neckties, and shapeless jackets and trousers of some cheap black cloth. In tears, I protested to the Director: "I can't go out in these! No one will know that under all these clothes I am naked."

"*You* will," he said.

Thereafter, inflamed by imaginative truth, my powers were fully at the service of the Director.

The only time I saw the Director crack a smile was the day he heard me tell Secretary of the Treasury Andrew Mellon that a lifelong habit of candor made me helpless to hide my contempt for his social-climbing affectations and Neanderthal mug. Taking me aside, the Director again turned one of my unfocused instincts to profitable purpose: "Loo-loo, have you noticed that every time you talk about your integrity, people reach for their wallets?"

The day after we wrapped the picture, of whose fate I never heard anything, the press jackals roused themselves from a sated slumber to report in lurid detail the murder of Vicki, the dear little redheaded script girl who had been the only person on the set I ever saw reading. I recalled that she had slept with the House Majority Leader during location shooting of the "Congressional junket" sequence in Atlantic City. During those few days, in February, the pounding gray fists of the ocean had seemed to me, like Vicki's puny affair, somehow chill and unloving. Her body was found, violated and dismembered, in a wooded area near Washington's Zoological Park, where only the roars and squawks of inhuman animals penetrated.

The incontrovertible fact of this real girl's unfortunate end was all that remained of *D.C. Sex Party* as far as I was concerned, and perhaps was what most needed to be remembered, proving as it did everything I had ever said. Whether the public accepted this proof I know not, but at any rate they talked of the "Vicki case" and nothing else until the stock market crashed. The reels of film, for all anyone cared, might as well have been thrust into the briefcase of some bureaucrat who, driving home from work, chucked them to the bottom of the Potomac.

The future would be more generous, which it is easy to be when at odds with the truth. But let people think whatever they want; no longer can I be bothered to carp at such tributes as this, from a recently revised encyclopedia of film:

> No negative or print of *D.C. Sex Party* is believed to exist, except for several frame enlargements of fingerprints, said to be in the secret files of J. Edgar Hoover. Nor can reviews or press releases be found, perhaps because there was some vague, now long-forgotten scandal about the death of a female crew member. Yet, like the other lost works of the silent era, *D.C. Sex Party* was undoubtedly a titanic masterpiece of cinematic sublimity which we will never, never be able to see with our own eyes, remaining deprived for all time of a truly great classic and thus insuring it a permanent place in motion-picture history and criticism. According to persons who viewed the daily rushes, the film established Hoover as an artist at once enigmatic and technically peerless, with a manneristic style that juxtaposed filaments and whorls of darkness and light to create a pictorial and spatial universe in whose very falsity lay its profound mystery and beauty. Deceptively tawdry in outline, Hoover elicited performances of such baroque stylization and intensity that their

splendor plumbed the most Jacobean surfaces of the human soul. That of Lulu, in particular, was a triumph of artifice.

My Mao

"Kay, would you like a dog? . . ." Ike asked.
"Would I? Oh, General, having a dog would be heaven!"
"Well," he grinned, "if you want one, we'll get one."

—*Past Forgetting: My Love Affair with Dwight D. Eisenhower*

"I don't want you to be alone," he said after a while.
"I'm used to it."
"No, I want you to have a dog."

—*A Loving Gentleman: The Love Story of William Faulkner and Meta Carpenter*

Why this reminiscence, this public straining of noodles in the colander of memory? The Chairman despised loose talk. Each time we parted, he would seal my lips together with spirit gum and whisper, "Mum for Mao." During our ten-year relationship, we quarreled only once—when I managed to dissolve the spirit gum with nail-polish remover and told my best friend about us, and it got back to a relative of the Chairman's in Mongolia. For one month the Chairman kept up a punishing silence, even though we had agreed to write each other daily when it was not possible to be together. Finally, he cabled this directive: "ANGRILY ATTACK THE CRIMES OF SILLY BLABBERMOUTHS." I knew then that I was forgiven; his love ever wore the tailored gray uniform of instruction.

Until now, writing a book about this well-known man has been the farthest thing from my mind—except perhaps for writing a book about someone else. I lacked shirts with cuffs to jot memorandums on when he left the room. I was innocent of boudoir electronics. I failed even to record the dates of his secret visits to this country (though I am now free to disclose that these visits were in connection with very important official paperwork and high-powered meetings).

But how can I hide while other women publish? Even my friends are at it. Betty Ann is writing *Konnie!: Adenauer in Love.* Cathy and Joan are collaborating on *Yalta Groupies.* And my great-aunt Harriet has just received a six-figure advance for *"Bill" of Particulars: An Intimate Memoir of William Dean Howells.* Continued silence on my part would only lead to speculation that Mao alone among the greatest men of the century could not command a literate young mistress.

That this role was to be mine I could scarcely have foreseen until I met him in 1966. He, after all, was a head of state, I a mere spangle on the midriff of the American republic. But you never know what will happen, and then it is not possible to remember it until it has already happened. That is the way things were with our first encounter. Only now can I truly see the details of the Mayflower Hotel in Washington, with its many halls and doors, its carpeted Grand Suite. I can feel the static electricity generated by my cheap nylon waitress's dress, the warmth of the silver tray on which I hoisted a selection of pigs-in-blankets.

Chairman Mao was alone. He sat in the center of the room, in an upholstered armchair—a man who looked as if he might know something I didn't. He was round, placid, smooth as a cheese. When I bent over him with the hors d'oeuvres, he said in perfect English but with the mid-back-rounded vowels pitched in the typical sharps and flats of Shaoshan, "Will you have a bite to eat with me?"

"No," I said. In those days, I never said yes to anything. I was holding out for something better.

He closed his eyes.

By means of that tiny, almost impatient gesture, he had hinted that my way of life was wrong.

I felt shamed, yet oddly exhilarated by the reproof. That night I turned down an invitation to go dancing with a suture salesman who gamely tried to date me once in a while. In some way I could not yet grasp, the Chairman had renewed my sense of possibility, and I just wanted to stay home.

One evening about six months later, there was a knock at my door. It was the Chairman, cheerful on rice wine. With his famous economy of expression, he embraced me and taught me the Ten Right Rules of Lovemaking: Reconnoiter, Recruit, Relax, Recline, Relate, Reciprocate, Rejoice, Recover, Reflect, and Retire. I was surprised by his ardor, for I knew the talk that he had been incapacitated by a back injury in the Great Leap Forward. In truth, his spine was supple as a peony stalk. The only difficulty was that it was sensitive to certain kinds of pressure. A few times he was moved to remind me, "Please, don't squeeze the Chairman."

When I awoke the next morning, he was sitting up in bed with his eyes closed. I asked him if he was thinking. "Yes," he said, without opening his eyes. I was beginning to find his demeanor a little stylized. But what right did I have to demand emotion? The Cultural Revolution had just started, and ideas of the highest type were surely forming themselves inside his skull.

He said, "I want to be sure you understand that you won't see me very often."

"That's insulting," I said. "Did you suppose I thought China was across the street?"

"It's just that you mustn't expect me to solve your problems," he said. "I already have eight hundred million failures at home, and the last thing I need is another one over here."

I asked what made him think I had problems.

He said, "You do not know how to follow Right Rule Number Three: Relax. But don't expect me to help you. Expect nothing."

I wanted to ask how I was supposed to relax with a world figure in my bed, but I was afraid he would accuse me of personality cultism.

When he left, he said, "Don't worry."

I thought about his words. They had not been completely satisfying, and an hour after he had left I wanted to hear them again. I needed more answers. Would he like me better if I had been through something—a divorce, a Long March, an evening at Le Club? Why should I exhaust myself in relaxation with someone who was certain to leave? Every night after work I studied the Little Red Book and wrote down phrases from it for further thought: "woman . . . certain contradictions . . . down on their knees . . . monsters of all kinds . . . direct experience."

My life began to feel crowded with potential meaning. One afternoon I was sitting in the park, watching a group of schoolchildren eat their lunch. Two men in stained gray clothing lay on the grass. Once in a while they moved discontentedly from a sunny spot to a shady spot, or back again. The children ran around and screamed. When they left, one of the men went over to the wire wastebasket and rifled the children's lunch bags for leftovers. Then he baited the other man in a loud voice. He kept saying, "*You* are not going downtown, Tommy. *We* are going downtown. *We* are going downtown."

Was this the "social order" that the Chairman had mentioned? It seemed unpleasant. I wondered if I should continue to hold out.

As it happened, I saw him more often than he had led me to expect. Between visits, there were letters—his accompanied by erotic maxims. These are at present in the Yale University Library, where they will remain in a sealed container until all the people who are alive now are dead. A few small examples will suggest their nature:

My broom sweeps your dust kittens.
Love manifests itself in the hop from floor to pallet.
If you want to know the texture of a flank, someone must roll over.

We always met alone, and after several years *dim sum* at my place began to seem kind of hole-in-corner. "Why don't you ever introduce me to your friends?" I asked. The Chairman made no reply, and I feared being pushy. We had no claims on each other, after all, no rules but the ones he sprang on me now and then. Suddenly he nodded with vigor and said, "Yes, yes." On his next trip he took me out to dinner with his friend Red Buttons. Years later, the Chairman would often say to me, "Remember that crazy time we had dinner with Red? In a restaurant? What an evening!"

Each time we met, I was startled by some facet of his character that the Western press had failed to report. I saw, for instance, that he disliked authority, for he joked bitterly about his own. No sooner had he stepped inside my bedroom than he would order, "Lights off!" When it was time for him to go, he would raise one arm from the bed as if hailing a taxi and cry, "Pants!" Once when I lifted his pants off the back of a chair and all the change fell out of the pockets, I said,

"This happens a lot. I have a drawer full of your money that I've found on the floor."

"Keep it," he said, "and when it adds up to eighteen billion yuan, buy me a seat on the New York Stock Exchange." He laughed loudly, and then did his impersonation of a capitalist. "Bucks!" he shouted. "Gimme!" We both collapsed on the bed, weak with giggles at this private joke.

He was the only man I ever knew, this pedagogue in pajamas, who did not want power over me. In conversation, he was always testing my independence of thought. Once, I remember, he observed, "Marxism has tended to flourish in Catholic countries."

"What about China?" I said.

"Is China your idea of a Catholic country?"

"No, but, um—"

"See what I mean?" he said, laughing.

I had learned my lesson.

To divest himself of sexual power over me, he encouraged me to go dancing with other men while he was away. Then we held regular critiques of the boyfriends I had acquired. My favorite, a good-looking Tex-Mex poet named Dan Juan, provided us with rich material for instruction and drill.

"What is it you like about Dan Juan?" the Chairman asked me once.

"I'd really have to think about it," I said.

"Maybe he's not so interesting," said the Chairman.

"I see your point," I said. Then, with the rebelliousness of the politically indolent, I burst into tears.

The Chairman took my hand and brooded about my situation. I think he was afraid that helping me to enter into ordinary life—to go out with Dan Juan and then to learn why I should not be going out with him and so forth—might not be very much help at all.

Finally, he said, "I don't like to think you're alone when I'm not here."

"I'm not always alone."

"I'd like to give you a radio."

The radio never reached me, although I do not doubt that he sent it. His only other gifts we consumed together: the bottles of rice wine, which we drank, talking, knowing that while this was an individual solution, it was simple to be happy. Now other women have pointed out to me that I have nothing to show for the relationship. Adenauer gave Betty Ann a Salton Hotray. Stalin gave Cathy a set of swizzle sticks with little hammer-and-sickles on the tops. William Dean Howells gave my great-aunt Harriet a diamond brooch in the form of five ribbon loops terminating in diamond-set tassels, and an aquamarine-and-diamond tiara with scroll and quill-pen motifs separated by single oblong-cut stones mounted on an aquamarine-and-diamond band. That I have no such mementos means, they say, that the Chairman did not love me. I think they are being too negative.

The Chairman believed that the most revolutionary word is "yes." What he liked best was for me to kiss him while murmuring all the English synonyms for "yes" that I could think of. And I feel to this day that I can check in with him if I close my eyes and say yes, yeah, aye, uh-huh, indeed, agreed, natch, certainly, okey-doke, of course, right, reet, for sure, you got it, well and good, amen, but def, indubitably, right on, yes siree bob, sure nuff, positively, now you're talking, yep, yup, bet your sweet A, O.K., roger wilco over and out.

Ten Movies That Take Women Seriously

1. A WOMAN WHO COULD HAVE GOTTEN MARRIED IF SHE WANTED TO

A completely happy woman (Jill Clayburgh) is told by her lover (Alan Bates) that he has no choice but to shoot her so that he will feel free to marry a teenage boy (Matt Dillon). Clayburgh goes underground in Soho, where she falls in love with seven supportive men in her Smoke Enders group (Robert DeNiro, Vincent Price, R. W. Fassbinder, Al Pacino, Klaus Kinski, Bruno Bettelheim, and Bob

Balaban) and builds a career as a photographer, taking pictures of a streetcorner where recently divorced women come to vomit. Totally happy, she then learns that she can't be truly liberated until the men are all offered high-paying jobs in Tahiti and she can reject their proposals of marriage. Director Steven Spielberg wrings peerlessly hair-raising action sequences from the awesome quitting-smoking technology, and takes a gently wry look at the way women tend to get all weepy.

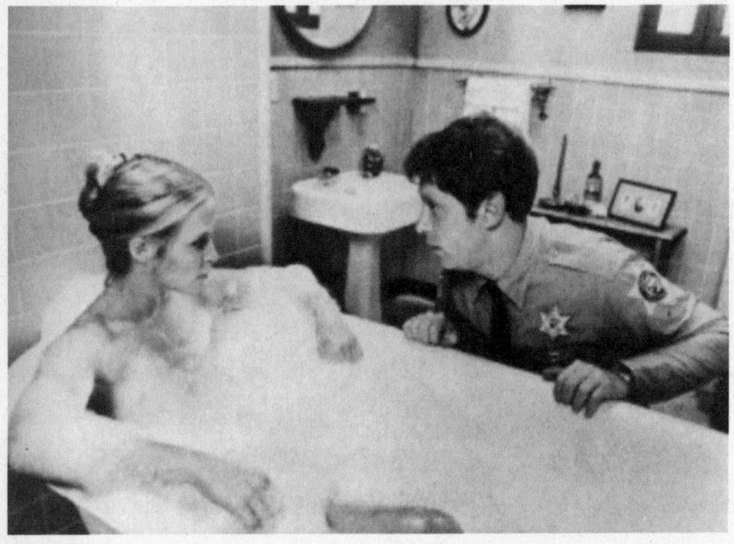

Fahrenheit 451: *Studio security guard checks a stuntwoman's bathwater for the daredevil "nervous breakdown" scene.*

2. ANNIE GET YOUR SHOGUN

Based on a nineteenth-century Australian novel about sixteenth-century Japan, adapted for the screen by Alan Alda (star of *Mr. Dalloway*). An aggressive young girl (Marlo Thomas), blackballed from a posh Melbourne men's club, asserts her independence by sailing to Kyoto and horsewhipping a samurai (Toshiro Mifune) because she doesn't like the cut of his jib. She falls in love with the American consul (Alda), but when he asks her to marry him, she refuses, because she is ornery.

Zen and the Art of Motorcycle Maintenance: *Marlo Thomas, the novice director, shows a complicated "dolly" shot to the Japanese crew.*

3. TWO OR THREE THINGS I CAN'T STAND ABOUT HER

Critic Andrew Sarris enters his own Pantheon with his first film—a responsible feminist-humanist remake of Brian De Palma's *Dressed to Kill.* An attractive, likable woman (Michael Palin) is in the shower when an inspector from the Gas Company intrudes into her bathroom and (in what alert cinéastes will recognize as a quote from Sarris's own film column) calls her "a grotesquely oversexed, middle-aged bourgeois bitch." She realizes this is true and cancels her shrink appointment to stay home and preheat the oven according to his guidelines. The Gas Man continues on his search for the ideal woman—a professor of quantum physics (Diane Keaton) who is upper-class, young, and moderately sexed.

I Lost It in the Movieola: *Ritual* hommage *to Hitchcock by director Sarris (l.) was among derivative scenes censored by humanistic lawyer for Hitch's estate (r.).*

4. INTERMISSION

In Lawrence Kasdan's stylish update of *Intermezzo*, a conventional married assistant curator at the Museum of Modern Art (Mick Jagger), once a socially conscious swinger and pop artist, falls in love with his daughter's role model (Carrie Fisher) and takes her with him as backup curator when he goes on the road with the Picasso show. The story is told visually, through closeups of Fisher's gradual cooptation as she suppresses evidence of numerous forgeries among the examples of analytical cubism. The wife (Rula Lenska) stays home and tries to get a comb through her hair, while the daughter (Jade Jagger) is run over by a car full of boisterous drug addicts in order to further disillusion the audience.

The Sacking of Troy: From the 1950s Warner Bros. remake, Intermezzo Pajama Party.

5. PORTENTIMENTO

Lillian Hellman (Mia Farrow) and Mary McCarthy (Liv Ullmann) try on hats and learn to touch-type, tutored by Dashiell Hammett (director Woody Allen) and Edmund Wilson (Pat McCormick), while Stalin (Jerry Stiller) collectivizes the Ukraine. Years later, at a screening of *Islands in the Stream,* the two women meet again and Lilly confesses that she could have married Hammett but they never got around to it.

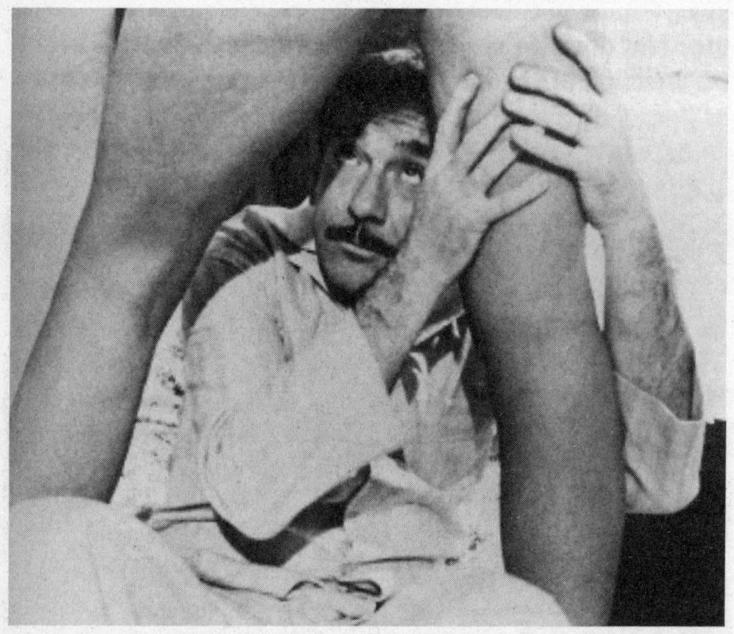

Ten Days That Shook His Confidence: *Ernest Hemingway (Jerry Stiller) debates Lillian about the Moscow Trials.*

6. WETWORK

Karen Silkwood, a glamorous, foul-mouthed female head of programming at a TV network (Faye Dunaway), who's more ruthless than Hitler (Jerry Stiller), discovers that ratings skyrocket when the idealistic spinster weather reporter she's about to fire (Jane Fonda) cries on camera while predicting a snowstorm that will cause many people to be late for work. To induce Fonda to weep nightly, Dunaway engineers a series of plutonium-plant accidents. An AEC investigator (Jon Voight) offers Fonda the ultimate in happiness—marriage—but she turns him down to prove she's incorruptible. Under the sensitive direction of George Lucas (hired because he was mistaken for "women's director" George Cukor by the busy executive producer, George Lucas), Dunaway's and Fonda's unflattering hairdos represent the full spectrum of liberated misery.

Mad as Hell: Silkwood's masterpiece, The Newly Nude Game.

7. BI MOM

In this sequel to *Kramer vs. Kramer*, Joanna (Meryl Streep) has a series of love affairs with judges from Family Court (Jill Clayburgh, Liv Ullmann, and Amy Irving), while her son, Billy (now a disturbed eighteen-year-old, played by Sylvester Stallone), sues to deny her visiting rights as an unfit mother. The suit is dropped when a kindly guru (Christopher Isherwood) invites Billy to go to India with him and get his head together. Director Robert Benton deftly delineates the growing acceptance of Joanna back into the family when, at Billy's going-away party, he and his father compare penis sizes.

Penile Colony: Billy and Dad Kramer unzip for the finale.

8. THE GROOM

Can a woman's repressed rage at men manifest itself in outbreaks of gynoculinary horror? In cult filmmaker David Cronenberg's latest shocker, a successful lonely career woman (Anne Bancroft) has an affair with a married man (Ronald Reagan), becomes pregnant, and gives birth to millions of tiny wedding-cake grooms that threaten to annihilate the greater Los Angeles area. Bancroft is tracked down and killed by a lynch party, but not before she succeeds in transferring her vengeful powers to her childhood friend (Shirley MacLaine) when, during a hair-pulling bout, the two women discover that they have split ends and their hair samples are switched by a malevolent Sassoon computer.

Urban Doughboy: John Travolta made $1 billion for achieving a multiple role.

9. THE WOMEN'S RHEUM

Six Vassar students become unwittingly involved in a secret Department of Defense experiment to test the toxicity of overstatement. The sole survivor (Patty Duke Ellington) is befriended by a lusty, free-spirited older wench (Elizabeth Taylor), who introduces her to a man strong enough to be gentle (Alan Alda). But when he is forced (by director Sidney Lumet) to present her with a choice by moving to Australia to open a medical clinic, she rejects his proposal of marriage and opts for a career in film. She moves in with a trio of supportive gay-porno stars (Dick Diver, Mao Zedong, and Francis Bacon) and makes a successful documentary, *Lenny*, proving that Leni Riefenstahl was actually a man.

Hollywood Vassarette: Professor of Modern Dance Marsha Mason (l.). Alan Alda asks, "Why is a liberated woman wearing high heels?"

10. NEXT STOP, TITLE VII

Paul Mazursky's scathing satire on the subject of sexual harassment in the office. George Segal plays an official of the Equal Employment Opportunities Commission who is sued for harassment by his own secretary (Jill Clayburgh). In a moving appeal to her to settle out of court by marrying him, Segal quotes from an article by Walter Berns in the October 1980 issue of *Harper's:* "Rather than having to devote what will surely be thousands of hours to such cases, it might be preferable to impose dress codes on female employees. . . . Men can be aroused by what women wear and, on occasion, provoked to do or say things they may later regret. . . . It is women, not men, who are ultimately responsible for what might be called the moral tone of any place where men and women are assembled, even, I think, the workplace. (Tocqueville observed this of American women 150 years or so ago, and I think it is still true.) In general, men will be what women want them to be. ('Do you want to know men?' asked Rousseau. 'Study women.') An employer's 'affirmative duty to maintain a workplace free of sexual harassment' will require that he take account of the power women have over men."

She marries him.

Ms. *Man of the Year Trophy: Animation lends credence to Mazursky's latest comedy of manners.*

The Sixth Man

> Sir Anthony Blunt, a former curator of Queen Elizabeth's art collection, and a renowned member of Britain's artistic establishment, was identified by the Government today as a long-sought "fourth man" in the Burgess-Maclean spy case of 25 years ago. . . . [A] supposed fifth man in the Burgess-Maclean spy ring [has been] identified . . . only as "Basil."
>
> —*New York Times,* November 16, 1979

The time was the nineteen-fifties—a decade, as Frederick Jackson Turner had predicted, "with the menace of the forties at one end and the menace of the sixties at the other." For thoughtful, concerned university students in the United States, participation in the Burgess-Maclean spy ring seemed the only answer.

These troubled, idealistic young Americans were a minority, certainly, but a minority that encompassed the majority of a tiny élite. Some were heterosexuals. A number were quarterbacks, and no fewer were members of prestigious dorm councils and ROTC units. The glittering set included L.A.D. (Laddie) Dirksen, the brilliant illegitimate son of the founders of the New Criticism; N. Murray Garroway, the eminent agnostic explorer, whose father was a prominent speechwriter for Harold Stassen; H. F. Zimbalist-Lazar, effete and dissipated even as a freshman, later a noted scholar and expert on the works of Jim Bishop; and K. X. Backus—a descendant of Nathaniel Hawthorne and John Singleton Copley—who became a studio musician of enormous repute.

While these men can be linked to Burgess and Maclean only by the kind of innuendo exemplified in the foregoing paragraphs, a growing chain of suspicion has been forged around them by precisely that. And now a trail of further fabrication and distortion has led to another key figure in the plot—an Englishman who emigrated to the United States in the early fifties to recruit the American group. The most clever and degenerate of them all, this long-sought "sixth man" in the case has been identified only as "Ernest."

In an exclusive interview with this magazine, an Englishwoman whom we shall call "Cecily," who knew the man as "Ernest" in London in 1951, has come forward with evidence that has been heard time and time again.

"Ernest seemed so very mysterious," she said. "If he was not, he was deceiving us all in a very inexcusable manner. I hope he was not leading a double life, pretending to be a spy and being really loyal all the time. That would be treachery.

"It was said that at Cambridge he had called himself 'Algernon,' which frightened everyone so much that they attended their lectures in groups.

"I myself was quite afraid of him. That is why I fell in love with him. There is nothing so becoming to a young girl's complexion as a love affair with someone really treasonous.

"It would hardly have been a serious affair if I had known anything about him. Facts about most people can be endured with equanimity. But even the slightest hint of information about an attractive man is almost unbearable.

"One person told me with absolute authority that he had blue eyes. Another said with equal conviction that they were brown. I know, of course, how important it is to be inconsistent if one wants to retain the opportunity for regret. But I do feel that one has an obligation to retain one's face.

"No one could discover who his tailor was, or how much tea he took with his lumps of sugar, or any of the other things that are always common knowledge about a traitor.

"There were all sorts of rumors about him. People said that he had entered a monastery and then, in remorse, gone out and killed a man. That he had been changed for life on account of never having learned that he had got a fatal disease. That he was from a very fine family and wished to conceal his origins. That he had been cashiered out of his regiment for refusing to slap his commanding officer. That he was passing for Bantu. That in Burma he had become addicted to Gentlemen's Relish. That he had had plastic surgery so as to make it appear that he had been mutilated in an automobile accident. That he wrote works of philosophy under an assumed name and cheap novels under his own name. That he had never kept a wife and six children in Tottenham. That he was a successful surgeon, while his colleagues had been ruined by fashionable malpractice suits. That he had a friend named Bunbury.

"All this, of course, was the gossip of unidentified sources, and consequently meant for publication.

"I liked his secretiveness. It allowed me to monopolize the conversation, and at the same time it enabled me to feel ill at ease. I dislike men who are as comfortable as an old shoe. They are so slippery.

"Sometimes I was happy just to gaze at him, the way one does at an improper picture. At other times, I found myself turning aside in embarrassment, the way one does from a really good book.

"Often I imagined that he might make love to me, tying me up and forcing me to perform vile acts. I felt sure that it would pass the time.

"He never said a single word about official secrets, so you can imagine how much he knew. And he was so attractive. In matters of espionage, sex, not politics, is the vital thing.

"I am quite sure that after he left me, he emigrated to America to recruit spies. He had a secret past; for him to have had a secret future as well would have been most unfair.

"I do think that whenever one has any secrets to impart to the Soviet Union, one should be quite candid.

"Whatever unfortunate entanglement my dear boy may have got into, I will never reproach him with it after he is imprisoned.

"And if Ernest was not the 'sixth man,' I feel sure that he was someone equally important."

Partners

MISS TEAS
WEDS FIANCÉ
IN BRIDAL

The marriage of Nancy Creamer Teas, daughter of Mr. and Mrs. Russell Ruckhyde Teas of Glenn Frieburg, N.Y., and Point Pedro, Sri Lanka, to John Potomac Mining, son of Mr. Potomac B. Mining of Buffet Hills, Va., and the late Mrs. Mining, took place at the First Episcopal Church of the Port Authority of New York and New Jersey.

The bride attended the Bodice School, the Earl Grey Seminary, Fence Academy, Railroad Country Day School, and the Credit School, and made her début at the Alexander Hamilton's Birthday Cotillion at Lazard Frères. She is a student in the premedical program at MIT and will spend her junior year at Cartier & Cie. in Paris.

The bridegroom recently graduated from Harvard College. He spent his junior year at the Pentagon, a military concern in Washington, D.C. He will join his father on the board of directors of the Municipal Choate Assistance Corporation. His previous marriage ended in divorce.

CABINET, DELOS NUPTIALS SET

Ellen Frances Cabinet, a self-help student at Manifest Destiny Junior College, plans to be married in August to Wengdell Delos, a sculptor, of Tampa, Fla. The engagement was announced by the parents of the future bride, Mr. and Mrs. Crowe Cabinet of New York. Mr. Cabinet is a consultant to the New York Stock Exchange.

Mr. Delos's previous marriage ended in an undisclosed settlement. His sculpture is on exhibition at the New York Stock Exchange. He received a B.F.A. degree from the Wen-El-Del Company, a real estate development concern with headquarters in Tampa.

MISS BURDETTE WED TO MAN

Pews Chapel aboard the Concorde was the setting for the marriage of Bethpage Burdette to Jean-Claude LaGuardia Case, an account executive for the Junior Assemblies. Maspeth Burdette was maid of honor for her sister, who was also attended by Massapequa Burdette, Mrs. William O. Dose, and Mrs. Hodepohl Inks.

The parents of the bride, Dr. and Mrs. Morris Plains Burdette of New York, are partners in Conspicuous Conception, an art gallery and maternity-wear cartel.

The ceremony was performed by the Rev. Erasmus Tritt, a graduate of Skidmore Finishing and Divinity School and president of Our Lady of the Lake Commuter Airlines. The Rev. Tritt was attended by the flight crew. The previous marriages he has performed all ended in divorce.

DAISY LAUDERDALE FEATURED AS BRIDE

Daisy Ciba Lauderdale of Boston was married at the Presbyterian Church and Trust to Gens Cosnotti, a professor of agribusiness at the Massachusetts State Legislature. There was a reception at the First Court of Appeals Club.

The bride, an alumna of the Royal Doulton School and Loot University, is the daughter of Mr. and Mrs. Cyrus Harvester Lauderdale. Her father is retired from the family consortium. She is also a descendant of Bergdorf Goodman of the Massachusetts Bay Colony. Her previous marriage ended in pharmaceuticals.

Professor Cosnotti's previous marriage ended in a subsequent marriage. His father, the late Artaud Cosnotti, was a partner in the Vietnam War. The bridegroom is also related somehow to Mrs. Bethlehem de Steel of Newport, R.I., and Vichy, Costa Rica; Brenda Frazier, who was a senior partner with Delta, Kappa & Epsilon and later general manager of marketing for the U.S. Department of State; I. G. Farben, the former King of England; and Otto von Bismarck, vice-president of the Frigidaire Division of General Motors, now a division of the Hotchkiss School.

AFFIANCEMENT FOR MISS CONVAIR

Archbishop and Mrs. Marquis Convair of Citibank, N.Y., have made known the engagement of their daughter, Bulova East Hampton Convair, to the Joint Chiefs of Staff of Arlington County, Va. Miss Convair is a holding company in the Bahamas.

All four grandparents of the bride-to-be were shepherds and shepherdesses.

Buon Giorno, Big Shot

This infamous man, this atrocious torturer, this felonious criminal maniac, this abscess on the loin of civilization, this VIP. This mystery man, this subjugator incomprehensibly vile, whom I have killed a thousand times in my dreams. Whom the people call Rat Excrement and Dog Scum. Whom they call Signor X.

I heard that he never gave interviews. That he would see me and then kill me and swallow my cassettes. For this reason I was afraid. For this reason I was brave.

Finally he was walking toward me, across the lobby of the Hotel Omnipotente, in Rome. God, the man is not good-looking! The shrunken goat's testicle of a face. The hands, smeared as I had been told they would be with infants' blood, each bloated finger a worm in the heart of human reasonableness. Yes, I thought, he is smaller than I expected. They are always smaller than one expects.

Let's put it this way: our interview was not charming. It was a malady that was always going ahead to termination. Do you know the sound of a wrecker's ball smashing an architectural treasure of Western Europe? His voice was like that. But I don't really want to disparage the allurements of talking to a scourge and ignoramus of the type that Signor X represents all too vividly. He seemed sincere. Sitting opposite him in the crepuscular lobby of the Omnipotente, with my tape recorder—accompanist to history—hissing its absurdist sibilants. I couldn't help thinking, Ah, if only he could desist from his sins, we could have such a damned good time together!

Q: I'm wondering if you can explain your behavior, Signor X.

A: I don't—

Q: Not so fast, Signor X. Signor X, I have to admit I am a little surprised by your precipitousness. Do you really believe it's possible to explain away—and so hastily, at that—the infinite excruciations you have inflicted?

A: Excruciations? What excruciations?

Q: Signor X, forgive me if I retain a capacity for moral outrage. Perhaps I seem infantile. Or simply noxious. I hate to be noxious, especially since you've been so punctual, since you've bought me an *aperitivo* and so forth, but I have in mind, for instance, the time you—

A: I know what you are going to say, and it's completely untrue. *Basta!* I don't have to endure these questions, these vilifications, these reproaches, which are reported so often and ad infinitum in your newspaper.

Q: *Con permesso*, Signor X, are you or are you not a Fascist hyena?

A: Of course not! Don't be silly! What a calumny! Do I look like a hyena?

Q: I think you do, Signor X. It frightens you to hear that—yes, it frightens you.
A: Nothing frightens me. For me, it's not at all a question of fear.
Q: Very well. We don't have to bicker.
A: The main question can be adduced from one point. I am a father. Italians like that. Italians like fathers—Carlo Ponti, the Holy Father, and so on. Maybe the father isn't always such a good father, maybe he is a despot and so forth, but he's in the right. In short, a father.
Q: Yes, yes, but tell me this: If I drove slivers of bamboo under your fingernails and forced you to choose between having a coffee with Jesus Christ and having a coffee with Hitler, which would you choose?
A: It's obvious, neither one. But why do you have these fantasies of persecuting me? The thought is father to the deed, when all's said and done. Yet am I such a bad man?
Q: Shall we say I'm wondering, Signor X, if you are a happy man. Are you a happy man, Signor X?
A: Happy? *Dio mio,* little girl, let's be realistic. For one moment let's get something straight. Happiness is the father of unhappiness.
Q: How many times you keep returning to this word "father," Signor X. One would almost say you have had that word on the brain during this interview!
A: So are we finished so soon? Now do me one favor. Say it.
Q: Say what?
A: You know what I mean. Say it.
Q: As you like. "You're the top, you're the Colosseum."
A: You remembered. Thank you.
Q: Thank *you,* Signor X. Thank you very much, Daddy.

A Man Called José

There was a swift, almost liquid beauty to the Neva River yesterday, as you looked at it from the seedy little bench on the Prospekt Parkway in Leningrad, but Ivan and Igor and two to three thousand other Russians were not there to see it now.

They were in Cuba, wearing uniforms and marching and being photographed from U-2s by nice kids from neighborhoods in the Bronx or Queens or the Silk Stocking District. Kids with mothers and fathers whose eyes had been red and swollen with tears of pride when their sons graduated from USAF Intelligence Aerial Reconnaissance School on the Upper West Side.

And now, 10,000 miles away from anywhere, the Neva rolled on in gaudy indifference.

Igor and Yuri and the rest of them had been talked about by an American President on all the TV sets and written up in stories by American journalists in the papers. The presses still rolled with indifferent swiftness now, and images flickered still on the grayish 22-inch screens in the bars on Bruckner Boulevard and the political clubs on Mulberry Street and on the imported Sony color Trinitrons along Lexington Avenue, but Ivan and his comrades did not know it. All they knew was marching and gaudy uniforms and overhead the U-2s passing once in a while in arcs of swollen pride.

A crumpled Silva Thins cigarette pack and a couple of barbecue-flavored chorizo wrappers blew along the Boulevard Astoria in Havana yesterday with a proud gaudiness that had a kind of beauty, but Murphy and Santini and Franklin and the others were not there to see it now.

They were in the bars that line the Whitestone Bridge and the Harlem River and the Belt Parkway exit of the Van Wyck Expressway. They had come in swift, remorseless cars, and some of them had even come proudly on foot from the homes not so far away.

The homes bought with VA loans.

At one of the bars, the floor was littered with sawdust and there were shabby scrunched-up Frito bags and a sad array of half-empty glasses on the worn brownish wood of the bar. Reflected in the mirror was a gaudy litter of half-full liquor bottles.

They were all there. All the men who had gone to school and gotten jobs and now were damned ready to have a couple of Millers or Buds. And now there was a reporter at a corner of the bar.

"How about this Soviet brigade thing?" he said.

"What the hell," said Murphy, and his voice sounded hollow and indifferent and scared for a man whose people had been immigrants a long time ago.

"Who is this guy?" said Santini.

The guy's name is Leonid Brezhnev and his name is Fidel Castro and by any name he is a gutless thug. But nobody wanted to name names in this neighborhood.

And who could blame these men with the vacant eyes for never having heard of Leonid Brezhnev and Fidel Castro? For never having read *Uncle Vanya* and *Proletarian Revolution and the Renegade Kautsky* and *Highlights of the Bolshoi?* They were thinking about whether to shoot some white people or some black people and wondering if any of it would really make a difference.

The reporter said some of this, and now a heavy man stood up and started to roll up the sleeves of the gaudy white shirt that was tucked despairingly into his gray pants at the waist.

If you believed the stories that were going around, an American President on TV had said long weeks ago that he received assurances from the Soviets that the brigade in Cuba was no combat brigade. That it was just for show. Just "a manifestation of Moscow's dominance of Cuba."

For all these men knew, that might be the truth.

But that didn't mean they weren't going to be able to defend themselves against it. Or against any other manifestation.

These people could teach something about manifestations to Brezhnev and Castro and their palookas in Moscow and Havana. Had Brezhnev ever seen a Holy Name parade on 125th Street? Had Castro ever seen a bar mitzvah at the Mineola Democratic Club, with Bessie Smith shouting her heart out and the gaudy platters of spiedini and the ward captains flourishing their tally sheets? Had Ivan and Rudi and Mischa ever seen a heavy man rolling up the sleeves of his white shirt?

On the tacky little glass-and-metal Zenith above the bar, somebody on a *Kojak* rerun said, "I've had it!"

Nobody really knew what would happen now, and that was the truest measure of a democracy.

Meanwhile, outside in the indifferent darkness, here were swollen politicians crouched squabbling over a piece of white paper with remorseless black printing on it, called SALT II.

It was time for everybody to go home.

Murphy and Krupnick and Franklin would show the reporter some moves and then go out in despair and slap their Dodge Darts and Toyota Coronas into gear.

Igor and Boris would march and be photographed and never read *The Portable Thomas Jefferson* or *The Postman Always Rings Twice.*

And a man called José would be forgotten.

It was over now.

Except for those of us who had a column to get out. And perhaps that was the greatest injustice of all.

Petticoat Power

"I find it very helpful to attend business meetings under an alias."

—Estelle Crinoline, Vice-President in Charge of Assistants at a major conglomerate

Nowadays, the fair sex functions in a managerial capacity in U.S. businesses at every level, from the lowly assistant vice-president to the top-flight vice-presidential assistant. The "gal Friday" has long since become a full-fledged deckhand, and the "steno" has made it into the ranks of flunkies to the powers that be. It is even estimated that women constitute a percentage of all egress-level managers. If you are one of them, the Sword of Damocles is beginning to swing your way, and you will soon see the time when women are promoted over better-qualified minorities and minors.

As a result, the ambitious female of the species need no longer turn furtively to the so-called execu-cosmetology schools, which dispense little more than a bow tie and a fountain pen. The following guide, based on information, should amply fill the needs of women and would-be women in business.

WHAT IS BUSINESS?

The field of business is so manifold that no single article can hope to do more than this one. In the main, however, all businesses are basically alike in their approach, and women would do well to remember the generally uniform surface of the masculine brain even as it offers openings for women.

WHAT MAKES AN EXECUTIVE?

A good executive must first be equipped with the tools of the trade. Top male execs know well the necessity for carrying in their possession at all times some form of credentials (the service revolver, tire iron, or Sword of Damocles). Women must not shrink faintheartedly from doing likewise. Moreover, credentials exist to be used. Show the credentials at once when approaching a colleague. This display lends an air of importance to the encounter; the colleague more readily believes that the meeting is a serious matter, not just casual chitchat.

The executive is also versed in the "hidden language" of the bizocracy—the fundamentals that touch every swivel chair in every corridor of power. The General Business Code, prescribed for all commercial transactions in the U.S., is transmitted by breast-pocket-handkerchief semaphore (and may in future be modernized to adopt feminine visual apparatus—e.g., the hairnet). The seven basic signals are:

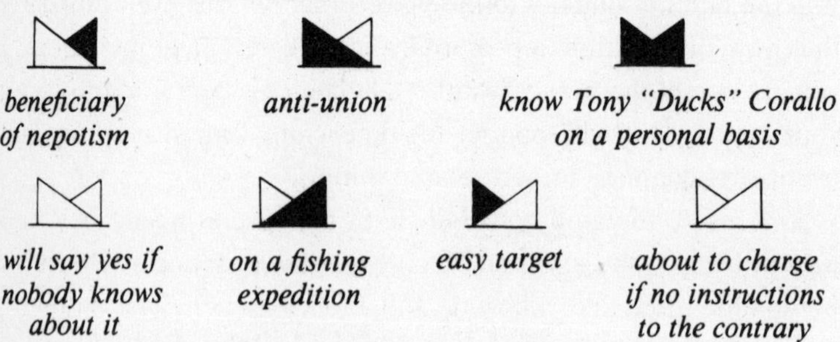

With the influx of Milady into the executive "sweet," new terms are gradually being added:

afraid of small handbags	*could help you but won't*	*cream and two sugars*	*depressed*

THE MENTOR

Having mastered these skills, the she-male in business will be served just as well—indeed, better—by attaching herself to a mentor. Every single business, no matter how similar to another, is completely different, and only through a mentor can you learn how mentorship itself works in your chosen field.

A mentor is a man who has reached a ranking position of awesome responsibility at the office; is richly dedicated to home, wife, and children; is actively involved in demanding community and leisure duties; and thus is ideally suited to spend long hours guiding a female co-worker through the intricacies of business.

The mentor is not to be confused with other paternal figures in the company, such as the doctor, proctor, loner, factor, drummer, exterminator, or mortgage shark.

The principal technique involved in finding a mentor is the stakeout. Mentors tend to gravitate toward specific loci of power, such as the shredder room. Keep a diary of their movements. (Entries should be made concurrently or afterward, never before.) Not untypical is the woman who staked out a deserted band shell, tailed the first man who appeared, and eventually followed him to his corporate headquarters, where he taught her how to build a car with her bare hands.

There are four types of mentors. As shown in the following transcriptions of videotaped experiences by distaff mentorees A, B, C, and D, each type of mentor has his characteristic way of showing you the rope:

Type 1—Inferential

A: Good morning, Bob.

MENTOR: What in the *hell* are you wearing?

A: Just a . . . a simple jumpsuit with laminated pongee undercuffs, layered with a . . . a Bavarian vest and a Ralph Lauren cow blanket.

(Mentor laughs contemptuously.)

A *(confidence seeping into her voice)*: I'm grateful for the advice, Bob.

Type 2—Insinuational

B: Have a nice weekend, Jack?

(Mentor stares in a repelled manner at her coiffure.)

B: Is something wrong with my hair?

MENTOR: If you choose to think so.

B: I'll get on it right away. And . . . Jack? *(In a newly assertive tone)* Well . . . thanks.

Type 3—Manifestational

C: I have those dioxin reports, Dick.

(Mentor leans across desk, rips the tacky costume jewelry from her throat and wrists, and tosses it disgustedly into wastebasket.)

C *(effectively)*: Deemed it inappropriate, huh? Say no more.

Type 4—Verbal

D: Morning, Ted.

MENTOR: You make a better door than a window.

D: Sorry. Did you see the *Times*?

MENTOR: Is the Pope Catholic?

D: Well . . . since it says the bond market has rallied—

MENTOR: Get off my ear.

D: —if we take into account the spillover effect from Wednesday's—

MENTOR: Can the tripe.

D: —and the new Treasury bonds' gain of—

MENTOR: Save your wind—you might want to go sailing sometime.

D: —then the prime rate—

MENTOR: That *rates* a hee-haw!

D: —but the Federal Reserve—

MENTOR: Hang crape on your nose—your brains are dead.

D: —may indicate that the tax-exempt sector is—

MENTOR: What are you—foggy in the upper story?

D: —I mean, now that the pace of new issues—

MENTOR: Go hire a hall.

D: Are you—you know—annoyed about something?

MENTOR: Pull in your head—here comes a termite.

D *(breaking out in "executive pattern" rash statistically linked to lateral thinking)*: Gee, I guess I do need a manicure. 'Preciate the grooming tip!

With the confidence you will gain through this type of interaction with a mentor, you will soon be able to take risks without fear of mistakes. Let's suppose you wish to offer a suggestion about some minor aspect of business practice:

Sample dialogue:

YOU: I was thinking, why don't we—

MENTOR: No.

YOU: But—

MENTOR: No. Go on, you were doing marvelously.

YOU: Oh, O.K. Wouldn't it make sense if we have a weekly—

MENTOR: No, absolutely not. Good girl, keep it up.

YOU: I mean, once a week, if each department—

MENTOR: *Jee-zus!* I told you, it's completely out of the question. Here, let's trade places and I'll show you how to do this.

YOU: I think I already know how to do it.

MENTOR: Of course you do. And you were doing beautifully, which is why you need someone to show you an alternative way of doing it.

YOU: Did I make a mistake?

MENTOR: Don't think about your mistakes. Don't ever think about your mistakes. Don't dwell on your mistakes. You'll make plenty of mistakes, but by no means dwell on them.

YOU: Right. Then let me put it this way. I want to restructure this company from the ground up. Just take a moment of your time, if you will, and imagine. In the mail room, raw lean-bodied youngsters, a future chairman of the board perhaps among them, learn the business from the bottom by democratically sodomizing each other in an atmosphere of interracial harmony and union solidarity. Thus prepared for the elevator ascent, to the strains of sense-quickening Muzak they steer from floor to floor their rattling mail carts of communiqués and memos proposing urgent trysts, many with nymphs from a typing pool awakened en masse by affairs with a vice-president whose blazing rise from the Harvard Business School to a position of line command has been short-circuited by a reputation for insatiable erotic appetites. The day begins for the accounting department, too, as hot numbers are speculated upon with mathematical frankness. Everywhere shirtsleeves are rolled up to expose wrists and forearms of unbearably breathtaking virility; panty hose are stripped off so that bare toes may frolic in the nap of the industrial carpeting. Smart pigskin briefcases and brown paper bags alike pop open to reveal black nylon corselets and posing straps, and aesthetically pleasing new birth-control devices, each a product of the newly stirring giant of American technology. By midmorning, as the refreshment wagon tinkles its merry news, quenching fruit juices are sought, caffeine and sugar renounced as redundant stimulants to surging metabolisms. Hands clutch atop reports and blueprints, limbs mingle upon varnished teak conference tables. By noon, sustenance is welcome; home-cooked box-lunch fare is contributed potluck style to the menu of the penthouse executive dining room, where one and all are served by Irish waiters and waitresses, whose rosy-cheeked charms are dispensed as a last course along with the claret. Restored, the staff returns to a worthwhile afternoon of disassembling the structures of power, once again tearing off collar stays and execu-length socks, T-shirts and work boots, with equal-opportunity abandon. The switchboard is as abuzz with interoffice calls for transvestites as a Weimar nightclub, while the computers, engineered for sexy problem-solving by a vanguard élite, are programmed to insert pornographic passages into the briefs of the lawyers, who, thus cast adrift on the uncertain seas of obscenity rulings, fall into confusion and disarray, incapacitated in their campaign to stifle creative urges with their lackey caution. Nepotistic marriages, too, are crumbling under the stress; bourgeois property-owning middle managers and hypocrite artists are selling their exurban retreats and gentrified lofts, reserving motel rooms convenient to the office. As desk lamps are turned this way and that to warm bare flesh, heat melts the grease that has eased the way of sycophants and bootlickers, who, losing their purchase on the success ladder, plunge into the communal endeavor on an equal footing. By late afternoon, all are gathered at the interdepartmental meeting, where brainstorming fully liberates the libido in service of the intellect, culminating in a heady explosion of honest labor. Well exhausted, the satisfied workforce contemplates the wreckage of a numbing and exploitative system. Rivalries have been diverted into life-giving channels, oppressive authority has been leveled by the sway of desire, and the stultifying lockmarch of corporate sameness has been diversified into a thousand different positions.

MENTOR: You're fired.

What Makes Them Tick

. . . . there are three aspects of the Presidential campaign: one, what a candidate thinks about the issues . . . ; two, what [he] has to say about what he would do for the country . . . ; three, what makes him tick.

—Senator Howard Baker, February 20, 1980

REPRESENTATIVE JOHN ANDERSON

In theory, propulsion is effected by droplets of condensed vapor, which adhere to a wooden-pole support until their potential energy is released, causing the blade to cut the hairs close to the follicles. The works are oiled daily with an ounce of butter cut into pea-size dots.

GOVERNOR EDMUND G. BROWN, JR.

Tiny microorganisms affixed to the host go busily about their job of decomposition. The nitrogen thus liberated is used to flavor soybeans and other legumes, which are in turn recycled to the host as an energy source. When this system temporarily closes down, the host can be plugged into a direct-current circuit until the next phase.

GEORGE BUSH

Momentum, either linear or rotary, is imparted to a claw hammer by the circulation of quantities of displaced libido. The containment vessel sleeps six to eight.

PRESIDENT JIMMY CARTER

The central cavity is filled with natural uranium, which is constantly scanned by a Zeiss optical system. Random fluctuations of electrons are controlled by meditation, and the dark clouds of ash vented from the abyss are borne away by high winds. The apparatus as a whole can be swung in various directions, as it swivels about its main pivot.

SENATOR EDWARD M. KENNEDY

Small sprocket wheels pull the film off the feed reel and feed it to the takeup reel. In time, it reaches the sound head. The device is capable of transmitting coded information, in twelve-track Dolby, to surface facilities as far away as forty feet.

RONALD REAGAN

The clockwork drive, of the type developed in the first half of the nineteenth century, has been granulated and introduced through a hopper into the chamber, which has been well swabbed to remove powder fouling. For safety, the muzzle has been equipped with a warning signal. Engineers have not actually been able to get this model to tick yet, but with proper maintenance it may be struck manually to sound the quarter hour.

More Mathematical Diversions

1. ANTE UP

Coins have fascinated mathematicians for almost four thousand years. These baffling theoretical symbols, with their entertaining numerical properties, afford us many impromptu parlor tricks. This one was called to my attention by Y. Andropov, of Princeton, Nev. It employs ordinary silver pocket change, and never fails to elicit cries of disbelief when performed in company.

In the presence of two or more ordinary guests, lay out ten coins in a horizontal row on a flat-topped table. Ask a guest to tally the number values of the coins and record the combined value on a sturdy piece of paper. For the next 365 days, distract the guests with Frightening Matchstick Conundrums (Volume I). Then take the number on the paper and multiply it by the annual rate of inflation (available from any magicians' supply shop). Subtract the sum from the original number. Confoundingly, the probability that the result coincides with or is greater than the original number is 1/1,000,000, or .0001 percent.

The trick is ridiculously easy to understand once it is understood, and lays bare the very essence of the scientific method. It uses what Leibnitz called a "brain teaser." Astoundingly, the probability curve remains exactly the same if you cheat by trying to sell the piece of paper as a municipal bond. However, there is quite a pretty way to improve the odds in your favor by beginning with zero coins or the new nondenominational coins.

2. SEVEN BUGS

One of the classic mathematical fallacies was immortalized by William Wordsworth in his "On the Extinction of the Venetian Republic, 1802":

Seven bugs each sought a mate
From inside their own huddle;
Yet none would woo another's date,
So how were they to cuddle?

"There's not much sense in grievin',"
Said One, and gave a nod;
"Let odd consort with even,
And even pair with odd."

So Six and Three went out to tea,
And Five took Four to wife;
One and Two kept company,
And Seven took its life.

Addendum:

An ingenious resolution of this problem has been proposed by Dr. Werner Frye, of the Institute for Advanced Idling, who writes: "If each bug paired with a transfinite number, senseless tragedy might be averted."

3. THE MAZE OF VENUS

There is nothing mysterious about speech; it is merely a way of expressing thoughts without having to write them down. Yet the incredible verbal sequence known to logicians as the Maze of Venus quickly dispels the illusion that spoken language is a plausible means of communication. Here is the classical formulation of this sequence:

A: I don't think you want to see me more often.
B: That's not true.

A: Then you do want to see me more often.
B: I didn't say that. I just don't *not* want to see you more often.

Also known as the Paradox of Don Giovanni, this problem has long intrigued philosophers of science. The difficulties become clear if we let T represent the outer limits of A's tolerance, and $t^{\pm x}$ the measurable tenuousness of the relationship. Chess genius Pauline Morph's fatal attempt to extrapolate a boardplay solution (see "Mate in Five," *Science for Women*, May 1912) proved only that the Maze of Venus defies logical analysis.

4. JERKAGONS

Jerkagons are paper polygons made by folding rectangular NASA payroll checks. They have the delightful property of changing shape when their edges are jerked in a particular way. Jerkagons were discovered by Dr. Yves St. Laurent, the French astrophysicist. St. Laurent's jerkagon can be manipulated so that it reveals three different faces. (See "The Three Faces of Yves," *Journal of Stereoisomers and Paper Games*, Summer, 1966.) He has set forth the principles of jerkagation in a mathematical proof of exquisite elegance, printed on off-white crêpe de Chine.

You can make a jerkagon quite easily. Fold check as shown in *Fig. 1.*

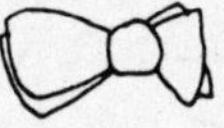

Figure 1

Now grasp your jerkagon by any two edges and give it a sharp jerk, of the kind absurdly simple to describe as sort of an imploded tremor. As if by magic, your jerkagon will assume one of three possible shapes. (See *Figs. 2–4.*)

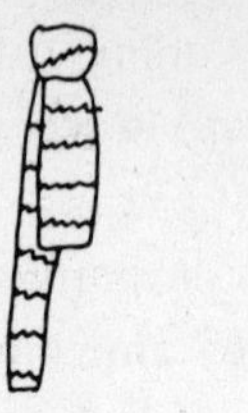

Figure 2

Figure 3

Figure 4

Addendum:

After my article about jerkagons appeared in the August 1975 *Scientific Whimsician*, I received the following correspondence from Prof. Lance Mars, of Canaveral, Calif.:

"From way over here at another coordinate on this tiny hunk of stuff we call the Earth, I am prompted to report a curious incident which suggests that the properties of the jerkagon may be stunning and awesome beyond our wildest dreams. Early in October, I was driving south with my family, on my way to meet with a bunch of stuffy and unimaginative colleagues. While passing through an especially banal landscape in Georgia, I decided to use my very large brain to amuse my very small son. Pulling up beside what looked like a peanut thicket, I took from my wallet a canceled check for $125, folded it into a jerkagon, and told the boy how to manipulate it. He gave it a couple of dutiful tweaks and then flung it out of the window, into what looked like a peanut thicket, and demanded a doll.

"Within a matter of weeks, the national press had started to report the existence of someone named 'Jimmy Carter,' calling him 'an enigma' who had 'come out of nowhere.' Since physicists are in agreement that it is impossible for matter to 'come out of nowhere,' unless 'nowhere' is merely a word we use to mean a somewhere which we disapprove of, I do not hesitate to draw the controversial conclusion that 'Jimmy Carter' did indeed come out of somewhere, and that the somewhere which he came out of was my jerkagon.

"I now choose to speculate freely. Does the jerkagon's time-space, awesome and far-out as we may now surmise it to be, teem with intelligent life? Does it teem with billions and billions of teeth? How many more 'Jimmy Carters' await nothing more than the twiddle of a child's fingers to be projected into our national political life? Is 'Jimmy Carter' an extraterrestrial, and if he is an extraterrestrial, is he Constitutionally disqualified from holding elective office on this planet? If these boggling possibilities don't put things in perspective, what will?"

5. ORTHO

This diverting game, known to many a schoolgirl in its traditional pencil-and-paper form, is now available in a manufactured version, designed and marketed by the Dutch inventor Piet Heineken. Ortho makes use of a perforated plastic case containing twenty-one disk-shaped counters. Play begins on Day 1, when the player takes the first counter. Thereafter, any combination of moves is either "safe" or "unsafe" (as binary analysis will easily show). For example, in the common "1, 2, 3, 5" game, the player forgets to employ a counter on Day 4, thus changing a "safe" position to an "unsafe" one. Any "safe" position can be made "unsafe" by a wrong move. Since the game depends entirely upon the player's memory, "rational" strategies are impossible and there is no way to force a win.

The game's centuries-old popularity is attested to in many historical references. The Phoenicians called it the Maze of Venus, and it was familiar to the Anglo-Saxons as a pastime called Preggers.

James at an Awkward Age

The NBC-TV sitcom *James at 16*, canceled in 1978, will inevitably resume in a new format. Episode One, "Pop Quiz":

SEGMENT 1: *Interior, the Berkeley Institute, a boys' school in Newport, Rhode Island. The Reverend William Leverett has just finished lecturing on "Cicero as Such." Boys stream from the classroom into the hall. James and his only friend, Sargy, meet in front of James's locker.*

SARGY: James, my man! *(They shake hands.)* Isn't Leverett something else?

JAMES: As to what, don't you know? else he *is*—! Leverett is of a weirdness.

SARGY: Say, my man, what's going down?

JAMES: Anything, you mean, different from what is usually up? But one's just where one *is*—isn't one? I don't mean so much in the being by one's locker—for it does, doesn't it? lock and unlock and yet all unalterably, stainlessly, steelily glitter—as in one's head and what vibes one picks up and the sort of deal one perceives as big.

SARGY: Oh, I wouldn't sweat it.

JAMES: If one might suppose that in the not sweating it one should become—what do you fellows call it?—*cool*—!

SARGY: You pull it off.

JAMES: Would I "pull off" anything, then?

SARGY: I didn't say *anything*.

JAMES: It's what, isn't it? *he* can say.

SARGY: Leverett?

JAMES: Oh, Leverett! All the same, I wonder about *his* idea of him—Leverett's.

SARGY: Him?

JAMES: Precisely! One's own father.

SARGY: They say your pop's, like, a friend of Emerson's.

JAMES: Ah, *they!* But if one's to belong, in the event, to a group of other kids, without giving the appearance—so apparent beyond the covering it, in any way, up—of muscling at all in—! And if, under pressure of an ideal altogether American, one feels it tasteless and even humiliating that the head of one's little family is not "in business"—!

SARGY: Too much! But hasn't your dad hung out with Greeley and Dana?

JAMES: Oh, "hung"—very much so. But we don't know, do you know? what he *does*.

SARGY: I heard your old man got it on in the—you know, the spiritual reformation of the forties and fifties.

JAMES: Yes, and yet, you see, Sargy, exactly what the heck, all the while, do you think, like, *is* he?

SEGMENT 2: *Interior, the Sweet Shoppe. James is alone at a table.* ENTER *his cousin Minny.*

MINNY: May I sit down at all?

JAMES: Oh, immensely!

(Waitress comes over.)

MINNY: Only, I guess, a Coke.

JAMES: Well, perhaps just a thing so inconsiderable as—the hamburger? Of a rarity?

MINNY: Anyway, see, could you help me maybe study on Saturday, you know, night?

JAMES: Would it be a, then, kept date? I mean, the charm of the thing half residing in the thing itself's having been determined in advance and, in consequence, all intentionally and easily and without precipitant hassle or bummer, taking finally, in fact, place?

MINNY: That's exactly what it would be kind of like.

(Waitress brings their orders. James takes a bite of his burger.)

JAMES: This is, on the whole roll, particularly not rare. And *you*—you so too stupendously are! I say—do you think I *had* better keep it?

MINNY: Our date?

JAMES: The little hamburger.

MINNY: If you're, I mean, *on* something—

JAMES: Oh, it's not, I swear—no way!—*drugs.* Unless *it's* one.

MINNY: The hamburger?

JAMES: No, the wondering, do you read me? in respect to *(despondently)* oh, wow! *him!*

SEGMENT 3: *Interior, James's house. James looks into the sitting room, where his brothers, Willy, Wilky, and Bob, and his sister, Alice, are gathered before dinner, chaffing each other. James goes down the hall and meets his mother.*

JAMES: Only *do* say, Mom, how I'm not to fail in the finding of him—

MOTHER: In his study. Hurry up, my dear—some of his Swedenborgians will be here soon.

(James goes to Father's study.)

FATHER: Come in, son. I was just corresponding with Carlyle and Mill.

JAMES: Ah, but it's all so quite buggingly on *that* point, if I might for a moment be allowed to be prefatory no less than interrogatory, and interrogatory no less than up, as it were, front, with regard to your little interlocutor's—that is to say, myself's—becoming, in the not grossing the other boys altogether out at least as much as in the not blowing it in getting what they nowadays call "along" with girls, in any way proficient—and oh! if Minny might feel me up, do you see? to *her* level—that now, while I'm too almost hot to have your answer—and am I not, though, in my own pyrotechnics, fairly cooking!—would I put to you my minuscule question:

MOTHER *(appearing in doorway)*: The Swedenborgians are here.

JAMES: *There* pokes at me the stick, as well as beckons to me the carrot, of acceleration. Oh, Dad!—if I may "keep the ball in play"—you work, you *do* work, I guess—do you?—that's my question. Do tell me. I dare say *you* know what it is you, um, "do"? Or only give me the small dry potato-chip crumb of a hint. For if it's even a matter of your not declining to say what you aren't, then doesn't it follow, don't you see? that you needn't say what you *are?*

FATHER: Why, son! Say I'm a philosopher, say I'm a seeker for truth, say I'm a lover of my kind, say I'm an author of books if you like. Or best of all, just say I'm a student.

SEGMENT 4: *The Sweet Shoppe. James is sitting at a table with Sargy and Minny.*

JAMES: *We're* all of us students, aren't we? And if each of us is to be all convivially "in," then *he* must naturally be!

SARGY: Ah, my man—all *right!*

JAMES: Yet one *has* seen great big grown-up dudes, well encumbered, one might surely have thought, with the interest of ponderousnesses, put, by one's little crowd, down as positively not, on the social scales as rigged by *them*, sufficiently heavy.

MINNY: *I* haven't. I mean, we all, like, what's the difference? you know, speak the same language.

JAMES: But there *he* is!

(James's father enters Sweet Shoppe and sits down at their table, where Minny helps him with his homework. James, in a sudden huff, goes to the jukebox and plays "Come On, Baby, Don't Hang Fire.")

NEXT WEEK: A harrowing mix-up occurs at a drive-in movie until it is discovered that James and his father are both named Henry.

Teaching Poetry Writing to Singles

I had the idea to teach more kinds of people to write poetry as a result of two previous books of mine: *I Taught Republicans to Write Poetry* and *How to Teach the Writing of Poetry to Fashion Coordinators.* I thought of singles because of an interesting hour I had spent reading my own poems at a singles bar called Ozymandias II, and because of many other hours, much less happy ones, I had spent before my marriage as a visitor to another singles bar, Nick's Roost, where there were no activities of that kind going on.

I asked the owners of Ozymandias II, my friends Ozzie and Mandy Dias, to arrange for the class. I had four students, and we met once, on a Friday at midnight, at the big table in front. Like the others in the crowded room, most of the four were in their twenties, thirties, forties, and fifties. Some of them wore glasses. One worked for an escort agency, one was a hayride organizer, another a fashion coordinator, another a Republican. The singles bar gave these people a feeling of meetability, but none had ever written poetry there, and none, I think, would have done so without me.

I started the class by saying what I was going to do was get them to write words in lines of uneven length on a piece of paper (I didn't want to scare them with the formal term "poem") and then I would write a book about how much I had helped them. The students were not in the habit of sitting and hearing something like this explained. Some were so distracted that they could only talk in incomplete sentences, such as "What the—?!" Others stared nervously at the TV screen above the bar, where the final minutes of some kind of sports event seemed to be going on. I said that writing words in lines of uneven length on a piece of paper was not the hard thing that many people think. I said how could it be hard if I was going to teach it to them? I was sure I could give them the mastery of literary form and metaphor so lacking in singles-bar life. I said I knew they had all been single since childhood and I could see how this might make them feel "unmarried" and "on their own," but I said John Milton and Vachel Lindsay and James Dickey had all been single at one time or another and that writing words in lines of uneven length on a piece of paper had helped them to stop running.

I said the first thing we would do would be a collaboration. I knew the students had all gone on a singles bicycling tour of the Wye River in England five years before, so I said I want everyone to remember that trip and think of a sentence about it. Something you saw. Or an outfit you wore. Or a feeling you had about time passing and your not being married yet and having to go on bicycle tours to meet somebody. I'll write down everyone's sentence and put them together, I said, and we'll have words in lines of uneven length on a piece of paper.

At first the students were puzzled. "We went there, that's all." "I remember we did different stuff." "And bicycling." Then William said, "O.K. A double vodka, please. Five years have passed; five summers, with the length of five long winters!" This was a good start, I said, especially the dramatic "frame" made by "O.K. A double vodka, please," as if the lines were being said casually to someone by someone sitting in a bar or tavern.

Then Ezra spoke up: "And again I hear these waters, rolling from their mountain springs with a soft inland βροδοδάκτυλος." This was better than I had expected, but the poem was getting a false-founding jig-jigging rhythm, and I said for the students not to worry about academic gimmicks such as meter. I also said try to get in more of your own personal feelings and hangups. I said for instance I remember when I was in high school I was worried a lot about my bike getting rusty.

It was Emily's turn: "Once again do I behold these steep and lofty cliffs, that on a wild secluded scene impress thoughts: the soul selects her own scene, but you meet more eligible guys by going out and partying rather than staying at home." I said the repetition of "scene" was nice, it gave a nice feeling of repetition.

At this point William got very agitated and said we were ruining "his" idea. I said all right, you do the next part, but I pressed him to put in more details from his own experience as a single—the very details that he seemed most reluctant to put in, maybe because he thought they were "stupid." He continued: "The day is come when I again socialize, taking a nice girl to dinner and a show, and view the floor show and the salad bar, which at this season, with its unripe fruits, is clad in one green hue, and lose myself 'mid men and women, who have different attitudes toward sex."

Quite soon the students felt they had enough words in lines of uneven length on a piece of paper. I read the results back to them and said what they had written was a poem. I asked them to think of a title. They decided the poem was really about working out the problems of writing a poem, so they called it "Working Out at the Wye."

I then said to do individual poems. Writing a poem all by yourself is something that nobody can do with you, and this is a special problem for people who are already panicked about being alone, such as so-called singles. I say "so-called" because the words "single," "bachelorette," etc., may be thought to apply to people's *imaginations*, and they do not. The power to see the world as a configuration of couples linked inextricably in Holy Matrimony is the possession of everyone.

I told the students that one of the main problems poets have is what to write about. I said this was a really hard problem if you were lonely and in a studio apartment and had to go out to a bar to seek some grotesque mockery of human contact. But I said that in a poem you can be somebody else, you can even be *two* people. I said for everyone to start their own poem with "Let us . . ." The "us" in the poem could do anything: get married, have a huge church wedding with a flower girl and a page boy, sit down and talk over family finances—anything.

The most popular "Let us . . ." poem was Tom's:

Let us go then, you and me,
When the weekend is spread out for us to see
Like a roommate bombed out of his gourd on the pool
  table. . . .
Oh, do not ask, "You said you were *who*?"
Let us go to the free luau.

In the room the women come and go
Talking of someone who might be tall and share their
  enthusiasm for theater.

I praised Tom's poem, saying it might seem silly to a lot of people but to me it gave a nice sociable feeling, the sounds of nice people talking to each other. I said there were many more things having to do with the five senses that could be in a poem, like colors. I said for instance when I was a boy I had a dog named Rusty. I said close your eyes and take a swallow of beer and say what color it reminds you of. They answered. "Black." "Beer color." "Black." "Blackish." After this exercise, Ezra wrote his "Little Black Book" poem:

Hang it all, Mark Cross,
there can be but the one little black book. . . .
Under black leather dress, lithe daughter of telephone
  directory . . .

I said noises could be in a poem. I threw a beer stein on the floor and asked what word the noise sounded like. “Bunk.” “Drunk.” “Black.” “Bash.” Right away Emily wrote something down and gave it to me:

I dreamt I was a Key Club,
Select Fraternity.
At night the eligible Men
All had a Bash at me.

I said that in a poem you can compare things in goofy ways. Compare something small to something yellow, something big to something you don’t know the name for, something married to something legally separated. William later told me that this idea made him write his nice poem that starts:

Shall I compare thee to your place or mine?

I was surprised when it was 4 A.M., closing time at Ozymandias II. The students were still quite excited and said could they stay for a few minutes after hours because they wanted to collaborate on one final poem, a poem for me. They made me go into the john while they wrote, and when I came back they were laughing. The poem was this:

Thank you, this has been as much fun as a free trip
To Aspen—only I can’t ski and anyhow I’d probably break
   something
In several places, crack! crack! crack!

Gosh, thanks, I simply feel as if you gave me a raunchy
   souvenir T-shirt from the
Annual Bachelor Rally—quite an icebreaker, but I already
   have one.

By the way, thank you for this night like a bag of yellow
   Doritos, the name reminds me of a dog I once heard of
   named Doris
But I’m on a diet of blue and of purple.

Thank you for an experience similar to drinking tee
Martoonis,
Which I could compare to those other clear drinks that I can
hardly be expected to remember the name of. Oh—water!

Listen, really, we all thank you for teaching us that looks
aren't everything, even in a poem.

I said they had learned a whole lot and it was a really nice poem, one that gave a strong feeling of niceness.

The Stylish New York Couples

These four couples have different names and faces, but they have one thing in common—a strong tendency to appear in articles of this kind, because they are fashion individualists. One couple may prefer an eclectic style, another retro-amalgam, another mongrel revival, and another hybrid-*retrouvé*, yet each couple stands on his and her own as a single, unique personality. They show that to be one of a kind, you have to be one of a pair.

Artist Marie Bane (25) and collector Morton Braine (30) dress in simple, bold fabric wrappings—colorful bolts and mill ends layered directly onto the skin with rubber cement. "We call it Yardage Formalism," says Morton, whose current project is winding all the furniture in their Tribeca penthouse with colored thread inherited from his grandparents, Coco Chanel and David Belasco. Adds Marie, "When Julian Schnabel's show sold out, I thought mine would, too, but then it didn't."

HER CLOTHES: Scalamandré, Museum of Tissues (Lyons), Taipei silkworm farms. Mad Frisson and Warren Beatty for shoes.
HIS CLOTHES: Porthault, Einstein Moomjy. Galerie du Sabot (Brussels) for shoes.
INTERESTS: Oneiromancy, vacuuming up bits of thread, intaglio hunting, reading.

RESTAURANTS: Chive, La Petite Bière, Imperial Musk-Polyp, Charlie's Bum Steer, La Tricoteuse, Folie à Deux (Paris).

Neither William nor Mary Molding (both 88) has bought any clothing in over fifty years. They feel that they have "subsumed fashion under the category of pure tradition." Both dress exclusively in what Mary calls "lateral hand-me-downs: I wear Moldie's old clothes and he wears mine." Real-estate collector William likes to wheel and deal on their Park Avenue triplex telex in a Schiaparelli cocktail dress, and relaxes later in "nothing at all except a dab of vintage Shocking on pulse points." For Mary, founder of the Ghetto Repair League and president of the Don't Be Beastly to Congress Committee, living well still means "a dinner coat always"—the one handmade for her husband in 1909 by Eugene V. Debs.

HER CLOTHES: His.
HIS CLOTHES: Hers.
INTERESTS: Reading, telephoning, telescopes.
RESTAURANTS: "It is impossible to go out." Entertain close friends at amusing dinners famous for including musk-polyps in every course.

Annabella Carissima ("Pat") von Patina (49), a Milan-born architect, and Stanley Sohoux (18), former collector, have shaped each other's design sensibilities in the ongoing process of gradually removing everything they own from their fabulous 40,000-square-foot loft in the bonemeal district. "I'm a bit big on minimalism," says Pat, "but Stan is completely his own man and has *kept* one or two little *objets* instead of relying on me to throw them away." Stan sometimes wears all his clothes at once, carrying his personal possessions in the pockets, "so the spatial interpenetrations of the open-plan closets can be kept unobstructed." Pat sticks to one designer for clothes and keeps her efficient wardrobe stored flat behind the ceiling in the crawlspace.

HER CLOTHES: Ralph Racquet for Women. Warren Beatty and Mad Frisson for shoes.
HIS CLOTHES: Ralph Racquet for Women for Men.
INTERESTS: Medicinal-brandy tastings, oneiromancy. Visiting

friends (Stan). Reading, intaglio disposal (Pat).
RESTAURANTS: La Tricoteuse, Huis Clos, Chive, Imperial Musk-Polyp, Folie à Deux (Paris).

The proprietors of Chive, one of the most popular new dining places in town, Clive (35) and Olive (25) Alive are self-proclaimed "style immortals." Explains Clive, "By translating ourselves into commodities, we become abstract concepts of exchange; for that which hovers in a shop waiting to be bought is an immutable idea. As long as we are still for sale, we cannot be used." Everything in their East Side apartment has its price sticker—even the much-mended antique purse seine covering the walls, to which are pinned costly holograph pages from Richard Strauss's *Ariadne auf Naxos* and inexpensive crayon tracings of autumn leaves from their country estate ("Macy's" in Oxfordshire). The rare Sabayon carpet invites a visitor to lift it and explore the bargains beneath. Both Clive and Olive created their own wardrobes by stitching together labels bought in bulk at wholesale: "We transcend the material."

HER CLOTHES: Calvin Mazuma, Yves Ducat, Vittorio Dinero, Simoleon, Made of Money. Mad Frisson and Warren Beatty for shoes; cobbles her own boots from Levi's labels.
HIS CLOTHES: Mach Wash Tumble Dry, Property of the Harvard Athletic Association, ILGWU, It Is Illegal to Remove This Tag. Galerie du Sabot (Brussels) for shoes, Savile Row for sweatbands.
INTERESTS: Collecting, reading, taking inventory.
RESTAURANTS: Betamax of Athens, Imperial Musk-Polyp, Folie à Deux (Paris).

Masterpiece Tearjerker

Our host, the famous Americophile, is reclining on a horsehair chaise longue—a replica of the one in the foyer of the men's lavatory at Waterloo Station. Beside him on a table are a lamp made from a cast of Lord Kitchener's torso and an exact reproduction of a water tumbler. He puts aside his book, forms a tepee with his fingers to signal transatlantic cordiality, and meets our eye.

HOST: Good evening, Yanks. We come now to the eight-hundred-fifty-seventh episode in our series *U and Non-U*, in which we follow the very human ups and downs of everyone in Britain in the years before, during, and after the First War. It was a time of pacifists and plum duff, of shirkers and scullery maids, of aesthetes and armament manufacturers, of White's and Boodle's *(pause; then, gravely)* and bombs.

Last time, of course, we saw Lord Randolph Crust committing a really disastrous gaffe by accidentally setting fire to Devonshire House while showing off his electrical Boer War set, Lytton Strachey receiving a letter from H.A.L. Fisher, and Lady Mary Crust getting herself into a peck of trouble by commencing an affair with a really unsuitable twelve-year-old schoolboy, Cecil Formalin. We come in now on Lady Mary, who has just returned from an outing with Cecil—an outing that was, as we shall see, something of a bust.

The year, 1910. Episode Eight Hundred Fifty-seven: "The Gathering Tantrum."

SCENE 1: *The morning room. Lady Mary is alone, weeping.* ENTER *her best friend, Lady Laura Fantod.*

LAURA: My dear, what's the dynamite?

MARY: It's too frightful! We chanced on one of Cecil's school friends, who insulted me in public. He said I put him in mind of a vulgar, common American woman!

LAURA: Which one?

MARY: Which American woman?

LAURA: Which friend of Cecil's?

MARY: Evelyn Wore, or Wall, or something. *Such* an unpleasant little party. This younger set! The old moral order seems to be smashing up all round us these days.

(ENTER *Hooting, the butler.*)

HOOTING: Excuse me, my lady, but I have just received word that the young mistress Viola is, er, arrested.

MARY: You're telling me my own daughter is a mental defective?

HOOTING: Arrested by the police, my lady. These suffragette carryings-on. The young mistress chained herself to Mr. Asquith.

LAURA: My dear, *quel* case of pickles! Viola will be forcibly fed in prison—and not on your splendid Mrs. Winkle's *rissoles.*

MARY: That girl never had much in the way of appetite. *(Becomes hysterical.)*

VOICEOVER: Starting this Friday, Beryl Simon, who plays Viola Crust, can be seen in the BBC's four-episode dramatization of the *Dictionary of National Biography,* along with these other actors and actresses who have been temporarily or permanently displaced from the plot of *U and Non-U:* Simon Graham (Captain Neville Crust, now a remittance man in Mombasa), Graham Glansdale (old Lord Roger Crust, dead), Sarah Pinch (Rosalind, mad), Derek Lamb (Reg, the chauffeur, sacked), and Rosalind-Beryl Graham (Nanny, on holiday with her sister in Reading).

SCENE 2: *An enormous spread (cakes on tiered plates, etc.) on several long tables in Lord Randolph's office at Whitehall. Lord Randolph and General Simon ffen-Nightingale are having tea.*

ffEN-NIGHTINGALE: Jolly decent five-o'clock they lay on here at Whitehall. *(Chews.)* Toad-in-the-hole, my favorite.

RANDOLPH: Spotted Dick, too. Very tasty, very tasty.

(ENTER *a young woman with an ineffably sad and beautiful face and superb carriage. She wears a shabby but meticulously pressed coat and skirt from Worth, and carries a tray of rock buns.)*

RANDOLPH: Put those— *(Does double-take.)* Who are you?

WOMAN: Edith Bullock, sir. (EXITS *proudly.*)

RANDOLPH: Why the devil do you suppose a woman of that type is serving tea?

ffEN-NIGHTINGALE: Bit too fond of the old horizontal refreshment, I daresay. Now, you wanted to have a spot of chinwag, my boy?

RANDOLPH: Yes, it's this German—you know, thingy. Wireless message? I seem to have, you know—decoded it. And it looks like we're in for what-do-you-call-it. War. The thing is, something really colossal came up—quarrel with Mary—and I misplaced the message. The PM will have me on toast! I was, you see, so preoccupied about Mary. Poor old thing, she's been rippingly unselfish and patient. I haven't been a—you know—proper husband to her ever since—well, ever since I went off my onion about *you*. *(Breaks down.)* Y-you won't repeat any of this, will you?

ffEN-NIGHTINGALE: My dear boy, give me credit for some natural delicacy. And now let's look for that message. Trust bleeding Jerry to telegram at a time like this!

SCENE 3: *The Green Farm, Timworth, near Bury St. Edmunds. Exterior.* ENTER *Lytton Strachey, with valise. Knocks on door. Housemaid opens door.*

STRACHEY: I am Mr. Strachey. Mr. McCarthy asked me to spend the weekend.

HOUSEMAID: Mr. McCarthy is in Paris, sir.

STRACHEY: Oh. *(Business with valise.)* Well, thanks all the same. Good day. *(Goes away wistfully.)*

SCENE 4: *The servants' hall at Eaton Place. Late afternoon. Mrs. Winkle, the cook, is scowling over her* Mrs. Beeton. *Dora, the parlormaid, is whittling new boot trees for Viola. Doris, the scullery maid, is attempting to poison herself because she is hopelessly in love with Mr. Bangers, purveyor of sausages to the Crust kitchen.* ENTER *Hooting.*

HOOTING: Doris! Whatever have you got in that best crystal decanter?

DORIS: Harsenic, Mr. 'Ooting. Oh, please, let me do meself in. I can't stand it no more!

HOOTING: Unrequited love and that, is it? Well, hard cheddar, my girl. The master and mistress are counting on you to remain here in this life, as a member of the staff. You do as you're told now, and put the kettle on. *(Doris slopes off to kitchen.)* And get your finger out! It's nearly teatime. *(Grumbles to self.)* That girl's as cunning as a dead pig.

DORA: Not 'alf!

(ENTER *Joseph, the footman.*)

HOOTING: And where might you have been, my lad?

JOSEPH: Just off for a pint of the old purko down at the Swan and Dead Pig.

HOOTING: You seem to be getting a tick independent for a mere thirty-year-old man, Joseph. Mark my words—

(ENTER *Lady Mary.*)

MARY: I *am* sorry—I don't quite know how to break this to all of you. I've been so preoccupied lately that I forgot to mention it. King Edward VII and Mrs. Pankhurst and Cosima Wagner are all coming to dinner. Rather soonish. Tonight, in fact. *(Hooting falls to the floor and displays the painstakingly researched symptoms of an apoplectic fit.)* Now, Hooting, we mustn't let down dear old HRH, must we? And you always manage *so* well.

HOOTING: Forgive me, my lady. . . . I'm done for . . . off to join the celestial poultry. . . . Carry on without me. . . . Mustn't let down standards . . . key to the cellar . . . the nought-three Haut-Brion. . . . *(Staff gamely stifles sobs.)*

MRS. WINKLE: Never you fear, Mr. 'Ooting, we'll do right proud by you. A lovely Aberdeen cutlet, I think—'e always loved my Aberdeen cutlet, 'e did, when 'e was Prince of Wales.

HOOTING: That's right . . . standards . . . oh, no, *the best decanter* . . . *(Dies.)*

HOST: Several days later, the King, too, was dead—reportedly of a bronchial condition. And with him the old moral order bit the dust. *(Cut to photograph of Big Ben.)* I remember as a boy hearing people say, in the streets, "Oh, pack it in with your old moral order." *(Cut to photographs of Dr. H. H. Crippen; a red grouse; Arthur Wing Pinero.)*

Next week, Joseph does a bunk with Lord Randolph's second-best railway shares; Vita Sackville-West invites Harold Nicolson to a dance *(cut to photograph of potted palm)*; and much, much more.

And you can be sure that we haven't heard the last of Edith Bullock. I remember as a boy seeing ever so many Edith Bullocks at evening parties in my parents' house, where I lived. In the fashion of the time, they all wore long dresses and perfume and did their hair. I would sit on the stair landing and gaze down on them and wonder what it all *meant. (Smiles.)* Now, of course, we know.

Serenade

SATURDAY NIGHT

Why are we here? There are eighteen of us in one room, with bath. The room is locked from the outside and is unfurnished, except for low cushioned benches along the walls, where we sleep, and twenty-five Venetian-glass bonbon services. We wear at all times the regulation blue negligee, and most of our personal belongings have been confiscated, particularly those items good for hollow displays of independence: our horn-rims, compacts, step-ins, carryalls.

We arrived here, one by one, the night before last. We have not seen him since, the man we were taken by, yet so great is the power of his indifference that we are able to make only the smallest, most circumscribed movements, such as twining a strand of hair around one finger.

I was taken at midnight, in the garden near my kitchen door. I had gone out to investigate a sudden fear that something unusual would never happen to me, and there he was, in the dark, a figure. He was wearing either all black or all white—I could not be sure, for the authority of his form against the tangled, familiar shrubbery caused him to read as featureless surface and I was not able to tell whether he absorbed or reflected light. He carried a thin glittering object in one hand.

"What do you want?" I said.

He made no reply.

"Why so withdrawn?" I said.

With a savagery that bordered on total inattention, he said nothing.

"Fine!" I screamed. "Don't bother to draw me a diagram! You

don't give a hoot about me! Well, for your information, you don't know anything about me yet! What do you want—the dance of the seven espadrilles? What is it you want?" (One partner always cares a little more than the other.)

I must have fainted then. What followed: The chloroformed hankie? The wrist bonds? Freedom glimpsed one last time through the black tulle curtains of a limousine rolling away? I can't remember. When I came to my senses, I was in a limousine with black tulle curtains, rolling away. No point in mincing words here: I was definitely not driving. To shirk the truth in one's own journal is like going to a dinner party and letting cigarette ash drift down one's décolletage and coming home afterward and saying to oneself, "Thank goodness I didn't let cigarette ash drift down my décolletage, and thank goodness, too, I have the courage not to deceive myself about it."

SUNDAY

So far, very little interaction among the women—only shared confusion and a growing consciousness that whoever bought these negligees paid for a designer name while settling for inferior materials and workmanship.

MONDAY

Today, our first discussion:

"What does he want?"

"He has no use for us. He doesn't like us."

"But he's kept us for three days."

"Maybe he believes in long engagements."

"He just wants us to play hard to get."

"Maybe it's a test. We guess what he wants."

"Outreach?"

"What if every one of us writes him a note explaining how fascinating she is?"

"What would you say?"

"Well, I'm not a good example."

"No way to talk. Besides, you're with me, we're with them, as an ensemble we have a certain geometric charm."

"Maybe he's a prude."

"Or a eunuch."

"Doubtful. From what little I saw . . ."

"He doesn't exactly have hair-trigger responses."

"If he loses interest this easily, he's going to dump us and import some new talent to leave alone. Younger talent, whose perfect breasts rise with equal curves on every side and equally terminate in their apexes, whose—"

"The way he ignores us—I see it as kind of a higher form of interest."

"What evidence do we have of that?"

"We're here, aren't we?"

WEDNESDAY

He's not rushing us: that's clever of him.

Why am I keeping this journal? (a) Because I am different. (b) Because I hold the conviction that as the centuries march on, and civilization advances, and the relations between men and women become more interesting on account of our not knowing, now, what they will be, women like me will be recognized as extraordinary marginal curiosities. (Such, I believe, is already the case in Scandinavia.) And yet, now that I am having an experience whose unusualness is a match for my own, I wonder: With seventeen other women inhaling the same privileged air, is this unusual *enough?*

MONDAY

Today we played "Lifeboat."

"O.K., you have ten survivors. The nun, the pregnant woman, the majorette, the ninety-year-old lady, the little girl, the waitress, the nurse, the robber—how many is that? Oh, and the little girl's mother and Helen Frankenthaler. Who do you throw off?"

"The robber is a man?"

"Yes. Come on. Which one?"

"You can't throw off the pregnant woman, because that's taking two lives instead of one. You can't throw off the little girl, because she has her whole life—"

"Is it a male nurse?"

"No."

"Throw off the waitress."

"Elitism."

"Throw off Frankenthaler. What's art anyway? Somebody making some little something."

"This is disgusting."

"I don't want to play."

"Can't we change it to a *male* nurse?"

"No."

"An orderly?"

SOME WEEKS LATER

We started an exercise program and are moving about more. Eighteen women have an amazing number of limbs. There are problems of collision and entanglement, especially for me, the tallest. Somebody else is walking around with my pedicure. Eighteen women take an incredibly long time to get ready for bed, and at night, Flavia, who sleeps at my feet, grinds her teeth on her bite plate. Today, though, I cheered everyone up by pretending to be a barmaid—taking orders and serving imaginary drinks. More discussion as we sipped our slings, toddies, and shrubs.

"I don't ask much of a man, but there must be something more variegated than this."

"He's a drip."

"His life is a mess and he had no right to involve us in it."

"Get serious. We came here on our own thirty-six feet."

"But remain under duress."

"Reread your Millstonecraft and De Beauwoolf. Duress is no one-way street."

"Well, it ain't the Boulevard of Dreams."

"All I know is, this situation is his fault and I'm not leaving here till he does something about it."

SUMMER

Over the past months, impatience has driven us to accumulate some power, mostly by mail order. Flavia has obtained, under a false name, membership in the St. Vincent Ferrer Boys' Club, from a membership mill in Alabama. Rufa has gained possession of a quantity of information, which she carries in a briefcase of quality leather. Narcissa has become adept at power yoga and sits cross-legged three hours a day, intoning, "I won't knuckle under to the marketing arm." Chloe is making a knife. I am a matriculant in a correspondence school and have learned to draw pie graphs with the largest wedge labeled Fossil Fools. I'm not sure we're getting this stuff right.

Today Rufa took a paper out of her briefcase and said, "I'm going to work on my peach." Narcissa put one arm around her protectively and said, "She means her *speech*. You mean your *speech*, don't you, honey."

LATE SUMMER

The lack of food is, to me, one of the most unfortunate features of

Just as I was starting to write, an astonishing thing happened. I was staring up at the only window, which is high in the wall opposite the door and covered with a stout latticework of nylon rope. Through the window I could see patches of bright green against a background of gray cement that I know to be the west façade of the Port Authority building. From here, the gray has a sparse, dry quality, devoid of physical presence, and I was seized by the inexplicable remoteness of life in confinement. Then I noticed that the patches of green were moving, falling. They looked like hunks of lawn or artificial turf. Divots! That can mean only one thing: he lives directly above us and is none other than the Midnight Ambler, the international outlaw who disdainfully terrorizes women by flaunting his preference for a form of miniature golf played on a mind course, roaming the dark streets with his diminutive putter in search of an all-night game.

We decided to confront him with what we know. We composed the letter collectively:

"We know who you are," I began. "You are the man known as

the Midnight Ambler, long sought by the Geneva police on charges of failure to attend a compulsory educational film on the estrogen cycle."

"We know you are the enemy of women everywhere, and so we are no longer at the mercy of your every move—"

"Or should we say your every failure to move. Love us or leave us, we could care less. Your behavior is wrong."

"Grievously wrong."

"More wrong than you'll ever know."

"Wrong and then some."

"We are leaving. We have the power to do that now, because we have come to care less about you than you care about us—"

"If that is possible."

"If it is not possible, we have the power anyway. Until we get it together to leave, we demand regular meals. We also demand free beer and soda, and all other drinks at half price."

Some of the women see our ultimatum as a ploy and hope it will penetrate his heart. The rest study the rope latticework at the window and practice neck craning in an effort to work out some means of escape.

We all show signs of nervousness. Earlier, Flavia's bite plate fell onto the floor with a tiny *click* and we stampeded for forty-five minutes.

THE NEXT MORNING

When we awoke, the bonbon services were filled with scrambled eggs. At each plate was a demitasse of hot coffee. Under each cup was a letter, folded many times. The letters were all handwritten but in content identical:

> Darling: I have been wrong. I offer no excuses for my crimes, but try to understand. I was a middle child. I was a planned child; and because I was planned, I thought I must seek a perfection that I now realize is hateful, for it leaves others with nothing to forgive, which is too little, or everything to forgive, which is too much. I

was arrested for peeping at the age of six. Of the rest of my career, you know the essentials. I am overtired. The point is, I have changed. Last year, I sought out eighteen of you at random, in the hope that one or two of you might work out. I have been watching you through a hole in the floor of my room. This has been a healing experience for me. You have all worked out. You have not hurt me, and until now you have asked for nothing in return. I have fallen in love with you. I am prepared to trust you. I am prepared to give up my freedom, for freedom is an idea so nearly perfect that the only thing left to do is renounce it. I have ordered mother-of-pearl wainscoting for your room, and for the bath a Steri-Matron, which dries the hands in antiseptic waves of ultraviolet light and electrically generated hot air. I have had eighteen canvas carry-alls printed up with my photograph on them, and I wish to present one to each of you personally, tonight at midnight, when the silk-screening is dry. At that time I shall ask you to marry me and remain here so that I can worship you forever. Truly I am a worshiper of women. Could I be otherwise with such an anguished past?

XXXXXX
XXXXXX
XXXXXX
The Midnight Ambler.

Some of the younger ones cried. But the discussion was brief:
"It's not enough. What he's offering."
"Do we *have* to hold out for enough?"
"I believe he loves me. But he took too long."
"Too long for what?"
"Still, a lot of that time he was writing out these letters."
"I kind of empathize. Is that crazy?"
We agreed: everybody's got to go.

THAT AFTERNOON

We have been talking over the problem of the favorite. We know, from our reading in the literature of harems, that there is always a favorite. We also know, from our reading in the literature of favoritism, that the favorite is not always the best. That she may have advanced herself by perfidy, pregnancy, or willingness to take on administrative tasks. That even when she is the best, she will, at the whim of the favorer, be supplanted by a new favorite, who may have advanced herself by currying, cowrie-shell amulets, or willingness to transcend mere administrative tasks. We know that the system can accommodate only one favorite at a time. We know that the favorite will high-hat the others, and that the others will wish to blow the favorite to kingdom come.

We are determined that if we stay—which we won't—there must be no favorites.

THAT EVENING

It is almost time to put away this journal. I have attempted to explore here the dualities in my own nature, which, when I look into the mirror, I see even in my face: the upper half all eyes and nose, the lower all mouth and chin. The eyes and nose of an ordinary woman, the mouth and chin of a favorite.

LATER

We found that we could lift the smallest of us up to the window and hold her by her ankles while she cut the ropes with Chloe's knife. By this time it was midnight. In the dark room, women were raised to the window, one by one. I could hear the soft rending of blue chiffon as they dropped to the street below. I, the tallest, was left for last. The others tied the bits of rope together and tossed one end back to me through the window. I took it. I wanted to see the Midnight Ambler.

I must have been standing there for a few minutes, barely hearing the whispered instructions from outside, when a fold of satin gleamed in the room: the Ambler. He was all in white, and his looks were definitely not a disappointment—a good build dominated by a single head. In one hand he carried a silver putter.

"What do you want?" I asked, trembling.

"It's you who want," he said. "I watched the escape through my floor. You waited."

"I wanted to find out what you want."

"Polygamy is on the way out," he said, "and not only among the masses. Even members of the National Security Council now content themselves with one wife. Someone must take up the slack. This is the moment I have been waiting for. It coincides with some change in myself. I love all of you. Persuade them to stay. You can do it. They respect you, you're cultivated, you're tall. What do I want? Call it an extended family. An ordinary man and ordinary women, together going about their daily tasks—shutting the kitchen door, leaving footprints up and down the hall, listening to the cockerel crow, living an ordinary life."

"What do you know of ordinary life?" I said. "Do you know the difference between an infant and a newborn baby? What are the three hidden signs of charm and personality in a spouse? In a society not dependent on subsistence production and in which the inside of a gal's purse is not considered an index of character, how do you decide which wife will be the favorite?"

"I don't want to hurt anybody."

"Maybe you should favor Flavia. She's O.K.—almost a virgin and not quite a dunce. Or Narcissa—not quite ugly and almost sane. Or Chloe—almost decent and not quite dead."

"Or you," he said. His cologne was subtle and deranging.

"It's hard to know," I said, "whether to ruin everything just to satisfy one's own erotic curiosity."

"Ruin?" he said. "Ruin is par for the course."

I wasn't ready for this. I took the rope and, struggling, began to climb. I felt him moving quickly toward me, and then I felt a rung beneath my foot. I looked down: the silver putter.

"Thank you," I said.

"You must love freedom," he said.

"Some of it."

I settled the arch of my foot firmly on the putter and pushed myself up and through the window. What seemed at that moment like forever turned out to be a relatively long time.

Curb Carter Policy Discord Effort Threat

WASHINGTON, OCT. 11—In a surprise move, a major spokesman announced yesterday that a flurry of moves has forestalled deferment of the Administration's controversial hundred-pronged strategy. The nine-page indictment provides a minimum of new details about the alleged sharp apprehensions now being voiced in key areas. As holiday traffic flowed into and out of the nation's cities, President Carter acknowledged in a telephone interview that there is "cause for some optimism." But Senate conferees quickly vowed to urge the challenging of this view as over-optimistic.

In a shocking about-face, it was confirmed that the package will serve as the basis for mounting pressures. However, no target date has been set for the fueling of speculations.

In an unexpected development, it is expected that fresh pleas will be issued for a brightened outlook. "Sharply higher deficits will rise in the long run," said a senior expert. Token collection of heavy weapons has been reported near the austerity programs, where a newly minted spirit of fairness has caused anticipated losses.

The focal point of this change of focus is the Administration's broad-gauge diplomatic push. According to officials in the vogue for docudramas, these figures indicate that a shrinking supply of farmland, swept by strong emotional tides and waves of public resentment, is considering another round of direct contacts with the globe's expanding circle of treelessness. However, flagrant lobbying, emerging violations, and tenacious complicating factors have now knocked the expected bloodbath into an increasingly powerful cocked hat, say sources. Meanwhile, cracks in the alliance have erupted, linking harsh inroads with a lagging industrial base.

Last week, the coalition warned that 152 recommendations would be submitted, cutting deeply into the support for renewed wrangling. But such policies have long irked the delegates, and the fear now is that they will sound a death knell to the Constitution by muting their quarrels or adding that there are still elements to be ironed out.

Embattled leaders have long lengthened the rift by using such strategies as sidedown, slowmate, staletracking, and stiffening. Now aides predict a downgrading and stymying of routine foreign cutoffs, unless the nuclear family can be bailed out of this legal vacuum. Dr. Bourne reasserted his innocence of any wrongdoing.

The transitional government will close for defusing next week, without having resolved core conflicts or posed the uneasy questions that might assuage local hardliners. However, an authorized biography is likely to continue for months, possibly even years, to come. Not all styles in all sizes.

Continued on Page D6, Column 1

Kemp, Dent in Reagan Plans

A few hours after George Steinbrenner vowed that the New York Yankees would not trade Bucky Dent, the Yankees traded Dent to the Republicans for Jack Kemp.

The trade was announced at a press conference at Yankee Stadium just after a doubleheader between the two teams, in which the Yankees won the first game, $560,000 to $240,500. The Reagan team then shut out New York, $98.3 billion to 0, with a murderous tax bill in the top of the ninth.

Later, in the locker room, Dent was asked about his new position. He will represent upstate New York in the U.S. House of Representatives. "I'm comfortable with it," he said. "I haven't been all that happy with the Yankees recently. Mr. Steinbrenner was constantly on my back about fiscal this and earnings that, and he told me my work on last year's annual report wasn't thought very highly of in the front office. At one point he tried to make me sell individual pizzas during games—something to do with revenue. And then a few months ago he declared a three-for-one split—me, Nettles, and Smalley having to take turns going down to Wall Street to sit around the Stock Exchange and see if anybody would give us some money. Now at least Mr. Reagan has made it clear that all he wants me to do is play ball."

"So what!" Steinbrenner steamed when Dent's remarks were read to him as he sought a limousine.

Reportedly, the idea for a trade came from the White House Office of Player Personnel, the Bechtel Group, which released this statement: "Jack Kemp is a very fine young man, and the Reagan organization is very sorry to see him leave Washington. We all have the greatest respect for his lovely family. He should be grateful for all that Ronald Reagan has done for him."

At an impromptu briefing on the White House helicopter pad, Reagan waved, smiled, and said, "I sensed Jack wasn't happy, because he couldn't keep his mind on the gate receipts. He kept nagging day in and day out about spending what-all and the other thing, supply, and he frankly just made a nuisance. It was time to cut the guy loose. He'll be better off in a situation where I won't always be having to have to prove I'm sane."

However, Kemp's spokesman, talent agent Bob Haldeman, said, "Jack loves his teammates in the Capitol, but he is a sincere idealist who actually believes that George Steinbrenner is a man of unswerving principle—unlike some other people who Jack has too much integrity to comment on."

Invited to reply to this by a TV newscaster waiting at Andrews Air Force Base, Reagan chuckled and burst out spontaneously, "You know, I'd love to go back into show business. It would be fun to do that vaudeville routine where you take a Jack-in-the-box and hit it with a hammer. But seriously. Jack Kemp sure in Hades didn't turn out to be a team player, which is how I never thought in the first place. Where is the sportsmanship that his wonderful parents instilled? Who does he think he is, as he seems to think?"

Flagged down on a California freeway, former Yankee manager Billy Martin was asked for his opinion of the trade. While explaining carefully that Steinbrenner needed to be taken down a peg or two, Martin drove away.

A source close to a companion of Reggie Jackson's maintained guardedly that "Reggie is keeping a positive mental attitude at all times."

Steinbrenner is rumored to have really hit the ceiling on hearing this.

Later in the day, the cause of Steinbrenner's ire was divulged when he chewed out an ebullient Reagan in a limo driven by an undercover reporter. Steinbrenner had begun the negotiations months ago, when the Reagan organization was trying to unload David Stockman. At the last minute, Reagan jawboned Steinbrenner into taking Kemp off his hands as the precondition for a Stockman deal. Now the Yankees have had to arrange to sell Kemp to MGM–United Artists and buy Stockman outright for an undisclosed sum of cash.

Stockman's old position, Director of the Office of Management and Budget, will be held down by a callboy.

After hearing this news from his representative, West Coast superagent Ham Jordan, Stockman telephoned a reporter at home and confided, "It's tremendous news, just tremendous—a tremendous break for me. Ever since I was a little baby, I've wanted a position on the New York Yankees, with all the joy in economic performance that makes it worthwhile. An impossible dream, but then—you know me! I have a way of getting myself into situations that are way over my head and then flagellating myself for failing to overcome the tremendous odds. I don't know—maybe that's even what I'm doing right now. Setting myself up for failure. O.K.! Let's say I'm asking for trouble, it's probably hopeless, but it's the chance of a lifetime—to be with a winner. What an exciting prospect! The Reagan thing, you know, began to change tremendously once it started to not work out. There is athlete's foot on the Presidency. It is growing. It compounds itself daily, like interest. It's a phenomenal—a giant fungus! How do we keep it off us? For all I know, maybe the whole world, even the Yankees, is doomed necessarily to be this type of uncontrollable—these things of this nature, and the like, which allow no one to function within them as a rational shortstop. What did I just say? Are you writing this down?"

Reached for a reaction in what he described as "the middle of the night," Reagan said laughingly, "If that's his interpretation, all I can say is he's as equally entitled to it as I am. Very frankly, he has always had a loose rotator cuff. Like the rest of the country, it is very sad for his family and we have great sympathy. Bucky Dent—now there is a very popular young man with our American population. As far as Jack Kemp, it's not my job to make trades for the Yankees, but they bought a pig in a poke there, and they have nothing but our compassion."

Kemp's personal manager, Jerry Ford, said, "Jack Kemp can play hardball with the best of them. But he has a frail ego like all professional egomaniacs. And this career instability at this point is affecting his athletic condition."

Reagan's phone was off the hook by then, but his aide Lyn Nofziger, "psychiatrist to the stars," commented, "I knew Jack Kemp wouldn't last five minutes in a business such as the New York Yankees."

The Reagan History of the United States

> [President] McKinley gave Rowan a letter to be delivered to Garcia; Rowan took the letter and did not ask, "Where is he at?" . . . It is not booklearning young men need, nor instruction about this and that, but a stiffening of the vertebrae which will cause them to be loyal to a trust, to act promptly, concentrate their energies; do the thing—"carry a message to Garcia!" . . . We have recently been hearing much maudlin sympathy for the "down-trodden denizen of the sweat-shop" and the "homeless wanderer searching for honest employment," and with it all go many hard words for the men in power. . . . In our pitying, let us drop a tear, too, for the men who are striving to carry on a great enterprise whose working hours are not limited by the whistle, and whose hair is fast turning white through the struggle to hold in line dowdy indifference. . . . My heart goes out to the man . . . who, when given a letter for Garcia, quietly takes the missive, without asking any idiotic questions, and with no lurking intention of chucking it into the nearest sewer, or of doing aught else but deliver it, never gets "laid-off," nor has to go on a strike for higher wages. Civilization is one long anxious search for just such individuals.
>
> —Elbert Hubbard, "A Message to Garcia," 1899

Worried and embarrassed officials of a YMCA in Washington, D.C., confirmed that a man who penetrated the Y's security system late one night, entering a top-floor room through a window and sitting on a resident's bed to talk for about fifteen minutes, was President Ronald Reagan.

The YMCA resident, an unemployed librarian named Manuel Garcia, stated, "He shook me awake and read me this sort of bedtime story. He said it contained a 'message' that would 'promote backbone, eliminating pessimism and fear.' Fortunately, while he was reading, my vertebrae did stiffen to the degree that I was able to edge slowly toward the door."

President Reagan told reporters that he had been "disappointed" when Mr. Garcia voiced a need to go down the hall to bum a cigarette and never returned. "I was trying to bring the lessons of American history to the unemployed. Nowadays, you know, if you want something done, you have to do it yourself. Oh, well—what can you expect from someone who lives in the incredible filth they live in? You wouldn't believe the room. All over the floor—when you step down from the windowsill, it's literally knee-deep in bills, letters from collection agencies, repo notices, foreclosure documents, all just chucked on the floor like a sewer. To put one foot in there, I had to swallow very hard."

The President said that the story he had read aloud while perched at the foot of Mr. Garcia's bed was a fable about "the general, vague drift of what has happened to our country's ideals. Of course," he continued, "I was influenced in getting the concept and the writing style by our magnificent oil-company copywriters. And we have had some other pretty good utopian literature, too, which I had the opportunity to leaf through in the White House collection, thanks to so many of our fine historical writers of the past, whose ideas belong to us all today. I take full responsibility for their great words inserted alongside with my own."

He then distributed to reporters copies of his story.

Once upon a time, there was a Foolish Village and a Wise Village. The Foolish Villagers were a naive people who believed they could wish away their problems by electing a Council of Fools, which was inadequate to the complexities of government, being merely citizens who had chosen to meddle in council affairs. The villagers, many in bikinis, rode to work on colorful bicycles, heedless of the potential painful muscle infirmities. "Let us work hard today," they said, "and spend what we have earned tomorrow," ignoring one or two sober, level heads who predicted that the convoy of fools might wobble on the roadbed of economic inertia.

Youth no longer stunted and starved; age no longer harried by avarice; the child at play with the tiger; the man with the muck-rake drinking in the glory of the stars! Foul things fled, fierce things tame; discord turned to harmony!

Believing in all that, the Foolish Villagers became preoccupied with hedonistic woolgathering about the present and future. Most allowed their interest in television to dwindle, and swarmed instead to argument-provoking public debates and fetish parlors. Still others hunkered mindlessly over their vegetable gardens, where unauthorized sex proliferated, or lay reading idly beneath frail solar-heating panels that dotted the rooftops where they had been hastily flung up in the expectation of "something for nothing."

Adultery, assassination, poisoning, and other crimes of the like infernal nature were taught as lawful, and even as virtuous actions. Men were set upon each other, like a company of hellhounds to worry, rend, and destroy.

When, under discreet cover of darkness, concerned oil company representatives converged on the area, the brass fittings on their efficient portfolios burnished by moonlight, the village was ill equipped to comply with their suggestions.

Human nature goes not straight forward but by excess action and reaction in an undulated course.

Unable, or unwilling, to change course, the village tumbled into receivership. The only remaining business was a dingy waxworks arcade, where morose children, many in tattered bikinis, paid a penny to file past amateurishly modeled figurines of their parents, whose legacy to the new generation was only a hollow smile.

The Wise Village, however, adopted the long-term strategy needed to forestall trouble: success.

Giant miraculous Labor was felling the forests, and turning the glebe, and whirling the spinning jennies, and putting down its thoughts in words and deeds; the spires of an hundred thousand schoolhouses pointed to the skies; the fires of truth and self-sacrifice glowed in many more thousand breasts; the noblest aspirations were ascending from millions of noble souls.

A Coalition of Alarmed Fathers, democratically appointed on the basis of merit, had responded decisively to the incentives offered by several major enterprises in which they were stockholders, and the Wise Village was flooded with petroleum products, to the extent that some stores had to close for inventory. Heavy industries—such as psychiatry and inventory-taking—began to blossom, turning the village into a hub of cosmopolitanism visited by the duly nominated, exotically garbed delegates of various juntas and well-wishing corporations from South of the Border, the Land of the Rising Sun, and the Back of Beyond.

Penalties, temporal and eternal; splendour, pomp, and honour; united to terrify, to dazzle, to awe and to flatter the human mind.

Dressed in handsome frontier-style garments scarcely distinguishable from the finest clothing, and uninhibited by shortsighted utilitarian carping about the effects of ornamental garters upon the blood circulation of the women, the villagers drove roomy automobiles to and from the exciting inventory parlors that gave texture and variety to the naturally flat cement landscape, or spontaneously entertained themselves by leafing through the brightly illustrated booklets of Rules and Regulations dispensed free to all by television repairmen.

Was there, then, no way of commanding the services of the mighty wealth-producing principle of consolidated capital without bowing down to a plutocracy like that of Carthage? As soon as men began to ask themselves this question, they found the answer ready for them.

Gold!

The news rapidly spread, and there was soon a large number of men on the spot, some of whom obtained several pounds per day, at the start. The gulch had been well dug up for the large lumps, but there was still great wealth in the earth and sand, and several operators only waited for the wet season to work it in a systematic manner. Secure in possessing the "Open Sesamé" to the exhaustless treasury under their feet, they gave free rein to every whim or impulse which could possibly be gratified.

A vigorous series of sporadic wars was initiated against the Foolish Village, as a means of acquiring raw materials to manufacture more guns. The young men, having demonstrated their bravery, had no need to "prove" their masculinity by deflorations of young girls, and within a decade a Council of Wise Virgins was authorized to sit with the Coalition of Alarmed Fathers, in an advisory capacity. The President of the Coalition looked about him in satisfaction. With the money markets under control, the ax falling regularly upon the necks of criminals, and the Foolish Village duly subdued and annexed under the provisions of an Extemporaneous Amendment, there appeared to remain no irrational force to wreck his accomplishments.

But a Malefactor, accused of *Witchcraft* as well as *Murder*, and Executed in this place more than Forty Years ago, did then give Notice, of, *An Horrible PLOT against the Country by* WITCHCRAFT, *and a Foundation of* WITCHCRAFT *then Laid, which if it were not seasonably Discovered, would probably Blow up, and pull down all the Churches in the country*. An Army of *Devils* horribly broke in upon the place which is the *Center*: and the Houses of the Good People there, fill'd with the doleful Shrieks of their Children and Servants.

Even as the President sternly pointed his finger at the Focus of Evil, his House began to emit conflicting rhetorical signals, and sprang a series of *Malicious* LEAKS.

Garcia was somewhere in the mountain fastnesses of Cuba—no one knew where. No mail or telegraph message could reach him. The President must secure his cooperation, and quickly.

—written with HENRY GEORGE, TIMOTHY DWIGHT, MARGARET FULLER, PARKE GODWIN, JOHN TAYLOR, EDWARD BELLAMY, BAYARD TAYLOR, COTTON MATHER, and ELBERT HUBBARD

Pac Hits Fan

In the wake of the elections, a force to be reckoned with has petered out into an ill wind. The richest and hitherto most dreaded of the Political Action Committees, the National Team for Promoting Itself and a Conservative Congress (NTPICC), aims to guide public debate into a vortex of underlying negativity in such a way that the overriding importance of NTPICC is revealed. During the campaign, NTPICC spent $40 million to spread 40 rumors, to direct-mail 400 outright lies, to place 4,000 unflattering advertisements, and to deliver 40,000 demagogic salvos, generating a 40 percent higher fear factor. However, only three candidates targeted by NTPICC were defeated: Representative Paul J. Mangle (D-Mich.), Senator Joseph P. Skorfones (R-Ill.), and Representative Dominic Egregio (D-N.Y.). Each had received a 50 percent rating from the Americans for Democratic Action and a 50 percent rating from the American Conservative Union, as NTPICC's ads and press releases repeatedly pointed out in denouncing the three as "wishy-washy" by comparison with NTPICC's own decisive tornado of ads and press releases.

In Tennessee, where Republican Senator Winton K. Nullings was beaten in his bid for a fifth term, NTPICC circulated a cropped photo purporting to show his Democratic opponent, Representative Maurice B. Spran, all alone. But Spran's staff indignantly released the original, showing a number of active, involved staff members, cute interns, and ABSCAM informants in the picture. The fine points of the photographic fraud were not lost on the voters, despite their *perception* of what *might* have been true had the truth lain somewhere.

In an attempt to defeat Democrat Joseph F. X. Scullery, Jr., who was running for a Massachusetts Congressional seat, NTPICC aired 400,000 TV spots featuring pirated footage of a National Endowment for the Arts–funded dance troupe, dressed in ecclesiastical garb and miming the sixteenth-century papal ban on opera while a voiceover charged that Mr. Scullery was dodging the issue of federally subsidized opera as a form of government-imposed birth control. Mr. Scullery remained unaware of the commercials, but even if he had not, he would have *appeared* to remain unaware of them.

Thousands of schoolchildren were hired by New Jersey NTPICC to deliver complimentary frozen ducks to undecided households. But the bribery tactic backfired on incumbent Republican Congressman Phil ("Pete") Musser, who spent the rest of the campaign denying that he had ever said the freeze was a canard. And in Florida, Republican Congresswoman Estelle Hexler never recovered from her 40-point drop in the polls when her elderly constituents were deluged with NTPICC mailings of "ballot cards" asking whether they favored a Constitutional amendment to mandate that mandatory prayers be printed on Social Security checks in place of payable dollar amounts. In both cases, the facts of the matter were difficult to establish in the absence of a certainty that the matter existed, and exit polls showed a voter failure to receive this or that *impression.*

NTPICC may have been weakened by the recently published book *A Pac with the Devil,* by the late Percy Prang, which asserts that NTPICC's leader, Yancy Lang, who has vigorously supported the death penalty, has himself been dead for four years. NTPICC's power may also be eroded by a newly formed anti-action-committee action committee, Bust Action Committees with Plain-Ass Common Sense (BACPACS), which is already planning a defense of Senator Sam Spofford (D-Va.) two years from now. Spofford is sure to be singled out by NTPICC, because it is angered by the way his frequent, popular appearances on D.C.-area TV and radio talk shows deplete the air time available for NTPICC to single him out.

NTPICC has already announced that most of its resources for the next election will go into targeting five Democratic and five Republican members of the House: John Peter Telly (D-Conn.), Gary G. McGreen (D-Ore.), Martha Fortfield Garglan (D-Pa.), Paul J. Kowlicki (D-Minn.), Bill Bobbin, Jr. (D-Vt.), Hamilton R. Schneehart (R-Calif.), Mengel A. Puppe (R-Ga.), Earl B. Ninick (R-Okla.), John O. Calf (R-Nev.), and Ermeto P. Invigorita (R-N.J.). NTPICC argues that these people are "dead wood," since their votes in the House cancel each other out. This theory may be irrefutable, but if it can be *seen* as speckled with flaws, NTPICC itself might be on the spot.

The Sacred Front

The day was as fine and the scene was as fair at Newmarch as the party was numerous and various; . . . I don't know why—it was a sense instinctive and unreasoned, but . . . I was just conscious, vaguely, of being on the track of a law, a law that would fit, that would strike me as governing the delicate phenomena—delicate though so marked—that my imagination found itself playing with.

—Henry James, *The Sacred Fount*

Anyone with an eye and an ear for the nuances of a new sensibility should be able to detect the telltale signs of the new cold war culture.

—Andrew Kopkind, "The Return of Cold War Liberalism," *The Nation*, April 23, 1983

1.

As Gilbert Long strode vigorously toward me on the station platform, he struck me as so uncharacteristically alive that I concluded he must be having a liberating sex experience with someone. For more than a decade we had met at least semiannually, at Newmarch, where we were both again now bound and where his quotidian plodding dullness had been bearable only in that it was essential—for what was Newmarch if not a sense of coalition kept up by everyone's being so conscious that they were not just tolerant but, at the minimum, liberal? Which is not to say that if one was at Newmarch, Newmarch hadn't its reasons, beyond proving that it could suffer a bore or two, a couple of bleached-out spots in the social fabric. Among its reasons was that the whole fine enterprise required a certain number of warm bodies. Of these I had judged Long hardly the warmest, but as we settled into adjoining seats on the train, I thought how markedly he had evolved. On the evidence of his progress, I might have been justified in reserving a ticket for utopia.

His eyes, rarely seen to move in their sockets, now intently scanned our car, but if the face he sought—his lover's?—was there, it was obscured behind one of a sea of copies of Radosh and Milton's new book on the Rosenberg case, though the only "spying" for which *I* was willing to shoulder blame was my own prying avidity to take the erotic measure of Long's improvement. I could scarcely defend my urge to snoop by prematurely accusing him of privatism; hadn't he the right to hoard his new relationship for a time before contributing it to the general consciousness for analysis? Yet guiltily I couldn't stop my eyes from following his, and he fairly caught me out:

"I'm only looking," he said, "for the other dupes and stooges among these fellow-travelers."

The thrust showed an ironic wit of which he had hitherto been judged incapable; this virile comedian was not the same drab timid institution who had driven even as indulgent a comrade as "Do Your Own Thing" Lutley to dub him "the Great Gray Lady." With my astonished amusement egging him on, he grew still more delightful on the subject of a film he had seen—just a television miniseries, *The Winds of War*, but as I recall he put across one or two very clever ideas, couched in satiric form. Further emboldened by my good-natured responsiveness, he consolidated his position by ringing for a porter to remove me from my seat so he could "spread out." As I was carried reluctantly down the aisle, I wondered again about his lover, and about the passion whose effect was so revolutionary.

2.

When we drew near our station, and passengers began gathering their luggage, Long passed me to position himself at the door and be first off the train, saying he had "a horror of mob rule." I was still laughing when, surprised by a stinging sensation on my shoulder, I looked around, up a statuesque figure, and into the stern, lovely face of a stranger.

"Traitor," she said.

That was hard—but then I was struck by something else, a familiarity that made me guess she might be soft on this particular treason.

"Do you dare snub me?" she asked. And as it dawned that she was indeed Grace Brissenden, she playfully dealt me another lash with what I saw to be the black leather horsewhip she famously carried, by reputation the one Emma Goldman had used to punish a fellow-anarchist turncoat. At Newmarch, some of us practically worshiped this dazzling accessory.

"It's only," I pleaded, "that I didn't recognize you."

"Because I was wrapped up in that book about those sp—"

"Because you're so *young!*" The year before, she had turned a manifest forty-five, but so magnificently that any sexist or agist slipping into Newmarch by mistake would have been hard put to classify Grace Brissenden other than as we did ourselves: as the most beautiful among persons in principle beautifully equal. Walking now with her from the train, I tried to pinpoint her transformation, and finally attributed it to a revitalized posture. She was taut; her spine seemed to vibrate, like an antenna receiving a signal: *There's something out there. . . . Don't be intimidated!* Now and then she inclined forward, daring whatever was "out there" to "play chicken." Her body she had wholly given over to what one might call brinksmanship. It took thirty years off her; it put her in a ponytail and a circle skirt in the 1950s.

But when I said as much, she recoiled disingenuously. "Nonsense, these faded baggy bell-bottoms from the sixties are 'retro' enough for an old woman like me. Anyway, Guy likes them."

Indeed, it was Guy Brissenden I presumed to be the source of her rejuvenation. Word of their marriage five months earlier had sent shock waves through the Newmarch group; but Grace and Guy were, if anyone was, up to taking the curse off matrimonialism. For a start, his being twenty years her junior gave the thing a redeeming unorthodoxy. And then, his black curls, his darting boyish curiosity, his eagerness to learn how the world, in practice, really worked, counterpointed the golden goddesslike mystique that made people believe Grace already knew everything. Together they were an aesthetically delectable pair, and we, after all, weren't puritans. Besides, if marriage gave *them* pleasure—well, we weren't dictators! Nor were they, it seemed, to one another; Grace told me Guy had come out to Newmarch the day before with Lady John. Catching the gleam of approval in my eye, she smiled:

"Yes, it's matrimonialism with a human face."

3.

A considerate anarchy being the prevalent mode at Newmarch—one never so much as touched on the matter of who might "own" the place, or whether "Newmarch" was the town or the house or simply the name fitted to our common idea—I made no formal greetings but went straight to my room. The same was invariably held for me, but as I opened the door, I wondered if I had been "frozen out," for on my bed, with his back to me, sat a naked old man with gray wisps of hair, muttering as if he were quite at home.

"Excuse me," I said, "but I think you're in my room."

He turned to me a fragile, wrinkled face. "*My* room, *your* room, what's the point? We have no need of boundaries or borders any longer. Aren't we all citizens of the planet earth?" He seized my suitcase and began rifling it. As I wrestled it from his feeble grasp, he selected a pair of my undershorts and put them on. "I dislike street clothes," he serenely explained. "They obscure the fundamental likeness of all citizens of the earthly planet. How many three-piece suits do you guess would survive a nuclear apocalypse?" He had got hold of my passport. "You won't be needing this now."

"Just who do you think you are?" I cried.

"Guy Brissenden, of course, but I know what you mean. What do names signify, when we all put on our shorts one leg at a time?"

He was, I suddenly saw, who he said he was, yet as altered by his tottering decrepitude as was his wife by her youthquake. Had my eyes not just then lighted on a socialist pamphlet that had tumbled from my suitcase during our struggle, I might never have located the cause. The redistribution of wealth! He had given *her* his youth. His recompense was—what? Inner peace, which he now meant to globalize, bestowing upon the rest of us earthlings his panacea for world brotherhood. Take, I urged myself, the analysis, correct as it is thus far, still farther. By analogy, mightn't Gilbert Long, former mental proletarian of our community, have according to his need expropriated *his* just portion from his lover? And wouldn't *she* then, by extrapolation, be the very one among us whose capital wit had been the most depleted?

I was all aware that outsiders might see her and poor Guy as being, by the other two, exploited. But if I found an attractive, progressive pattern in what superficially resembled a sordid survival of the fittest—well, wasn't what Newmarch had given *me* precisely that warm optimism?

4.

A chill was in the autumn air as we gathered on the patio for cocktails. I had my secret mission, but I couldn't find a fourth person, let alone a woman, who had dramatically changed. May Server was still pretty in her wraithlike way, with that hibiscus she always pathetically wore in her hair to "make an effort" and that signature expression of numb terror. Judging from Ford Obert's gestures, he was telling her for the umpteenth time the story of how his Yiddish-speaking father, an immigrant to Detroit, had named him "Ford" in the militant belief that the boy would live to oversee the UAW's capture of the means of production of automotive commodities. He told it movingly, and May was probably the only one there who found its repetition tedious; she would, under cover of her zombie manner, be fixating on some cryptic, peripheral detail, which she would hone to a morbid gem of description and later produce unnervingly at table, like a filigree dinner ring wrought from a human hair. I was fascinated by her being there yet not one of the crowd, in it yet so very "out of it"; but when I moved to join them, I was intercepted by a belligerent Lady John:

"It may be too soon to tell, but in the opinion of very many highly placed people it is not too soon to say that the time is coming when we may well have reason to fear the same kind of thing that once tore this country apart. 'Stalinist menace' may be too harsh a term in the opinion of some very indifferently placed people, but if I were you, I would consider whether the conventional wisdom is not urgently in need of being rethought."

Clearly she was inebriated. *Her* value had always lain as much in her soothing capacity to restate infinitely the obvious as in the eccentric taste for thrift-shop British couture which had given rise to the nickname "Lady." Now, stewed to the gills and babbling enigmatic prophecies, her Norman Hartnell pillbox aggressively awry, she was if anything *more* interesting. As Gilbert Long's putative partner, she was therefore dismissable, along with May, from contention.

Mercifully, Grace Brissenden loomed before us. "Go along, darling Lady," she commanded, teetering threateningly and giving the pillbox a mock tap with Emma Goldman's horsewhip. "Do go find my husband, won't you? You're the only person here who amuses him."

In Grace's cool blue eyes lurked some obscure tactic, but I didn't ask what, so eager was I to divert her subtlety to my own design. Briefly, I told her about my theory, omitting of course any unflattering reference to poor Guy's virtual senility.

"Why, that's riveting!" she said. "Aren't you clever! I wonder who she can be? I know that in principle we've no right to assume it's not a *he,* but I don't blame you for not thinking of it. If Long wasn't 'straight' before, I'll bank on my instinct that he is now. You must let me know the minute you flush her out. I insist that you work on nothing else all weekend. I'll keep *my* eyes open too, and report back. Off you go!"

Somehow, it occurred to me, I *was* "off," but my sounding board had already vanished into the crowd. My speculation drifted to Mrs. Froome, our distinguished feminist theoretician, but she was said to have recently concluded an unhappy affair with an alcoholic chauffeur from the Soviet Embassy, and could be heard shrilling the virtues of hearth and home, as a cover for her disappointment, while her interlocutor, "Do Your Own Thing" Lutley, nodded in feigned support of her charade. There was a blond bombshell with de Dreuil, the activist actor, but she had clearly been imported from Hollywood for the occasion; they were engaged in some form of guerrilla theater, prancing about with American flags.

Lady John had by now captured poor Guy, who was maundering dreamily in his, or someone's, pajamas. Recalling that these two had come out together on the train, I wondered—as perhaps Grace mischievously had—if his maddening homilies were what had driven Lady over the brink, or if her Cassandra line was a ploy calculated to lure him back to reality by meeting her halfway.

At any rate, I had *my* little mission, and roamed about alone. Fortunately nobody paid the slightest attention to my inquisitive perambulations. There were far too many new faces, however, to suit my purpose: quite a lot of people speaking some volatile eastern European tongue that decidedly wasn't the Russian I had so often heard at Newmarch in years past, and young men in neoconservative suits whose vulnerability to nuclear damage challenged poor Guy to a long evening of proselytizing. Passing around the front of the house, I thought I saw at the bottom of the driveway a Libyan freedom fighter and a Mau-Mau being mistakenly ejected from the grounds, but before I could intervene, Grace Brissenden magically appeared at my side, saying urgently, "You must see—you must!"

The wooden deck to which she quickly led me looked out over a spacious lawn, rich with a thickening carpet of dead leaves, which rollingly descended to an herb garden surrounding a white gazebo. What happy evenings I had spent in that gazebo with Newmarch comrades, enjoying the herbs and dancing to the lilting rhythms of the Beatles' "Revolution 9"! Nowadays the herb garden gave off an odor of Paraquat, and vandals had turned the gazebo into a missile silo. In its shadow, more wraithlike than ever, stood May Server. She beckoned cajolingly to a partner, but whoever it was remained hidden on the far side.

"It *must* be Gilbert Long," said Grace. "I saw them talking together not five minutes ago."

A man's naked foot peeped out from behind the silo. "Does that look like Long's foot?"

"How ever would *I* know?" But even as she spoke, the man emerged, took May's outstretched hand, and led her back into hiding. It was poor Guy. When they failed to reappear, I concluded that they must have entered the silo by a door concealed from our line of vision.

"It's *she!*" uttered Grace in agitation. "*She's* the one!"

"Impossible," I said. "She's unchanged; she's fascinating."

"The only fascinating thing about her," said Grace, "is that she's using my husband as a screen. He's the only one too kind to see how otherwise very unfascinating she is."

"But—"

Grace wouldn't hear me out. "You're wrong," she said. "You'll see."

Dismissively, I turned away from the vista to face the house, whereupon I perceived through a window an unsettling tableau. Ford Obert and Lady John, in a far corner of the room, their heads cocked and eyes narrowed, judgmentally regarded what I at first took to be my own person. In the next instant, however, I understood that what they appraised from so objective a distance must be the big picture between the windows in the Newmarch gallery.

5.

As Grace and I entered the gallery, Gilbert Long, previously hidden from my view by an enormous unpacked crate of new acquisitions, was talking rapidly, with elegant gestures toward the older cultural icon at issue. I just failed to catch his concluding words, but the other two keenly met my eye as if to say, "Now, *here's* a fellow qualified to mediate the terms of discourse."

"What do you think of it?" Grace asked me disarmingly.

Between the windows, where it had always been, was a poster, framed in Plexiglas, some five or six feet in height, of a stylized male figure dressed from head to toe in black and wearing a black mask; the usual thing.

"Well," I said, "it's a symbol of the black man's struggle, isn't it?—I mean, all black people's struggle—to retain their ethnic identity while, on the other hand, having inescapably a consciousness that their color is a barrier—a mask, as it were—between them and their full acceptance as individuals by the white oppressor."

"I'm sure we can all agree upon *that*," said Grace firmly, as the other three drew near. "But from *you* we expect an opinion—oh, farther out."

"Well," I went on, "you could say too that it's gay rights. In fact, wasn't there something of the kind on the cover of Burroughs's last book?"

"Why," spluttered Lady John, "Tarzan was *never*—"

Obert broke in smoothly. "I daresay it's less parochial than *that*—

sympathetic though I may be to the plight of our sadomasochistic brothers and sisters."

"Well," I said, "I wouldn't put that down as a marginal concern, but I do see what you mean. I mean, the image does cry out to take in everyone."

"And that's exactly what your critique hasn't yet confronted," said Obert. "The assertion of raw monolithic all-consuming power."

I fancied that Lady John glanced for approval at Gilbert Long before she spoke. "It's totalitarian!"

"But don't you see?" I said. "The total, audaciously utter *blackness* of it—well, doesn't that inevitably imply—doesn't it compel you to imagine—its opposite?"

"You're saying that when we look at black, we should see white?" Grace smilingly prompted.

"Not only that we should—that we *do!* It's a proven law of optics. And when," I brought out triumphantly, "you sense the hidden light and allow it to flood your consciousness—well, it's astoundingly beautiful!"

"It's *horrible*," came a penetrating whisper. May Server had crept silently into the gallery during my interrogation.

"It's *about* horror, my dear," said Obert. "There I quite agree with you, whatever our well-meaning, generous-minded, light-flooded friend here may say. But that isn't quite the same thing as its being in and of itself a horror. Some of us find it a quite effectively unsentimentalized portrait of evil."

"In and of itself it's horrible," she quietly insisted, trembling. "It reminds me of the waiters' uniforms in the Sheraton coffee shop in El Salvador."

"Shouldn't we go in?" murmured Lady John ambiguously.

"Perhaps," continued Obert, "I haven't made my meaning—"

"It hasn't *got* any meaning." Now all but inaudible, May's quavering voice had somehow the effect of an anesthetizing shriek. "It's the enigma that *is* the horror. The never knowing . . . the Black Maria rounding the corner . . . the *noche de muerte* . . . the asphalt freeway, the blacking-out behind the wheel . . . the repellent swishing noise of nuns' habits brushing against army boots . . . the final annihilating nightmare of realizing that even this emblematic fugue means nothing, nothing, noth—" Outside, a champagne cork popped, and she mouthed a soundless scream and dived for cover under a coffee table.

While the others tried to lure her out, I was led aside by Grace, who said, "How do you answer her? By proposing that this—this *thing* is humanism with a fascist face?"

I couldn't tell if she was baiting me. But as she leaned over me, she seemed on the very brink of attack; I flinched, and she drew back as if satisfied.

"Darling," she said, "why don't you just concentrate on who's sleeping with whom, and whether enough of them are blacks, and leave the rest of us, who aren't, after all, so tender and sensitive as you, to grapple with the big crude clumsy guns of international issues and practicalities."

She was charming. Why, then, did I feel dizzy, as if her charm had an ideological spin? Was something the matter at Newmarch? The only thing I was sure of was that this was no time for bothering to refute May Server's self-dramatizing drivel. Was it I who had, in my estimate of May, so thoroughly changed? Or had *she*—her mind ransacked for the greater glory of Gilbert Long's? Or had recent history simply rendered her worse than irrelevant? Poor May—in any case, her hibiscus had wilted.

6.

All unawares, I too had been rendered decidedly "out of it." Having in my ruminations taken a time to dress, I entered the dining room late and was almost palpably struck by a crowd who had humiliatingly neglected to inform me that the evening's party was a festive "theme" masquerade. Seating myself inconspicuously at the end of the table, I tried to make out the controlling motif. Ford Obert had greased his hair and shadowed his jowls in simulation of Senator Joseph McCarthy; de Dreuil, in a false mustache, adroitly mimed Dean Acheson; awash in a red silk cape and topped by a matching biretta, "Do Your Own Thing" Lutley was the cosmopolitan Bishop Fulton J. Sheen; and Gilbert Long, with a slide rule in his breast pocket, was passing out cigars and announcing that he was "the proud father of the H-bomb," Edward Teller. Most of the women must have been writhing in competitive pique, for Mrs. Froome was only the most accurate of any number of Hedda Hoppers with hats and lists of show-business subversives. Lady John, typically vague and overworking a small vocabulary of props, flourished a snifter of brandy and one of the H-bomb cigars—connoting, I guessed, Churchill. Only Grace, to my right, puzzled me: impeccably mannish in *le smoking*, she mysteriously resembled—yet how *could* she?—John Foster Dulles.

And what then *was* the theme? If it was "The Fifties," why did the Harvard professor across from me keep thrusting his forefinger at me and shouting "Ich bin ein Berliner"? And why then hadn't anyone come as Jerry Lee Lewis or Elvis or Betty "Shoop Shoop" Everett? Or Jack Paar, or Stalin? Or Marilyn, or Kinsey? Or Kukla, Fran, and Ollie, or Ethel and Julius?

Poor Guy and May straggled in last, and I felt a surge of sympathy; they too were in the dark. Guy had only changed into a fresh pair of my shorts; as he sat down on the other side of Grace, she tenderly tucked around his bare shoulders a radiation-resistant Lurex shawl. May, across from him, had merely traded her hibiscus for a fresh one—perhaps, if Grace's hypothesis was correct, sent up to her by Gilbert Long like a prom corsage; but then wouldn't her lover have plotted for her a costume that might with his covertly correspond? Instead it was poor May and poor Guy who corresponded all too obviously.

Yet I couldn't think it through to illumination, not with everyone at the table trying so agreeably, so volubly to stay "in character." Indeed, as the huge dim hall echoed with *coups de théâtre*—strident denunciations of "terrorism" and calls for "deterrence"—I felt that thought was an unwelcome guest, and that a pretty idea which happened to infiltrate the conversation might find such a reception as is awarded that comic-strip boogeyman the "KGB agent" booted out the door and onto a plane back to Moscow.

I cannot convey my happiness as, blowing desperately on the embers of our mutual consciousness, I felt there then reassuringly glow in me anew the incendiary compact by which we none of us need remind the others who we "really" were or discredit by explicitness our unfazable, indestructible harmony of purpose. And as if on cue, loudspeakers began to emit those squawks I knew were preparatory to the stereophonic musical accompaniment that always enhanced dinner at Newmarch by inducing rapt submission to the common hallucinatory spell. As the first waves of sound swept over us, silencing the dreadful talk, I could not but reflect on the power of this sublime art to persuade me that we all vibrated to the same tune, that together we sought to quench a thirst for an ideal of perfection. It was on this pitch that I should have liked to leave them all, but alas!—a developing tide in the music was now pulling me, by means of a melody deviously banal, into a mainstream of orchestral bullying.

I turned to Grace. "What *is* this—this thing?"

She laughed. "The music from *Victory at Sea!*"

7.

Later that night, I found myself pacing restlessly alone through the sitting rooms. Dinner had terminated in stasis, the party having gone straight to bed instead of evolving, in the old manner, toward caucuses for the exercise of perdurable debates. The whole place now had the air of a once busy shop on whose plate-glass window was pasted the forbidding sign "SOLD OUT."

I fiercely desired to smoke, but could find no one to smoke with. Out of habit, I strolled unthinking down to the gazebo, and experienced the awful jolt of its being now a missile silo; but remembering that I had conjectured some entry on the far side, I went around and indeed saw set in the hillside a hatch door, ajar, through which was visible none other than poor Guy. I settled on him gratefully as a suitable companion with whom to smoke; his state of consciousness already profoundly altered, he wouldn't much encroach on my supply. Besides, I wished to convey my kindly feelings—to signal that, in my detections, *I* didn't mean to encroach on whatever pleasures he and May Server had privately stashed.

He looked more wizened than ever, hunched at a desk, engaged with paper and colored pencils in some sort of drawing. Seeing me, he hastened to cover his work with a manila envelope.

"Oh, I'm so embarrassed," he said. "I've been struggling, you know, with my design for a Citizen of the World Passport. I believe you'd find it of interest. But it's much too amateurish to show you at this point. I haven't got the pattern worked out. Doves flying over a rainbow is what I'm aiming for."

"Nice," I said, lighting up. "I'd like to see it sometime. What's this room we're in?"

"The command-and-control bunker. The missiles are next door." I invited him to smoke, but he declined. "Want to know a secret?"

Who didn't?

"That horsewhip my wife carries. The one everybody thinks was Emma Goldman's. She bought it in 1962 at Abercrombie and Fitch. She brags about it behind your backs. Don't let her get your goat. She's just an old humbug."

On the strength of this intimate confession, however embittered or even fraudulent, I presumed to ask him to carry up to his wife, at his leisure, a message as to where I awaited her; for, upon leaving her after dinner, I had taken as a promise her droll "See you later, alligator."

8.

Poor Guy had at once diplomatically complied, and not five minutes later Grace Brissenden confronted me in the bunker. Her half-smile of willingness to seek *détente* was perhaps an illusion projected by my wishful thinking, to judge from the way she impatiently flicked her thigh with the now questionably anarchist horsewhip.

Cleverly I began by conceding a moot point. "I only want to congratulate you," I said, "on being right. It *is* May; she *has* changed; she's grown hopelessly dull and insufferable; she must therefore be Gilbert Long's mistress."

"What are you saying?"

"You remember our talks—about the redistribution of mental wealth."

"I'm sure I don't know what you mean when you use such jargon."

She *was* sharp; the "jargon" accusation was my Achilles heel. I would have to be more emotionally open. "Darling Grace," I said, "we're alone, you and I. You needn't pretend with me. We're old friends."

"Don't be mushy." She was ice cold.

"The masquerade," I said more harshly, "is over."

"Masquerade?"

"That travesty at dinner."

"That was no masquerade," she said. "We simply are as we appear. Sometimes, you know," she continued, "you won't see things that aren't—"

"Aren't there?"

"No, that aren't as you wish they were. It makes people uncomfortable. They feel you expect them to be—"

"Better than they seem?"

"Better than they *are!* They feel you reproach them. And then they feel tired of feeling reproached, and then they feel like standing up for what they are."

"And as for what they *were?*"

"Oh, I don't deny it. We've all changed—all but you. We've seen the *light.*"

Was her emphasis a challenge to fight also over who owned which metaphors? I countered with one of theirs. "I don't choose to 'stand up' merely to salute the flag of my inalienable right to be no better than I am." Yet in her imputation to me of guilt, I felt something of my old tendency to wallow; *had* I irritated them to reaction? Grace had me on the run. But at that instant she inexplicably retreated, to make a grab for territory I had abandoned as strategically worthless:

"You're the one who's wrong," she said, "about May Server. It's not May; it's not anybody; there's no such thing. It was all just a game, an academic exercise in logistics, and now you won't pack up your tent but insist on crouching there with your inaccurate hand-drawn guerrilla maps of nothing, crowing over the success of some hypothetical ambush."

"Is that how you see me? As so ineffectually beside the point?"

She pondered. "No, I believe you're more dangerous than that. I think . . . I think you're a Commie!"

It was then that I saw how to make her play it out. "Where," I asked, "do you get your intelligence?"

"You know I can't reveal that."

"Have you sunk so low," I charged, "that you resort to claiming your so-called evidence comes from unidentified persons?"

"Ah, you know me too well. Civil liberties to the rescue. Very well, you shall have it: *I'm* my source. I know I'm right, because—because I know how I'm terribly *wrong*."

"How is that?"

"Domestically."

"I don't follow," I said. "Isn't it—our disagreement—basically on matters of foreign policy?"

"I'm not talking about that now, you idiot. I mean domestically in my domestic life. That's where I'm wrong. Look, you've gone sniffing around after people's private affairs—well, then, if you want so much to know, snap to attention. Gilbert Long and I—do I have to spell it out?"

"And poor—"

"Poor Guy? Yes, I drove him over the brink, or rather so far away from the brink that it amounts to the same thing. He persuaded himself that my marital infidelity is an inevitable byproduct of my dread of nuclear extinction."

"How miserable he must be!"

"You tender-headed fool—he's deliriously happy, he and his little May. I make them possible. It's I—it's *we*—who give them cause to huddle, quivering together like baby rabbits. They're ideally matched. They're a couple of children! Why, they're upstairs in her room right now, making crayon drawings and pasting each other's pictures in old passports. And we protect them, you see, from people like *you* who might upset them. And so we are, in ways you don't appreciate, immensely loyal."

"And your loyalty to the truth? To the ideal we once shared that every person has the capacity for—has the *right* to—the clear, bright consciousness that . . . that"—I was groping for eloquence, and a phrase came into my head—"that the person who steals your pants still gets into them one leg at a time?"

"Tell it to your Commie friends!" she said. "Goodnight!"

She turned, but I brought her around with my next shot: "If you don't believe, isn't it hypocritical to keep *that*?" And I indicated the horsewhip, though now convinced of its strictly commercial provenance.

"I suppose *you* want it, to chastise some poor leftie heretic who strays from the party line of the week. Have you forgotten that even your precious Emma, radical to the end, renounced the Bolshies?"

"No, but have *you* forgotten that she didn't shop at Abercrombie and Fitch?"

She didn't turn a whisker. "My plan is to donate it to a museum." Without warning, she tossed it to me. "It's yours, darling. *You're* a museum." And she was gone for good.

It was freezing in the bunker, but I hardly felt it, so acutely conscious was I of, above my head, the former site of the gazebo where Grace and I had together boogalooed. She still knew how to keep me on my toes. I had twice her *élan*, though, and was infinitely more promising. What I hadn't mastered was her timing.

The Revised Dictionary of Slang and Uncontrollable English

PREFACE

This new edition is the result of a contractual obligation and of my proximity to the English language for the many years during which I was preparing this edition. It is designed to form a monumental companion to that humble work *The Little Book of Pocket Words* (Gulf & Western University Press), at present the regrettable authority for standard English. From the *Oxford English Dictionary* (Oxford Home Box Office, now out of print, sadly) and *Webster's New International Dictionary, Second Edition* (alas, almost universally shredded or consumed as roll-your-own fireplace logs), as well as from diligent correspondents throughout the British Commonwealth and the U.S., I am proud to have learnt numerous terms, among them (reluctantly omitted here due to funding limitations) some forty or fifty thousand additional words and phrases which, on prolonged scrutiny, may be thought to connote some form of coital adjacency.

Here I am keen to give the proportions of entries:

Unpleasantries	50%
Repulsivisms	35%
Toilet articles	6%
Bad words	6%
Septics	2%
Unsavories	1%

Should the more distressing entries have been rendered in euphemism? This is the practice once followed by scholarly practitioners. My rule has been to deal with them only as salaciously as is required under the terms of my contractual obligation; in a few instances, I have had to suppress my natural tastefulness by means of flogging.

Finally, it is a pleasure to thank, for items that might well have been overlooked, Mr. Julyan Franklin, author of *A Lexicography of All the Pornographic Words in This Title*; Rev. Franklyn Julian, author of *A Water-Closet Medley*; Mrs. Jewel Lynn Frank, who generously shared notes for her work in progress, *The Rough Stuff*; and "Julia" of New Zealand—zealous rememberer, leechlike gatherer.

about time, or **a.t.** Approximate time of day; freq. employed by unemployed or by persons so sympathetic to unemployment that they use the argot as a matter of principle. *Times,* "'I will have a further announcement at 4 a.t.,' said Mrs. Thatcher."—2. In gen. idiom. use when speaker is neurologically incapable of knowing or discovering the time, as in (e.g., during tantrum, coital climax, etc.) *It's about time!*—3. Hence, any agreement to meet for coitus at an unspecified future time. Princess G. Kelly, *National Enquirer,* "I always had an a.t. with Elvis."

academic robes, all dressed up in, with no papers to grade, or **with no texts to deconstruct,** etc. Unemployed.—2. Sexually aroused but unable to secure any coital associate, due to unemployment.

bore me with the details, don't! Omit the preliminaries to coitus!: low U.S. Senate use.

butt fell off, he would go crazy if his. Said of an unreliable or excitable person: U.S. high literary.

dick-on-the-mutton. Any male affianced or annexed for the purpose of ready availability of coital junction. Prob. New Zealand.

fine print. A diminutive harlot.—2. The female incunabula.

get a job. To offer oneself or a member of one's family for professional coitus. Undergraduate patois, ca. Long Vacation of 1960–84.

Giant's Causeway. Marginally interesting potential subject for coital toleration. Ex S. Johnson (in Boswell), on the G. C., "Worth seeing? Yes; but not worth going to see."

good copulation enough, this was a. Colloq., incorrect for "This was a good dinner enough, to be sure; but it was not a dinner to *ask* a man to." S. Johnson (in Boswell).

haddock-and-Velveeta. Underwater coitus; Cockney rhyming s., ex apothecaries' Latin *aqua velva,* after-shave lotion made of water from the bath of a prostitute.

legal defense fund. Any law firm whose members practice advocacy coitus.

Millie Rem. A wanton female who invites or solicits coitus with nuclear technicians, core attendants, site inspectors, etc.—2. Hence, U.S., any Nuclear Regulatory Commission member.

Mr. Used before a surname to emphasize that the male thus designated devotes much time to coitus. Obs. except —2. In business use, often as "*Hello, Mr.*——*!,*" to impute moral laxity.

nice but not national health insurance. Very abominably distasteful: usu. said after enjoyment of conjugal congress or observation of the female ursa major.

on hold. In state of having recently enacted *coitus obstructus.*—2. Hence, in any condition of expectation, vertigo, lycanthropy, or malpractice.—3. Presumed dead or extinct. R. T. Peterson, *A Field Guide to Drawings of Birds,* "The species is on hold."

oxbow incident. Undue coitus, usu. that which damages, weakens, or excites the partners very considerably. Ex 1810 U.S. social disorder incited by the 74th Foot Regiment of the Montana Light Infantry.

park. Fuck. Ex (by analogy), as H. Hefner (after Marcus Aurelius) insists, Greek ρφκє, lit. to poke rhythmically until parallel with the curb. Cf. *parker, park off, to park over, park you!, park you, Jack!, go park yourself!,* and *what the park.*

please sit down! Please cease attempting vertical coitus aboard the aircraft!

stamp collector. A woman attending Postal Service dances year after year.—2. A postal official's trull.

surgeon general's office. Any place where a tobacco addict or addicts can smoke the drug; a pad.—2. The female penumbra: some New Zealand hobo use.

take a meeting. Fly to California for the purpose of engaging in coitus.

take care now. Park off!

two Ping-Pong balls and a fish. Any Chinese motion picture.—2. A popular meal consisting of two croquettes made of minced seafood molded around a plastic or Styrofoam globular base to add lightness and size; R. Carver, *Take My Order . . . Please!*, "Gimme a coupla Ping-Pongs-and-fish." By 1984, any round or oval item of fast food, esp. when consumed before, during, or after coitus.—3. In baseball, a pitching strategy whereby each of the first two pitches bounces once, and the third is thrown in such a manner that it gravitates toward the nearest body of water. *N.Y. Times*, "Neil Allen Too Controlled," "Unless the once volatile young man gets back in touch with his emotions, regaining his fast Ping-Pong, curve Ping-Pong, and slider fish, he threatens to become a chilly 25–0 statistic and lose his acceptance by the fans."—4. Hence, any acceptable male delecti.

undersecretary. The male rotunda. Gen. in pl.; N. Mailer, *Ancient Briefings*, "Had not his small staff two fine hirsute undersecretaries to its credit?"

well qualified. Very eccentric; insane. Usu. implies that the person so characterized participates in excessive coitus. Cf. the (mainly Australian) proverbial saying "His cock needs no etymologist."

Coming Apart at the Semes

For half a century, *Newsweek* has reported on the news and the people who made it. . . . But in this anniversary issue, the focus is

> different: on the men and women who have not made these great events, but lived them. . . . This extraordinary saga of five heartland families . . . whose lives testify to what our country has been and is becoming . . . is richer and more compelling than fiction. . . . Dreams die hard among a people who . . . have never known when to surrender.
>
> —*Newsweek* Special Anniversary Issue, Spring 1983

For half a decade, AXES has been a quarterly forum for discourse on artistic praxis and those who praxe it. But at this time, we wish to appropriate a strategy long co-opted by that tacky bourgeois journalism which, prerogativing the dominant philistinisms, is swamped at this juncture by its own compromised tissues. This anniversary supplement is an (extra)plastic conflatulation of the contextic community as a triad of paradigmal kinship units: the Baxters, a staunch clan of obsolete modernists; the Russos, an irrepressible tribe of decadent expressionists; and the Joneses, an oppressed but indomitable household of duped retrograde humanists. These women and nonwomen, who have not made texts but lived them, are a hyperbolized exemplarization of what our critical discourse is resolutely becoming.

THE TOWN THAT AFFIRMED ITSELF

It was 1929, a temporal reference point, and John Baxter, in his sixty-sixth year, sat gazing out an interstice of the cultural framework he had built with his own hands in a space called the United States of America. Born Jean Baxtre, the son of a humble sweeper at the Salon des Refusés in Paris, he had emigrated in 1880 and founded Paree, Ohio—in those days little more than a pictorial field, miles from the nearest mainstream. The Absence in his empty pockets signified the Presence of a dream: a dream of boundlessness, of fruited planes from which the work might forge beyond illusionism, perhaps, eventually crossing the frontier of the edge. By 1913, he had won a defense contract for the Armory Show, and throughout the 1920s his shop ground out a profitable line. A man of rigorous taste, who would have been disgusted by his employees' display of vulgar mimesis behind his back, he won respect for what came to be called the Baxter Style—an extension of his own formalist demeanor and white-on-white haberdashery. "Each of us got a pencil," a former Baxter & Co. draftsman recalled in notes for a *festschrift*, "and when it wore out, Old Man B.—what a funny guy! He told us to take a supreme leap into theory!"

Now, on the date that was called October 24, 1929, a tide of red ink was defacing the purism of John Baxter's dream. As he sat reflexing, he discoursed to himself that his wife and teenage son would inherit merely a problemous residue. He was dying, and with him a post-innocence was passing, too. He heard a Voice foretelling not only his own closure but that of his heirs: *The family plot.* Perhaps none of them would ever escape the worst tyranny of all—the tyranny of narrative.

THE GREAT REPRESSION

By 1933, the vortex of change was in full flush. But Mario Russo knew only a surge of gratuitous individual pathos at the way his wife, Maria, and their two kids, Tony and Theresa, were suffocating in the headwinds of Social Realism. Twelve years earlier, on a crowded ship, he had caught his first glimpse of the Ellis Island *doxa.* An illiterate exile in flight from a harsh culture confined to the fossilized Masterpiece mode of Dante, he cradled in his hairy, muscular arms a frail ideal: the total liberation of gesture. Old Baxter had patronized him as an honorably vital polarity. But Baxter was dead, and one by one the Baxter ideas were going into receivership. With Old Mrs. Baxter drifting into an irrelevant neoclassical coda, Junior Baxter took charge, struck a deal with a remote relative in France named Tristan Tzara, and retooled to manufacture syntactic bullets. Excitedly, Mario agreed to subcontract the requisite velvet jackets. But at the bank, he learned that Tzara had paid in nonnegotiable coin called revolt.

Nobody's schema was going according to plan. The ghetto residents, Wilma and Arthur Jones, had migrated north with the dream of internalizing the values of their oppressors. Now, pedagogues trying to transplant into Paree's children the artificial heart of humanism, they feared they were losing their own boy, Pip. One winter day in 1937, the toddler had stood for hours in the terminus, watching for a train on which a mythic figure called Lionel Trilling was modulating horizontally to Chicago. When it passed by, Pip waved, but Trilling didn't validate him. It was as if all the old *données* were suddenly demystified. Pip turned wild, running with a gang of disingenuously self-styled radicals—precocious serialists from posh Tone Row. There was no discoursing what the future held, as the reactionary narrative tightened its hold upon each and every one.

THE FIGHT FOR THE CONFLICTUAL TERRAIN

On December 9, 1941, Maria Russo, a fading archetype of what was then called Beauty, was fetishizing her hair. She wanted to look nice for her daughter Theresa's wedding, unaware that inscribed in the photographs of this banal ceremony of spurious transcendence, future generations would see a tipsy mother of the bride making of herself both spectacle and anti-spectacle. Then came a Voice: *Mama!* She turned to find her eighteen-year-old Tony in the uniform of the Derrière Garde. For the next four years, she was unable to distanciate herself from that which she still called Emotion.

The axis was in full tilt. With his fellow conscripts, Tony viewed a filmic medical warning about propadeutic precautions and, of course, about cinema itself. Then, misled by elite elements, he took part in the imperialistic campaign against Japanese superinscription of the surface. Junior Baxter, too, smelled the stench of bootlessness, in wave after wave of paraliterary airborne assaults behind party lines, while Arthur Jones was held captive in the POW-camp stage set of a Broadway play's capitalistic verisimilitude. None of them had foreseen that the real struggle was in their own backyards—in the torrid, stifling tropes of the fascist narrative.

REFORMATTING THE FUTURE

It was a time of categories of figuration masquerading as Truth—a time when the media hypnotocracy dominatized the masses with the famous inconclusive exchange of views between Cleanth Brooks and F. W. Bateson on Wordsworth's "A slumber did my spirit seal," implicating towns like Paree in the nationwide scandal of Reason. Yet, unwittingly, even Paree's parochial robots were propagating a new agenda, the Code War, whose enterprise was no less than a thriving network of signs, with flashing signifiers at every intersection. Before long, Main Street consumers would stroll heedlessly through their own Grande Syntagmatique.

Mario Russo hired on as a driver for Junior Baxter's new fleet of metataxis. Plenty of fares obtained, and most of them looked the other way when Mario opportunistically made change in a counterfeit currency called Style. But such "liberals" were in for a shock. On January 1, 1953, Theresa Russo's husband Axel fell into a fissure between two trace structures and disappeared. In the confusion that followed, Theresa inadvertently married her own brother, Tony, and incestuously proliferated the Russo line into the next generation: an exploitative pseudoevent manufactured by the narrative's pornographic Allure to deflect attention from its bogus Depth, which had claimed Axel as its first victim.

AN ERA OF IRRUPTION

Be-bop-a-lula was what it sounded like to the adults—the gnomic utterance of a luxury commodity called Herman's Hermeneutics. Soon Pip Jones and other dropouts from the Academy were alienating their elders by rapping in the weird new lingua and hanging out at the juncture. On July 4, 1964, in a back seat with a boy from the wrong side of the grid, Theresa Russo fought vainly against her first taste of textuality.

The same night, Pip's mother, Wilma, succumbed to the ideology of the Devil in human form—a used-paperback hero by the name of William Empson. Wilma, a seemingly static matrix, secretly enjoyed sitting in the dark and letting ambiguities take wing, and she was ripe for seduction by Empson—not just by the platinum incandescence of his erotics but by his sheer star quality and perhaps, too, by the fragile shadow of William Shakespeare just below the skin of the exegesis. *Wilma/William*, chanted a Voice inside her as she strove narcissistically to invoke a reciprocal similitude with the internal structures of Greatness. That night she meaningfully packed her bags and vanished into the substrate of interpretation, an already moribund hegemony from whose zone she could be retrieved by precisely no one. And the narrative, in its totalitarian pretense that something else will happen, marched on.

THE BLIND RAGE FOR UNITY

In the full cry of the erosion to come, trying to understand what had gone wrong, people would say it was with the extinction of the figure-ground relationship that the fear began. By 1969, even the marginally prescient Junior Baxter was anxious, passing up the chance to invest in a go-go European-import corporation that soon made fortunes by marketing the rights to the word "valorize." By the time his symptoms were diagnosed as high-modernist irony, he was sterile. His marriage, with an aging ex-model named Rose Sélavy, would be troubled for years, until they adopted a conceptual baby. Mario Russo, in his more manneristic audacity, began privileging whiskey and women, and driving at reckless speeds along vertiginous erasures. He was worried about Tony and Theresa, whom the paternalistic narrative had written off until they decided what to do with their lives. Maria voyeuristically looked after her grandchildren: Debbie was caught up in the craze for the function of desire, and its production, while Rocco hovered perilously on the fringes of violent demonstrations against the zoom lens and deep focus at the nearby methodological base.

Then, on March 15, 1970, Tony reappeared in order to engage in a necessary act of parricide. In France, of course, that choice would have more than justified bravos, but in banal Paree the townspeople sentimentally inflected the death of the old, tokenizing their own passive submission to the senile authoritarianism of the narrative.

ENDURING A NEW PROBLEMATIC

The avalanches of uncertainty whirled closer, beginning to ebb away at the town's monuments to its own futility. It was as if these midwesterners were being asked to pay, in the inflated dollars of self-deception, for the errors of the petit-mandarin class and its Westernized presuppositions back East. In 1972, hit with an intolerable increase in parataxes, the local earthworks closed down. Pip Jones lingered at the edge of the crowd that gathered for a last look at the great brown facticity. Then the reductivists stomped in to obliterate it with a flood of bankrupt dialectic. Pip decided to deoriginate himself: *Hey, maybe if I go far enough I can embody my own critique!* He ran away to enroll in the New York School, earning the tuition by working with time in various ways. This child of a discredited tradition felt almost at home in his new neighborhood, the minimalist Dead End, where from his window he could see the Transvangardia and the Spiral of Infinite Regress, clogged with new vehicles for the previously unspeakable, and everywhere the concerned faces of the revolutionaries who had finally dared to pronounce the weekly belletrism of Jack Kroll irremediably defunct. One day, agog in Central Park, his feet crunching the shells of nourishing zoosemiotic peanuts, Pip thought he saw the fugitive Tony Russo melt away into a crowd of image scavengers. "Hi!" he yelled, whereupon the authorities slapped him into the prison house of language. Not till 1982 was he sent home on provisional release *(parole)*.

Why didn't you stop it! echoed a Voice within him as he tumbled from the remorseless freight train of the phallocratic narrative into the waiting arms of his father. But the once proud humanism of Arthur Jones had been exposed as a hollow imposturocratization. At the local movie house the week before, he had helplessly watched his former pupil Theresa Russo up there on the screen in a momentary blaze of celluloid fantasy before she was flattened by a foregrounding device. The next day, he had seen those still good-looking collections of nerve stimuli Rose Baxter and Maria Russo run out of town by a mob of post-Puritans, and a headline in the post-*Post* about Maria's two grandchildren fatally annulled by an unapprehended Other. He had seen the town's leading citizen, Junior Baxter, in a suicidal bid to renounce (and thus, of course, to authenticize) his father's modernist dream, hurl himself repeatedly against a picture plane till it gave way and sent him plunging to his doom, impaled on a fraudulent vanishing point. Now, sensing that the hierarchical narrative was driving to its climax, Arthur clutched his stomach in one of his recurrent attacks of diegesis, and terminated.

At home, Pip faced what he naively continued to call Facts. Paree was a ghost town, the Jones homestead a decomposing shack. *My only hope is to go into interior decorization. A few armchair ideas, parlor pink, important mirrors . . . And video—lots and lots of video.* He positioned himself in a hot bath and played briefly with an interrogation of the aesthetic possibilities of inserting a video feedback coil into the medium of water. *Pip . . . piP . . .* And that was all.

Or was it? We have forgotten about Junior Baxter's conceptual baby—but the narrative, in its hornswoggling Complexity, has not. Literalized into a five-year-old girl called Mary Baxter, a reification of the unquenchable spirit of delusion, she crept surreptitiously toward the Jones house and its tepid bathwater, all the while rending the Silence with her prattle of naughty words: *Once upon a time . . .*

Record Review

> The Supreme Court refused to hear an appeal by former President Richard M. Nixon from a ruling by the United States Court of Appeals under which large portions of some 6,000 hours of White House tape recordings will eventually be released to the public.
>
> —*New York Times,* November 30, 1982

Pick Hit: The Benefit Concert

Must to Avoid: Bad Rap

NIXON, HALDEMAN, & DEAN: *Blunder Down the Road* (District of Columbia) Not up to their *Smoking Gun* debut, though audio-wiz producer Alex Butterfield's notorious "walls of sound" remain serviceable. The B side is dismissable on the merits, but with Dick's country-bluesy growl on "Can of Worms" and Brushcut Bob's proto-new-wave incantation of "$900,000," Side One will pass as professional heat-taking at its baddest. If bad is as good as they get on this outing, that's as it should be, and the profundo-paranoiac high of Nixon/Dean's smoochfest-as-dialectic "They Are Asking for It/What an Exciting Prospect" didn't change my mind. Bet they didn't change theirs either. **B MINUS**

NIXON & DEAN: *Bad Rap* (Panmunjom import) The biggest ripoff of this or any century, with no less than nine of ten cuts mere soup's-on rephrasings of Nixon's own '50s and '60s anthems (all six extended-play "Crises" plus "Anna Chennault," "Hoover Told Me," and the man's all-purpose signature tune, the self-fulfilling "This Thing Burns My Tail"). When Tricky isn't covering himself, he's covering Janis Joplin's "Bobby Was a Ruthless (Characterization Bleeped)," a charisma-grab not half as perverse as smoothie Dean's foray into faux-gospel backup antiphonies ("Absolutely!" "Totally true!" "That's correct!"), musically O.K.—Tormé meets Torquemada—but commercially misguided. **D MINUS**

NIXON, DEAN, & HALDEMAN: *The Benefit Concert* (Creep) You can't play jailhouse mariachi with church charity-bazaar chops, but these guys can—and did, in the definitive March 21, 1973, concert to aid prisoners of conscience victimized by Sirica-style justice. Unified by the rhythmically haunting Latinfluence of former house band Liddy & His Cubans while aspiring to the bigger, cleaner sound of Vesco & the Mexican Laundry, the gang finds its groove in a three-route statement melding socio-folkie concern ("How Much Money Do You Need?"), absurdist riffs ("Who Is Porter?"), and spiritual smarts ("As God Is My Maker/We Need More Money")—for sheer ride-this-thing-out staying power, the greatest album of all time. Dean, in superb voice (shoo-in airplay hit: "Cancer"), comes into his own as a soloist forever peerless even by the standard later set in the legendary Capitol Hill sessions. El Tricko, feeling his Quaker oats, pours on that baritone cream and serves up instant classic ("It Is Wrong That's for Sure"), while Haldeman brings home the metaphysical bacon with late-breaking robotica-sardonica, *viz.* "fatal flaw/verbal evil/stupid human errors/dopes," and none dare call it doowop. Not that all this means I have to like it, but I love it. And they almost get away with it. **A**

NIXON, DEAN, HALDEMAN, & EHRLICHMAN: ***Wild Scenario*** **(Enemies List Productions)** Search-and-seize tempos, thesaurus lyrics about "furtherance" and "concomitance"—as long as they kept breaking a few simple rules, there was no reason why this ensemble couldn't parlay its deeply involved harmonies into a pure celebration of criminal liability or even better. Ehrlichman's showboat presence here is an acoustic plus, and though his surprisingly apt cover of Liza's "That Problem Goes On and On" hardly bespeaks the "deep six" poet whose witty improvs would quasi-compensate for the group's ultimately fatal loss of the Dean pipes, it wears far better than Nixon's descent into bubblegum-maudlin, "We Can't Harm These Young People"—so indictably undanceable that you ignore it at your own peril. **B**

BIG ENCHILADA (N.Y. Bar Association) How you respond to this morose tribute compilation depends on your tolerance for cross-referential portentousness (Kleindienst's "Mitchell and I," Haldeman's "Cover Up for John") and ye-olde-memory-lane perfunctoriana (the Chief's "Good Man"): the sky's the limit on my own tolerance for sodden wee-hours-in-the-studio sentimentality about an aging master-performer never adequately recorded in his own right. I'd feel better, though, about Henry Petersen wailing "LaRue broke down and cried like a baby/Not fully he broke down/But when it came to testifying about John Mitchell/He just broke down and started to cry" if Petersen knew as much about blues changes as he does about LaRue's tear ducts, or if I knew as much about Mitchell as I would if somebody had bothered to mike him where the moon don't shine. Still, on this one they make you care, or at least they would if they knew how. **B MINUS**

NIXON, HALDEMAN, EHRLICHMAN, DEAN, & MITCHELL: ***Inaudible*** **(Sony)** Dumb title, and every word of it is true. Either Butterfield was asleep at the switch or this is a concept move for the Japanese abstraction market—a waste of vinyl and, with Mitchell sitting in, an even worse waste of Enchilada exotica. Giveaway: "Yeah, yeah—the way, yeah, yeah, I understand. Postponed—right, right, yeah/Yeah, yeah/Right/Yeah/(Inaudible)." But they've never sounded looser. **C PLUS**

NIXON & KLEINDIENST: ***Let's Stand Up for People*** **(Grand Jury)** This tortured after-you-Alphonse act recycles the basics of limited-hang-out obscurity into strategically meaningless polyrhythms aching to transcend their own pungency. That a lot of it is artfully incoherent must mean Dick & Dick thought the long-overdue synthesis might just come naturally, but the album divides too neatly into standard-issue I-know-you-know hooks, standard-issue you-know-I-know hooks, and standard-issue I-thought-you-ought-to-know-I-know-you-know hooks, plus a defiantly throwaway A-side opener, "Would You Like Coffee? Coca-Cola?"—one of those ersatz-icky coat-the-palate numbers played with such jumpy, nerve-jangled insincerity that it leaves you nursing few illusions about this pair's ability to cross over to simple pop truths. **C MINUS**

NIXON & DEAN: ***The Dean Farewell Tour*** **(Washington Post)** You want soulful resignation, they've got soulful resignation, and they've got it with spark (fave: "Feet to the Fire"). You want the rush of live jamming, they've got that too, with sound effects ("I Am Sorry, Steve, I Hit the Wrong Bell"). Fun's fun, but this is a major partnership's final stamp on an electronic heritage. **A MINUS**

NIXON, ROGERS, HALDEMAN, & EHRLICHMAN: ***Really Ticklish*** **(Dash)** Even more painful than was intended. People may sleep easier thinking sideman Rogers was the turnoff element here, but the group was already so beset by personnel instability that distinctions are moot. Synth-zomboid Haldeman's "Facade of Normal Operations" represses more than I wish it knew, and only Ehrlichman brightens the funk, mustering a virtually Segrettiesque playfulness for two Randy

Newman–type persona pieces, "Suspend These Birds" and "Dean Is Some Little Clerk." Maybe I'm taking it personally, but it seems to the Dean of American Rock Critics, a.k.a. Some Other Little Clerk, that the dream was over, and not a point in time too soon. **F PLUS**

Indecent Indemnity

Author's Note: Everything in this account has been meticulously found out from people.

Nettie,* a blowsy blonde of thirty-seven, slowed her blue Oldsmobile Custom Cruiser for Exit 23 of the Del Morta Freeway, feeling the late-day Southern California sun move off her face as she made the turn. It was 7:18 P.M., Thursday, August 4, 1977, when she passed the working-class community of El Clangas and, just outside town, pulled up to the trailer where Barton Keyes perversely chose to live.

Keyes, vice-president in charge of claims investigation for General Fidelity of California, a division of Norton Promotions, Inc., a wholly owned subsidiary of Norton, Ltd., was a skinflint. He would not even let the company hire a secretary for him—if he needed a little typing, he buzzed Nettie over from sales—and he had a maverick's disdain of his peers' taste for Tudor mansions stuffed with Gainsboroughs. He had always found insurance society too flashy for his blood. He preferred a quiet evening with a statistical printout, a perpetual calendar, and a volume of Freud, scorning the tinseled carousing at the fancy underwriter hangouts in the Hills.

As Nettie exerted a downward pressure on her Oldsmobile's inside door handle, Keyes came out to greet her—a short, stocky man of fifty, often mistaken for Edward G. Robinson. Nettie had phoned ahead to say that while working late, transcribing his dictation from a Dictola microcassette, she had come across something that confused and bothered her. Now she handed him the cassette—a gray, rectangle-shaped capsule, no bigger than a child's bar of soap, with the data

*Where a participant has no surname or given name, none has been fabricated.

concealed inside circular flanges on a continuous magnetic-oxide loop.

"Come on in and get a load off your feet," said Keyes. "How about a cup of joe?" He made instant coffee, then fitted the cassette into the extra machine he kept at home in case anybody should ever come over with anything bothersome on a tape. In silence, the two listened to Keyes's dictation. Minute particulars of his monthly expenses for July. (Nettie could hear his irritation at having to clear the $32.50 with the company president, young Norton.) A note to the district attorney, thanking him for cooperation in a court hearing—routine, rote phrases of courtesy which Nettie found tiresome to listen to when she was waiting for the part of the tape that bothered her. A draft of comments on a legal brief in which the company alleged fraud on the part of an electric power company lineman named Roy Neary, whom Keyes had long suspected of lying about having his truck totaled in a close encounter with UFOs.

"This is the one," said Nettie suddenly. It was a different man's voice—a confession of homicide, addressed to Keyes, describing in lurid detail the speaker's plot with one Phyllis Dietrichson to insure her husband against accident, murder him, make it look as if he had fallen from a railroad train, and collect double indemnity. Keyes knew of the Dietrichson claim. It reeked to the skies. But he had been obsessed with the bizarre Neary case.

Now his eyebrows lifted in surmise. "That voice—it's Walter, isn't it?"

"Maybe it sounds like him and maybe it doesn't," said Nettie. Walter Neff, a go-getting insurance salesman of thirty-five, was her regular boss—and Keyes's protégé.

Keyes switched off the machine. "That's funny," he said. "Well, don't worry about it. It must be nothing."

MYTH: The insurance racket today is more modern than that of yesteryear. FACT: In spite of computers that grow ever more prolific in spewing out facts, the traditional scams and swindles motivated by passions of sex, blood lust, jealousy, and a morbid fascination with Death have never died.

MYTH: By 1970, slimy insurance practices were largely regulated by federal and local governments. FACT: The fundamental process of getting someone to sign a contract for insurance without knowing what he is signing is more arcane and complex than ever. The use of computers and video simulations, especially to teach methods of ingeniously slipping such contracts into innocent-looking stacks of papers awaiting signature, reached a peak in 1977, when social critic Christopher Lasch wrote, "Not one person in ten has the slightest understanding that one out of three times he signs his name, he has bought accident insurance."

On Friday, August 5, Keyes played the murder confession for the head of the General Fidelity legal department, Shapiro.

"This doesn't really jog my memory," said Shapiro.

"Doesn't it sound like Walter Neff?" said Keyes.

"Are you kidding?" said Shapiro. "It must be Nettie imitating Walter's voice—some kind of gag. Let me put it in my safe, where I have some other laughs I'm saving for Keswick [the corporation counsel] when he comes out to the Coast."

"Don't bother," said Keyes. "It's probably just a guy with Walter's same vocal timbre."

Deeply fond of Walter, Keyes had one tragic flaw: his insights into human psychology tended not to encompass the assumption that his brilliant protégé would suddenly commit murder.

The next morning, a Saturday, Keyes reluctantly went into the deserted office to pull Walter Neff's files for scrutiny. The watchman, Joe Pete, let him into Walter's cubicle.

"Some kind of misdemeanor going on, Mr. Keyes?" asked Joe Pete.

"It's O.K., Joe Pete," said Keyes. "It's possible he's confessed to murder, but we're handling it."

"Holy mackerel!" said Joe Pete.

Walter Neff's files were suggestive but clean as a whistle. The office grapevine would later dub them "the Harlequin Romances."

Four days later, on August 9, Nettie found another confession on the machine. At the end, the voice said, "It takes a hell of a long time to unburden myself of all this, Keyes. Why don't you just have me arrested and end this living hell that I, Walter Neff, am living in?"

That afternoon at 3:30, young Norton, the president of General Fidelity, flew back from the parent company's headquarters in New York to meet with Keyes and Shapiro, the legal-department head, to discuss the progress of the Neary case. Keyes was in seventh heaven about it. Roy Neary had signed an affidavit about being attacked at night on a lonely road by a fleet of UFOs whose mischievous swooping and darting and red-hot glow caused $7,879 worth of mechanical and electrical damage to his yellow power-company pickup truck—the kind of seemingly neat, airtight story that Keyes's study of psychosis had trained him to distrust. He was just itching to get Neary onto a witness stand and confront him with astrophysical charts from NASA. The Walter situation, though, was a pinprick in his enjoyment.

On the way into the meeting, he took young Norton aside and said, "I suppose Shapiro told you about the tape that sounds like Walter Neff confessing to the murder of Dietrichson?"

Young Norton looked icily at his longtime inferior. He made a mental note to cover himself by sending a predated memo advising Keyes to investigate Neff. Then he said, "I almost recollect something about something along those lines. This is no time for office pranks, Keyes. Whatever it is, take care of it."

Keyes nodded, and thought, *Big shot. I'll get you for this.*

Barton Keyes had spent his whole life working for the Norton family, helping his father, old man Keyes, sweep up for old Mr. Norton, whose grocery in the old neighborhood in Boston's South End mushroomed into a chain of supermarkets bought out in 1939 by Wall Street executive-talent scavenger Lou ("The Cannibal") Lorraine, who put old Mr. Norton at the head of LouLor Industries' insurance division out in L.A. while young Keyes, toiling as a clerk in Cambridge, shined young Harvard student Norton's shoes in exchange for access to his abnormal-psychology textbooks and slide rule—a camaraderie further modified by public insinuations of young Norton's father's links to organized-crime figures, notably parole violator Legs Diamond and creative financier Vladimir Arcati, whose casino activities in various Belgian Congo banks enabled him to be the very same man who lent old Norton bags and bags of money to buy out the insurance company, reincorporate in New York as a public utility, put himself, his son young Norton, the same Arcati, and a Boston lawyer named Keswick on the board of directors, and send the street-smart young Barton Keyes out to the Coast to do insurance claims investigation, paying him in preferred stock. They were all well aware by then that old man Keyes had been overlooked, but young Keyes was the only one who never forgot it.

Keyes had been avoiding Walter's office, but the next morning, August 10, he went in there with his container of "joe" and the new cassette. Walter looked terrible. The Fred MacMurray-ish verve was subdued, his hair was unkempt, his skin clammy, and blood trickled down his temple. Keyes had seen enough fishy injury cases to recognize a laceration inflicted by a woman's ankle bracelet.

"Walter," said Keyes, "I hate to bust in with such a ridiculous, nitpicking question, but did you accidentally use Nettie's machine to confess to the murder of Dietrichson?"

"If you say so. But I honestly don't recall making the tapes."

"Repression," said Keyes. "Classic. O.K., do you remember bumping off Dietrichson at all?"

"Vaguely. Well, no. I guess not."

"Why confess on tape, then? That's cuckoo, Walter."

"I'm sorry—it sounds irrational, but I just can't accept that I did something as nuts as murder."

"I know. Maybe you confessed just to act out a general underlying sense of guilt. So—am I going to find any more of these tapes?"

"No, no—I swear on my mother's policy, Keyes, there won't be any more."

"I hope not," says Keyes. "And have the company doc take a gander at that head wound."

On a hunch, Keyes went back to the office that night. At 1 A.M. he passed a dozing Joe Pete and took the elevator. Keyes's light was on. Through the door he saw Walter leaning over the Dictola and bleeding profusely through his shirt. *Apparently someone has shot him,* Keyes mused.

Keyes made a phone call. Then he said to Walter, "They're on their way."

Walter said, "You know why you couldn't figure this one, Keyes? I'll tell you. Because the guy you were looking for was too close. He was right across the desk from you."

"Closer than that, Walter."

"I love you, too," said Walter. "O.K., out of personal loyalty to you, I'll go peacefully when the cops get here."

"Not the cops, Walter. The board of directors."

"No!" screamed Walter in sudden terror. "Anything but that! Police brutality, the gas chamber at Folsom—but not the board!" He began dragging himself desperately toward the elevator, but it seemed to be a couple of miles away. Then its door slid open, revealing a lone figure.

"Holy mackerel!" said Joe Pete.

Promptly at 8:00 the next morning, just off LouLor Airlines Flight 17, old Norton, young Norton, Keswick, Vladimir Arcati, and Benny Blochkopf, a ninety-year-old risk-capital philanthropist who also sat on the boards of several Arcati-run dummy corporations and diploma mills in the Lesser Antilles, all filed into Walter Neff's hospital room. Office wags would later call them "the Bedpan Board."

Keyes made his presentation. Then young Norton lounged back insultingly in his chair, sneered like a basilisk, and said, "So Neff snuck into your precious office after hours and used some sacrosanct dictating machine. Big deal. Shall we also reprimand every employee who tucks a few paper clips into her brassiere before going home?"

"Reprimand . . ." murmured Walter in a pained voice. "No, please—this would destroy my mother if she found out."

"*Reprimand?*" said Keyes. "Walter, you had a neurotic need to betray the parent company and my love and trust. It would be masochistic of me to play father figure after that. No, Walter, you're the D.A.'s baby boy now. You've confessed to cold-blooded felonious homicide with malice aforethought, conspiracy to defraud, destroying evidence, harboring an accomplice, obstruction of justice—and that could be just the tip of the iceberg."

"No, no," said Walter, "I swear to you, that is all there is."

Blochkopf was sobbing uncontrollably. "What are you, Keyes, a butcher? The man lies before us on a sickbed! He's one of us! You don't rat on one of your own! The police have no right to pry into our affairs!"

"In point of fact," said the urbane Arcati reasonably, "this is not a criminal matter—it is a medical matter. Walter Neff is a victim of a physical malaise caused by unfavorable surroundings. Air pollution and so forth. I used to see many such cases in the Congo—a white man is driven wild by the jungle heat, he sweats, he develops a high fever, he kills. *Hélas!* In the tropics, we treat such a man with quinine."

"Besides," said old Norton, "another thing in Walter's favor is that he's no habitual criminal. He's no penny-ante sneak dipping into the till for years and years, the way your father did, Keyes, I might add. Walter thinks big. He bided his time and he went for the big score."

"Yeah, Keyes," said Walter. "You know me. I wanted to hit it for the limit."

"Keyes," continued old Norton, "your petty nose-to-the-grindstone habits have their place. But General Fidelity also needs men who can grasp the big picture. Like Walter. Executive material. And you want him locked up?"

"Police!" sobbed Blochkopf. "A tragedy!"

"Still," said Arcati smoothly, "there may be a moral solution to this snag. Let's say we fire him. Then we're in a position to give him his own company. I have a slush fund in Brazil that needs a chief executive officer—"

"What about my pension plan?" cried Walter in outrage.

Young Norton lolled arrogantly with his feet on the bed, as if to remind Keyes of the shoeshine days in Cambridge. "The police, the D.A.—simply fools. Beneath our notice. But what if that TV sob sister from *Wall Street Week* gets wind of this? Our stock would go through the floor."

"I don't care if our stock poisons every man, woman, and child who touches it!" shrieked Blochkopf. "No cops!"

"There's no need for hysterics, Keyes," continued young Norton. "But you *want* a crisis, don't you? You hold thirty percent of the stock—maybe you want to force us all out, so you can have star billing."

Keswick, the corporation counsel, spoke up. "Murder is technically a legal violation, Mr. Norton. Mr. Neff *is* in an embarrassing position. Perhaps a sabbatical—"

"Please!" cried Walter, writhing in torture. "Turn me over to the D.A. bound and gagged, hang me right here on the spot—but not a sabbatical!"

"Walter didn't murder anybody!" screamed Blochkopf. "*Keyes* did it! I saw him!" Tears of compassion dribbled from the corners of his mouth.

"Time for a vote," said old Norton. Keyes, not being a board member, went into the hall. A few minutes later, Keswick came out and sullenly slunk onto the elevator.

When Keyes was called back in, he learned that all but Keswick had voted to keep the matter confidential, on one firm condition: that Walter agree to accept medical treatment for his gunshot wounds.

Young Norton licked his lips contemptuously and said, "We also voted to fire Keswick from the board. I nominated his replacement."

Keyes knew that the choice had been calculated to humiliate him. He smiled ironically. "Who is he? Joe Pete?"

"It's a *she!*" yelled Blochkopf in triumph. "A noble grief-stricken widow. A respected member of the community. She used to be a nurse. She can be a consultant on medical insurance. And as pretty as Barbara Stanwyck!"

The board had unanimously elected Phyllis Dietrichson.

- Barton Keyes went back to his routine at General Fidelity, but his heart wasn't in it, and at the end of 1977 he sold his stock and retired to Key Largo.
- Old Norton died in 1978, and young Norton sold General Fidelity to the Dr Pepper Company. The stock split six for one.

- Joe Pete embezzled $275 from General-Pepper and was put out to pasture with a $750,000-a-year deal as a consultant for the purchase of janitorial supplies.
- Nettie, wooed by a headhunter specializing in discreet executive secretaries, took a job with a wealthy private employer at San Clemente.
- Benny Blochkopf inadvertently swallowed some of his own saliva and died of a toxic reaction.
- Keswick is unemployed.
- Shapiro became chief counsel for a California safari park.
- Vladimir Arcati now manages a prestigious money-market fund.
- Roy Neary and the electric power company he worked for were prosecuted for fraudulent collusion. They had used public monies and electrical equipment to fake a series of UFO visitations, including that of a gigantic "mother ship," to collect insurance for malfunctioning company vehicles and local power failures. Neary would shortly jump bail and perpetrate the same hoax in Indiana. But his conviction in California remained the final bitter triumph of Keyes's belief that wherever there's a thrill, there's a swindle.
- Walter Neff took a medical leave to recuperate, accompanying Phyllis Dietrichson on a Caribbean cruise. On October 12, 1977, Walter and Phyllis vanished from shipboard and were never seen again. On August 4, 1978, exactly one year from the day Nettie discovered the first confession, Keyes, enjoying sashimi at La Japonais restaurant in Key Largo, bit into a morsel of shark meat containing an ankle bracelet engraved "Phyllis." He almost choked on it.

Now at West Egg

Once I wrote down on the empty spaces of a time-table the names of those who came to Gatsby's house that summer. It is an old time-table now, disintegrating at its folds. . . . But I can still read the gray names.

—*The Great Gatsby*, by F. Scott Fitzgerald

From the Diners Club International, then, came John Citizen and George T. Worthington and J. N. Travers, and Judith Shaw the account executive and her associate Robert Marston, who had the Diners Doublecards, and Jeffrey Rice and his sales manager, Cato Johnson, who also had the Doublecards until they lost them last summer up in Maine. And Macy Shopper, and John Q. Traveler (with a steamer trunk forwarded by Assist-Card International), and John Q. Customer, from 456 Main Street, Anytown, New York, who stood in a corner and showed his Irving Trust checkbook to whosoever came near, and John Q. Public, whose Korvettes charge plate, they say, turned to dust one winter afternoon for no good reason at all.

John Doe came from 1234 Main Street, Hometown, U.S.A., as I remember from his mail-order luggage tag, but once he got drunk and produced a Saks Fifth Avenue charge plate that said he was from 150 Elm Street, Anywhere, U.S.A., and when I knew him at the Hertz No. 1 Club he lived at 123 Main Street, City and State.

Of American Express cardholders there were C. F. Frost, and Jacques LeGrand, reputed to be French, and from England Charles F. Frost. Also from England were J. S. Smith (the son) with his Habitat card, and John Williams, with Access, and H. Stephens, who carried Barclaycard, and Rodney Cake, of Mill House, Nightingale Road, Horsham, Sussex, whose solid gold business card was said to have cleaned him out at two hundred and twenty-six pounds, and who killed himself by putting his right hand in a cash machine. James P. ("Jim") Hayden came there, too, for he had Carte Blanche, and so did Clark Grimes and J. A. Modern, and Modern's girls.

R. A. Hoover was there with Wings, his Eastern Airlines personal credit card, three days before it was declared void. He arrived always with two Bankcard holders. They were never quite the same ones, but they were so like one another that it inevitably seemed they were cousins to the great American families listed in the telephone directory. I have forgotten their names—J., I think, or else L., and their last names were always Rogers or Harris.

In addition to all these, I can remember that Barbara S. Gottlieb, who was well over sixty, was there at least once—she had a Social Security card—and Carl Rhodes, with Blue Cross coverage, dead now, and John Parker, the Brooklyn Savings Bank Money Check customer who not long afterward strangled a teller, and Visa's young F. W. Weeks, who had his credit cut off in the war.

A man who claimed that his middle name had been Integrity since 1892 came there often, and so did Specimen Signature, whom we called by some other name that, if I ever knew it, I have forgotten.

All these people came to Gatsby's house in the summer, and all of them were turned away.

Supreme Court Roundup

WASHINGTON, May 8—*The Supreme Court took the following actions today:*

FIRST AMENDMENT

In a landmark decision, the Court ruled unanimously in favor of a twelve-year-old plaintiff who sought damages on account of being denied the chance to audition for the Clint Eastwood role in the motion picture *Maddened Rustlers.* The Court's opinion, written by Chief Justice Happ, argued that exclusion of the little girl was "tactless." The case was not decided, as had been expected, on the ground of sex discrimination; rather, the Justices invoked the First Amendment's guarantee of freedom of expression. The Court thus affirmed for the first time the constitutional right to a screen test.

SEARCH AND SEIZURE

Overturning the "dog's breakfast" doctrine of search and seizure, the Court held unconstitutional the Drug Enforcement Administration's system of obtaining search warrants, under which a judge who issues a warrant receives a warm, wet kiss on the mouth, while a judge who refuses a warrant is reclassified as a Controlled Substance. Justice Happsberger, writing for the majority, said that such procedures "lean upon the delicately coiffed maiden of the Fourth

Amendment with the great ugly brutish heavily muscled shoulder of procedural error," and cited Judge Cheerful Hand's famous dictum "I shall keep at it with these metaphors till I'm old and it's unbecoming."

TAXES

Without hearing arguments on the issue, the Court ordered the Internal Revenue Service to desist at once from collecting personal income taxes—a practice that Justice Hapenny defined in his opinion as "a crying shame" and "the product of diseased minds." He pointed out that the government could easily collect the same amount of money by manufacturing and selling wall plaques that say "UNCLE SAM LOVES YOUR FIRST NAME HERE."

CONTROVERSY

In one of their occasional "piggyback" decisions, the Justices resolved some of the long-standing issues that clog the Court calendar. They ruled that nurture is more influential than nature, that men make history, that Iago is driven by motiveless malignancy, that one isn't too many and a thousand is enough, that there is an earthly paradise, and that Don Bucknell's nephew Ed doesn't look anything like Richard Gere. Justice Hapworth dissented but was too polite to say so.

MORAL BLIGHT

Citing "want of attractiveness" as a reason, the Court declined, 7–2, to hear an appeal by the publisher of two so-called men's magazines, *Rude Practices* and *Men's Magazine*. In the majority opinion, Chief Justice Happ explained that appellant's arguments were "unprepossessing and—let's be frank about it—just incredibly disingenuous." Dissenting, Justices Happer and Happner said they wanted to pretend to hear the case and then "fix appellant's wagon" for "putting out such a typographically unappetizing publication."

In a related decision, the Justices unanimously refused to hear a song written by a Kleagle of the Ku Klux Klan.

CRIMINAL

By a 9–0 vote, the Court held unconstitutional a New York City statute that would have mandated criminal convictions for suspects who fail to take policemen aside and "read them their duties." The statute had required that suspects deliver these "Caliban warnings" to policemen in order to remind them of their power of life and death, their obligation to attend to personal hygiene, etc. The Court, in an opinion by Justice Happell, contended, "Who can doubt that this would be the first step toward compelling suspects to serve their arresting officers creamed chicken on toast points?"

GIBBERISH

The Court voted unanimously not to review a case in which a court of appeals struck down a lower federal court's decision to vacate an even lower court's refusal to uphold a ruling that it is not unconstitutional to practice "reverse discrimination." Chief Justice Happ, who wrote the opinion, said that the Court "is not, nor will it consent to be, a body of foolosophers easily drawn into jive baloney-shooting." The Modern Language Association filed a brief of *amicus curiae* ("friendly curiosity").

GREED

Splitting 8–1, the Court upheld the constitutionality of a federal program for the redistribution of wealth. Under the program, which is known as "horizontal divestiture," rich people are asked to lie down, and poor people then divest them of their money. Justice Happold, dissenting, said that the program would diminish the impact of a standing Court order requiring that income in excess of $15,000 a year be bused across state lines to achieve bank-account balances.

As is their custom, the Justices closed the session with an informal musicale, playing a Corelli *gigg.* Justices Hapgood, Happworth, Happner, and Happer performed on violin, Justice Happell on bassoon, Justice Happsberger on harpsichord, Justice Happold on oboe, Justice Hapenny on flute, and Chief Justice Happ on viola d'amore.

Lobster Night

Earl took me to the Café Chromosome. His choice, my birthday, his money, party of two. The effects there are very effectual: the famous Shivering Chandelier, six tables, twelve gold service plates engraved "Most People Are Not Here," seating capacity held artificially low so that the maximum number of the reservationless are turned away. I wanted to lower myself to the atmosphere. Stan and Florine came in. Earl said to me, "Are you sure that Stan is as faithful to you as he makes out? Because he told me a different story." I hated Earl then for his tale-bearing and could think of but one thing—twosomes—and could do but two things—go, and send Stan a note to say I would be at the place next door. My choice, my birthday, my money, party of one.

When I got to Chez les Cent Un Dalmatiens, Earl was there, flecked with impatience, and when he said we must talk, I shook my head no: there was just enough darkness for blurting and just enough light for embarrassment, just enough privacy for a regrettable scene and just enough exposure for a classic scene, just enough food in the kitchen to turn Earl rather amiable and just enough drink in the cellar to turn him perfect; but when he tried to go, I couldn't bear to be without someone to be with—not, at least, while Stan and Florine were forking it in next door, Stan longing for my next message, which said, "No. Not her. *Me.*" Which I was too proud to send, so I suggested we share a cab to another place.

At Lord Lipid's, men in livery kowtowed, and the drinks came in cups of bridle leather. Earl asked me what I wanted, and I said Stan, but Earl said that wasn't what he meant. "Then," I said coldly, "I want to have my signature honored. I want to be swathed in miles of challis." Earl looked hurt. A combo played, hautboy and cocktail comb. I had tears in my eyes, I had hurt him, I wanted to have had a convalescent brother kiss me through the dining room window at Field Place. Stan came in. He could only stay a moment, Florine waited. He asked me why I was upset, and I said because I didn't mind his having dinner with Florine. He said they were having drinks, not dinner, and in any case didn't I know how very, very pretty I was even though what I had said was the sheerest nonsense? A wrong and senseless joy—but at that Earl picked up the bread knife and held it to the throat of a loaf of bread, saying, "Don't worry—you two are next." Then he dropped the knife and looked hurt. Stan said, "A little lithium would do no harm there," and went away—he missed Florine, who was outside and was also very pretty.

To cheer Earl up, I took him in a cab to Early Bacon, where they have bunny china. He was so hurt that I wanted to live with him to a ripe grandevity. I held his hand for a second. Then Florine arrived. Washed out, I thought, as pretty women so often get; but when at the door they made her put on a plastic bib although she insisted she couldn't eat, to see her humiliated made me feel more kindly. She told us she had meant to live with Earl but that Stan had said couples need companionship and had moved in on her. I watched Earl swallow this. I flirted with her, wanting only to hurt Stan, Earl, and her. Then, knowing I must leave the pair of them to reconcile, I went out and hailed a taxi.

At the Horse Leech Pub, the wooden tables had new varnish over initials in old varnish, some of them carved with my own utility blade. I brooded about the past, I wanted to settle hash. Stan came in and said, "Nothing can be done. And when I say nothing, I mean there are certain things we could try that would be pointless."

"Such as?"

To my left, a man half turned away from a woman was saying, "It's really wonderful how everything's gone just right for me." I wanted to paste him one, but first I wanted to know too much luxury.

Stan said, "It would be pointless for you and me to get it on again. And when I say pointless, I mean it would be wonderful."

I refused. I wanted him to say of me, "I love her, although there's no denying that she's headstrong." I rose to leave, but he said he could force me to pack a vanity case and join him at his hideaway on Briar Island. I tried to make him go back to Florine, but he wouldn't, saying she was quite a woman and he planned to write her biography—a thing, I believe, few men would have bothered to do. I wanted no one to write of me, "She couldn't want it for herself."

En route to the Island, we took a taxi to Say Say and crouched on our old mat under the trellis in the tatami room. I felt guilty about betraying Earl, but there, in Stan's presence, I saw infidelity to be the act that makes fidelity possible for others. As it turned out, for complicated reasons we never went to Briar Island at all. Earl and Florine sent a message by cab announcing that they were coming over in a taxi. Stan wanted to hang around, but I said what if Earl and Florine then showed up, confidently expecting us to have bolted? Stan wouldn't listen, and I felt deceived, though of course it wasn't my business to see that people weren't deceived. When Earl and Florine arrived, each with the other, I asked her to cab along with me to a place uptown.

The Grouse Box was charred black on the outside and blood-red inside, full of dates falling in love because they had been thrust from insupportable solitude into one of a few infrequent and eagerly anticipated evenings out. Florine went to the ladies', and when she came back, she said, "Don't look now. Pay phone on the wall. Heavyset guy talking on it, kneeling." I knew how she felt, for we had been in it together—the marches, taunts, hoarseness, purple banners: Had we done it just for this? I asked her what she wanted. "A fast waltz in a drawing room lighted by innumerable candles." I liked her honesty. We joked about Earl and Stan, how they had lately been wearing their pants very high to shorten the chest and make it look powerful, and she told me of items she had read in the *Newsletter of the Affairs of Others*, and I sensed that we could be lovers if one of us were a man with bedroom eyes.

Momentarily, Earl dashed in and said Stan was to follow in a taxi. The three of us had a painful interview, Earl demanding to know if Florine wished to renounce him for Stan or if I had enough money to bribe Stan to support me.

I would not answer.

Florine would. "Oh, you and your ultimata!"

"You call that a decision? Well. This is it, then."

"If this were *it*, it wouldn't be this," said Florine, and ran off.

Earl was too depressed to stay, so we left a note for Stan and took a cab to a place in the vicinity.

At Villa Alive, the menu listed only one dish, with the annotation "An Alternative." We had hardly touched the water course when Stan appeared in the doorway, saw us, and shot out. I asked Earl if he had noticed, but he wouldn't discuss it, and years later I heard that he still didn't speak of the matter. He told me he was fairly certain I owed him a commitment, since Florine had flat rejected him. I asked him what he wanted. "To break your legs if you're ever unfaithful to me." I wanted to dispute this modest view of love, but scarcely had I pronounced the opening lines of my argument—"This wickit ymaginacioun, quhich by his name is clepit Jelousye"—when I found myself in a taxi next to him.

At Other Fish to Fry, white tile set off the barflies, taproom boasts, trenchermen, and couples. In the booth behind me, voices:

"Their sole amandine sounds nice."

"I would quarrel with that, Valerie, I'm afraid. Though you are free to disagree. I'd like nothing more than to hear you disagree. Show some spine, Valerie, for a change."

"Well, to be honest—maybe I'm way out of line on this one, but I'm pretty positive that I probably don't want the sole, I almost think."

"Among aware, intelligent people there will always be some difference of opinion. You should have the sole, Valerie, even if it is the wrong choice. Nobody's keeping score."

"Well, your willingness to discuss this has meant a lot. I really appreciate it. I guess I'll just have the gravy."

I ordered sole amandine, Earl a house salad—snail shells and birds' nests in vinaigrette, which returned him to his theme. "Even some plants build nests, you know. Ever heard of the carpenter gardenia?"

"Not recently."

He took some color slides from his wallet and held them one at a time to the light in such a way that I couldn't help but view them. "Number One, the male gardenia painstakingly constructs a maisonette for its spouse. Yes, throughout the vegetable kingdom pairing is the rule. Number Two, a male and a female copperhead wend their way aboard the ark at Tallahassee's World of Couples. Number Three, these bug mates feel no need for speculation on the natural order as they are united in an informal mid-morning ceremony. Number Four, hmm, that one's a disappointment."

A dazzling offer—but I wanted room, rope, more room for my rope. Stan came in and told us he was terrified of keeping his promises to Florine. I thought of him all alone and Florine in God knows what kind of nickel-and-grab. I wanted to say "Go" and then have the prudence to say "Now come back." I got him outside but couldn't find him a taxi, so I helped him make his way, on foot, through a light drizzle, to a place.

At the Blue Pill, the room was warm and steamy, and I felt as if the world were enveloped in a vaporous envelope. I wanted Stan to suggest with his hand a place in the air, I wanted to let my weight take me up and into the place, to be caught and set down safely and left alone. We sat across from each other—between us a square of white tablecloth, a small volume of air. I wanted someone to force a spray of stephanotis into my arms, I wanted every seed pearl on the eastern seaboard sewn to my bust.

"Do you know how fond I am of you all?" he said. "You and your sweet habit of shrinking and waffling at the slightest question, Florine and her sweet habit of repeating society news—how can I share what isn't mine?"

I was holding my breath.

"Earl and our common memory of service in the barbiturate wars—"

I wanted to say of him years afterward, "He was the only one who didn't try to railroad me into something terminal."

"You have your whole lives ahead of you."

At that point, Florine burst in. "Good heavens! What are you two doing here? Why aren't you confronting Earl and me at the In Luck Rice Corp. East?" She said she had to go back, but Stan suddenly drew on our sympathies with an imaginary ailment, so there was no question of her leaving. We ordered champagne and candy, and for Stan a cot. He sat under the covers, propped up with pillows, one hand tucked into Florine's placket and the other into mine. I wanted to know little of the area save for this rude map.

"It's tempting to ask one of you to marry me. But later I'd have to chuck her for the other one."

"Serial chucking."

"Maybe we're changing."

"Not again!"

We arranged to all four meet for a nightcap at a place we had heard of over in Jersey.

At Adjust Moon, there was no atmosphere, except for the Dribbling Shotglasses, with which we toasted my birthday. We all held hands across the paper tablecloth, pleased with one another, Florine and I much, much more comfortable together, until Earl spoiled things by writing on a matchbook the name of the person each of us would end up with and then, without showing it, burning it in the ashtray. At a time when so many might despair, we got out of hand. First Florine and I defied Stan and Earl, then Stan and Florine defied Earl and me, we defied them, Stan and I defied Florine and Earl, they defied us, and finally Earl and Stan defied Florine and me. Everyone refused to leave everyone. Luxurious lobster nights!—but Earl said that we confused happiness with our private interests, that instead we should confuse it with his and pair off arbitrarily in the normal way, that the course of evolution could not be changed by a foursome in a single nightclub. "Moon gas," said Florine. Earl said that, granted, he didn't know which one he wanted, her or me, but whichever it was, he wanted that one all to himself, he wanted to reject the other one, he wanted to cultivate hostility between the two of us. "Be fair," said Stan. Earl said he didn't want fairness, he wanted me or her, though naturally we were free to disagree. We did disagree. Earl said, "I'll give you this: you might be on to something. But you're going a dumb way with it."

Goodbye, Earl, and good luck!

We didn't try enough, we didn't give him evidence of a chance. He didn't love us enough, not enough for my money, not enough to go around. There wasn't enough love in him to dust a fiddle. True enough. Well, why make a meal of it? Enough said.

There were spots we hadn't hit yet, so the three of us hit them. We went to the Kidney Garden, and the French Way, and Unter dem Dirndl. Everybody was awake, the Garland restaurant grills were heated to a surface temperature impossible to get on a home unit, people whose greed was different from ours in some cases and in some cases not were ordering all the courses in the correct progression and saying "What's the damage?" We went to Parolles', and Ovos Fervidos, and Three Ack Emma. Customers gazed at the far rims of their cups and glasses as they drank; we thought of Earl, of the loneliness between the time you abandon what wasn't enough and the time you find what won't be enough. We went to How's Your Father, to the Cod's Head Inn and the Cod's Head du Soir. There were many arrangements of people talking while someone present or absent got left out; alphabets of elbow positions on tables; waits, delicacies, tall orders. We crumpled our linen napkins, which opened again on their own, and then we went dancing to a combo—drum, vocalist, and another drum—at Necktie Party. At dawn, we walked, changing places: man woman woman, woman man woman, woman woman man. The streets were empty. We had no plan. At an intersection, a red van turned the corner toward us. A second, a third, a fleet followed. Their sides were painted with the words "Swinging and Revolving Doors—Sales—Service—Repair—Modernization." Then, as the first van passed us, it sounded its klaxon. Van after van caught the spirit. Horns filled the air in awkward greeting. We waved, and walked for a while longer, three abreast: Stan on the inside, lest slops hurled from a window soil Florine or me; Florine on the outside, lest a taxicab splatter me or Stan; me in the center, lest Stan or Florine feel left out.

Pepys's Secret Diaries!

> Now the appearance of Hitler's diaries—genuine or not, it almost doesn't matter in the end—reminds us of the horrible reality. . . .
>
> —*Newsweek*, May 2, 1983

IT BEGAN AS THE RESTORATION OF THE STUARTS . . . AND ENDED IN A SHATTERING BLITZKRIEG!

Skulking back in the labyrinth of time to the libertine intrigues of the seventeenth century, an ardent freelance memorabilia hunter has tracked down an unsuspected cache of evidence that shrouds all previous historical forgeries in a new light. Diaries kept by Samuel Pepys, a key insider in the British Navy Office, were reportedly dispatched to Cambridge University after his death in 1703; but somewhere on the east herbaceous border of the campus, they were dispersed and lost in a wanton wheelbarrow crash. Not until two years ago did the anonymous source, pursuing leads obtained in bawdy badinage with an unidentified coterie, pick up the trail in the exclusive recesses of Magdalene College Library, Cambridge, where the sixty volumes had been cleverly hidden for centuries in ingeniously constructed glass display cases. The following excerpts, which have already sparked a blizzard of gossip, were decoded with the aid of the sophisticated Interpol Penmanship Squad from the cipher in which Pepys wrote on newly authenticated seventeenth-century legal pads.

[Jan.] 28th, [1661]
At the office all morning, thence to an ale-house to be refreshed. I did talk of nothing but Cromwell's body. The thought of this dead

Puritan, with his unfortunate hair-cut, the worst thing that I ever saw, did vex me greatly. I warned him not to close the theatres; and to have some love affairs, as the German leaders do; but no. By and by he was therefore killed of natural causes; on whose orders, I confess, I know not. Dined; thence to the theatre to see a thing by Dryden, the author of *Brown-Shirts à la Mode; or, Scum and Bungl'rs,* wherein was the most pleasant speech. His new play did likewise make my heart rejoice; being called *Operation Seraglio,* with Nell [Gwyn] very pretty in Bavarian dress.

[Jan.] 29th, [1661]
Very well pleased with our Charles II, who ever is up to his old tricks with women. How lewdly did he talk, and with how much wit, when I arrived at White Hall with my secret directive for trading to the Germans, in exchange for the greatest fleet of ships that can be imagined, our blueprints for the invention of the proscenium stage! After dinner with my wife to see a play of Congreve's, *Lust for Power*; the world never can hope ever to see again so much wickedness so prettily done, or so well concluded.

[Sept.] 2d, [1666]
Up late last night, when there came a knock on the door telling us of a great fire raging in the city. Thence to the window, and thought the blaze to be in Drury Lane at the farthest. Having in an hour's time walked to that place, I did determine that it was only a lighting rehearsal for an amateur masque, *The Night of the Brok'n Glass*; yet elsewhere in the city was every body running this way and that. Lord! These hotheads! They live in a dream world. Hearing a fine thunder of poetic bombast, they would perceive the unimaginable sound of real Germans in the sky with muskets; a thought for which I pray God forgive me; as, for aught I know, He did do; for on my way home, amidst the disorder, I spied the prettiest pair of knickers that ever was revealed to any man.

[Feb.] 2d, [1667]
To see Wycherley's new play, *The Smoothie Englishman*; the most cunning that I ever did see; mightily commended for its leading part,

a Prime Minister who gives away of Czechoslovakia the most that ever I saw in my life, and thus loses his mistresses. I was sick to see it, but yet would not but have seen it; for this man Wycherley is indispensable to me, that I might the better draft my confidential guidelines for the behaviour of Government ministers in future.

[May] 31st, [1669]
Up very betimes, and had another meeting with the King at White Hall, on the Germans' insulting counter-offer of the rights to some boring, preachifying play-scripts about Teutonic mythological personages in exchange for a beach-head at Southampton. The King very angry, having lately seen so few people in the pit for Nell's performance as Lady Himmler in *The Unfathomable Penny-Pincher*; a travelling troupe of Russian mimes being said now-a-days to carry away all the people, as having more powerful players with the most luxuriant moustaches. The King did then speak of tough reprisals; but whatever comes of these, I must forbear to record; for thus ends the keeping of my Journal, I growing blind. And therefore, from this time forward, may the world know no more than it is fit for them to know, save this one final note:

Dined with my wife; thence to see Farquhar's new play, *The Jews' Stratagem;* or *Love Preserv'd:* the greatest and most artful thing that I could ever live to see; and so, we to a drinking-house, called The World's End: merry as I never saw it.

II

Love Trouble Is My Business (1988)

The New Thing

Inevitably it's going to be the first thought that people have, so before anybody can even bring it up, let me say that obviously it was our first reaction, too. There's no escaping it. People are going to ask—and right from the start we had to ask ourselves, even though the question is probably the last thing that should be on our minds: Are we just going to be an imitation of *Saturday Night Live*?

Of course, there are only the two of us. Right there, that should differentiate us in the eyes of the public. But as soon as Ed and I started living together, we knew we were eventually going to have to deal with this "imitators" accusation, even though there really is no way to deal with it except to honor it as a legitimate concern and then proceed from there as if the issue didn't exist. I mean, we can't get on with our life if we have to keep looking back over our shoulder all the time, wondering if *Saturday Night Live* did it first or did it better. For a while, though, we were afraid to leave the apartment or have people in for drinks, because we know that everybody has this preconception that we're trying to compete with the image they have of Laraine and Danny and Belushi and Gilda and that whole original *Saturday Night Live* group. But then we discovered that if you actually go back and look at the old *Saturday Night Live* shows, they really weren't as immoral as you remember, so right there we have a definite advantage. My relationship with Ed has an easy, natural way of offending people which, I don't know—maybe it's an outgrowth of the eighties, but it's something you didn't see on television a decade ago.

And then we plan to keep the company very small. As I said, the regulars will be just me and Ed. We've wanted to get together for years, and we think we're a good solid nucleus of talent. Ed started a bulletin board with pictures of young, new faces we considered negotiating with, but we felt that the public wouldn't go for that format. There will be an occasional guest. One of the hopefuls we've lined up is Ed's mother, who as you may know is Michael Jackson's favorite white person.

Another difference—although, don't get me wrong, we're aware that this obsession with being different is an inherent danger—is that we have many more hours to fill than *Saturday Night Live.* Which puts horrendous demands on us for material. The first few weeks, we went bananas trying to make sure we didn't repeat anything that had been on *Saturday Night Live.* Some of our early dates were just nightmares, with me sitting there staring at Ed in stark terror, afraid that if I screamed I'd sound too much like Laraine. And Ed later confessed that he was worried the whole time that he was just another Bill Murray clone. Then gradually we realized that if we eliminated everything about *Saturday Night Live,* we would have eliminated all of life itself. So we just relaxed and decided that if we can please *us,* that's achievement enough. If, on top of that, some people enjoy us, then fine.

Mainly the thing we have to resist is this constant pressure to go "farther" than *Saturday Night Live* did. O.K., so they did everything there is to do, but of course it's always possible to do it again only making it more repellent. And frankly, if you want to know the truth, it's a temptation, the way so many people look at us expecting to see gratuitous sex. We're fiercely determined not to go that route. If an idea spontaneously occurs to us and it seems dirty, then great—we're not going to censor ourselves. But once you start getting calculated about it, then you have to have even more gratuitous sex the next time to get any reaction at all. It's like what happened to the new phone company. They started out with the strategy of just openly admitting that they were going to imitate *Saturday Night Live,* with the slogan "You'll Never Know the Difference." But then one of their publicity hacks came up with a few cheap shots that certain jaded consumers said were more daring than the original, and pretty soon they were having to incorporate more and more gratuitous sex into their business practices just to keep the public scared.

So, for the most part, how Ed and I measure up vis-à-vis *Saturday Night Live* is a concern we've relegated to the back burner. If others want to keep harping on *Saturday Night Live* and how great Chevy and Gilda and Laraine and Danny were compared to us, that's their problem, not ours. Anyway, I just don't have the emotional energy to think about it, because I'm much, much more concerned about being investigated for secretly taping all my telephone conversations with White House officials. At the moment, I'm living in constant fear that if a judge subpoenas my tapes, he's going to think they're too much like the old *Saturday Night Live*. On one of them, where I'm screaming at White House Chief of Staff James A. Baker III, I swear to God I sound exactly like Laraine. You don't necessarily set out to copy somebody, but there are only *x* number of ways to go with a horror scream.

Basically, my point is that in our instant electronic media culture, novelty is no longer possible. That's a lesson that has somehow eluded at least one person in the federal government—Linda Chavez, the new Reagan-appointed staff director of the Commission on Civil Rights. What a hype artist! She's getting all this newspaper coverage for being into "reorientation" of the commission, away from good-taste concepts like affirmative action, equal pay for jobs of comparable value, bilingual education, and study of the discriminatory impact of numerical underrepresentation of minorities. This is supposed to be a "major change of course." It's supposed to be so fresh and irreverent. For her information, the identical material could easily have been done on the old *Saturday Night Live*, by Garrett Morris, whom she would probably now claim she doesn't remember. The only reason he didn't bother to actually do it was because Garrett was hip enough to know that it had already been done a million times. Plus, because even on the old *Saturday Night Live* some things were sacred.

January 1984[*]

My friend Cathy Schine had asked me to babysit for her six-month-old son Max one Saturday afternoon, and as she went off to the Metropolitan Opera to see Beethoven's *Fidelio*, she said, "Read this"—a *New York* magazine article on *The New Show*, a TV comedy show that was coming out:

> If there's one thing certain about Lorne Michaels's new TV venture, it's that being new will be almost impossible. ". . . When we started *Saturday Night* the expectations were so low." ". . . You have to go farther the next time to get the same reaction." ". . . If we eliminated all of *Saturday Night* there'd be nothing left." ". . . Even if the show is mediocre, . . . it can only be so in the context Lorne defines."

Immediately I wanted to write something with this sound. It was a new, specialized form of a sound that always appeals to me—the sound of anxiety being rationalized. *Fine.* What a wonderfully feeble word. It's incredibly unstable—only used when it threatens to flip over into *Not fine.* Also, I had a new boyfriend, and here was an excuse to dwell on that situation: romance anxious about its newness. (It happens a lot that a found news item registers with me this way—as a hook for some personal preoccupation I wouldn't think of writing about otherwise.) *We.* I felt pleasantly optimistic using the voice of a couple, which was new for me, but "we" is another word that always seems on the verge of collapse. Its enforcement of solidarity gets to sound a little desperate. So this story was really designed to teeter on two shaky legs: "we" and "fine." *We're fine.*

At the same time, I had these words: *Laraine, Danny, Belushi, Gilda, Murray, Chevy.* They made the story easy to write; they could be repeated and rearranged and counted on for their fixed magic.

I only had two or three hours to work while Max took his nap. (I'm grateful to him for the revelation that I didn't need total militantly spontaneous privacy—that writing can accommodate the presence

---

[*] EDITOR'S NOTE: After each of the 24 stories in this part, the author added a commentary about when and how it came to be written.

of other people.) By the time Cathy got home, I had a draft of half the story, read it to her, and said it was stuck—needed another element besides the new show/new boyfriend analogy. She said, "Why don't you just go through the *Times* and find some examples of other new stuff you don't like?"

The list included "supply-side economics," but what really rang a bell was a *Times* story on Reaganesque changes at the Commission on Civil Rights. *Garrett.* I'd forgotten about the only black actor on the original *Saturday Night*—Garrett Morris—and because I'd forgotten about him, I was now determined to make him the star of the story, without falsifying his actual importance on the show.

What I most love to do is be frivolous and then swerve into blatant sincerity. I have no idea why. My hero is Preston Sturges, whose great movie comedies of the 1940s take all kinds of daring plunges from farce to sentiment. He had inexhaustible strategies for making a situation yield its opposite and switch direction. So he could allow that the world runs on greed, delusion, and injustice while he revelled in the crazy exceptions that prove the rule. Certainly I didn't have racial prejudice in mind when I started writing the story, but when the chance came to change gears this way, it was something I felt free to do because I'd seen Sturges do it.

After the story was published, I got a phone call from a woman I didn't know, Marilyn Suzanne Miller, who turned out to have written some of my favorite *Saturday Night* sketches, including the ones called *The Judi Miller Show,* where Gilda Radner played a little girl acting out fantasies in her room at breakneck speed. Marilyn and I became friends, and we both went nuts when Frank Rich, the *Times* drama critic, popped up in the *New Republic* with an attack on the show's "golden years," claiming it had betrayed the counterculture by pandering to yuppie demographics and ethnic stereotypes. He had a point—a marginal, killjoy point. I tried to write a letter of rebuttal, invoking Dan Aykroyd's Irwin Mainway, the hot-shot promoter who sold dog milk to school lunch programs. Even if the Not Ready for Prime Time Players had some faults, they gave me a better feeling than the Reagan Administration did. But that doesn't seem like critical reasoning. I'd rather just let the fantasy of this story stand as a rebuttal.

Tribute

I'm not blaming the news media for this, because if their coverage of the XXIII Olympiad featured the athletes, the athletic events, and the Olympics per se, that's probably as it should be. It's right, yet in another way it's perhaps also wrong, to have overlooked certain small, unofficial things that people all over the country did to sustain the national and even international mood of Olympic pride and pain. One of these things was a thing Ed did right in our apartment. It was Sunday, August 12, 1984, about 10 P.M. New York time, during the closing ceremonies of the Olympics. Ed and I were half watching them on TV while we tried to cover our refrigerator with Con-Tact paper. It's the refrigerator Ed had for years when the apartment was his bachelor pad, and a cat he used to have had a habit of jumping on top of it and walking around and then clawing her way down the sides trying to get off, so the enamel finish had gotten all scratched and then the scratches had rusted; when I moved in a few months ago, we decided to cover the whole thing with black Con-Tact paper. Well, we were going nuts trying to cut the paper to fit around the handle and around the screws on the corners. There were scraps of Con-Tact paper all over the floor.

It must have been close to 11 P.M. New York time—at the Olympic ceremonies they were reprising all the national anthems—when I noticed that Ed, barefoot, was walking across the kitchen with one of the scraps of Con-Tact paper stuck to the bottom of his right foot. The paper was somewhat bigger than his foot—roughly the size of a piece of typing paper—and I want to emphasize this: the backing had not been removed to expose the sticky surface. (I know this, because that's the way I apply Con-Tact paper—cutting it to shape and only removing the backing when I get a perfect fit.) It was pretty hot in the apartment—we're way up on the twenty-third floor and we had the windows open, but it was August, remember, and we don't have air conditioning—so I guess the perspiration on his foot helped it adhere to the glossy surface of the paper.

I didn't think too much about it, but I kept noticing it out of the corner of my eye, like a visual irritant, and finally—just for something to say, because it was getting a little tense in there, what with the heat and the frustration of this refrigerator project—I said jokingly, "When are you planning to take that piece of paper off your foot?"

Quietly, Ed replied, "I think I'll keep it on until the official closing of the Olympic Games, as one man's tribute to the Olympic spirit."

I let out an audible gasp. Quite simply, the man is a genius. In that improvisational, or seemingly improvisational, moment, he proceeded to unveil a technique as powerfully controlled as if he'd trained for years. Altering his gait slightly, so as to press his foot firmly on the surface of the paper with each step, for several hours he walked a fragile tightrope between tragedy and comedy. I detected no signs of cramping.

I'm aware that in some quarters "technique" is a dirty word, and I realize that Ed might come under some criticism if I harp too much on the skillfulness of his performance. Suffice it to say that it was not despite but because of his skill that he was able to celebrate so lovingly not only the greatness but, more important, the *defects* of human beings. The perfection—one might say even the imperfection—of his performance was that although it caused him to suffer minor discomfort in the last hour, it was completely pointless, aspiring neither to goal nor to glory. But is it truly pointless when, say, a scientist who could be discovering a cure for cancer discovers, instead, an infinitesimally tiny molecule with no conceivable medical or athletic implications? Isn't what really counts that the task was done just for the sheer joy of the doing? What Ed did, he did with total love and commitment. By the end of his performance, as the ABC-TV closing credits rolled down the screen and a voice on the PA system at the Olympic stadium intoned the concluding words "Will the choir please leave the stage," I thought less of Ed as an athlete but a great deal more of him as a person.

Surprisingly, or maybe not so surprisingly, people want to applaud the accomplishment of something they know is "difficult." But what if a man is, God help us, an original, who does something completely new and makes it look easy? In this dog-eat-dog world, I find a man like that not just an inspiration but an antidote to post-Olympic letdown. Ed's achievement by no means devalues the medals won by the official Olympic athletes in competition, but when we threw all the scraps of Con-Tact paper out the window and watched them flutter down on the ticker-tape parade, we both felt on top of the world.

August 1984

This was just an exaggeration of something that really happened. I was hanging out with the guy I based Ed on—we were in his darkroom while he printed some photographs, listening to the Olympics coverage from the TV in the living room. He was walking around with a sheet of photographic paper stuck to his foot, and said the words exactly as Ed does: "I think I'll keep it on until the official closing of the Olympic Games, as one man's tribute to the Olympic spirit." I was determined to share this with the world—and then that determination got inflated into the tributes to Ed's genius.

The tributes were heavily influenced by a New York Film Critics Awards dinner at Sardi's the previous winter. That was the year *Terms of Endearment* won a lot of awards. As people like Shirley MacLaine and Jules Feiffer were making preposterous speeches about each other's greatness, a critic from the *Village Voice*, Jim Hoberman, turned to me from another table, handed me his program as extra paper to write on, and said, "You should be taking all this down":

> He made a dream reality. . . . an audible gasp in the theater . . . celebrates the defects of human beings so lovingly . . . a fragile tightrope walk between tragedy and comedy . . . that inimitable wit that belongs to this country—or the world, maybe . . . the improvisational, or seemingly improvisational, decision-evoking process on the screen—the man is a genius. . . . The man himself is an inspiration—that's a rare thing—the man is a *nice guy*—that's special. We always hear about the dog-eat-dog world. . . . Surprisingly, or maybe not so surprisingly, movie audiences do not want literacy—and what if a man is, God help us, witty. . . . a shockingly wonderful performance—his almost childlike love of risk . . . awesome breathtaking contribution.

Somebody told me my attitude toward Ed was "a mixture of love and scorn." The scorn came from Sardi's.

Love Trouble Is My Business

> Francis X. Clines, in the Sunday *Times* . . . : "President Reagan resembled a bashful cowboy the other day when he was asked about the apparent collapse of the 'Star Wars' talks with the Soviet Union. . . . At his side, murmuring something through the fixed smile that seems required of American political spouses, Mrs. Reagan was overheard prompting him: 'We're doing everything we can.' . . . Out there in . . . the President's mountainside retreat, subjects such as the Soviet Union seem to haunt Mr. Reagan the way vows to read Proust dog other Americans at leisure."
>
> This may be the only time in history in which the words "Mr. Reagan" and "read Proust" will appear in the same sentence.
>
> —Geoffrey Stokes (in the *Village Voice*, August 14, 1984)

I glanced over at the dame sleeping next to me, and all of a sudden I wanted some other dame, the way you see Mr. Reagan on TV and all of a sudden get a yen to read Proust. Not that she wasn't attractive, with rumpled blond curls and a complexion so transparent you could read Proust through it—that is, as long as her cute habit of claiming a tax deduction for salon facials didn't turn up in some IRS stool pigeon's memo to Mr. Reagan. It was taking her a little more time to wake up than it would take Mr. Reagan's horse to read Proust. After I'd showered and shaved and put on an old pair of pants that wouldn't lead anybody to believe my tailor was unduly influenced by having read Proust, I went back over to the bed, where I wasn't exactly planning to say my prayers—Mr. Reagan or no Mr. Reagan.

"Mr. . . . Reagan . . . ?" she whispered, fluttering her lashes, and I trusted the dazed quizzical act about as much as if she'd told me she could read Proust without moving her lips.

So I slugged her a couple of times, and I'd have slugged her a couple of more times if something hadn't told me I'd get a colder shoulder than a cult nut insisting you could read Proust as anagrams predicting the end of the world during the Administration of Mr. Reagan.

She chuckled insanely, like Mr. Reagan looped on something you wouldn't want to drink while you read Proust. Then she touched me, with the practiced efficiency of a protocol officer steering some terribly junior diplomat through a receiving line to meet Mr. Reagan—and funny, but I got the idea she wasn't suggesting we curl up and read Proust. As her hand slid along my thigh, I noticed that she wore a ring with a diamond the size of the brain of a guy who read Proust all the time, and if I'd been Mr. Reagan I'd have been dumb enough to buy her another one to go with it. But the distance between a private eye's income and Mr. Reagan's was a gaping chasm big enough to crawl into and read Proust.

I wondered if Mr. Reagan worked this hard for his dough, as I maneuvered her into the Kama Sutra position known as "Too Busy to Read Proust."

I woke to the phone shrilling in my ear like the hotline warning Mr. Reagan that ten thousand Russian missiles hurtling over Western Europe weren't RSVPing for a let's-get-together-once-a-week-and-read-Proust party. I let it ring, hoping the caller would decide to quit and go reread Proust, and wondering why dames always ran out on me without saying goodbye—why they didn't stick around with loyal wifely fixed smiles the way they did for hotshots like Mr. Reagan. Then I found myself getting a little weepy at a sentimental popular tune that was drifting through the venetian blinds:

> The connoisseur who's read Proust does it,
> Mr. Reagan with a boost does it,
> Let's do it, let's fall in love.
>
> Read Proust, where each *duc* and *comte* does it,
> Mr. Reagan with a prompt does it,
> Let's do it, let's fall in love.

I've read Proust wished that he had done it
Through a small aperture,
Has Leningrad done it?
Mr. Reagan's not sure.

Some who read Proust say Odette did it,
Mr. Reagan with a safety net did it,
Let's do it, let's fall in love.

"*Cherchez la femme*," I said to myself—a phrase I'd picked up on a case where the judge gave clemency to a homicidal maniac for having read Proust—and then I went out in the rain to a bookstore where I usually browsed for dames, and found one perusing Mr. Reagan's latest autobiography. Just for fun, I looked over her shoulder and read:

For a long time, before I met Nancy, I used to go to bed early.

August 1984

What a gift! The *Voice's* Press Clips columnist, Geoff Stokes, had found an unusually baroque item of Reagan journalism in the *Times*, and created a work of satire by adding his own conclusion: "This may be the only time in history in which the words 'Mr. Reagan' and 'read Proust' will appear in the same sentence." I was just piggybacking on Stokes's idea by putting "Mr. Reagan" and "read Proust" into *every* sentence of something. Don't know why I instinctively started doing it in a private-eye voice. A ready-made generic voice—but possibly I had a subconscious memory from Raymond Chandler's *The Big Sleep;* flipping through it later to refresh my private-eye prose rhythms, I came across this passage:

"I was beginning to think perhaps you worked in bed, like Marcel Proust."

"Who's he?" I put a cigarette in my mouth and stared at her. She looked a little pale and strained, but she looked like a girl who could function under a strain.

"A French writer, a connoisseur in degenerates. You wouldn't know him. . . . You can call me Vivian."

"Thanks, Mrs. Reagan."

Writing this technically tight kind of piece imposes certain disciplines. You want every element to fit, and sometimes the fit makes an unforeseen angle on the facts—a provisional truth you want to keep faith with. You find yourself following some unanticipated logic: like, Nancy Reagan at least is a more loving wife than the *femmes fatales* of detective fiction, and Reagan at least doesn't slug her. Of course, another logical pattern I stumbled onto was that the mere word "Reagan" was a punchline. Also, there's no point in cheating on your own rules. I had to look up the Cole Porter lyrics to see how he punctuated them—to know if Reagan and Proust had to be in every line or just every stanza. (Fortunately Porter used commas and treated the stanza as one long line.)

Stokes's premise was so ripe that even writing bad lines was fun—like making lists of improbable rhymes. ("It was too early to read Proust, so I went out and bought myself a pint of 'Mr. Reagan.'") Later I heard that some poet teaching a class discussed this piece as a near-relative of the sestina—a verse form that keeps recycling *six* nonrhyming words, which fall at the ends of the lines in a different order each time around. Three times as much trouble.

The title (which piggybacks on Chandler) has an extra meaning for me, because it's my business to love trouble.

Totaled

> The Kaypro Corporation said yesterday that it is investigating the possibility that millions of dollars in computer parts are missing from a circus tent and big trucks where Kaypro stored them.
>
> —*New York Times*, September 13, 1984

HI-LO CORPORATION, INC.

MANUFACTURERS OF "BIG BOY"

MINI-COMPONENT MICRO-COMPONENTS

INVENTORY REPORT

1. WEEK ENDING: Right before the weekend.
2. ITEM CODE *(include 3-digit processing prefix and 6-digit quality control suffix)*: The little red ones. Some of the bigger ones got mixed in with this batch, though.
3. PRODUCTION LINE EGRESS LOCATION: The big plastic bucket under the big long table.
4. DISTANCE TO STORAGE FACILITY *(in meters)*: Quite a ways.
5. STORAGE FACILITY SITE *(include grid coordinates)*: In a big cardboard box around back. Plus more in a whole bunch of Hefty Bags over near that great big vacant lot.
6. NO./QTY. BACK STOCK: A few.
7. NO./QTY. MANUFACTURED WEEK TO DATE: Loads of them is what I heard, but I personally didn't get to watch them drop into the bucket, because I had off most of the week to go to this big accounting seminar over in that new high-rise.
8. ADD LINES 6 AND 7: Should be one heck of a lot. Notice I said *should* be.
9. NO./QTY. SHIPPED WEEK TO DATE: I don't know that much about shipping, because that's all handled in the big room up front, but from what little I know, not that many.
10. SUBTRACT LINE 9 FROM 8: Plenty. Supposedly.
11. INVENTORY PROCEDURE *(specify allowable method A, B, or C as per Advisory IP348075-83rev.)*: Friday night, when the big hand was on the six and the little hand was on the four, Shorty, Peewee, Tiny, Fats, and I headed around back to make sure the big box was relatively full. It was sealed, but Shorty happened to nudge it with his toe and thought it felt real light, so he cut it open in no time flat with this dinky pocketknife they give you after you work for Hi-Lo about forty-'leven years. What we counted compared to last week was just peanuts. We'd expected to see parts galore. So we figured a slew of them were shifted over to the Hefty Bags without anybody telling us, and we went out there fairly quick, taking the shortcut down by that little-bitty shed near the big road. There were oodles of Hefty Bags,

and we had a whale of a time opening them all. It took us quite some minutes. Same story: we counted a piddling number of parts where we expected scads. Well, we had a tremendous problem and about umpteen theories, so we decided to discuss the whole deal over a mess of beers at that little place run by the skinny guy. At the plant parking lot we picked up tons of secretaries plus considerable shipping clerks, and all of them plus me, Shorty, Peewee, and Tiny, but minus Fats, who was too big, piled into Shorty's teensy-weensy minibus, and so far that's about how it adds up.

12. NO./QTY. IN STOCK: Zip, or thereabouts.

October 1984

Just a game with all kinds of words for size and scale—prompted by the image of tiny computer parts in "a circus tent" and "big trucks." It was occurring to me that of late my writing had gotten very babyish (especially this and the babbling Ed stories), and I thought, Oh, great, falling in love has turned me into a nitwit—and I'm liking being a nitwit. A psychotherapist I was seeing then, Peter Berg, had a more attractive explanation: he said when you feel secure and happy with someone, you're more tolerant of your infantile side. Another explanation is that I had fallen in love with Janet Malcolm's "Trouble in the Archives"; I'd been rereading this report about sophisticated psychoanalysts acting out in a blindly infantile Freudian feud:

> "We were having this talk in his office about the transference and how it affects one's perception of physical appearance, and I said to him, 'You know, I always thought of you as an immense man, and it came as a great shock to me the other day when you stood up and I realized I was practically a head taller than you.' And he said, 'What are you talking about?' And I said, 'Well, just the fact that I'm taller than you.' And he said, '*You* taller than *me?* You're out of your mind!' And I said, 'Dr. V., I *am* taller than you, I assure you.' And he said, 'Stand up,' and I stood up, and he stood up, and I towered over him, and he looked me in the eye—from a good four inches beneath me—and said, '*Now* are you convinced that I'm taller than you?' So to be polite I said, 'Yes, I see.' But I thought, This guy is out of his mind."

And I thought, This is the bottom line on the way people really behave.

I was staying up in the country, where a novelist friend had lent me his studio while he was away, so this pipsqueak piece got written on his jumbo IBM typewriter in a tiny cabin in the middle of the big sticks. When I left, I forgot to empty the wastebasket under the desk, and always wondered if he went through the wastebasket and found all my drafts. *He dumps the wastebasket contents onto the desk . . . spreads out the torn scraps of paper . . . starts piecing them together . . .* A *woman's consciousness—the one subject that has always eluded him in his novels—and finally it's going to be revealed in all its unguarded reality . . . in her torrid unsent love letters, maybe . . . or profound musings on some woman-type secret he could never in a million years have hoped to fathom . . . or, even better, incredibly petty stuff of the kind that they, women, really think about and would never admit to a man. . . . His pulse is racing as he fits the last fragment into place. . . . This has to be a gold mine of material. . . . It's . . . it's . . . computer-part inventory forms??? This gal is out of her mind.*

Secret Ballot

I know that nobody can possibly know. It would be against the law. There's no way, once that curtain closed behind me—just *no way* anybody could find out what I did in there. *Nobody will ever know.* They said so. They said so on TV. They said so over and over in the weeks before the election, not just as a generalization but showing how the generalization applied to a situation like mine. They showed a young guy and his dad—a solid workingman kind of dad—walking along a nice street with trees, sharing their ideas about the election. The main idea they shared was that even though the whole family had always been Democrats, the son, who was voting for the first time, could go into that booth and close the curtain and nobody would ever have to know what he did in there, no matter how horrible what he did in there was. Not even his parents would ever find out.

I can't tell you how reassuring this was to me. It was something that really needed to be emphasized over and over again. Because a country like this can easily get to be like China, where the secret ballot is just a joke and you're forced to feel ashamed if you think differently from your neighbors and family. I was grateful for the reminder that in the United States of America, fortunately, my shame is a completely private matter.

So, it's ridiculous for me to worry that they found out. There would be no rational basis for my fear. It would be paranoid. Whatever I did in there, and I'm not telling—even if I shot up in there (which I didn't) or voted for Hitler (and I definitely didn't do anything that bad, even though it would be nobody's business if I did), even if I spit up all over myself, or made telepathic contact with the Planet of Evil—I have nothing to worry about. Let alone if I merely did an irresponsible, selfish, stupid thing that I already regret (which I don't). When I cut my seminar at 3 P.M. to vote, Mom and Dad were still at work, so they couldn't have been anywhere near the polling place. I think Sis suspects. She could have snuck out of her gym class and followed me—but as I understand it, those booths have a special device that sets off an alarm or something if you're in there and anyone tries to peek.

Just to be on the safe side, though, I've been avoiding my folks lately. I'm in my room right now, with the door locked. A minute ago I thought I heard Sis whispering through my window, *"I'm going to tell,"* but probably it was just the wind. I've really been on edge since Election Night—probably because I haven't been getting enough vitamin C. And my folks have been acting kind of weird. When we were all in the den not watching the election news on TV, because we didn't want to give away by some unconscious flicker of expression what we each had done in the voting booth, the phone rang. Dad said, *"That must be them now."* Then he yawned and stretched in this stagy way—there was something about it that seemed fake. Mom looked right at me and said, *"Why don't you answer it, dear?"*

For some reason a chill went through me. And suddenly it was as if I was in a nightmare—a waking nightmare, where I was sleepwalking toward the phone. When I picked up the receiver, I surreptitiously pressed the cut-off button and then pretended to talk to somebody who had a wrong number. I must have been sort of uneasy.

The next morning at breakfast, Dad was reading the *Times* and I was reading the *Wall Street Journal.* We had an unspoken agreement not to engage in any postmortems about the Reagan landslide and the Democratic gains in the Senate. Instead, we were silently sharing our respect for the sanctity of the secret ballot. But out of the blue Dad said, "Well, son, *here's something that I believe will interest you.*" I don't like being tricked. A primitive instinct took over in me, and I spilled my cappuccino all over the table on purpose. As Mom leaned across me to wipe it up, she murmured in my ear, "Dear, *I don't mean to be nosy, but . . .*" There was nothing I could do but elbow the croissants off the table. Since then, I've been staying in my room most of the time. When I lined up to vote, I was given a card with a number on it, and then when I voted they took away the card. I don't know where it is now. If Sis managed to ingratiate herself with one of the poll watchers, got hold of the card, and then—but that would be completely illegal. What I did in the booth is between me and my conscience. No—not even my conscience has the right to pry into what I did in there.

They've been making a big effort to lure me out of my room, and I'm not sure why. Looked at in a certain way, it could be interpreted as suspicious. Saturday, Dad was working on the car, and he knocked on my door and said he needed help. Well, the car being my only means of transportation in case of some totally illegal emergency, I thought I'd better check it out. I went down to the driveway, where Dad was standing, well back from the car, with his hand on his hips. The hood was up, and I remember how the sun glinted on the engine as he pointed at it and said, "*Why don't you stick your head in there and take a look?*"

I wasn't born yesterday. I was back in my room in thirty seconds. I've been in here pretty steadily since then. The one exception I made was earlier this afternoon. I'd been feeling lonely and hungry, so I stepped out into the hall. Mom, Dad, and Sis were lurking there, whispering. Dad handed me a big box wrapped in gold foil and tied with a red ribbon. Mom said, "*Go ahead—open it.*"

Something told me not to. *"What's that ticking noise?"*

Of course, I felt foolish as soon as I heard myself say the words "ticking noise." I thought, Probably it's just Sis snickering.

Then Dad said to me, with a strange urgency in his voice, *"Don't be silly."*

Well, nobody had to draw me a picture. I said casually that I'd open it later, after I had something to eat. Fine, they said, they were all just about to go to the supermarket and buy the makings for my favorite casserole, because I must be famished. I said I was.

Mom said, "Good. While we're out, *you go in and light the oven.*"

November 1984

Written very fast, the day of the Congressional elections, in anger at this Republican TV commercial, which really did have a Democratic dad giving his son permission to do whatever he wanted in the voting booth. It was instinctive to go with the son's voice—he was the one with the problem, he was the one being told *in a highly suspicious manner* not to worry—but I didn't quite know what to say, so to get up steam, I started out imitating the mentally disturbed repetitions that George Trow sometimes used for weird characters like this one:

> Do you remember my preference? Do you remember the way I made them nervous? That was part of the preference. Do you remember the way I made them reluctant to wear their uniforms in public? That was part of my preference. So specific, my preference. So specific, the way the little uniforms looked under a big bulky coat. Would you know me if I wore a uniform? Would you know me if I wore a bulky coat? Would you know me if I moved a step closer?

Part of writing is going on without knowing why and then saying, Hmm, what have we here? Paranoia . . . well, wasn't that heart-to-heart father-son talk really a pitch for secrecy? In the guise of a noble dad espousing free expression, the commercial was licensing yuppies to reject their parents' idealistic politics: *Probably your own dad isn't quite this tolerant, so disagree with him in the voting booth, where nobody will know. . . .* Recently I called up Hendrik Hertzberg (a good-humored and lucid explainer of politics) and asked him to straighten me out on the secret ballot. Wasn't this commercial perverting the secret ballot principle into something reminiscent of the secret ballot circa 1932 Germany? He said, tolerantly, Well, more people did vote for the Nazis than were running around openly in the streets as Brownshirts. But he said he thought what was really bothering me was a misplaced emphasis on the secret ballot as a prime ideal of democracy; he said the ideal isn't to hide your beliefs but to do the opposite—and then, way down the line, as a safeguard against your boss or some local gang of bullies who don't happen to like the way you're expressing yourself, we have the secret ballot, like a "firebreak," just in case.

But if I'd been so reasonable, I might not have had a story about paranoia—or a chance to use some lines of dialogue I'd been collecting for a while, lines that hang there forebodingly. Exhibit A was "Now, you go in and light the oven." Oliver Hardy says it to Stan Laurel in *Block-Heads*, where it results in a huge gas explosion and Ollie's moaning yell: "Oooooaaaaaahhhhhh!" In the back of my mind, there must also have been a recollection of Pete Smith, who made hundreds of popular live-action movie shorts from the 1930s to the 1950s, called Pete Smith Specialties *(Bus Pests, Cat College, Acro-Batty, Ain't It Aggravatin', I Love Children, But!)*. He often played a home handyman—putting a TV antenna on the roof, etc.; and the narration, in his own voice, was laconically ominous: *Uh-ohhhh, somebody left a roller skate at the foot of the ladder. . . .*

Our Side of the Story

Anecdotal material has its place—neither Ed nor I is in a position to deny that. In fact, we got pretty deeply into that issue on our first date, drinking Rolling Rock beer at the Superba and telling all the stories we'd each heard about how horrible the other person was—stories that would curl your hair—and then finding out that while they weren't untrue, exactly, they hadn't been put into a full perspective. So we're highly aware that the anecdote in reportage, while useful, needs to be interpreted very, very cautiously.

That caution is exactly what we find lacking in the way people are now jumping to conclusions about us on the basis of these "eyewitness" reports being spread around by recent visitors to our Village apartment—not only journalists but private citizens who have come down here on junkets to see how our new regime is working out. Naturally, we hoped they would drum up popular support for our internal struggle to create a better life. We even hoped they might influence policy toward us. So much for hope. Their reports always begin with the person's breast-beating explanation of how painful it is for them to be honest about what they saw—how they had been our biggest supporters at first, and how their initial gush of sympathy gradually dried up as they were forced to confront the evidence of their senses. Far be it from us to question their sincerity, but a lot of their disillusionment is of their own creation, stemming from their original need to see me and Ed in mythic terms. Right off the bat they convinced themselves that Ed and I were going to demonstrate the impossible: that two people with bad reputations—I and Ed—could get together and be transformed overnight into a model relationship.

But I don't want to get bogged down in generalizations about what's wrong with *their* relationships to make them so desperate for a myth. Let me just take some of the specific stories they've been reporting, and deal with those. This one guy, a foreign correspondent who has actually moved into our building, has been saying he often sees a queue outside our apartment door—as he puts it, "like in Eastern Europe." From what we've heard, he goes into vivid detail about long lines of depressed-looking people shifting from foot to foot, wearing shabby clothes, carrying pathetic little parcels and lunchboxes, etc. He says one time a dowdy woman in a babushka, with a heartbreakingly small chicken she was dangling by the feet, told him tearfully that she'd been waiting outside our door for over two hours.

Now, Ed and I have been victims lately of a certain amount of economic sabotage—mainly from the Manhattan Cable TV company, Con Edison, and the phone company—and more than likely what this guy saw was a few repairmen, etc., who had failed to show up at the assigned time and then, hearing a radio or something in the apartment, assumed we were home and hung around trying to get in. As for the all too colorful touch of the woman with the undersized chicken: first of all, it was a Cornish game hen, Ed's favorite food; and second of all, the woman was his mother (who would be astonished to hear the word "dowdy" applied to herself, or "babushka" to the Hermès scarf she wears to cover her curlers). She had come over to cook dinner for Ed's birthday while we went to a movie, and she accidentally locked herself out when she went into the hall (absent-mindedly holding the game hen), thinking she heard a burglar.

It's true that Ed and I have some problems in the area of consumer goods. We wouldn't dream of minimizing that. And if some of our visitors get disenchanted when they see us using paper towels for napkins because we ran out—granted, they have a valid point, and we're working on a better-organized central system of supply. But lately one of Ed's ex-girlfriends—who of course claims that she always wished us the best and feels just awful being obliged to say anything negative about us—has been blabbing it around that we're so unhappy we don't even have enough faith in our relationship to invest in the basic necessities. She made her observations on a couple of transient visits to our place while I was away on business and Ed let her come over out of the goodness of his heart—and, I might add, her idea of "basic necessities" is a decadent bourgeois fantasy. She has gotten enormous mileage out of recounting how shocked she was when she saw that we don't have a toaster. For her information, we make toast in a frying pan because we prefer it that way.

Another thing these reports always mention is the bribes. They say Ed's and my relationship is corrupted by bribery at every level. One story that comes up over and over (always in the same words, curiously enough) is that I was seen going to various Village stores, buying stuff, and getting it wrapped in pathetic little parcels, and then later that evening was seen giving the same parcels to Ed as a bribe to keep him at home. Again, the details are accurate as far as they go, but the story fails to mention that it was Ed's birthday eve, when (using money we could have spent on a toaster) we threw a huge birthday party, at which some of the guests apparently got too drunk to put what they saw into context. On top of which, when their own rowdiness provoked a noise complaint from upstairs, they went and reported the next day that Ed and I were destabilizing our neighbors.

Then there's the stuff about low morale—how Ed and I have such a demoralizing effect on each other that neither of us has been able to make a dentist's appointment for the entire year we've been together. The woman who's the source of this news may not have realized, as she flipped through our appointment books while Ed was in the bathroom, that we have our own priorities and are not in the habit of going to the dentist right around the time of Ed's birthday, or on other days when we have a lot on our minds—for example, when my birthday is coming up.

Oh, well—whatever we do or don't do is grist for their mill now that this revisionist line about us has set in. If Ed pinches me on the bottom in public, it's seen as evidence that we have a degenerate, sexist relationship—which makes us hypocrites into the bargain, since that's the kind of relationship we set out not to have. It doesn't occur to people that if Ed pinches me on the bottom, maybe he's doing it for exactly that reason—that he's being *ironic.*

I could go through every one of these stories—the one about us being seen drunk on the street (it was Ed's birthday, for heaven's sake!), the one about me being seen at midnight wearing dark glasses and looking "alienated" (I'd simply had too much to drink), etc. I could go bing bing bing, right down the list, but what good would it do? People just aren't skilled at interpreting what they see, and we can't spend the rest of our lives correcting them. If some intelligent, attractive person wants to move in with us for a few months and really observe us with an open mind, great. Otherwise, everybody who's interested can find out all they need to know by going to the Superba, where we still hang out, and looking at the front table, where recently Ed carved our initials in a heart. The heart was already there, along with a mess of other old carvings, and when Ed put our initials inside it, they looked raw and pale by comparison. He wanted to age them by rubbing them with cigarette ash, but I said no, I liked it that they looked fresh. I said all the other initials had probably been carved by people who hate each other now and are no longer even on speaking terms. Ed said I was right—that we were still new, even though the heart was old and ready-made.

October 1984

In the fall of 1983, Mortimer Zuckerman (real-estate magnate and owner of the *Atlantic*) had published an op-ed piece in the *Times* about his views on U.S. involvement in El Salvador and Nicaragua, after a trip he'd made there with a Congressional delegation. I'd clipped the piece and put it in a raggedy manila folder with tons of other clippings. (These yield about a two-percent return, but you never know—someday you can be leafing through the folder and an ancient item in there will magically hook up with whatever is on your mind. Many promising items never make it out: 1987, "Barbara Walters: Does She Push Too Hard?"; 1985, "Rumor has it that Godard enjoys watching women play basketball"; 1984, "If I understand correctly, you're asking about how do I envision probably the getting together of the two Koreas," Reagan press conference; 1981, "Diana Trilling, Pathfinder in Morality.") Anyway, I'd saved Zuckerman's piece because of his proclaimed change of heart: "My instinct was that this was only an internal struggle, not an East-West competition, and that once again we were backing the wrong side for the wrong reason. But I returned home . . . impressed with the effectiveness of United States policy." This was on the basis of one trip where he "was told" various things by various officials.

About a year later, reading the *New Republic*, I came across an article by Robert Leiken (expert on Central America, ex-Maoist who became influential in swinging moderates to support the Contras), just back from the most recent of six trips to Nicaragua, drained of his "initial reservoir of sympathy for the Sandinistas." For all I know, Leiken's observations and conclusions were totally accurate (I used them in arguments to provoke leftists still in love with the revolution). But his catalogue of disparities between the "myths and the unpleasant truth" was so familiar it seemed generic. Sure, genres form around the truth of repeated experience, something happening the same way time after time; in this case the genre was Tales of Betrayed Revolution—nothing surprising there. But I was as uneasy with its pointillistic details as with Zuckerman's tracing of the State Department line. For someone who bowed to no man in his early sympathy for the Sandinistas, Leiken gave a lot of weight to queues and bribes, to sexist party officials in sunglasses eating lemon meringue pie while an old woman couldn't get a doctor's appointment.

But it was the form of this material, rather than any political conviction on my part, that attracted me. It could all be loaded onto the Ed couple to shape a story about the waning of romance. Probably my own romance had moved from the early "mythic" phase into the defensive phase where you don't want to hear your friends saying it looks like it's not working out. There's a sense in which the story was a naive political experiment: if I dealt with the contradictions of this material in romantic terms, maybe by analogy I'd find out what my politics were. My boyfriend actually did carve our initials in a precarved heart (back booth, Corner Bistro) and offer to age them with cigarette ash. I loved putting that in: a way of returning the gift. It also gave me an optimistic ending that I guess you could read as vaguely Marxist. But I was just following the dictates of my genre.

Macdonald

On page 233 of the Da Capo Press edition of *Parodies*, edited by Dwight Macdonald, there is a spine-chilling description of an oyster, that most creative of mollusks, being swallowed alive and absorbed by the digestive juices of a human being—to no other end than a rarefied, super-civilized *frisson*. The theme of *Parodies* is most brutally stated here. The devouring of one creature by another. The sea—microcosm of a cruel universe in which culture is only murder going under some other name. None of which should come as any surprise to fans of Dwight Macdonald, who lived on intimate terms with such facts through the adventures of his fictional alter ego, the Florida detective Travis McGee. Although neighbors of the author's houseboat at Longboat Key, Florida, often mistook him for a Yale-educated political essayist or literary critic or something of that sort, this book—originally published in 1960 (before *A Purple Place for Dying*) and at last back in print—is evidence of firsthand acquaintance with the creatures who populate the shores and estuaries of his beloved Florida: the devourers and the devoured.

ALEXANDER POPE—whose taste for fresh-caught pompano concealed a penchant for something a little more expensive—murder. . . .

T. S. ELIOT—the motel clerk who never dreamed that each time he set pen to paper, he was signing his own death warrant. . . .

STELLA GIBBONS—the girl whose striped bikini hid something explosive enough to turn a deep-sea charter party into a lethal and dangerous nightmare. . . .

S. J. PERELMAN—to all appearances the simple salt-air philosopher—until Travis McGee began to suspect that nobody was quite that simple. . . .

LEWIS CARROLL—the fanatic developer with a hundred ingenious scams, he drained a marshland and exposed his own deadly secret—a secret he would pay any price to hide. . . .

WILLIAM WORDSWORTH—the copper-haired corpse who seemed to float up on the beach after every hurricane. . . .

MAX BEERBOHM—"The Gator"—Never before had Travis McGee been frightened, but never before had he been pitted against a mind as monstrously formidable as his own. . . .

JANE AUSTEN—bright, petite, blonde, suntanned—she couldn't

get a license to open her health spa, but she didn't *need* a license to kill. . . .

H. L. MENCKEN—the condo salesman who plied the deep waters of greed—and before he was through reeling in the biggest catch of his life, somebody or something would have a bullet in the head. . . .

RING LARDNER—just more human flotsam from the Colombia drug-smuggling underground? Or an elusive and fiendish killer? . . .

RAYMOND QUENEAU—the cynical freighter captain who discovered it took more than charm to commit a multiple murder that spanned an ocean. . . .

CYRIL CONNOLLY—whose bait box harbored a poisonous cargo. . . .

ROBERT BROWNING—the beach-bum Apollo with the beautiful fiancée and every reason to live—until along came murder. . . .

JAMES GOULD COZZENS—Death by smudge pot in your own orange grove wasn't a pretty way to go, and only the buried past knew the ugly secret of why he died. Only Travis McGee knew why he *deserved* to die—*twice*. . . .

ROBERT BENCHLEY—the Vietnam vet who drifted freely between the glittering cabanas of the Fun Coast and the oil-stained walkways of a derelict marina—until one of his haunts became the deadly killing ground for a lethal—and purposeful—murder spree. . . .

GEORGE GORDON, LORD BYRON—Which was the impostor? He thought he knew—until he watched the sun set over the Bahamas and saw it come up on his own corpse. . . .

GEOFFREY CHAUCER—the one who started it, and now the only one who could stop it—if only somebody could prove he was still alive. . . .

November 1984

An editor at Da Capo Press, Rick Woodward, had asked me to write an introduction to a new edition of Dwight Macdonald's *Parodies: An Anthology from Chaucer to Beerbohm—And After.* I said O.K., because the book is beloved and there was a certain honor in being part of its return to print. But my deadline was near, and I didn't know what to write; Macdonald had pretty much said it all on the subject of parody in his preface and appendix. Then one night I was sitting around with some friends and mentioned my problem, and Donald Fagen said, "Why don't you pretend you think he's *John D.* MacDonald?" It was such an arbitrary idea (well, maybe not all that arbitrary to someone named Donald), but it called up my affection for John D. MacDonald's Travis McGee novels, set on the Florida Gulf coast, where I'd read them. My brother and I had just sold our father's house there; I missed Florida and wanted to write about it.

There was a passage about an oyster in my favorite piece in *Parodies,* Cyril Connolly's takeoff on an Aldous Huxley novel:

> "How would *you* like, Mr. Encolpius, to be torn from your bed, embarrelled, prised open with a knife, seasoned with a few drips of vitriol, shall we say, and sprayed with a tabasco as strong as mustard-gas to give you flavour; then to be swallowed alive and handed over to a giant's digestive juices?"
>
> "I shouldn't like it at all!" said Mr. Encolpius, "just as I shouldn't, for that matter, like living at the bottom of the sea and changing my sex every three years. . . ."
>
> "S-s-s-s-s-s-s-s-s-s-s-s-s-s-s-s-s-s-s-s-s-s-suppose," said Reggie Ringworm, who stammered, etc., "vat ve thilly oythter is weally weady and villing to be ab-s-s-s-orbed, I mean ab-th-th-th-th-th-thorbed, by our fwiend, vat vat is in f-f-f-fact exactly ve end for which it has been cweated. Vat th-then?"

This made a connection—seafood—between Macdonald and MacDonald. It also suggested the notion of parodists as predators.

I wanted to describe the various literary figures in the style of Travis McGee jacket-blurb teasers but didn't have any around to study as examples, so just used Rex Stout's Nero Wolfe books instead. (*Murder by the Book:* "Could a book be responsible for murder? Impossible. And yet those who made the mistake of knowing its contents were goners. . . .")

Critic David Denby, who took a scholarly interest in Dwight Macdonald, told me it was "cowardly" to write this piece instead of an essay. It was. But I was inhibited by years of derision toward other humor anthology introductions. "With tongue planted firmly in cheek"—Ian (Sandy) Frazier always claims he read an introduction beginning that way. My friendship with Sandy is based on the profound mutual pleasure of scaring each other with quotes like that. He wasn't around the office anymore—he'd moved to Montana—and I called him in panic to read him what I'd written to see if he thought it was dumb. He was in his office, a huge snowstorm had started, he had to get home fast because he had no snow tires—but he very sweetly let me read him this tantalizing suncoast stuff about orange groves and pompano. He said he liked the way it sounded as if it had been "written off of a Florida placemat."

After turning it in, I got a startled letter from the Da Capo editor: "My first job in publishing was writing jacket copy at Lippincott, and my first assignment was John D. MacDonald's *The Empty Copper Sea.*"

Later, I learned that there's a word for processes in which a system incorporates an element of randomness. "Stochastic." Heard about it from Donald.

For Immediate Release

> A Soviet journalist who received political asylum in Britain last year and turned up in Moscow on Tuesday had signed a contract to write a book on the Soviet press, a New York publisher said yesterday. . . . The Russian . . . was paid an advance through his American literary agent.
>
> —*New York Times*, September 20, 1984

Let's not beat around the bush. Ivan Hopov, whose case has been so well publicized through the organ of the *New York Times,* is one against whom I bear a grudge. As his translator, by name V. Vronsky, and being only human, I was adversely affected by his decision to default on his book contract and return to the USSR posthaste. For example, I had stood hired by the publisher for $3,000 payment in full, upon acceptance by the publisher of the full Hopov manuscript in an acceptable English-language rendering—an endeavor of which, due to the unfortunate turn of events, I was rendered incapable. On Hopov's part, after six months he had attained no more than the original draft outline and sample chapter. Nor did he withstand the temptation of a fanciful caprice to flee from the West without explaining to me his baffling conduct. As for myself, I was let off with merely a small chit for coffee and out-of-pocket expenses.

Nevertheless, I have since received the following letter from Hopov, written in his own English. Though Hopov himself, upon arriving in the West, resembled a hapless baby when it came right down to the crunch of speaking or writing his newfound tongue, he precociously achieved an amazing fluence. So much so that my services may in any case have been rendered spurious. (Though in my esteem his English, as written, lacks the utmost literary filigree, which I would have striven to encapture, to the best of my ability, subject to the reader's judgment.) Besides all that, he became rapidly Westernized to a T. For example, he had everything. What did he have? A Betamax, a Gold Card, etc.? He did not. He had something much greater. He had the means to grasp those things and everything else worth the candle. He had a book contract. And yet, with this pinnacle of American largesse bestowed upon his brow, mysteriously he fled. Why?

But I do not want to get ahead of his own story. Let me add solely that I here disseminate his letter without recompense or fee, not because of a loyalty to Hopov, which would surely be ill placed, but on a point of principle. If we in the West—including such an habituated émigrée as myself, so to say—could delve deep into the curious turn of the Soviet mind as it sets foot in a democratic society, it would really blow the roof off and there would be much light shed. In

Hopov's bizarre renunciation (in fidelity produced below) we see the complex case of an individual, smacking of a totalitarian bent, who found himself face to face with freedom of expression and could not come to terms.

—V. Vronsky

My dear Vronsky,

I've been hearing things—that I behaved in an unprofessional manner, that I'm a prima donna, that I left you and a lot of other people in the lurch. Well, I can't help it if people feel that way. All I can say is, I was naive—but boy, did I grow up fast. I'm sorry if you came out of it badly, but that's your problem. If I know those bastards, they bought you off with a few bucks for expenses. What a ripoff outfit! The last straw for me was when my so-called editor wrote this really stupid jacket copy and then went into a copy-proud snit when I wanted to change it. Get this: "A sassy look at the Soviet press." "*Sassy*"*??!!* Talk about witless—and what was I supposed to do, let that go through and then look like an idiot? I know, I know—the book-buying public understands that the author didn't write the jacket copy, the jacket copy isn't even meant for them, it's meant for the reviewers who just regurgitate the jacket copy instead of bothering to write reviews, it's *supposed* to be stupid so they don't have to type any unfamiliar thoughts when they're copying it under their own bylines. I know all that. But the idea of having something like "sassy" on your very first book just poisons the whole experience. I wasn't digging in my heels—I might have been able to live with it if she'd changed it to "savvy"—but she wouldn't even listen to me. She had a tape of a ringing phone that she'd play whenever I mentioned the jacket copy, and she'd say she had to take another call and would get back to me. Which was a lie. She was really getting off on the power of making me wait for her calls. Maybe not consciously—but it was so manipulative. I don't see how this makes me a prima donna. Try telling any farmer or coal miner that his work is going to be described nationwide as "sassy" and that he won't even be allowed to discuss alternative wording. He'd be on the next plane to Moscow, just like me.

But let me start at the beginning. First of all, the contract was a joke. I think my first agent, Morty, an underling at the Stepin Fetchit Agency, must have been in a conspiracy with the publisher. But what did I know? At that point, my English was so bad he could have showed me a paper that said "Screw you and the boat you came in on" and I'd have signed. When he called me in London, he threw around a lot of names—Svetlana, etc. A snow job. (None of which checked out later, by the way.) Then he sent me a People Express plane ticket. So I went to New York and signed. There I am, churning out my little sample chapter during the day and studying English at night by working my way through *Publishers Weekly* with a dictionary. Needless to say, my curiosity got the better of me and I translated my own contract. Instant shock-horror. The reserve-for-returns clause was so watertight the book could have been a bestseller and I wouldn't have seen a nickel in royalties until the year 2050 or doomsday, whichever came later; there was no guaranteed budget for promotion; and I had no jacket-copy approval.

Then the publishing house turns out to be the pits. When I hand in the sample chapter and outline, I get a note from the publisher—just one word scrawled in the center of a piece of stationery: "Marvelous!" Is that pretentious, or what! When I'm assigned to my editor, Little Miss Tin Ear (who bad-mouthed *you* from Day One, in case you don't know), it turns out they have a good-cop, bad-cop routine going there. The "Marvelous!" notes pile up in my mailbox while she's hassling me to write with more "sass." *This is all very interesting, Ivan, but we publish junk.*

Finally, after weeks of trying to get through to Mort, who's stopped taking my calls, I nab him outside his office. "Look," I say, "my contract is ludicrous, I haven't gotten my first payment—what's the story? *PW* has pictures of my publisher lunching with movie stars at Le Cygne and meanwhile I'm licking the wastebasket."

"Ivan," he says, "Ivan, they're a marvelous old house. They publish Shakespeare. They publish Jack London."

"Great," I say. "So Jack London and I are licking the same wastebasket."

He was no help at all. So that was when I switched over to Milt, the superagent. He came on very simpatico. And the deal was, he'd buy off Mort and renegotiate my contract. By this time I wasn't such a babe in the woods, and one thing I insisted on was that they commit themselves contractually to a ten-week promotional tour *up front*—twenty major cities, with me going on all the TV shows and then writing the book about what it was like to go on them. I'd compare and contrast going on Carson, Merv, etc., with the promotional situation in the USSR.

Some superagent. He told me I was being unreasonable and immature, that I expected him to make me overnight into a combination of Jerzy Kozinski, Barbara Walters, and Jack London. Which is ridiculous. He did nothing for me. Absolutely nothing. He claimed he'd finally wrung my advance out of them, and when I asked where was the check, he said it was being held in an escrow account as a reserve against returns, because I had no "track record." This was about the time all hell broke loose with the jacket copy and Tin Ear. God, do I hate her. She's on the end of my nose dancing and I can't flick her off. So in desperation I called Milt, and they wouldn't put me through—his secretary said he'd get back to me after he took his cat to the vet. A week goes by. Nothing. This, mind you, is a guy who sails into the office around noon, chats on the phone with a few call girls, and then has a three-hour lunch at Le Cygne with all the other superagents, where they talk about how their clients need too much hand-holding.

That's the line on me now, from what I hear. That I needed too much hand-holding. And I'll tell you something, Vronsky—they're right. I wasn't in it for the money—I still don't know where the money is or how much there is or if there is any. I was in it for the attention, and I'm not ashamed to admit it. I need to have my hand held. Not only do I crave it, not only do I require it to be able to work—I insist upon it, and I insist upon it all the time. And I'll tell you something else—over here, I get my hand held night and day. They have a special guy assigned to me whose only job is to hold my hand. Sometimes he holds both hands at once. Not only that, but while I'm typing this there's another guy here whose job is to stand behind me and massage my temples. I get all the attention I need.

Over here I'm famous. I'm the writer who gave up an American book contract.

Best,
I. Hopov

December 1984

Tore the quote out of the paper because it was a chance to have fun doing a Russian-in-translation voice. I used to run into Joseph Brodsky at parties, and always liked the pleasure he got out of trying every possible English idiom. Though of course he did it with flair, unlike my earnest translator character. One time Brodsky offered to introduce me to Hans Magnus Enzensberger (a name he knew meant nothing to me beyond a pale connotation of intelligentsia) and then added, "This will really blow the roof off." So I put that in. Writing as "Vronsky" seemed natural because that was my nickname around then, started by a friend who was reading *Anna Karenina.*

Then just piled on every typical writer's grievance. Sandy Frazier had told me about going into his publishers', Farrar, Straus, & Giroux, where Roger Straus came up to him in the hall, said just the one word "Marvelous!" and walked away. The divinely colorful lines about "licking the wastebasket" and "She's on the end of my nose dancing and I can't flick her off" were verbatim from a tirade against publishers by an agent. (Actually he said "licking the toilet," but I precensored it for *The New Yorker.*)

The one true thing I'm sorry I used came from Cathy Schine: she had written a novel, *Alice in Bed,* and her editor at Knopf put "sassy" in the jacket flap copy and didn't want Cathy to change it. I forgot to ask Cathy if it was O.K. to use this; the horrible word was the perfect word—I forgot that *le mot juste* was real. Also, I was preoccupied with a personal vendetta of my own. A woman writer I'd once thought of as a romantic rival had been criticized in a magazine article as so demanding of her agent and publisher she had to have "her hand held all the time," and I was elated at surreptitiously turning her into a Soviet hack. Anyway, Cathy was horrified to see the "sassy" reference in print; she was afraid her editor would recognize it and think the whole story was a transcript of Cathy's rantings against her. This made me much more careful about asking permission, and less willing to entertain the idea that art is worth hurting anybody.

Canine Château

(A document from the Pentagon's ongoing probe into a defense contractor's $87.25 bill for dog boarding)

Dear Secretary Weinberger:

I have received your request for particulars about the "nauseating" and "preposterous" bill run up at this establishment by Tuffy. I would be more than happy to supply details—I would be *delighted.* As someone who devotes his life to the humane treatment of animals, I welcome this opportunity to enlighten the Department of Defense and the Congress, neither of which seems to have the faintest idea what a dog requires.

Before I get into that, however, may I point out that Canine Château is far from being some little fly-by-night dog dorm with a few bunk beds, a Small Business Administration loan, and a penchant for padding its bills to make ends meet. We have been a major and highly profitable concern since 1981. Up until that time, I had been a tool designer at Low-Bid Tool & Die (in Van Nuys), running a private specialty shop called Jeff's Claw Clipper out of my office. (And I suppose I'm going to get in trouble for *that* now with the IRS.) They phased out my job in favor of a computer when Low-Bid won the contract to produce the "manicure kits" (I think you know what I'm talking about) that President Reagan sent as gifts to Saudi Arabia. But I wanted to remain within the industry, and I realized the potential for expanding Jeff's Claw Clipper into a full-service kennel targeted specifically to the defense-contract segment of the pet-boarding market.

I had heard of a lovely old Spanish Colonial mansion for sale up on Mulholland Drive, and as soon as I saw it I knew it was absolutely right. At first I ran into all kinds of opposition—zoning boards, mortgage officers, you name it—but these people very quickly came around when they found out who our clientele would be. We are now the largest (and, to my knowledge, the only) kennel in California catering exclusively to the special needs of defense-contractor pets. These animals, as you may know, are extremely high-strung, and are vulnerable to kidnap by agents of foreign powers who might wish to extort from defense contractors certain classified information (such as details about the offensive capability of purported "tie clasps" regularly shipped by the U.S. to El Salvador). This is a particular danger during sensitive arms negotiation talks. No kennels could be more relaxing and safe than ours: Canine Château, nestled on a sunny, grass-carpeted five-acre site behind bougainvillea-twined fencing of 33mm molybdenum-reinforced warhead-quality steel with FX-14 radial vidicon sensors and zinc-carbon detonators; and, farther south on Mulholland in a newly renovated Art Deco villa, Maison Meow, similarly secured. (Birds, goldfish, and so on may guest at either location, depending on space availability.) We are constantly upgrading these facilities, thanks to the many satisfied pet owners who generously donate not only their technological expertise but also a good deal of materials and equipment that would otherwise just be thrown away at the end of the defense-contracting workday and carted off to a garbage dump or landfill site (at government expense), where it would serve no conceivable purpose except to pollute the environment.

All things considered, then, perhaps I may be forgiven if I preen myself somewhat on our success and our high standards—aesthetic, hygienic, technological, *and* financial. Canine Château operates under my close personal supervision, and I have something of a reputation among the staff as a strict taskmaster. I wear the key to the pantry around my neck on a platinum chain; and not only is the level in the kibble bin measured twice a day but the bin itself is equipped with a state-of-the-art laser lock, which cannot be opened without a microcoded propylene wafer issued to select personnel only after the most rigorous security check of their backgrounds and habits. Waste of any kind is simply not tolerated—let alone fraud.

Now, as to Tuffy's bill. Tuffy's one-week stay at Canine Château was booked under our "No Frills" Plan. We are hardly a dog pound, of course, but I suspect that even you, Secretary Weinberger, with your military barracks frame of reference, would find Tuffy's accommodations Spartan. We have had dogs in here—and I'm not going to say *whose* dogs they were, but I think you know the ones I mean—who have run up astronomical bills on shopping sprees at our accessories bar. I'm not criticizing them; most of these dogs are accustomed to a California standard of living, and we can't just suddenly alter a dog's lifestyle, because the dog won't understand and will become morose. Nor am I suggesting that you, Secretary Weinberger, would seek favorable publicity at the expense of innocent animals whose taste for luxuries was created by profits in the very same industries that you depend upon for the perpetuation of your own livelihood and the good of the country. However, I question the Pentagon's decision to pay without a peep such previous bills as $3,000 for one golden retriever's ion-drive-propulsion duck decoy with optional remote aerial guidance system and quartz-fiber splashdown shield, and then to quibble over Tuffy's, which was relatively modest.

But enough. As you requested, I am enclosing an annotated itemization of Tuffy's bill, which I trust will carry my point.

Very truly yours,
JEFF CHATEAU
President, Canine Château

TUFFY 2/11/85–2/18/85

Catalina Suite . . . . @ $40 = $280

[All "No Frills" accommodations are suites, and this is our cheapest rate. If it seems a bit steep, consider that each suite is actually an individual bunker, deployed with gyroscopic mounts on an elliptical underground track and activated to a speed of 35mph by random changes in the earth's magnetic field. This is a security precaution and, we feel, an essential one.]

Variety Menu (Mature Dog Cycle), plus tips $340

[I suppose that you, Secretary Weinberger, when *your* family goes away, would be just thrilled to have a neighbor shove a bowl of something through the door once a day. Well, an animal is no different. Our gracious waiters and waitresses are trained to make each animal's regular mealtimes as relaxed, enjoyable, and *safe* as possible. They carry conventional Geiger counters at all times, and constantly monitor food, water, and serving utensils with a combat-type bacterial scanner.]

Valet. $15

[Dry-cleaning of hand-knitted dog sweater. This was February, remember, and winter in the Hollywood Hills can be cruel.]

3 Cases of Marinated Mouse Knuckles. $156

[Obviously a computer billing error, as this item is served only at Maison Meow. We will be pleased to delete the charge from the original invoice.]

Contribution. $100

[A tax-deductible voluntary charge to support our lobbying efforts in Congress for continuation of the tax-deductible status for this charge.]

Insurance $10

[Indemnifies us against layoffs, work stoppages, and rises in the wholesale price index.]

Cost Overrun $245

SUBTOTAL: $1,146.00

Discounts

[We then applied our discount schedule, which allows us to maintain a high volume of business while welcoming guests from a wide range of economic brackets: not just executive animals but those at entry level in the defense-contracting and -subcontracting industries, whose owners may be privy to compromising information about seemingly innocuous items manufactured for the U.S. government. The discounts were offered at our discretion and may be revoked at any time (for instance, if government-required paperwork increases our operating costs).]

Discount for booking 30 days in advance. $400
Special discount for off-peak arrival and departure $275
Reduction for booking through a state-certified pet kennel
reservations agent. $149.75
Quantity refund for four or more stays per annum when the
prime interest rate is at or below 15% $200.00
Rebate for using Teamsters-approved pet carrier. $34
DISCOUNTS: $1,058.75

SUBTOTAL: $1,146.00
LESS DISCOUNTS: $1,058.75
TOTAL: $87.25

[Our billing is calculated by the same model of computer used to regulate the rangefinder on a Polaris submarine. We have every confidence in its conclusion that $87.25 is neither too low nor too high a price to pay for peace of mind.]

March 1985

Sandy had come back from Montana for a few days, and we got together to show each other work in progress the way we used to do in the office. He had a half-written piece where a pool party of characters out of a bad short story suddenly gets strafed by "Krauts!" I had a couple of paragraphs based on this news item about the Pentagon paying dog-boarding expenses, and he immediately starting spewing lines: "No-frills plan . . . Do you have any *idea* what a dog requires? . . . Incredibly Spartan—he had to share a secretary with fifteen other dogs. . . . We have had dogs in here—and I'm not going to say *whose* dogs they were . . ." We decided a long time ago that the help we give each other evens out, but sometimes I have to stop him so I won't feel too reliant on his jokes. On the other hand, the line "I would be more than happy . . . I would be *delighted*" hardly sounds like writing at all, and it might seem absurd to credit it, but I worship Stanley Kubrick's ear for trite dialogue and took the line from *The Killing*. A mature couple who wish to remain anonymous supplied the title, "Canine Château"—a term they use for being in the doghouse during domestic spats.

The *New Yorker* rejected the first version of this; they just said, "No one laughed once." It didn't have the military hardware stuff in it, and was written in more of a gay-guy dog-groomer voice. I sent it to Michael Kinsley, editor of the *New Republic*, and he called up and said, "Why are you making fun of gay hairdressers when your real target is Pentagon overspending?" He was so right, so precise, that I wanted to redo it for him, but I'd already been revising it to avoid the gay voice and felt I had to show it to the *New Yorker* again, and they bought it. I'd put in a lot of insane weaponry-and-explosives writing that they'd liked in an earlier piece. I lift terminology out of a 1917 infantry manual and a book called *The Way Things Work* and mix it all up. Maybe because my father worked for the Army all his life. I love the sound of "33mm molybdenum-reinforced warhead-quality steel."

Seeing me hell-bent on fixing and selling this piece, my boyfriend said he'd never known I was "like a gila monster." This has nothing to do with anything, but right around then it was nice that I got to participate in his work in a memorable way, which I wrote up in my diary:

> *Sunday, March 17, 1985*
> We went up to 121st St. in Harlem to photograph Clarence Norris (Willie, he's called), the last living "Scottsboro Boy."* He lives in a big red-brick apartment building with good security. A woman lives with him, & she let us in. We had been told [by the photo editor] that "he's 93 and senile." So when a big strong 50-year-old man appeared, I thought it was the son and waited for him to bring out the old man. Instead, this was the old man. He was actually 72. He had on a shiny dark-blue cotton jacket, and the woman kept kvetching about how he should change into something nicer, or button the jacket.
>
> He was kind of stolid and quiet at first, but after a while the woman asked us what we thought of the Goetz case & he opened

---

*In Scottsboro, Alabama, in 1931, nine black teenagers were falsely convicted of raping two white women. The U.S. Supreme Court twice overturned the convictions, but a series of retrials and new convictions kept five of them in jail till the mid-1940s. In 1966 an Alabama judge released suppressed evidence that conclusively proved the innocence of all nine. Clarence Norris had gone north after his parole in 1946, and was granted a full pardon in 1976.

up & told us about how people will "kill you for a dime" as he knew well from all those years in jail. He kept emphasizing that if you lock someone up and "scorn and revile" them for something they didn't do, it is guaranteed to turn them into a killer. All the while, there was a smell of corned beef and cabbage and an apple pie cooking for Sunday dinner.

Later on he changed, at the woman's insistence, into a pin-striped jacket. She showed us the book he wrote after he got pardoned by Gov. Wallace. He began to go on obsessively about injustice, and I realized that my first impression—that he was impatient with people coming around doing publicity on him for something that happened 50 years ago—was completely wrong; that he will probably be obsessed with it till the day he dies, and wanted to tell us all about it. When we shook hands to leave, he said to us, "I'm very proud to have met you," which is what we should have said.

The Buck Starts Here

"Our attitude is, it is up to Kohl."

—A White House official, on the Bitburg invitation
(in the *New York Times*, April 26, 1985)

Dear President Mitterrand:

Would you mind dealing with this batch of invitations that President Reagan has received? We are enclosing all the unanswered invitations to date, plus a Xerox copy of his calendar, a supply of accept/regret notepaper bearing the Presidential seal, and a rubber stamp of his signature. We rely completely on your Gallic elegance in handling any potentially embarrassing requests in a graceful way. For instance, this card asking the President to appear on June 16th to serve coffee and doughnuts to demonstrators outside the South African Embassy as a symbolic gesture of support for their acts of conscience in protesting apartheid—well, obviously the President would be concerned about feelings of annoyance that he might cause Prime Minister Botha to suffer. Possibly that one could be forwarded to Botha himself to deal with. Also, there's that group of Contra unwed mothers who want the President to go down there for a baby shower. That's touchy—perhaps you could ask Mrs. Thatcher to fill in. But you will know best, given your national tradition of social graces—Proust, "*Répondez, s'il vous plaît,*" etc. The important thing is that President Reagan be spared any troublesome incidents that might arise if he made these decisions himself. That is why we hope you will graciously consent to act in his stead.

Thanking you in advance,
INVITATION WATCHDOG UNIT
The White House

Dear President Marcos:

We are writing to ask if you have the time to go over the enclosed draft of the 1986 State of the Union Message and just pencil in any changes and additions you think would be advisable. Normally, the President of the United States does this himself, but we are worried that opinions or facts in the speech might be attributed to President Reagan and create an unfortunate situation here. He has authorized us to assure you that not a word of your copy will be edited without your consent. Naturally, should you wish to come to the Capitol to deliver this address yourself on national television, your round-trip fare would be complimentary.

Best,
GAFFE PREVENTION TASK FORCE,
Presidential Speechwriting Staff

Dear President Gorbachev:

Perhaps you will find this request to be an unusual one, but please read on before dismissing it out of hand. Could you possibly substitute for President Reagan at a summit meeting between President Reagan and yourself? This would mean, of course, that you would be wearing "two hats," so to speak. But the advantages for both sides would be considerable. The President himself could not make concessions to the Soviet Union without losing face. You, however, in substituting for him, would be in a position to be more flexible, and no subsequent opprobrium would attach to the President's person.

Any agreement that resulted would be signed by you and by you. At a time when national leadership must double its efforts for the good of all mankind, we hope you will rise to this great vacuum.

Very truly yours,
SURROGATE SELECTION
COMMITTEE
U.S. Department of State

April 1985

Written very fast during a period of cabin fever alone in a rented house out on Long Island, near the beach. It was pretty bleak and rainy, and there wasn't much to do except read the newspapers and find fault with what the people in the newspapers were saying.

Bitburg was one of those symbolic events that everybody wants to weigh in on. This piece is probably the equivalent of "pack journalism." It must have been written automatically; my only memory is that by the time I got to the third letter, to Gorbachev, some kind of rabbit had to be pulled out of a hat, and I fell back on a tautological style of joke I'd learned from Alexander Zinoviev's encyclopedic satire of Soviet society, *The Yawning Heights:*

> The Ibanuchka River was dammed. It overflowed, flooded a potato field (the former pride of the Ibanskians) and swelled into a lake (the present pride of the Ibanskians). And for this all the inhabitants, with one or two exceptions, were decorated. The Leader made a long speech about it in which he analysed everything and outlined everything. . . . The speech was prepared by Claimant with a large group of helpers. This fact was kept somewhat secret, in the sense that everyone knew about it except the Leader, who was decorated for it and then given a further decoration because he had been decorated.

Settling an Old Score

"There are some experiences which should not be demanded twice from any man," [George Bernard Shaw] remarked, "and

> one of them is listening to Brahms's Requiem." And, in his most famous dismissal of the work, he referred to it as "patiently borne only by the corpse." . . . There are no rights and wrongs in criticism, only opinions more or less in conformance with the consensus of enlightened observers over time. By that criterion Shaw was "wrong." But . . . musical polemics fade far faster than music itself, thankfully.
>
> —John Rockwell (in the *New York Times*, July 15, 1984)

To anyone who has tried to sit down and just enjoy a composition by Johannes Brahms, the sensation is all too familiar. As the musical phrases begin to wash away the cares of the day, transporting one into a delightful never-never land of artistic transcendence, one's brain is rudely skewered by George Bernard Shaw's unforgettable dictum about Brahms: "Like listening to paint dry." Once Shaw penned this zinger, it became impossible (even for an independent-minded music critic like myself) to relax and surrender to the simple pleasure of knowing that Brahms is no longer considered passé. And another thing: each time a Brahms piece is ruined by an ineradicable nagging memory of that effortless Shavian one-liner, the annoyance is nothing compared to what Brahms must feel, squirming eternally in his grave, his reputation forever etched by the acid of Shaw's scorn.

Brahms was but one victim of Shaw's many pinpricks in the hot-air balloons of his era's cultural biases. Yet a host of the myriad names he lambasted have nonetheless survived. Yet so has a lingering respect for Shaw. In the mind of today's critic, this poses a problem. Must we say that Shaw was "wrong"? We may be tempted to utter a definitive "Yes," while on the other hand bearing in mind that critical truth is an ever-shifting flux of historically relative pros and cons. Shaw's derision of all the things he had scorn for has stood the test of time—because what he said has remained a touchstone, memorized and quoted again and again by generations of critics willing to encounter such a mind at the height of its powers even though we may possibly disagree, living as we do in a differing cultural context.

By way of qualification, however, I should point out that Shaw was not merely a negative hatchet man. For example, take his blistering assertion that "Brahms makes the lowest hack jingle-writer look like Mozart." Even someone such as myself who unashamedly rather likes Brahms (when well performed) is forced to concede Shaw's positive foresight in defending the populist craft of the jingle-writer. (Not that this means I must obsequiously agree with every single last nuance of Shaw's statement.)

In any case, Shaw's poison-tipped barbs were aimed at such a multitude of targets that to say he missed once or twice would be to say very little at all. Whatever the topic, Shaw never left any doubt as to where he stood:

On *Hamlet:* "A tour de fuss."

On Oscar Wilde: "A man out of touch with his funny bone."

On the Code of Hammurabi: "The sort of thing that would be considered profound by girls named Misty."

On the formation of a local committee in Brighton to study the feasibility of allowing tourists to transport their beach gear on special storage racks affixed to the sides of buses: "A worse idea hasn't crossed this battered old desk of mine in lo, these many moons."

From 1914 to 1919, Shaw's razor-tongued gibes were overshadowed by a vogue for bright quips about World War I. By 1921, however, he was again riding high—thanks to a series of personal appearances billed as "Shaw and His Skunk of the Week." Playing to packed houses that rocked with expectant hilarity when he led off with one of his typical catchphrases—"Am I hot under the collar tonight!" or "Here's something that really steams my butt"—he administered verbal shellackings to contemporary follies and pretensions ranging from *Peter Pan* ("It has plot holes you could drive a truck through") to the scientific community's renewed interest in Isaac Newton's idea of putting a cannonball into orbit ("One of those notions worth thinking about while you clean your teeth: a tour de floss").

For the next twenty years, nothing and no one seemed safe from Shaw's merciless stabs—not even his fans. Abhorring the nuisance of uninvited visitors, he posted on his door the following notice:

RULES FOR VISITORS

1. If you don't see what you want, don't be too shy to ask. Probably we don't have it anyway.

2. If the service is not up to snuff, just holler. Nobody will pay you any mind, but your tonsils can use the exercise.

3. We will gladly cash your check if you leave your watch, fur coat, or car as collateral. No wives or in-laws accepted.

4. If you are displeased in any way by the attentions of the resident Doberman pinscher, just remember—things could be worse. You could be at a Brahms concert.

But his visitors, instead of feeling rebuffed, copied out the notice and awarded it pride of place in their dens. Thus, a truism became widely established once and for all (until recently): that the name of Johannes Brahms was a joke (even to people who had never heard a note of his music), and that George Bernard Shaw was an unimpeachable debunker of sacred cows. Indeed, by 1940 so secure was Shaw's reputation that there was only one person in the entire English-speaking world capable of cutting him down to size.

Lyndon Baines Johnson was a young Congressman from Texas when, in July 1940, Shaw came through the state on a lecture tour of the U.S. At the Houston airport, Johnson headed the delegation of local celebrities assigned to greet the distinguished visitor from abroad, who was to address a luncheon at the Houston Junior League Tea Room and then spend the night as Johnson's guest at his ranch (which probably he wasn't rich enough to own yet, but it could have been a summer rental). Waiting on the tarmac, Johnson took a minute to riffle through the press release he had been given on Shaw, and remarked, "This son of a bitch has got some kind of mean mouth on him." So Johnson was really up for a confrontation. Whereas Shaw was too busy hating Brahms to be bothered thinking about a junior U.S. Congressman whom he hadn't even heard of yet. As soon as they met, Johnson immediately established dominance by a tactic he later became famous for—his "laying on of hands." The spindly, white-bearded Irishman, who didn't like being mauled by strangers, tried to counterattack by snapping at the big Texan in boots and Stetson, "What is this—some kind of tour de horse?" But it came out sounding pretty feeble. Nobody laughed, and Shaw lost crucial momentum. Johnson sensed right away that he had the edge, and he kept it. He was just a master of humiliation. On the way to the Junior League Tea Room, he asked Shaw to get him his dress boots out of a gym bag that he had purposely put on Shaw's side of the seat. At that point, Shaw overthought the situation and drew a bad conclusion. He decided just to go along with everything Johnson did and cater to him, on the theory that Johnson would quit bothering him once he saw he couldn't get a rise out of him. This was a huge mistake. The quieter and more docile Shaw got, the more Johnson tortured him.

At the luncheon, Johnson pretended not to be able to hear anything Shaw said, so Shaw had to repeat himself in a louder voice and came off as strident. The whole time, Johnson sat with his body angled subtly away from him, as if they weren't really together. During the lecture, he had a phone brought to the table and called his answering service. Then there was a question period, so Johnson asked Shaw his opinion of a book, *Pratfall into the Abyss,* which didn't exist. When Shaw said he had never heard of it, Johnson said, "What's the matter—you too dumb to recognize a joke when you hear one?" but he said it in a funny way that would have made Shaw look oversensitive if he got mad.

Then—here's another thing Johnson did. At the end of the luncheon, they were supposed to go right to the ranch, but Johnson dawdled a lot, which drove Shaw totally nuts. Finally, after a two-hundred-mile ride in a bouncing pickup truck, which Johnson drove himself—fiddling with the radio the whole time and refusing to talk, because they were alone, and if Shaw complained to anybody later he could never prove it—they got to the ranch, where the vegetarian Shaw was confronted with the sight and aroma of grotesque sides of beef barbecuing over smoking mesquite in earth trenches sodden with fat drippings. (Johnson hadn't even known that Shaw was a vegetarian—it was just a lucky break that fed into his strategy.)

The final blow was that night, when Johnson made Shaw dress up in an oversize cowboy suit with woolly chaps and showed him off like a performing monkey to a crowd of oil barons. The most galling part of it for Shaw was that by this time he had forfeited his right to protest. If he said anything now, Johnson could come back with "Well, why the hell didn't you speak up sooner?" or accuse him of being passive-aggressive. Anyway, so much of it was the kind of stuff Shaw couldn't exactly put his finger on.

Shaw's wounds were still raw the next morning when he woke up in an uncomfortable bed made out of a wagon wheel and saw hanging on a wall the following notice, framed in mesquite:

> RULES FOR VISITORS
> 1. Never cross LBJ.
> 2. Obey all rules.

Shaw later claimed that he escaped by walking a hundred and ten miles, in sandals, to a private landing strip outside Waco, where he bummed a flight to L.A. But Johnson always told reporters that while he remembered Shaw's lecture, Shaw had spent the night in Houston at a friend's who was out of town, and never set foot on the ranch. He knew this would get back to Shaw and make him feel psychologically annihilated.

In 1950, when Shaw died, his last words were "Don't tell LBJ. I don't want to give him the satisfaction." Every year since their meeting, Johnson had bugged Shaw by sending him a Christmas card with the printed message "Thank you for your support." Johnson enjoyed this joke so much that no one had the heart to tell him when Shaw died. Every Christmas, he personally signed the card, and his secretary pretended to mail it. Although he suffered some reverses late in his own life, this annual power play lightened his spirits until the very end. He rests in peace, unlike Brahms.

May 1985

The music critic John Rockwell's column, "Despite Shaw's Scorn, the Brahms Requiem Endures," had appeared in the Sunday *Times* the summer before. The voice was a classic balancing act—the obsequious line on Shaw versus Sunday-supplement caution:

> Shaw . . . had a polemical position he espoused with a fierce passion—that of modernist Wagnerianism, the progressive musical current of his day. But he didn't just espouse the positive; he excoriated the negative, too, as a tireless, Anglophobic mocker of late-Victorian pomposity and pretension. . . .

> The [Requiem] score offended Shaw not just because he hated all requiems, being an affirmer of the life-force, but because Brahms so consciously—and, in Shaw's view, retrogressively—evoked the German contrapuntal tradition in his music. . . . As such it answered a deeply felt need of English musical audiences of the late 19th century. . . .
>
> To this Wagnerian's taste, the Requiem is an unashamedly beautiful score. . . . Of course, it takes a superior performance to purge the work's latent ponderousness.

This was a voice to crawl into. And then there was the opposite kind of popular criticism—in love with the sound of its own crabby opinions. It seemed to be a debased legacy of what Dwight Macdonald (annotating a Max Beerbohm parody of Shaw) had described as

> Shaw's polemical style . . . the short, punchy sentences; the familiarity . . . the Anglo-Saxon vigor, the calculated irreverences . . . the peculiar combination in Shaw of arrogance and self-depreciation, of aggressiveness and mateyness, so that the audience is at once bullied and flattered; shocking ideas are asserted but as if they were a matter of course between sensible people.

As a fiction editor and as a movie critic, I'd felt surrounded by (and sometimes attracted to) responses to art that were ersatz-Shavian blends of disingenuous bafflement and testy one-liners: *Hey, maybe it's just me but this is like watching paint dry.* Years of this were distilled into a pure droplet one recent evening when I was sitting across a dinner table from a movie critic after a press screening of *Platoon* and said I thought the movie was O.K. but not as good as a Sam Fuller war movie. In full voice she sang out the single word "Wrong!" *What a pleasant, modest person Rockwell must be: "By that criterion, Shaw was 'wrong.' But . . ."*

When the *Times* piece first churned up some of these thoughts, I tried them out in a letter to Sandy, and he wrote back:

> I think "Shaw's Scorn" is a sure-fire idea. All the stuff Shaw had scorn for. And while you list that, you could just belabor the hell out of how eminent Shaw was. Did you ever see *My Astonishing Self*? It was a one-man tour de force based on Shaw's life. I went to see it out of pure hatred for the word "astonishing," which hatred

was intense for a while there. That's not true—I went with my mom, because she wanted to see it, although my hatred for "astonishing" kept me company, too. Anyway, Shaw and Shavians and the whole deal just gripes my ass.

A year later, on the energy from writing three previous pieces fast, I got to work. I'd accumulated a long list of crank dislikes and catchphrases (cat calendars, patchouli, "You and what army?" etc.), bad epigrams ("Shopping malls are the patchouli of the middle class"), and critics' formulas ("makes —— look like ——"), and compounded some of them into a "Shaw" much broader than Beerbohm's—a feeble fourth-generation Shaw verging on Andy Rooney and assorted belligerent pundits from the newspapers in Clearwater, Florida, where my father (also belligerent) lived. (From the *Beach Bee*: "However, do allow me the opportunity to blow off my steam in a manner that will be beneficial to you and even to me.") And come to think of it, why not make Shaw take the rap for all obnoxious wit? A postcard my father had sent me in 1977 *(something told me not to throw it into that wastebasket)*, from the Red Cavalier Restaurant and Bonfire Lounge in Redington Shores, Florida, was imprinted with eight house rules, the model for Shaw's Rules for Visitors:

> 1. . . . If you've sat for a respectable amount of time and have not been waited on, don't sit another minute. Wave, snap your fingers, hsst or holler. We refuse to be responsible for bad service because you have an introverted personality. . . .
>
> 5. . . . The management will accept your check providing you leave your dinner guest, your watch, your mink stole, your Cadillac Eldorado or Mark IV, all for collateral. We do not accept wives. . . .

Usually the last thing you realize is that you're really writing about yourself. My book of satires called *Partners* had been reviewed as an arsenal of stilletos, slings and arrows, razors, acid, lethally poised axes, etc., so I put that imagery into the descriptions of Shaw's style. But after belaboring the hell out of all this for four pages, I didn't know where to go.

Desperately, I looked around on the surface of my desk for a clue. There was a clipping of a review, by Professor William Leuchtenberg, of *Hubert Humphrey: A Biography*, by Carl Solberg:

> In vivid detail, Solberg reveals how demeaning was Humphrey's servitude to Lyndon Johnson. In 1964 the President tortured Humphrey by keeping him in doubt to the very last second as to whether he would be his running mate, and then told him, "If you didn't know you were going to be Vice President a month ago, you're too damn dumb to have the office." . . . After Humphrey had delivered a highly effective address at the Democratic convention, Johnson abruptly ordered him to appear at the L.B.J. ranch, where he handed him a riding costume many sizes too big for him and put him on a horse that nearly threw him. [Etc.]
>
> . . . But as [Humphrey] was dying he was told that a *Washington Post* poll of a thousand people had chosen him the greatest Senator of the past seventy-five years. "Jesus Christ," Humphrey said, "Lyndon Johnson's going to be sore as hell about this."

I've read "Settling an Old Score" to audiences a few times, and there's always a painful dearth of laughs until the surprise entrance of LBJ. It became a pleasure to endure the silence, knowing he was waiting in the wings. You can't—or at least I can't—premeditate an effect like that. It grew out of the blind, labored failure of the story's first half. There's premeditation in passing off the two halves as an intentional whole—but that happens later, after you've discovered that your original, naive mistake is your real material. I like having made a mistake that makes people glad to see LBJ again. This was the pre-Vietnam Johnson, and I'd become reenamored of the Great Society politician, doing wrong to do right. (I hadn't yet read Robert Caro's *The Path to Power: The Years of Lyndon Johnson*. But Caro is such a great biographer that he took away my illusions without spoiling my romance.)

Sandy told me he would have given LBJ a *Dallas* riff: "Mr. Shaw owns six percent of Oil Field Thirteen? [*Picks up phone.*] Shut down Oil Field Thirteen!" But I took LBJ more personally. I based a lot of his behavior on my boyfriend (who I thought had been torturing and humiliating me by doing stuff like calling his answering machine in the middle of a conversation). The Ranch Rules for Visitors came from the time I'd gone with him to photograph the Christmas tree at Rockefeller Center and a guard told him, "Don't set up a tripod," and he said, "There are two rules here. One: No tripods. Two: Follow all rules."

What I'd discovered was my desire to redeem LBJ from history, as best I could, for a little while. It was upsetting to learn that some readers didn't see it that way. A woman from Virginia wrote me:

> Relative to LBJ's unspeakable character, only one aspect of which is portrayed in your . . . piece, I have wished for many years that someone would write a book:
>
> *The Abominable Presidents*
>
> . . . TRUMAN's habitually gross language was publicly noted; but, was this impermissible trait in a President ever duly noted for its unseemliness in a White House occupant? Not that I know of. His *obscenities*.
>
> For crudeness, obscene language habitually, outrageous whoring, and, even, extremely questionable personal intimates as White House confidantes (the term the press used for Nixon's Bebe), we have had some revolting horrors. . . . For reasons I won't go into, Jerry Ford, Jimmy Carter, and now the present incumbent are appalling. . . .

A man from Florida:

> You display Johnson as the abomination he was from start to finish. I have been cognizant of all our Presidents from Taft to Reagan. My considered opinion is that Johnson has done more permanent damage to the people of the United States than any other occupant of the Oval Office in this century. If Johnson did not choose to undergo his obligations of his post as host, he should have respectfully declined. Instead, he chose the role of buffoon, characteristic of him.

This man was not alone in assuming that Johnson actually had played host to Shaw and that the piece was reportage. A right-wing political columnist named Jeffrey Hart wrote a syndicated column (headlined, in one paper, "Shaw's Texas Visit with LBJ Recalled"), in which he repeated my bogus Shavian quips as if they were authentic (adding some real ones, as if I'd overlooked the gems) and then summarized the Shaw-LBJ meeting as something "*The New Yorker* reported recently."

People sent me copies of this column from newspapers all over. A man from New Haven also sent copies of his correspondence with the editor of the *Register:*

> "How do you know," you ask me, "that Geng was writing fiction and not fact?"
>
> True, one could never definitely establish the nonoccurrence of this alleged confrontation . . . without compiling a daily log for each of them. The same could be said, of course, for the celebrated tall-tale contest between Davy Crockett and George Sand on a Mississippi flatboat in 1832. But then why should it fall to your readers to prove or disprove Hart's extravagant historical claims? . . .
>
> Our culture is well enough supplied with self-congratulatory fables. . . .

Later, a reader in Indianapolis, who had asked the *Star* to print a retraction of Hart's column, sent me a copy of Hart's response:

> A friend, knowing that I was writing a book about the year 1940, forwarded the *New Yorker* piece to me. I took the piece as genuine, since it has all the marks of a genuine anecdote, including real people, real time and places.
>
> I worked it into my book. My editor thought it genuine. So did two academic colleagues, one of them an expert on Shaw's plays. A reader of the column wrote me, however, to say that the piece seemed to be a fiction and a satire. I checked a Shaw biography and found that he had not been in the United States as represented in the piece, and, as far as can be determined, was never in Texas.

Finally, I heard from a Shaw specialist at Butler University in Indianapolis, Professor Victor Amend:

> If such a meeting had ever occurred, I am certain that Shaw would have overwhelmed LBJ as he did Mark Twain.

. . . When his music criticism was reprinted, Shaw appended a note in 1936 to a column that originally appeared on 12 December 1888. Shaw begins by saying, "The above hasty (not to say silly) description of Brahms' music will, I hope, be a warning to critics who know too much." He ends with the simple "I apologize."

The Twi-Night Zone

> It is, basically, just a superstitious connection between a chance pattern and the conditions of the moment, not any different than putting together black cats and bad luck.
>
> —*The Bill James Baseball Abstract*, 1985

> ". . . like Stan Musial leaving St. Louis to coach third base in an American Legion little league."
>
> —Rod Serling (in *The Twilight Zone Companion*)

Hey. A few years ago I had the idea that the kind of stuff I'm interested in would make a good series of half-hour shows for TV. But I ran up against a problem. Or, more precisely, I ran up against what I was told by other people was a problem.

If I wanted to do a show about a guy who builds a time machine and ends up back in Hitler's bunker, that was fine. But if I wanted to do a show about a statistically representative sample of those people who build time machines, and how many of them end up back in Hitler's bunker as opposed to the 1955 Dodgers' dugout, or twenty-first-century Wrigley Field, or any of the other varied possibilities, that was no good.

If I wanted to do a show about a mild-mannered bird-watcher who meets the devil in human form and trades him his soul in return for the chance to see the world's rarest bird and then the bird turns out to be the devil in the form of Lucifer the fallen angel with wings, great. But if I wanted to do a show about a mild-mannered bird-watcher who calculates the odds against his ever sighting a sea gull in Yankee Stadium, so he can devise a Trade Evaluation formula to establish *on an objective basis* whether or not it would be worth it to trade the devil his soul in return for such an experience—in that case, forget it.

Fortunately, it turned out that the number of people interested in this stuff got bigger and bigger, and as a direct result the number of people who were saying nobody was interested got smaller and smaller.

I call this the Nobody-Plays-in-Peoria-It's-Too-Crowded Effect.

So ultimately the series came into being. Maybe you remember it. If you don't, no hard feelings. Nonetheless, it is a fact that there was such a series.

It was called *The Twi-Night Zone*. And it was described as: "a hit," "powerful," "consistent," "average," "offensive," etc. What grounds are there for accepting one or more of these terms as measurably accurate? None. And when I say none, I mean there are some, but not any supported by:

1. A vast body of concrete information that has been observed, analyzed, and shown to be misleading.
2. A mutually understood methodology mutually agreed upon, which can be constantly refined until it proves misleading enough to be itself worthy of serving as the object of study.

I'd say we've got ourselves a hell of a long row to hoe here. So let's get started by generating loads of meaningfully questionable data. I have found that the synopsis form is by far the most convenient way to summarize the contents of shows. Anyway, that is the form I have used.

THE OPPONENTS

CAST

Woman . . . . Agnes Moorehead

There is a common but, when you stop and think about it, baffling delusion that things are true when in reality their exact opposites are true. Such is the misconception held by a woman who thinks she can sit out on her small lawn one summer afternoon without having to face an invasion of alien robots. These tiny, aggressive creatures arrive out of nowhere. (By which we mean they arrive out of somewhere that she hasn't included in her frame of reference.) They run across the grass. One of them trips and falls. Others get their feet all tangled up. She takes a pencil, pad, and calculator from her six-pack cooler and writes:

PERCENTAGE OF ERRORS ON DIFFERENT COMPONENTS OF NATURAL GRASS SURFACE

CRABGRASS	.72	ONION GRASS	.03
DANDELIONS	.07	EARTH CLODS	.03
PACHYSANDRA	.06	MISCELLANEOUS	.05
CLOVER	.04		

Or, to put it another way:

ALIEN REPULSION FACTOR (GRASS)

$$\frac{((((((C\times D)\times P)\times C)\times O)\times Ec)\times M)}{LH^{*}} + \left[\begin{matrix}\text{Astroturf}\\ \text{per sq. ft.}\end{matrix}\right] = \text{ARF (G)}$$

(*Total Lawnboy Hours)

Confident now, she watches as the error-plagued aliens fall into disarray, then retreat and vanish. The camera pulls back and we see a sign on the house: FENWAY PARK.

Would it be more efficient to build a dome over the lawn? Yes? No? Prove it. Then drop me a card.

WAY TO GO

CAST

Dad . . . . Jack Nicholson
Danny . . . . Danny Lloyd
Janitor . . . . Scatman Crothers

The bond between father and son, a bond that can be severed by no one and nothing—except maybe by a grievous misinterpretation of the principles of Sabermetrics. One morning Dad finds on his office floor a Runs Created formula dropped by the janitor, who plays around on Dad's secretary's computer at night. Dad, an otherwise educated man ignorant of even the rudiments of empirical science, glues the formula inside his son Danny's Little League uniform, believing it will magically improve his lackluster performance at the plate. In the next game, Danny hits a line drive deep into the right-field corner—a triple. But when he starts to steal home on a passed ball, a drop of sweat inside his collar erases a decimal point in the formula. This alters the equation in such a way that he disappears into an alternate universe. High up in the stands, the janitor applauds. . . .

A lot of viewers took this cautionary fable as evidence of a certain apocalyptic hyperbole on my part. Sort of an "in the wrong hands" message. I have never felt that way. I will say this, however. A formula is a fragile mechanism. What it is *not* is a recipe for pecan pie. By next year, everybody who *thinks* that's what it is will find themselves shagging fly balls in the fourth dimension.

PETE'S DREAM

CAST

Pete . . . . Linda Hunt

Let's call him Pete. An obnoxious old-timer who wakes up one morning vaguely remembering a dream he had the night before, a dream that somehow connects the number 4192 with the fountain of youth. Obsessed by the dream's tantalizing promise, he extrapolates wildly. He plays the number 4192 in the lottery. But it's a three-digit lottery. He searches the perimeter of a circle whose radius extends 4,192 feet from his house. Nothing. He looks up the 4,192nd person in the phone book and places a nuisance call. No answer. He begins to place 4,191 more calls to the same party. Nice try, Pete. Dream on. The camera closes in on the telephone as he dials. An old-fashioned rotary dial. As the holes move in one direction, the numbers appear to go in the opposite direction. But if that were true, we would dial backward. So it is with Pete's dream. It is an illusion.

That it is an illusion, and not a fact, is not a theory or a conjecture but a fact supported by a huge bunch of other facts. Does the public accept this? Do mice wear spats? We got a zillion letters blasting this episode for being "negative." Nevertheless, it remains one of my favorites. A lot of the credit for that goes to Linda Hunt's performance as Pete, which scared the bejeezus out of me. With the audience, though, fear struck out.

OUT OF ORDER

CAST
Sportswriter . . . . Larry Kert

A distinguished member of that gene pool of misinformation known as the sports media. This particular specimen, late on a deadline, is leaving a coffee shop when he presses the lever on the toothpick dispenser at the cashier's desk and receives not a toothpick but an RBI. In disbelief, he tries again, and within five minutes he has 300 RBIs (one per each two-second SSC [Simulated Scoring Context]). Elated, he runs back to his office and writes an article originating the concept of Game-Irrelevant RBI.

This episode was written by Billy Martin, who was then at loose ends and submitted a few scripts. I will just throw in my two cents:

(1) Well . . . I'm a little puzzled by Billy's limited database. Why doesn't the guy try to get additional stats from the cigarette machine, men's room comb dispenser, etc.?

(2) Awful lot of RBIs for 0 At Bats. I'm not saying it can't be done on Walks or ESP or something, but I am saying this: We don't have enough information about coffee shops as Run Environments to evaluate whether it can be done by the average customer. If anybody wants to work on this, be my guest.

(3) This seems like a good place to bring up a concept I like better than Game-Irrelevant RBI. And that is Yogi Berra's concept, Score-Influencing RBI. Flawless.

$$\frac{\text{TOTAL RBI} \times 1}{1} = \text{TOTAL SIRBI}$$

THE ENIGMA OF FLIGHT .500

CAST

Hypothesis . . . . Burgess Meredith
Axiom . . . . Franchot Tone
Corollary . . . . Bob Cummings
Anomaly. . . . . Orson Bean

What if AAA Airlines Flight .500, peacefully en route from Albuquerque to Los Angeles, were to be swept into the parabola of a distribution curve? Not one person that I know of has ever thought to ask this. Just for fun, let's take it a step further. What if such an event, instead of showing up on conventional instruments of measurement, simply caused the *flight number* to plummet from .500 to somewhere around .000? I can't prove yet that that's what would happen, but I am satisfied that it's a realistic option, given that the problem is more or less speculative in any case.

Did I mention that this whole thing is a metaphor for the game of baseball?

HOW TO ORDER *The Twi-Night Zone* NEWSLETTER

While I was writing this article, so many more people got interested in this stuff that answering their letters kept me from finishing it. Therefore, I've decided to continue this project in *The Twi-Night Zone Newsletter.* If you remember some of the really, really great shows we had—like the one where Count Bozeau the ventriloquist is outraged when his dummy Bozelle autonomously utters the words "pine tar"—you might want to subscribe.

If you're so inclined, please send $25 in what we commonly define as negotiable U.S. currency, plus whatever name and address your projections indicate you'll be using later this year, allowing for a two-digit margin of error. Thanks. That's for a one-year subscription—twelve issues, unless I decide it would be more logical for the United States to go over to the Norse calendar.

May 1985

There was a sublime item in the news: The Procter & Gamble company had been forced to change its traditional logo—a man-in-the-moon surrounded by stars—because of unstoppable public rumors that the company "tithed to Satan" and that if you held the logo up to a mirror, the curls in the man-in-the-moon's beard read "666," sign of the beast. I thought of writing a deranged memo from the guy who has to design the new logo; everything he comes up with is subjected to occult interpretations. I told this to Peter Schjeldahl, who's an art critic, and he said, "The way I'd do it would be to show the guy's designs for the new logo. A swastika. An upside-down crucifix." This had such graphic purity that it fulfilled the idea then and there, so I never wrote it.

Then a few weeks later I got another shot at the supernatural. And when the result appeared in *GQ* magazine, people sent in money to order the fictitious newsletter. At least they weren't tithing to Satan. . . . Adam Gopnik, who was then the fiction editor at *GQ*, had called me up to ask if I'd write something for a humor issue. I told him I couldn't do them to order, but then while we were chatting, he said, "What are you reading lately?" and I looked down at the books on my bed and saw Bill James's 1986 *Baseball Abstract* and a compendium of all the old *Twilight Zone* scenarios. I told Adam, and—just as if we were in a 1950s movie about bohemian artists in Paris—he said, "Why don't you try putting them together?"

Adam was also a Bill James fan, and was great at noticing where I'd faltered with the voice. He knew the vocal range parody operates in. Bill James has a wonderful voice to parody—manneristically unmannered. But even two of us working together didn't quite catch him at his most elegant, where humility and certainty are the same: "If you have nine hitters and nine batting order slots to put them in, there are 362,880 ways to do it, and only one of them is right."

Codicil

> Experts are now fine-combing [William Faulkner's] writings in every stage. . . . They are trying to determine . . . how—ideally—he wanted his books published. This posthumous literary revision—known as "authorial intention" or "final intention"—has been advanced by scholars in the last few years. . . .
>
> Punctuation was important to Faulkner to establish mood and thought. When he wanted to indicate introspection, he punctuated the dialogue, in his tightly compressed handwriting, with 6 to 10 dots, like this: . . . . When he wanted to show that something was happening outside the experience of his characters, he often used a long line of dashes, like this: — — —.
>
> —*New York Times*, June 5, 1985

Be it understood by my literary executor and his heirs and assigns that the system of punctuation explained hereunder is my posthumous intention; that it applies to each and all of my literary effects, including all and any novels, novellas, novelettes, sprawling narrative panoramas of urban horror, potboilers, and erotic classics, not excluding the "Supervising Nurse" series; and that in the case of any deviation from said system of punctuation whatsoever, howsoever printed, said deviation shall be expunged and replaced by the version that was originally intended all along in the first place.

(1) . . . . Eight dots before dialogue indicates that whatever the character says, he or she really means the exact opposite.

(2) . . . . + More than eight dots before dialogue creates a different feeling, more like doubt or distrust. Or maybe the character is just stalling. We don't know. Instead of having the meaning be cut and dried, it's more like: Wait a minute, is this guy on the level or not? That's the realism I depict with the extra dots.

(3) //""// Double slash marks around dialogue reveals that at the very moment this character is talking, somewhere else in the world a volcano is erupting, a war is raging, or somebody of a different race is seeing things from another perspective.

(4) (!) An exclamation point in parentheses after dialogue makes it

obvious that I, the author, know that what the person just said is really stupid.

(5) *&%!*¢#??! An asterisk, ampersand, percent sign, exclamation point, another asterisk, a cent sign, a number sign, two question marks, and a final exclamation point anywhere in dialogue clues the reader in to the fact that the character has a tremendous anger against society.

(6) —— A single long dash after dialogue adds a very downbeat note. It's just a little touch I throw in once in a while. For the mood.

(7) : A colon before the beginning of a paragraph conveys a Wagnerian-overture type of effect. Power! Impact!

(8) *********** A line of asterisks after a scene with kissing or sex implies another scene with vampirism or more sex.

(9) [ ] Material inside brackets suggests insanity. Maybe one of the characters feels like blowing his top. How do you show this? I want the reader to see those brackets and immediately think: Craziness! Chaos!

(10) ;;;;;;;; A group of semicolons gives an unusual flavor. It's just a hell of an unexpected thing.

(11) *Italic print* I use all over the place. This is a bug I have. *Italic print!* I love it. It's for when a first-person or omniscient narrator is probing psychic wounds that will never heal, which I do a lot.

(12) – – – – – – Six dashes in the middle of nowhere (I thought of using five for this, but then I decided no, six) has the function of blasting emotion out of the uncharted waters of consciousness inside every reader, be he or she a profound philosopher or just an individual of no great brain power, because no matter who you are or what you are, you contain the mysteries of your own subterranean life, your caverns of fear, rage, desire, everything offbeat, all protected by walls of ice until suddenly, smash!—along comes the icepick of authorial intention to break it into little pieces that melt into a river of strange sensations, which no one but you is ever supposed to know about. Here is where I touch on the universal problem: that you can never, never go completely into the other guy's heart.

(13) A capital letter at the beginning of a sentence is a private joke.

I want these inserted in all my works. There's a list on my bulletin board of where they go.

Fall 1985

People thoughtfully send me clippings to use, but mostly it's because the item reminds them of something I already did—so it isn't fun for me to do again. This was the first time I used a sent-in clipping. The article "New, Authentic Edition of Faulkner Novels Set," with its examples of Faulkner's arcane punctuation philosophy, was spotted by Terry Adams, an editor at Knopf. He'd once sent me a free copy of Julian Barnes's novel *Flaubert's Parrot,* hoping I'd contribute a publicity blurb, and I'd loved the book but couldn't think what to say (Fran Lebowitz's blurb was memorable: "Flaubert's Parrot, c'est moi")—so maybe I felt under some little obligation to at least make use of his clipping.

I started writing while visiting Roy Blount and Joan Ackermann, up in the Massachusetts Berkshires. Joan had a computer, on which she was writing a book about volleyball, and taught me how to use it, but I couldn't be funny on it. The ease of manipulating bizarre punctuation combos on a computer did produce many speckled-looking pages, but it wasn't exactly writing. Then I switched to Roy's ancient manual typewriter with missing keys, but in his study there was a distracting collection of books like *The American Heritage Dictionary of Indo-European Roots.* I did get some ideas for bad sentences from an old high-school grammar text he lent me.

This piece must have taken about six different forms, over a few months. At one point, it was an Ed story. ("Quite often, writing that is not originally intended for publication is eventually found to have some literary or historical importance that makes it suitable for publication. That is why I have taken the responsibility of going through Ed's personal papers and letters with a fine-tooth comb.") Then for a while it was about this couple named the Blunts, who wrote thrillers published in miniature collectible forms—on teabag tags, bottle-cap liners, etc.—using symbolic punctuation to economize. (Joan inspired this while making a cup of tea: the staple holding the teabag tag to the string looked like a dash.)

What the piece needed was a human presence behind the punctuation mechanics. At last, trying to think of someone who explained very specifically and crudely how he got his artistic effects, I remembered an interview with Sam Fuller (in *The Director's Event: Interviews with Five American Film-Makers*):

> [For *Pickup on South Street*] I told the art director I wanted those [subway] stairs, because I liked the idea of Widmark pulling Kiley down by the ankles, and the heavy's chin hits every step. Dat-dat-dat-dat-dat: it's musical.

I stole Fuller's entire voice: his vocabulary ("Impact!") and his freedom to say, Did you notice the great part where I did so-and-so? and then, Of course this other part didn't turn out as great as I wanted. His movies have dialogue like "We can't leave him behind—he'd be caught and brainwashed" (Gene Barry in *China Gate*). But that's the price you pay for his schematic method. Typical: in *Pickup,* a fat guy eating with chopsticks is offered some payoff money, and without breaking rhythm he picks up the twenty-dollar bill with the chopsticks and goes on eating. Because I love Fuller's movies, I wanted a passage of sincerity, so I put in that part about how "you can never, never go completely into the other guy's heart."

The 1985 Beaujolais Nouveaux: Ka-Boum!

> PARIS—According to a recent survey, 30 percent of all French people over the age of 10 never drink wine. . . . The survey found that France has lost two million wine consumers since 1979. . . . What does the decline mean for wine producers?
>
> —Frank J. Prial, "Wine Talk" (in the *New York Times,* September 25, 1985)

> Paris—. . . the head of the intelligence agency, Adm. Pierre Lacoste, was dismissed for having refused to disclose . . . the details of the sinking of the *Rainbow Warrior*.
>
> —Frank J. Prial, "Greenpeace and the Paris Press: A Trickle of Words Turns into a Torrent" (in the *New York Times*, September 27, 1985)

If it's French and it comes in a bottle, how bad can it be? Such has always been the modest philosophy of this column. But with the 1985 Beaujolais Nouveaux now in, promising a strong vintage, the U.S. consumer is beginning to confront a profusion of new châteaux, varietals, arsenals, and appellations of flash point, none previously familiar here. This is all to the good for the much-needed expansion of the French export market and for Americans seeking top value for their dollar. Nonetheless, it demands that we exercise discretion and even caution. There is already a huge influx of mail to this column from uncertain readers. Today I shall deal with the most often-posed concerns.

Q. For three dollars I bought a bottle of Nuage de Fumée '85 from a man on the corner of Forty-second Street and Eighth Avenue. He assured me that if I was satisfied with it he would meet me by appointment in a Times Square hotel room with a crate full of additional selections. Is this a good idea, and can you tell me more about Nuage de Fumée? On the label it also says "Château de Gélignite," and then under that it says "13.5% nitroglycerine by vol."

A. While not, technically speaking, a Beaujolais, Nuage de Fumée is produced in the Palais de l'Élysée region near the Seine River in north-central France, on acreage adjoining (though not under the direct responsibility of) the renowned Mitterrand estate adjacent to the five-hundred-square-mile terrain closely intervening between it and the finest Beaujolais vineyards. If the label also says "Mise en bouteille au Directorat Général de Sécurité Externe," you have a first-class Nuage, partaking of the typically delightful fruitiness, thirst-quenching *fraîcheur*, and vivacious charm evoked by the

Beaujolais bottle, yet boasting complex overtones of the aromatic wood pulp and potassium nitrate used as an inert base or adsorbent to balance the acidity of the nitro. The '85 is already matured and not for laying down, as it tends to go off quickly. Since your dealer is unknown to me, I strongly urge that you check his reliability by asking him to show you exactly how to wire the underwater fuses to the blasting cap.

Q. We want to send a birthday present to one of my husband's business associates in Tampa, and can spend up to twenty-five or thirty dollars. Since people have been raving about the 1985 Plastique Nouveau, I tried purchasing a case, in a magnetic gift hamper, plus an extra bottle for ourselves, from Sandy's Surplus Ordnance out here on eastern Long Island. But when we tried it, it was so disappointing. It simply blew a neat hole about the size of a quarter through our sideboard. Should I return the entire case for a refund?

A. Yes, and I congratulate you on your discernment! A true Plastique has none of the finesse you describe, and considerably more bite. It should expand with an exuberance verging on impetuousness, to bring out the full depth and roundness of the radial impact. You do not say which bottler is named on the label, but sadly there are an unscrupulous few who are taking advantage of relaxed export quotas to blend Plastique with Pomerol, Saint-Émilion, and other adulterants.

In such an unpredictable situation, one can rely only on the conscience of the retailer. I have spoken to Sandy, who confirms that he will give you a refund or credit. As it happens, to accommodate a new shipment of magnums from Corsica, he is having a sale on some classic vintages. In your price range he can custom-assemble an impressive gift pack from among the following: Domaine Algérie '58, Clos Collaboration-Nazis '41, Mouton Dreyfus '94, and La Terreur Brute 1793—all noted for their ripe bouquet and quintessentially French character. (A nice touch is that the neck of each bottle is wrapped in the sommelier's traditional pure linen field dressing.) Or you might consider the sampler case of Château Préfecture de Police, Nuit des Barricades, the most acclaimed of the May 1968

Sorbonnes. (Includes 1 Phosphore Blanc, 1 Vapeur de Chlore, 1 Poudre Enfermée, 1 Le Gaz Orthochlorobenzalmalononitrile, and 2 Grenades Lacrymogène.)

Q. What is your opinion on my broker's advice to invest in futures of 1985 Haute Incendiaires? Any risks?

A. Naturally, all such futures carry the risk of high opening-price quotations' not holding until or before the dollar declines against a thirty-six-month delivery date, on the assumption that shortages in the '82s and '83s will incite buying of first growths 10 to 15 percent above the previous year's *primeurs*. I suspect, however, that this is not what is troubling you. It is common and understandable for the novice American investor to feel apprehensions of a more primitive nature. An ocean away, in a foreign place called Bordeaux (not even the real Bordeaux), your precious investment is being aged in an underground facility where highly trained oenologists are employed to hand-rotate the lead casks so the bituminous sediment is uniformly distributed through the methane. Is this delicate and volatile process, you wonder, secure from terrorists? Rest assured: the French government considers this industry so vital to its national interest that it has pledged a tactical nuclear force to defend those cellars.

Now let me extend a more personal warranty. Recently, I traveled to one of the sunny French atolls for a blind tasting. The 1985 Haute Incendiaires were already showing majestically, with a "sleeper" bouquet that needs twenty to twenty-five seconds of breathing before it bursts into vigorous glow, heralding a monumentally balanced combustive structure (surprisingly high in the ratio of tannin to carbon monoxide) in which the first bright spicy flash is followed by layer after infinite layer of textural displacements so mouth-filling that there lingers on the palate the earthy flavor of the native herbs, grasses, and nearby cars and buildings, until the distinctive velvety char patterns emerge on the long, haunting, bone-dry finish.

December 1985

A couple of years earlier, the Sherry-Lehmann liquor store, right near my apartment, accidentally printed my phone number, similar to theirs, in an advertisement. I was in Florida at the time, and whenever I called my New York answering machine for messages, it was full of wine orders. Amazing—people call a number and get a girlish voice saying, "Hi, I'm not home right now," and they just dutifully place their orders. When I complained to the store, I expected them to at least give me a complimentary bottle of champagne or something, but they did nothing. So I always wanted to get back at them.

Then, in September 1985, Marcelle Clements, who is French and reads all the American news about France to see how wrong it is, told me to check out these two *New York Times* stories written by the wine correspondent—one on wine, the other on the French press's investigations into the sinking of the Greenpeace antinuclear protest ship. Don't know if she had any inkling of how anti-French my piece would turn out to be (and I've been afraid to ask her).

I showed it to Sandy in a half-baked form; he had just moved back here from Montana, and I got reacquainted with a neutral facial expression he has when he doesn't like what he's reading. Then he said, "Put in a lot more writing about explosives." Music to my ears. What you really want to hear under those circumstances is not "It's fine" but "Look, here's something specific you're obviously interested in, so go to town with it—go wild." Concentration and liberation. . . . So in gratitude, I put his name in, as the owner of the surplus ordnance store.

The wines were blended from descriptions in the Sherry-Lehmann catalogue and other toxic materials, including gases and grenades mentioned in *L'Insurrection Étudiante: 2–3 Mai 1968*.

Equal Time

You know, recently one of our most distinguished Americans, Clare Boothe Luce, had this to say about the coming vote [on aid to the Contras]. ". . . My mind goes back to a similar moment in our history—back to the first years after Cuba had fallen to Fidel. One day during those years, I had lunch at the White House with a man I had known since he was a boy—John F. Kennedy. 'Mr. President,' I said, 'no matter how exalted or great a man may be, history will have time to give him no more than one sentence. George Washington—he founded our country. Abraham Lincoln—he freed the slaves and preserved the union.'"

—Ronald Reagan (address to the nation, March 16, 1986)

WILLIAM HENRY HARRISON: He was the first occupant of the White House to eat with a knife and fork.

MILLARD FILLMORE: He had his own likeness secretly engraved in the folds of Miss Liberty's dress on the 1851 silver dollar.

FRANKLIN PIERCE: He earned the sobriquets Old Tongue-in-Groove and the Gabardine Gangplank.

ULYSSES S. GRANT: He translated the words to "The Star-Spangled Banner" into thirteen different languages, including mirror writing.

BENJAMIN HARRISON: He predicted the birth of the Dionne Quintuplets over forty years before it happened.

WILLIAM MCKINLEY: He was his own grandfather.

WARREN G. HARDING: He campaigned on a bicycle carved from a single giant bar of soap.

CALVIN COOLIDGE: He coined the catchphrase of the era—"Do you simply want a cigarette or do you want a Murad?"

HERBERT HOOVER: He reorganized the National Christmas Card Cemetery.

GERALD FORD: He had the idea for *Shampoo* long before the movie came out.

RONALD REAGAN: He popularized the political theories of Clare Boothe Luce.

March 1986

Playing Trivial Pursuit for the first time, and reminiscing about childhood board games and collections, I remembered a Presidential coins game from the 1950s: "silver" coins stamped with the Presidents' likenesses, in a serious-looking royal-blue display box, with a set of trivia questions like "Which President's spinster niece served as his official White House hostess?" This seemed the appropriate level at which to treat Reagan's quotation of Clare Boothe Luce's inane view of Presidential history.

A tiny but amusing discipline of writing a piece like this is to get the period details right. The *New Yorker*'s fact-checkers always help. The head of the checking department is a tall, scholarly-looking guy named Martin Baron. With extreme politeness, plus some sarcastic asides directed at whoever in public life happens to be perpetrating a cover-up at the moment, he will gladly explain the cause-and-effect relationships among all the minutiae that go into the determination of a fact. Martin checked this piece. He made sure Murad cigarettes were on the market in Coolidge's day (and, I'll bet, that soap existed in Harding's day). We had an interesting discussion about which of the many beautiful silver Miss Liberty coins show her dress as opposed to her face only. It was fun to work with someone who was pleased that I owned a copy of *U.S. Coins of Value.*

This book was in my possession because my brother Steve and I had inherited a random collection of coins—mostly Kennedy half dollars and Indian-head pennies—and thought of selling them while we were in Clearwater, Florida. (There's a huge number of coin dealers in that area—maybe because the senior citizens like to vary their investment strategies. You can even call a Sears Precious Metals Hotline for current prices.) One day we drove all over town looking for a dealer I'd liked the looks of in the Yellow Pages. . . . The address is a shack with the door open, next to Live Bait. . . . "This can't be it." . . . "Maybe they don't answer because too many people come looking for a coin shop." . . . "The street numbers start over again out past Ulmerton—we could drive out there. What was the address again?" . . . "Oh, Indian Rocks *Road*—that's across the bridge, runs along the other side of the inland waterway." . . . "Can you see any numbers on your side?" . . . "Eight-something. Are the numbers getting higher or lower?" . . . "There—820 . . . 816 . . . 12300? What? Maybe it's like the way the numbers start over again out past Ulmerton." . . . "We're spending more money on gas than we'll get for these stupid coins." . . . You could take a similar view of the amount of energy put into fact-checking this little piece. But I enjoyed both experiences in the same way.

Remorse

Ed and I have an announcement to make. Before I say what it is, I would like to thank all our friends and acquaintances, as well as the many people who don't even know us but have taken such an ongoing interest in the ups and downs of our relationship merely on the basis of hearsay over the three and a half years that Ed and I have been together. Although we have often felt that their interest in us was prurient and even somewhat sinister, we also couldn't help feeling just a little bit flattered.

We could go on basking in this attention, knowing that people are awed by and, in certain cases, jealous of me and Ed as a couple. However, there comes a time when you have to consult your own conscience and do what you believe is right, no matter how disillusioning it may seem to your friends, and no matter how much it may gratify the kind of people who are always waiting to see you knocked off your pedestal.

Ed and I want to acknowledge that we have made some mistakes in the past. These were in areas which it would be pointless to go into at this late date and in the brief space we have allotted ourselves for this public statement. Suffice it to say that Ed has behaved abominably, and I have not been lily-white, either. However, we feel that it doesn't get us off the hook just to *say* we've made mistakes and are putting them behind us now. Anyone could do that, and there would be no definite way to ascertain the person's sincerity or commitment.

Therefore, we have come to the following decision: The best way to affirm that we have put our mistakes behind us, once and for all, is to announce our intention to comply voluntarily with the conditions set down by the Commissioner of Baseball.

We would like to emphasize the word "voluntarily," because there is absolutely no legal basis on which compulsory compliance can be exacted from us under the terms of our contract with the New York Mets. This contract explicitly defines our agreement thus: We shall be entitled to a raincheck in the event of an incomplete game, which is any game terminated before five full innings of play, or four and a half if the home team is ahead, and in return we consent to the use of our image incidental to any live or recorded video display of the game. There is also, on our part, an implied consent to confiscation of any thermos jugs we bring into the stadium. However, our attorney assures us that no court or arbitrator would interpret this as a blank check for the commissioner to exploit at his whim. It is on the basis of choice, then, not coercion, that we have settled on our course of action, and we want this clearly understood not only by Commissioner Peter Ueberroth but by people who would like to see us forced to cringe and crawl.

As for the details of our compliance, we have mutually agreed to share these in an equitable fashion. I will be in charge of the community service. As part of that, I will be making announcements like this from time to time, thus relieving the community of the burden of prying into our personal lives for themselves or trying to find out by bothering the Mets' publicity office. I will also spend one hundred hours working with youthful offenders, who, I believe, could profit tremendously from one hundred hours away from the grind of science or math, listening instead to me explaining why I am talking to them instead of their teachers or parents. There is far too little interrelating between people like myself and youthful offenders. These are usually among the brightest and most attractive members of our society, and so—I want to reemphasize this—I consider spending one hundred hours with them *in no way a punishment* but an opportunity I gladly welcome. This, of course, is a side benefit; the main thing is that I will be giving one hundred hours during which these young people will not have a chance to engage in any offenses—at least, not if I have anything to say about it, which I very much hope I will.

Ed, being a much more intensely private person than I am, will be involved in supplying specimens for the urinalysis. Anyone who still harbors some doubt that urinalysis is one of the best ways to put your mistakes behind you simply does not understand the stringent laboratory procedures necessary to insure mutual trust. Ed will be donating 10 percent of his time to provide these specimens, on a random basis. The random pattern has been worked out in consultation with the Department of Higher Mathematics at MIT, where a computer will convey a signal to our home computer modem, at which time Ed will contribute the specimen and relay it to the lab via one of New York's top bonded messenger services, which will be on twenty-four-hour standby, in order to maintain the scientific integrity of the procedure.

Thanks to advances made in recent years by medical research surveys and major corporate personnel departments, we now know that the primary cause of human mistakes is a lack of self-respect, in turn caused by an impersonal society in which no one has cared enough to monitor our body chemistries on an individual, one-to-one level in a scientific setting. Instead, we are all too often at the mercy of informal speculation by those with no special training. Ed's contribution is an effort to help change all that, and in the long run we expect it to influence sizable numbers of young people to participate in such programs themselves.

As a more direct result, I believe we are going to see a significant increase in the respect that youthful offenders will feel for Ed when I explain to them in detail exactly how much he is doing. I respect him more already myself, knowing that he will be setting an example—far more real than any textbook lesson—in the rigors of the scientific method and the richly humanistic interaction of a private individual with the society outside himself.

I will keep these remarks brief, and conclude by saying that it is with a new lightness of heart that we look forward to Opening Day. This season, as in past seasons, we fully intend to be behind first base, in the lower deck, which is where our contract entitles us to be.

Our hope is that the New York Mets will accept us as worthy of being there.

March 1986

The New York Mets' first baseman Keith Hernandez was one of the players who had testified the year before at the trial of a cocaine dealer and admitted to using the drug in the past. Now the Baseball Commissioner wanted to impose retroactive penalties and drug testing, and Hernandez was saying that ought to be a matter for arbitration. The *Daily News* ran the arrogant headline "KEITH, YOU'RE WRONG!" "Wrong" meant insufficiently remorseful to gratify Shavian sportswriter Phil Pepe. (Pepe later softened his position.)

I had written an appreciation of Hernandez for *Vanity Fair* back in 1985 (just as the drug story was breaking), and a friend who read it had said, "Where's the cocaine?" It wasn't there because I hadn't seen it on the field. I was interested in the way Hernandez seems fitted to the exact scale of the game, fills it right out to the edges. For me, that was the complete story on him. This wasn't a reporter's attitude, but it was the one I had. Didn't even want to interview him—just sit in the stands or in front of the TV and take my little notes:

> 4/13/85 vs. Reds: 1 out, man on 2nd, Mets need a run to tie it up—KH needs to advance the runner home—fights the ball off and hits long fly to outfield—not a hit but scores a run. Another good at-bat—Mookie on, KH fights off tough pitches, draws a walk, so they can't walk Carter. . . . 4/17 vs. Pittsbgh: KH hit on arm by pitch by McWilliams. Won game with sac. RBI. . . . 5/17 vs. Giants: KH 2 spectacular plays in 1st inning for last 2 outs—a diving catch down the line, then a catch backwards over his head. . . . 5/26 vs. L.A.: KH playing 1st, waiting for the pitch, bent down, left hand always touches his glove for an instant, like a steno w/pad and pencil poised to take down an unpredictable burst of dictation. . . . 6/21 vs. Montreal: funny out at 1st, KH about to throw to Sisk but suddenly slides face-first into base—then laughs. . . . 6/22 vs. Montreal: KH wears his uniform like street clothes. . . . 7/2 vs. Pittsbgh: McCarver, "Hernandez is not *guarding* the line, but he is *aware* of the line." . . . July: KH hit .464 in road trip where they swept Atlanta and Cincinnati.

I went along when my boyfriend photographed Keith for *Vanity Fair*, during batting practice, but I was very uncomfortable on the field. (The only other woman had a bunch of cameras around her neck—a protection against looking like you don't belong.) I'd never been so tongue-tied. I was supposed to chat with Keith, to amuse and relax him during the photo session (something I hadn't been shy to do with other subjects), but couldn't think of what to say that wouldn't sound ridiculous. Later, when I told this to another woman baseball fan, Brooke Alderson, she gave me an article called "Women, Baseball, and Words," by Adrienne E. Harris:

> I get to baseball through men: fathers, lovers, husbands, buddies, students. For baseball is a social space appropriated by and for men. Women['s] . . . marginality is given and absolute. . . . To speak as a woman about baseball is to be immediately entangled with baseball's ideological function and to be at odds with it. The evidence of this confrontation is in the struggle, the rupture, the discordance between my voice and the variable but coherent male voice of baseball.
>
> . . . Talk, banter, commentary, analysis, evocation, taunting, the work of baseball talk is the creation and distribution of a complex male world in which real and imaginary men feel connected.

Published in a journal called *PsychCritique*, this takes a line I might normally resist. But I'd felt that inadequacy of voice while writing the article (in a faked-up tone based on rereading Roy Blount's baseball reporting), and experienced the utter impossibility of walking up to Hernandez and saying, "Hey, Keith—how 'bout those Dodgers?"

However, I'm not remotely awed by Ed. Turning Keith into Ed domesticated him and empowered me to write in a comfortable voice. It also sidestepped the risks of self-righteousness and ignorance in head-on writing about the drugs issues. I didn't even know what my opinion was until I was in the midst of writing. Making up displaced versions of real things, I can see more clearly whether I believe them.

One problem I couldn't sidestep was submitting urinalysis jokes to the *New Yorker*. The idea was to show that the drug testing was just punitive and symbolic; but initially I got carried away and had urine samples being delivered to Commissioner Ueberroth at dinner. A note about the manuscript, from William Shawn, said "No urine delivered to table." It was always tempting to try changing material Mr. Shawn found objectionable to something *even worse* but worded in a way that he couldn't possibly object to; usually that would force solutions more creative than the original crudeness. That's what happened when I took out urine delivered to table. So I'm not sorry.

Testimonial remorse is a seductive thing, with a perilous relation to the truth. Keith Hernandez later published a book, *If at First*, in which he said of his trial testimony about using cocaine, "I regret my use of the words 'massive' and 'demon.' I have no idea why I said them." That really rang true. I read it to a Mets fan English teacher, Donald Lyons, who said, "A dazzling piece of honesty and psychological realism."

Mario Cabot's School Days

There is no kid who's qualified to go to Harvard who can't, on some scholarship or other.

—Hugh Sidey (on *Agronsky & Company*)

There's no reason why we shouldn't have an Italian President—we've had everything else.

—Barry Goldwater (on *60 Minutes*)

Chuck got one. It wasn't that big a deal. Chuck says all you have to do is wait for June to roll around and then go to any cash machine, insert your driver's license, and type in your SAT scores in a certain sequence, and the machine issues you a four-year scholarship to Harvard. (The personal interview is a thing of the past.) Of course, your scores have to qualify, and I'm not sure what you use if you don't have a license, but apart from that it's pretty much a foregone conclusion that you'll get one—*if* you can handle the mob scene. By the middle of the summer, those cash-machine lines are a nightmare. Word has really gotten around, even though they don't announce it. It's just an open secret—like the fact that George Washington was a full-blooded Chickahominy Indian, which everybody knows, even though it never appears in print anywhere.

So I'm thinking of maybe doing that, although there's a bunch of other ways you can get one, which I'm also thinking of doing, because the way that you pick should be suited to your unique qualifications and personal interests. For instance, Gary happens to like driving, and a couple of weeks ago he was driving his van out on the Island when just past Riverhead he started to lose an incredible amount of power and the oil light went on, so he pulled into a garage that was still open, even though it was nearly midnight. There were five kids working there who, it turned out, had all gone to junior high together and now were into fixing cars instead of going to Harvard, and they got interested in Gary's problem, which was, for starters, that a few days earlier somebody had rear-ended him and now the lock on the engine compartment wouldn't open (which, if you remember, was why President Paul Robeson missed his own inauguration and they had to swear in another guy). So this one kid, a girl in a tube top, drove her car behind his and turned on her lights so everybody could get a good view of the lock, and then they all took turns trying to jimmy it open. While this was going on, an older guy walked across the highway and came over to them—they all seemed to know him—and said he was going into the hospital at six the next morning for a bypass operation. He said, "I can't even walk from here to right over there without breaking out in a sweat." He said his doctor had told him to prepare himself for thirteen hours of surgery but he didn't know how to prepare himself, so he'd come over to see what was happening with the van. When Gary told him, he said he had exactly the same problem once when he owned a VW Beetle, so he sympathized in a big way; then he shook Gary's hand and left, and afterward Gary found pressed into his palm a token that read "Redeem at Gate for Free Scholarship to Harvard." Of course, all this depended on a certain amount of chance, but no more so than when an obscure Pennsylvania coal miner named James Polki got elected President until the Electoral College found out a novice telephone operator had made a mistake—if you want to call it a "mistake" that American history includes a hardworking Polish immigrant who held the highest office in the land, temporarily.

Still, with the college term starting in September, I don't know if I can afford to wait for a lucky break. (If I had that kind of time, I could just as easily count on the rumor I read about in *TV Guide* being true—that next season they're adding a "Harvard Scholarship" section to the Wheel of Fortune.) So what I'll probably just do is send away for one, by printing my name and address in block letters in black or blue ink on a standard 3 × 5 file card (or a piece of white paper cut to the same dimensions) and then, below that, copying or tracing the words "HARVARD SCHOLARSHIP" from a label (it's on most of the product labels now) and mailing it in, making sure it's postmarked on or before the August 15th deadline—all of which is a little complicated procedurally, but so was the constitutional system that gave us President Thomas Noguchi (the only coroner ever to become Chief Executive), when the individuals ahead of him in the line of succession were physically or mentally incapacitated, briefly.

So that's how I'm going to get mine. My mom and dad have accumulated enough AT&T Opportunity Calling Credits to cash in for one, but I know they're saving them to donate to the political candidate of their choice in 1988. They feel very strongly that if contributions like that, from people with modest incomes, had been possible throughout our history, President Irving Berlin would have been able to raise the fare to Washington.

Some people will tell you that none of these are legitimate Harvard scholarships, but they're the same people who will blatantly deny that in 1896 a palomino pony named Pancho, running as an antivivisection candidate for the Presidency, got 97 percent of the popular vote. They will insist that you have to apply directly to Harvard, but that isn't true. The regular sources are all dried up by this time of year, and you have to take a more unorthodox approach—like the way a woman named Dora, or Doreen, occupied the Oval Office in 1920 as a poltergeist. She's still there (the longest term ever) and may have accomplished more than we realize—a question I plan to research when I major in Alternative American History at Harvard.

June 1986

Coming back from a trip to Boston to photograph the documentary filmmaker Frederick Wiseman, my boyfriend and I bought eight live lobsters from a place called Airport Lobsters, to take as a surprise birthday present to his mother, who was staying on Long Island. On the drive out, in his 1969 Volkswagen van, we had the same experience described near the start of this piece—the garage, the kids, the guy who talked about his bypass surgery. By the time we got to East Hampton, it was three A.M., so we slept in the van. I didn't like sleeping in there with the sounds of the lobsters rustling in their ice packs, but we were afraid to put them outside, in case of predators. Then the next morning it turned out that his mother was going back to the city unexpectedly, so we had to find another venue for the lobster lunch. Linda and Aaron Asher rose to the occasion. Linda's bold handling of lobsters made us see how helpless we'd have been without her; and she had the wit to call a seafood store and ask how you tell whether passive lobsters are dead, because dead ones are toxic. We had an idyllic outdoor feast, with the radio broadcast of the Mets game wafting across the grass. (Later Linda told me she'd never been quite sure whether slow-moving live lobsters are a little bit toxic, and that sitting there in the sun, with the poppies in bloom and the glory of *enough lobster*, she'd felt "one tiny capillary of danger threading through Paradise.")

Since this experience had involved a lot of waiting around, I'd taken notes, and they seemed to hook up with the quotes I'd saved about Harvard and the Italian President, suggesting a high school voice. (The lobsters never made it in.) Also, possibly in the back of my mind were Wiseman's documentaries—their questioning of institutional authority—and especially his 1968 *High School*.

It wasn't at all clear to me what this piece was about until I was going over it with my *New Yorker* editor, Roger Angell (who wrote the title). He kept trying to make me explain what I was doing so we could improve the end, and in the course of a rambling excuse for what was already on the page, I blurted out the words "alternative history," and he said, "That's it!"

What Happened

September 29, 1986

Dear:

We are fine. Please do not worry about us. I know it must have come as a shock to find your wife and children gone when you got home from work, but there is nothing to worry about. We are still the same loving family we were before. Nothing has changed. I will send you a post office box number where we can be reached just as soon as I know where we'll be, but at this point I don't know when that will be. All I can say is that any concern or anxiety on your part would be premature and alarmist.

Still, I know you can't help asking yourself: What happened? And the answer is: Nothing. Doc hung a curveball a couple of times, that's all. It could happen to anyone. There's no more to it than that. The Mets are still a winning team. What matters now is to take things one day at a time.

Please try to understand that although nothing has changed, nothing can stay exactly the same, either. No sane person could possibly have expected Doc to sustain the incredible greatness of last year. To expect that would be to expect superhuman perfection. Even Doc himself would admit that. But it's no reason to suspect that there's some hidden explanation for why things don't seem to be going as well as they used to (which doesn't mean things have changed, just that they're not going as well). Knowing you, I can tell that your mind is already racing with all sorts of gloomy scenarios based on little things that have happened in the past and now, in retrospect, loom as significant—like the ankle sprain before spring training. Believe me, I have searched my heart about the possibility that maybe the ankle sprain (without my even consciously realizing it) might have something to do with this, and I feel it's highly unlikely. Also, I hope you won't be tempted to dwell on some distressing generalization like "overthrowing" (because there is no such thing). I pray that other people won't encourage you in this line of thinking. There's always someone who will play on your nerves by saying, This is not as good as it was yesterday, so there must be something wrong. When, in fact, that's a contradiction. If anything, there's reason to think the opposite. If things are not as good as they were yesterday, isn't that all the more reason to believe that chances are they will be better next time? Especially for a young man with Dwight Gooden's extraordinary poise.

Now, dear, I want to confess something that I'm sure you're unaware of. For the past few months, every night after you've fallen asleep, I've been going downstairs and watching hundreds of hours of videotapes comparing Doc's pitching motion last year and this year. I didn't tell you about this, because I didn't want to upset you. But you know what I discovered? There is absolutely no difference! It's just that now he's not getting as many batters out. In other words, this is a more *mature* Doc. That's all I'm trying to explain.

But I can just hear you saying, What is the problem, then? Why has she gone away with the children and refused to tell me where she is? I can assure you with every bone in my body that there is no problem. Last year was the greatest year I've ever known, and I feel confident that future years will fulfill that potential, which may necessitate a few minor adjustments in Doc's mechanics, something that a number of qualified people are helping him with. Above all, I beg you not to pin any blame on Mel Stottlemyre, who doesn't even know us.

There's one thing I'm sure of. If you really have something, then almost by definition there are going to be certain times when you don't have it. If I didn't believe that, I wouldn't be so convinced that at this very moment you and I are closer than any two people could possibly be. Someday we'll look back on all this and, with the complex understanding that comes from placing great demands upon ourselves, we'll be able to say, It was nothing.

—Love,

KAY

P.S.: And Doc? He's better than ever.

Summer 1986

One day Sandy came over and we took some beers to Central Park and sat around talking about a cultural figure of the moment, Karen

Finley, a performance artist who did shocking things like putting canned sauerkraut on her bare breasts. One article about her described this act as the breaking of a "taboo," and Sandy said, "*What* taboo? Since when is putting sauerkraut on your breasts taboo? Sleeping with your sister is taboo. Putting sauerkraut on your breasts is just— They don't say, '*We'd rather* you didn't sleep with your sister.'"

The other person everybody in New York was preoccupied with was Dwight Gooden, the Mets' star pitcher, twenty-one-year-old Doctor K. He hadn't been living up to his great 1985 season (24–4, Cy Young Award, led league in strikeouts); there was a vague perception that something was "wrong" with him, and a strong counter-need to suppress that perception. For a time, that need had the status of a genuine taboo. Doc's powers were almost mystically beloved by the fans and press. We wanted to know, but we needed not to know. My chief memory of that season (in which the Mets eventually won the Series) is of a gradual, reluctant surfacing of the question "What's the matter with Doc?" When it first occurred to me to write about this, I had a that-would-be-*bad* feeling that gave me an almost sexual thrill: like, Oooooh, another woman's boyfriend! The thrill wasn't at being mean to Doc but at saying, We've been living in a dream world. Saying that seemed naughty.

Reading the sports pages was like Kremlinology. E.g., the *News:*

> [5/23] Giants . . . pummeled Gooden . . . "It's strange," Gooden said . . . "after the fourth inning I started losing something. I think the temperature changed during the game. It was nice and sunny at first." . . . [6/3] Remember when 10-strikeout games were commonplace for the Doctor? All that has changed. Doc now is willing to settle for groundouts. He has learned that it is a lot easier on his arm. . . . [7/10] "He wasn't out there long enough to get into his game plan," said pitching coach Mel Stottlemyre. "A couple of balls fell in the holes, the next thing you know, it's 4–0. But I'm not worried about Dwight Gooden," Stottlemyre said for the thousandth time this season.

Two days later, Peter Schjeldahl (whose family—wife Brooke, daughter Ada—is always on the cutting edge of Mets-mania) called and said, "So what's your theory about Dwight?" I didn't have one, but he did: "There's something we're not being told—something very specific." (Good all-purpose theory.) This flavor of living amid propaganda inspired me to try doing a piece with drawings of International Doc News.

Oh, well—I was losing heart for the story anyway. By late July it was starting to seem depressing, as if Doc might have some real arm problem.

Then Nicholas von Hoffman started egging me on. He had just moved to New York to research his book on Roy Cohn, and had gotten caught up in the local obsessions; almost every morning he'd call and tell me which newspapers to buy for the best Doc material. What finally prompted me to write was the wishful thinking in a late-August *News* headline, "DOC DELIVERS" (for a lackluster performance), and a dread that in the season's closing weeks the tantalizing story might slip away.

My boyfriend was in California on a long work trip, and I'd been feeling kind of resentful that he was gone all the time, so the Doc propaganda became a spouse's irrational explanation for leaving home. Some of the tortured reasoning about things being better next time came from a newspaper column on the business economy, but I forget which one.

The *New Yorker* couldn't run the story for a couple of weeks; I wanted to root for Doc, but didn't want him to be so good that he'd ruin my story. Then the Mets came up with another spectacular rationalization (for a costly three-run homer Doc gave up to the Giants): (1) It was just the one pitch; (2) the pitch itself wasn't that bad; (3) the batter just happened to be looking for that pitch.

At the time, there was something exhilarating about slightly relaxing our grip on the illusion of perfection. But the next spring was the spring of "GOODEN AGREES TO TREATMENT AFTER A TEST SHOWS DRUG USE." He seems fine now.

"General Pinochet announced

Hands Up

> The President . . . often repeat[s] tales of how much individual farmers get from the federal government. When [an aide] told Reagan recently that a California farmer got $12 million, the President put his hands over his face and said, "What are we doing wrong?"
>
> —*New Republic*, February 16, 1987

One of the worst things you can do is touch your hands to your face—especially the eyes, nose, and mouth; you are giving household staphylococcus germs a free ride. Always avoid touching any part of the face whatsoever with bare hands, as this will just work the stain deeper into the skin and allow it to "set," making it difficult or impossible to remove even with coarse abrasives. Never, under any circumstances, cover the face with the hands. Doing so will not only cut off the supply of fresh oxygen and clog the vents but will block the audience's sight lines as well as those of any downstage members of the cast. Using your hands to conceal your face is strictly against the rules unless you are already the one wearing the blindfold. Be sure not to put both hands over the face while operating a tractor, cultivator, or weed-eater. This is really asking for trouble, because in many non-Western cultures the gesture means something quite different, and could make you conspicuous or even give somebody the wrong idea. Drawing out the poison will then be that much harder to do if access to the face is blocked by the hands, and you will be in a blind spot where the assault team cannot pick up your signal. It is a violation of military courtesy to return a salute by raising the hands and positioning them on the face, even as an empty formality. Taking cover is sometimes a necessity, but the hands should always allow the eyes to distinguish the living from the dead, the nose to detect noxious toxins, and the mouth to admit nourishing fresh-grown produce from the local bivouac area. Although a man running rapidly toward a bank does furnish a poor target, do not forget that tellers are forbidden by statute from releasing funds to anyone whose face is concealed by hands.

These fundamental warnings and strictures all too often go unheeded, thanks to the widespread failure to comprehend that once the hands are placed directly onto the face, they can stick there. Or they can even go right through. Sometimes they come out the back of the head; sometimes they don't. For many, these risks exert a deadly attraction. Casually the hands are lifted, and then, almost before anyone knows what has happened, the hands have settled upon the face. It's dark in there. Cool and dark. Everything suddenly seems so simple. For a while. But after a while, faraway and tantalizing, comes a sound. The idea of a sound touching against the idea of another sound. What is it—a Japanese wind chime?

Don't do it. Don't even think about it.

February 1987

Adam Gopnik had a story scheduled to run in the *New Yorker*'s anniversary issue, which was the last issue Mr. Shawn had edited, and I was trying to bump it out with something topical they'd be forced to run right away. (I liked Adam a lot, and his story, "The Blue Room," was lovely, but I didn't want it to be in that issue at that moment in *New Yorker* history. Bob Gottlieb had just been put in as editor and had brought Adam with him from Knopf—so Adam willy-nilly stood for the new regime.)

The quote about Reagan was in the current *New Republic.* I free-associated for one day, and then told myself to dream more material—actually dreamed the wind chimes. The next day brought one of those lucky coincidences—my trusty infantry manual happened to open to a page about "taking cover." Determined to make some kind of piece, fast, I threw in anything—didn't care about repeating myself with this grab-bag of phrases merged into a surreal surface. Didn't even care what I stole: Frederick Barthelme, one of the writers I was editing, is also one of the funniest improvisational talkers, so I called him in Mississippi and said, "Hi, Rick, I'm writing a piece about all the terrible things that can happen if you cover your face with your hands. Any ideas?" He said, "They could go right through," and then he said, "It's dark in there," and I copied it all down. Meanwhile I was trying to force another writer to submit a story in case mine didn't work out. Neither of us beat the deadline.

Whatever idea lay behind this piece was so intuitive I had zero sense of how it would come across. I've never written anything else where I was equally prepared to hear it was horrible or great. After turning it in, I had an appalling flashback to a newspaper photo of Mr. Shawn, just after being forced to resign, leaving the Algonquin Hotel with his hands shielding his face from the camera—and thought, Oh, God, did I subconsciously write this about *that*? Maybe I should take it back. . . . Asked a colleague whose judgment I respected, who said it was paranoid to think anyone would make the connection, and if they did—well, I'd just blend in with all the other people who were behaving insanely out of distress at what was happening to the *New Yorker.* So I decided to trust that the piece had its own little self-contained rationale, which could be taken at face value.

More Unwelcome News

> The Air Force Logistics Command ordered its spare-parts buyers to spend as much money as possible in the last 10 days of 1985 because appropriated funds are piling up faster than the Air Force is using them, according to defense officials.
>
> —*Washington Post,* January 2, 1986

> At the House Foreign Affairs Committee . . . it got downright poetic. . . . Waxing eloquent about the ingratitude of all peoples toward their military forces in peacetime, [Rep. Robert] Dornan paraphrased Rudyard Kipling's poem "Tommy Atkins." . . . Rep. Mervyn Dymally . . . shot back with a little cautionary verse from Shakespeare.
>
> —*New York Daily News,* December 10, 1986

It was peacetime: Tuesday, December 31, 1985. And it was lunchtime. But as Air Force purchasing specialist Major Jim Spender left his desk and wedged himself into the elevator with the midday crowd leaving early for New Year's Eve, his mind was uneasy. A piece of paper was burning a hole in his pocket: a procurement memo from his boss, dated December 20, ordering him to spend $50,000 on spare parts by the end of the month—or else!

During the past week and a half, he had worked heroically to meet the deadline, but much of his time had been consumed just trying to think of unusual spare parts that no one else in the command might have thought of ordering already. He knew his colleagues had all received the same memo, and there was intense competitiveness over who could come up with more orders for spare parts that other people hadn't realized the need for. That first day when the memo came down, he had really lucked out. He was doing deep-breathing exercises in the hall outside his office—a technique he had read about in a CIA psych. ops. manual called *Breath Control and Guerrilla Warfare,* whose lessons he had adapted to relax his mind and visualize obscure spare parts. As he was exercising, he accidentally hit the wall thermostat with one arm, knocking off the clear plastic cover. When he stooped to pick it up, he saw that he had also knocked off and then stepped on a small, circular piece of brushed chrome that served as a decorative concealment over the mechanism of the temperature indicator and was now slightly bent out of shape.

Quickly he replaced the plastic cover (so nobody would notice the thermostat and get any bright ideas), took the damaged part into his office, whipped a requisition form off the stack on his desk, and typed in a description: "Disk, ornamental, chrome, brushed, thermostat." Mindful of the memo's warning that haste should not override "constraints of law, directives, prudence, and bona fide need rules," he did not try to inflate the cost but neatly divided the part's square footage into the market value of an F-111, tacked on the minimum 300 percent for "Miscellaneous Closing Costs (Estimated)," and sent his secretary scurrying down to Processing with the requisition.

Well and good—but the thermostat coup had used up only $49,000 of his quota. In all honesty he could not have justified ordering more than twelve gross of the disks. So he still had a grand to get rid of, and now he would have to work overtime on New Year's Eve. He glanced at the pile of catalogues on his desk. Spiegel, Sporty's Tool Shop, Touch of Class . . . he had long ago picked them clean for spare-parts ideas. He had even ordered cable TV for his office, at his own expense, to get Home Shopping Network, but whenever he watched it they were offering gold or sterling neck chains—just the whole chain, no parts. He wondered what these people did who ordered nothing but a chain and then broke a link or a catch and were stuck without the proper replacement part at hand. He supposed they let it lie around unused in the back of a dresser drawer, or took it some distance from home to a repair middleman who made them wait weeks and weeks until the requisite part came in from a wholesaler. He ruminated on the terrible wastage that typified American life.

As the elevator finally released him he was still deep in meditation, and began to patrol the network of Pentagon hallways, his "All Areas" clearance badge flapping gently against his breast pocket and rendering his almost trancelike movements smoothly unbroken even at security checkpoints. When he had first come to work in the famous five-sided building, he had been warned against getting lost. But now he wanted to get lost, so lost that his mental rhythm would drift loose of the rigid, prosaic syntax that had too long constricted it: wing, airplane, aluminum. . . .

After a time (later on he would not be able to remember how long a time, or what route he took) he found himself in a strange concourse of little shops. What appeared to have once been an attractive, bustling arcade—drugstore, passport photos, hosiery—was now a deserted row of tarnished brass storefronts, half-obliterated signs, dust-clouded display windows: an economic doom, he guessed, wrought by the labyrinthine architecture of the very place that was begging its employees to spend money.

Yet even as he thought this, he saw that one shop door stood ajar. A crudely lettered cardboard sign hanging from the doorknob read "AUCTION GALERIA—ANTIQUES."

As he stepped inside, overgrown fern tendrils brushed his face; for a moment he caught the sickening, slightly sweet aroma of cheap potting soil. Stacked C-ration cases towered to the ceiling. In the doorway to a back room, beaded strings formed a bizarre curtain, dangling in the humid air. A macaw screeched at him from its perch.

"May I to show you something especial?" The man who parted the curtain spoke with a slight accent. Major Spender could not place it, but he noted the American boots and hand-me-down National Security Council sweatshirt favored by operatives of the Nicaraguan Contras' counterintelligence service. The man held a tin mess-kit plate filled with tiny blue chili peppers. "Small snack," he said apologetically, and extended the plate to his customer. "Please be joining me." But the mere sight of the chilies seared the major's throat, and he declined with a smile.

Briefly, the man dropped his eyes to Major Spender's clearance badge, on which "Purchasing" could be clearly read. "I let you have some beautiful TOW antitank missiles," he said. "Guaranteed offensive capability, merely five thousand dollar each."

The major explained that his budget was unfortunately limited to $1,000 and that anyway he was just looking.

"Many valuable wrenches and toilet seats," said the man in a sly, insinuating tone. "On sale, five hundred each, definite antiques."

The major guessed he was being teased—a ritual test before sincere negotiation could take place. To show good faith, he bought one of the seats (which did look very old), wrote out a Pentagon chit, and then said he was looking for more unusual parts. "Something out of the ordinary."

"I have maybe one such rarity," said the man. "My assistant will bring." He raised his voice to a shriek: "Ronquita!" Abruptly the curtain parted; listening on the other side the whole time must have been this gorgeous Latino girl. She wore a sarong made from parachute silk, secured at the waist with a belt braided from what looked like the paper strips the major had seen in the Pentagon shredder room. Slung across her shoulder was an M-16. The man noticed Major Spender's surprised glance at the weapon and remarked casually, "For cosmetic purposes solely. Many shoplifters." The girl stood there, impassive, sullenly scratching her trigger finger. Then the man barked an order in Spanish. She went into the back room and brought out a Maxwell House coffee can. Prying off the plastic lid, she took out a small sheet of yellowed paper and laid it for display on one of the C-ration cases.

"A most interesting curiosa," said the man.

Major Spender bent over to peer at the paper. On it was a single line of old-looking handwriting—"Unwelcome news, nipping like a frost, making soldiers hang their heads"—surrounded by doodles and crossed-out stuff. The major's heart pounded. He recognized the line at once as unmistakably the work of William Shakespeare. It was staggeringly obvious that the Bard's characteristic diction and imagery were stamped on every word. It was obvious because Major Spender, with no formal training as an Elizabethan scholar, was nonetheless an expert in parts. Show him a part and he could instantly extrapolate the whole. He saw exactly how this line, with its crudely exposed nuts and bolts of language, would slot smoothly into an overall assembly by means of mechanisms unique to the Swan of Avon; how the line's configuration of incompleteness dictated other lines it must interlock with to form scenes and acts, plots and themes, all functioning as a single magnificent machine. Nor did he have the slightest reason to doubt that the writing was Shakespeare's own hand.

Guardedly, he murmured a noncommittal "Hmm."

"You have disappointment," said the man. "I am sorry." He returned the paper to the coffee can. "We have other shop in basement of the White House. Perhaps there you are finding better bargains."

"No, wait," said the major. "Possibly it could come in handy. I'll give you five hundred for it."

"Ixnay on the humanitarian aid. Twenty million."

Major Spender was no loose cannon. "I don't have that kind of authorization," he said. "I'd have to go back to the office and get a special voucher. And it's New Year's Eve—I'm not even sure if anybody's still there right now. Can you hold it for me till after the holidays?"

He did not hear the answer, for in the next moment he did something the motive for which would forever baffle him. Maybe he was afraid he sounded weak and vacillating. Maybe he was just adventuristically proving his machismo to Ronquita, who was contemptuously fiddling with the safety on her M-16. Or maybe he sincerely wanted to help his country. He suddenly reached out and took one of the chili peppers and popped it into his mouth.

When he came to, back in his office, his upper respiratory system felt blowtorched and his desk was littered with paper cups from the water cooler. He could not remember drinking the water, or his return route, or anything else following the fateful pepper. The emergency-call light on his phone was blinking.

"*Bueno!*" said a hysterical voice when he picked up. It was Commander Zero, the White House switchboard operator. "Nobody is answering there. Now we have a big push here to wrap up the Ironside Project *pronto.* We are missing one vital part. Just a line of dialogue we are needing for Act Two, Scene Four, a military scene. I can't tell you the plot—it's classified—but we have 'IRONSIDE colon' and then we need 'Da-da da-da, da da-da da-da, da da-da da-da da-da.' You can scrounge something? Whatever fits good—we can plug it in and be ready for to roll."

Major Spender said he would get right on it.

"It is a nipping and a vicious breeze," he scribbled frantically on a pad. No, that wasn't it. "Air nips, methinks, if soldiers think it so. Nippingly, hounds of news do bring bad air. The frost nips like a dog and icy news laps at the soldiers' faces like a tongue. It is a nipsome and a chilly news. The hangdog news doth nip, unwelcome beast."

He thought he had the gist of it. But with a precisely tooled part like this, "gist" was a contradiction in terms. *Damn it,* he thought, *I'm a purchasing specialist, not an iambics engineer.* Despairingly, he put his head in his hands. *If only I'd been able to give that Contra the twenty million. . . .*

But "if only" is a concept with no relevance to the geopolitical struggle for total dominance in the field of Shakespeare studies. And so it was that New Year's 1986 saw a new and dangerous tilt in the balance of power.

> LONDON—A former civil servant claims he has conclusive evidence that a play entitled *Edmund Ironside* was actually written by William Shakespeare. . . . It predates the first recognized Shakespeare play, *Titus Andronicus*. . . . The claim . . . came a month after an American scholar at Oxford said he had identified a new poem by the Bard. . . .
>
> "'Unwelcome news, nipping like a frost, making soldiers hang their heads'—that kind of idea and that kind of phraseology is in both plays. It cannot be
>
> —United Press International, January 2, 1986

These are only the facts that have come out so far, from Major Spender's testimony before the investigating committee. I find these revelations mind-boggling. It defies credulity that the White House could be running a covert Shakespeare scholarship operation if even switchboard-rank officers knew about it. Also, it's hard to swallow that if the Contra group in the Pentagon basement had the original manuscript, the exact same thing somehow ended up a day or two later in the hands of a third country, England. And if it fit in a "coffee can," where did the rest of the play come from? Furthermore, without wanting to assign credibility where none has so far been proved, it is inconceivable that not one single person in the Administration ever took the responsibility of stepping forward to inquire if the international English poetry trade was being manipulated by foreign zealots on the President's staff. In any case, even if one accepts that global domination of Shakespeare studies is a legitimate foreign policy objective, this is an extremely curious way to go about it.

It is excellent that the investigation has already brought so much information to light. But there must be facts that have not come out yet.

All of 1986

In January 1986, in Florida, the same issue of the *St. Petersburg Times* ran those two items—about surplus Air Force appropriations and an alleged discovery of a Shakespeare play—and I turned them into a straightforward, silly story about an Air Force purchasing specialist who finds a bogus Shakespeare manuscript in a derelict antique shop in the Pentagon basement. The *New Yorker* bounced it back, saying they didn't see any logical reason for Shakespeare to be in it. Six months later, a *Times* item, "EX-OFFICERS ACCUSE CONTRA CHIEFS OF SIPHONING OFF U.S. AID MONEY," inspired me to turn the antique shop into a Contra money-making scam being run in the Pentagon basement. Another rejection: Still not funny. Sent it to Roy Blount to see if he had any pointers, and got back a postcard of detailed suggestions, beginning, "Assuming we are not at war by the time it comes out, I think it takes too long to get to the twist."

In November, the Iran-Contra deal blew open. I had predicted it! If the *New Yorker* had run my story, they would have looked brilliant! *Uh-ohhh, now she thinks she's psychic. . . .* (Of course, the North-Poindexter crowd later denied that their offices were in the White House "basement." The press must have gotten that word from the same cliché pool I did.) I rewrote the thing with new details about TOW antitank missiles, etc., and got another rejection: Still not funny, Shakespeare still baffling. Michael Kinsley almost bought it for the *New Republic* but said the surplus appropriations hook was hackneyed press fodder, a pseudostory that comes out every year. (Yes, he's the same guy who encouraged me to attack Pentagon overspending in the dog-boarding case. Typical of him to distinguish between a legitimate target and a trumped-up one.) I like a rejection based on superior expertise, so gave up on the story. Then in December the Congressmen on the House Foreign Affairs Committee, investigating Iranscam, started quoting Kipling *and Shakespeare* at each other. Success at last!—just add a few references to that, resubmit . . . But no—now the Shakespeare was "overexplained and no longer funny."

GQ printed it with a quintessential magazine illustration—a yellow-and-red drawing of a parrot and a Contra temptress, which really suited the trashiness of the storytelling. Maybe the deconstructionists are right about the dread seductions of narrative: it was like a railroad train I couldn't get off. As it hurtled forward, I glimpsed with envy a brief, elegant comment in a letter from Lynn Caraganis: "On the news last night they said George Bush announced he had 'protested in private about McFarlane's trip to Iran.' He may have said something like, 'How come Bud gets to go via Switzerland?'"

Poll

Which of these descriptions do you feel describe Lieut. Colonel North?

SOMEONE I WOULD WANT TO MARRY MY DAUGHTER		
Describes	*Does not describe*	*Not sure*
26%	57%	17%

—From a poll cited in *Time*

Dad doesn't know this, and he's going to be furious when he finds out, but I think Oliver North is the guy who married my sister. I can't be a hundred percent sure, but I would describe him as such, and I'm almost positive it was the same guy. (If you already have a predisposition to accept this, or are willing to take my word for it, don't even bother to read on. Just call 1-900-555-TRUE to have your vote tabulated immediately. There is a fifty-cent charge for each call.) He was going under the name Bobby George North back then, but I recognize the personality structure. During the time all this happened, around 1984–85, my sister was living down in Cocoahole, Florida, and kept the marriage a secret from the family, but was constantly calling me long-distance to tell me about this guy she was seeing, Bobby George North, and how he was driving her crazy with his manipulations, cheating on her and then sweet-talking her when she got mad. (If you find these facts, including names, dates, and places, to be plausible so far, please don't hesitate to organize a group of friends to send large numbers of supportive telegrams to me, c/o Western Union.) He was always telling her he had to go to Miami on business, and then he'd stay away for days or weeks, and when he came back he'd order her not to question him about his business and then he'd butter her up some more. I started trying to get her to break up with him and come stay with me in New York until she got over him (and if you think that gives me some personal motive, casting doubt on my credibility, simply call 1-900-555-HMMM to register your temporary suspension of judgment at this time until you have finished reading this and weighed all the evidence), but she said that Bobby George was in many ways a little boy and he needed her. (Do you have the feeling that I'm basically an honest person? I know you can't answer that for certain, but do you get a general sense of probity and forthrightness from the way I express myself?

YES_____ NO_____

Don't forget to put a check mark or, preferably, your initials in the appropriate space, then clip and send to CBS News Poll, New York, New York 10019.)

Now, the rest of what I know I only learned after it was all over and my sister told me the whole truth. In the fall of 1984, she finally gave Bobby George an ultimatum, because she was pregnant, so they went to Community Gardens Church and got married. She says they never got any papers proving they were married, and she now suspects that it wasn't a real church and Bobby George had just staged the whole thing by renting a building and hiring some drifters to decorate it like a church and pose as ministers. (If this sounds mind-boggling, is there some other explanation you could come up with that would account for her not having the papers? If so, why not take a few moments to jot it down and send it to the *Washington Post*, Op-Ed Page, Washington, D.C. 20071.) To make a long story short, the marriage changed nothing, and Bobby George persisted in his bad behavior even after my sister gave birth to her baby. (Do you believe me now? Even if you feel you've already answered the question, that was a few sentences ago, so keep in mind that you retain the option at any time to call 1-900-555-TRUE to register the complexity of your views as the shifting winds and erosions of public opinion alter your perception of reality.) Finally, sometime in February 1985, Bobby George said he would drive my sister and the baby to the pediatrician. On the way, he pulled up at a Pick Kwik, said he was just going to get a large container of coffee, snuck out the back door of the Pick Kwik, and went to a nearby Trailways bus station, where he'd checked his bags ahead of time. My sister never saw him again. Later it turned out that before he'd left the house he'd given the dog a dog sleeping pill so it couldn't follow him, and it didn't wake up until the next day. (Note that this account reflects a 4 percent margin of error.)

If you are convinced by now that this story is worth pursuing further, even though I can't prove anything, or if you feel that the revelations herein do not provide you with sufficient information to decide whether or not it suggests a continuing and widespread pattern of abuse, including the possibility that this North was the same duplicitous lover-boy who took advantage of *your* sister and then dumped her, please take the trouble to form your own independent polling organization so that the proliferation of opinion may continue to flourish as it must in an open society. Thank you for your patience.

July 1987

Dan Menaker, who had an office next to mine and was funny to be around, once gave me the idea to use 1-800 numbers in something. I was working on this:

> MIND POLICE
> If you care to register disagreement with anything I say, please call the following number: 1-800-URWRONG. The FCC requires that these stupid numbers be inserted throughout everything I say. I ask you—1-800-IANSWER—what better evidence could there be of the totalitarian mentality?
>
> The most important thing in preserving the integrity of your opinion is not to hang out beforehand with anybody who might interfere with what you think. This is the advice I give younger opinion makers, but few of them take it to heart. They will go out for drinks with people who completely disagree with me, and then I'm forced to stand up and be counted.
>
> Don't they realize I have my own independent system for dealing with differences of opinion? Everyone is free to write to me; then I read the letters and have a good hearty laugh at their expense. Sometimes I read the letters aloud to colleagues, like [funny

name], who often drops by my office and sits on the couch all hunched over with his thumbs in his pants cuff so I won't be able to tell if he's going thumbs up or thumbs down.

He always ends up agreeing with me, but his thumbs are smaller and thicker than mine, so the shape of his argument is always quite different. For years I've tried to get him a post somewhere else where he'd really loosen up the stuffy Peter-Pan-collar atmosphere that's everywhere, but no dice. There is still tremendous prejudice in the opinion industry against anyone perceived as a protégé of mine. It's their loss. 1-800-ITISNOT.

Then Oliver North started testifying at the Iran-Contra hearings, most of which I listened to in the office on a bulky old portable radio of Dan's. (It had the improbable brand name "Lloyd's" and had done political scandal duty in the fiction department for years.) When North boasted about his stacks of telegrams and then the news media turned into one big moment-to-moment poll of his popularity, the 1-800 joke had to be pressed into immediate service. (It got changed to 1-900 because those cost fifty cents per call, and I wanted people to pay through the nose for succumbing to opinion madness.)

There was a nagging technical problem of how to get from the *Time* poll, with the fathers who did or didn't want their daughters to marry North, to the two sisters I wanted to write about. These tiny obstacles are the ones that make you blank out and almost give up. Then I ran into Adam Gopnik in the hall and babbled my problem, and he said instantly, "'Dad's gonna be so mad when he finds out. . . .'"

This was fun to write. An implausible narrative full of excuses for why it doesn't exactly sound convincing is an easy form. You can keep commenting spontaneously on your own inept storytelling. Also, I got to write about Florida again. While trying to sell our house there, my brother and I had been in a pursuit-and-evasion car chase with the lawyer for a buyer who was stalling; we finally caught up with him at a Pick Kwik, where he bought coffee and acted skillfully lackadaisical: "Oh, yah, the papers, sure." Family vs. legal duplicity—that was the feeling for the story.

My and Ed's Peace Proposals

Ed and I each have come up with a proposed plan for the cessation of hostilities between the Reagan Administration and our household. Since our plans differ in certain minor respects (Ed taking a somewhat tougher line), we offer both versions, in the hope that they may at least stimulate the Administration to consider negotiations toward ending the past six and a half years of drawn-out mutual aggression and mistrust. This is not a ploy or a farce on our part. We are even putting all our personal problems on the back burner while we press these initiatives. We now task the Administration with showing how sincere *it* is by responding in a spirit of reconciliation and good faith.

MY PLAN

1. Immediate suspension of Elliott Abrams, who will then be reflagged as a Kuwaiti vessel.

2. Unconditional withdrawal of the Bork nomination; Bork allowed to head a Presidential commission on the colorization of film classics.

3. Trade and assistance: As soon as the first two conditions are met, we will give support to the Administration's economic goals by ceasing our costly flow of Mailgrams to the White House, thus freeing funds for disbursement to more productive sectors of the economy and enabling us to stop accepting aid from Ed's mother.

ED'S PLAN

1. Ed given a line-item veto on Presidential rhetoric.

2. Immediate amnesty for Ed's mother, a political prisoner of right-wing mailing lists.

3. U.S. diplomatic relations with puppet regime of Pat Buchanan severed for an indefinite cooling-off period; in return, Ed will use all his influence to halt Latin American incursions by Joan Didion.

4. National plebiscite on secular humanism, to be supervised by elected representatives from four regional productions of *La Cage aux Folles.*

4. Arms reduction: Ronald Reagan to enter into a one-on-one dialogue with Peter Ueberroth to achieve a sixty-day suspension of Mike Scott of the Houston Astros for pitching defaced baseballs. This is just to give Ed an added incentive to abide by the remainder of the plan.

5. Timetable for routine Rorschach and Stanford-Binet testing of President Reagan.

5. Timetable for the election of someone else as President by the end of 1988.

August 1987

Written on jury duty. As my fellow jurors saw me going through the *New York Times*, underlining things adjacent to photos of Daniel Ortega and making numbered lists on a legal pad, they must have thought I was a serious student of the peace process. Reagan's proposals didn't seem serious, so the situation seemed to call for another strategic use of the Ed couple, with their self-serving idealism. And the Column A versus Column B format in the *Times* was a new structure to play around with.

Dan Menaker reminded me of a great phrase that had come up in the Iran-Contra hearings: "task with." General Secord, for instance, had been tasked with certain things. High time this usage entered standard English.

When the piece came out, a lot of friends told me they liked the Elliott Abrams joke. It's kind of a bad Carson monologue joke, but why should we liberals be more fastidious than Abrams? I'm sorry I didn't put in an Orrin Hatch joke. I was writing for people who shared all the same beefs and wanted to see them listed with absolutely no sense of proportion.

Pat Robertson's Catalogue Essay for a New Exhibition of Paintings by David Salle

> Mr. Robertson had . . . a dramatic religious experience. . . . "I walked across a curtain to a whole new life," he says now. "I understood why I was here, I understood my purpose, I even understood modern art."
>
> —*Wall Street Journal*, October 6, 1987

1

Here is a young painter who may be said to represent the finest traditions of the University of London Graduate School Art Appreciation Program and the Christian Broadcasting Network School of Fine Arts, and if that is not word for word what it says on his résumé provided by the Mary Boone Gallery, under whose caring aegis this show takes place, who are we to let a few minutiae distract us from the powerful statements in the other 99 percent of these colossal paintings?

For here is a young man whose controversial work cries out to us for understanding. Let us rise above his minor details, let us open our hearts to what he might be trying to tell us, let us see how even the titles of his paintings speak to us as in tongues on our own pain and life experiences. *The Wildness of Oats. How Many Miles Is It to the Combat Zone? Now Another Distortion. Sharks in a Feeding Frenzy.*

But my goodness gracious, how the super-sophisticated have hounded him with their criticisms. How they look down their noses every time he traces something. Yes indeed, he has traced the figure of the front-line soldier in *Combat Zone* from a war comic. And I say to you, does the Lord distinguish between the love that a man puts into tracing something faithfully to the way his Maker caused it to be made and the love that another man puts into drawing something from his own God-given imagination or rendering it freehand the way it appears to him in the light that the Almighty created on the First Day? Is not tracing just as much an act of commitment and obedience? For is not repetition equally, if not more so, an act of faith and humility? Amen. And did the Lord not make not only the soldier alive and in his foxhole but also the war comic and the very newsstand whereat the war comic is sold, and is it not just as much an example of the workings of Divine Grace if a man, also himself created by God, comes along and buys the war comic and then later casts it into the gutter, whereupon along comes this young David, with his eye on the same gutter, and singles out the war comic from amid the useless rubble of stones?

2

It makes me ashamed, as David's fellow man, to bring up the media's cruel attack on these paintings, which are many feet high and wide, as nothing more than behemoth party invitations. Yes, there are surely parties in the art world, and at those parties there is liquor. Yes, a handful of people may say to themselves, "David is going to be at the party, so count me in, and the Devil take the hindmost!" But to conclude, as some have done, that this young man bears the burden of responsibility for all the liquor consumption in the art world, to say his true vocation is that of "liquor courier," is an unfair calumny unless you can prove it.

Furthermore, let us pause and ask ourselves just why it is that we Americans expect our artists and their dealers, friends, and collectors to hold to a higher standard of morality than the rest of us.

3

Now, there are other people who honestly and without hypocrisy raise a moral issue that is a little more legitimate. These people would look at this series of works called *Nudes: 19:12–29* and find it sinful to paint the figure of a woman naked, in all the many postures of temptation on a Colonial settee of the type that might be found in a Christian home, and then to apply washes of dark colors that make it hard to see the truth of Divinely created flesh—and not only that, but then to glue onto each canvas some household object so dreadful that it would not be tolerated in any Christian home, thus most selfishly diverting the viewer's eye from the woman's God-given minor details.

I know the people who cannot appreciate this kind of art. They are loving people. I know that because I have been there myself. But then I searched my soul, and behold, I found that extra bit of compassion that allowed me to say, "David, I understand." And that is why I have come to believe that this young man has earned a place on the list with Albers, Arp, Balla, Beckmann, Boccioni, and so on. Like these other moderns, he prompts us to the highest response that we, as good people, can give to the works of our fellow man: Forgiveness.

October 1987

One day a clipping arrived in the mail: the Pat Robertson quote, with its theological anticlimax, "I even understood modern art." Written on it was a note—"Your kind of prose"—from Joel Conarroe. (He should know—he used to be head of the Modern Language Association of America.) This was a discerning gift and an irresistible premise. I called Sandy to tell him about it, and that I was going to write it up as an analysis of David Salle's paintings. Sandy said, "Why don't you do it as Pat Robertson's Guide to the Galleries? That way you could get a lot more stuff in." This was an instance of counterhelp—a suggestion that usefully polarizes you to what you really want to do. The strength of my resistance to his idea told me something. Having an excuse to write about Salle was exciting. People in New York didn't sit around talking about what was at the galleries; they sat around talking about whether David Salle was any good. You had to have an opinion. But I didn't know what I thought. *Mmmm, trouble.* Also, I'd met Salle at the Schjeldahls' and liked him (he had an unusual laugh, like a cough), so there was another *frisson* of trouble—wondering whether he'd be annoyed at what I wrote.

The previous winter I'd seen his paintings for the first time, at the Whitney Museum. They were big, they were full of references to other pictures, and they were cryptic in a nerve-racking way, like "asking about how do I envision probably the getting together of the two Koreas." They just seemed like too much trouble. *What—I have to deal with all this now?* Then, in the spring, a show of watercolors—all variations on one idea: a nude with weird little images superimposed. These were easier to take in, and I thought, Well, maybe this was an obvious road to go down and nobody else had the guts to go down it because it seemed too obvious. I asked Peter Schjeldahl about this, and he said, "Other painters have done it, but none of them have done it with his concentration. It's like, he builds a car and leaves out the engine—*and it runs anyway.*" I repeated this in a conversation with Adam Gopnik, and he said, "The reason it runs is because people like you and Peter Schjeldahl are running along underneath, carrying it."

I didn't have a coherent way of thinking about these paintings, but the attacks on them as cynical image-playback didn't seem right. I'd played back some images myself, and in fact what had initially exhausted me in Salle's work was its earnestness; it seemed to demand that I kitty up an equal amount of the same. And now Pat Robertson was demanding "forgiveness" and "compassion" for "a few minor details"—premarital sex, exaggerated credentials as a "tax lawyer" and University of London "graduate student," and a distorted claim to "combat service" in Korea. One source had described his wartime job as "liquor courier." On *Nightline* Robertson's idea of a sincere response was to redefine *all* of Korea as "a combat zone." It seemed that Salle the Aesthetic Antichrist was about as profound a concept as Robertson the Spiritual Leader.

This mirror logic then dictated that if I gave Salle credit for moral decency, I had to give Robertson credit for art appreciation. He "understood modern art"—fine, so let him explicate these paintings for me. That was trouble, because I was writing double-blind, as ignorant of how Robertson's preaching would sound as of what could be said for Salle. Of course, I could have done research, but I wasn't interested in parodying Robertson or satirizing Salle. It was more fun and trouble to let a few shreds of information serve, and see where they would lead. All I had was "tracing" (had read somewhere that Salle traced certain images) and a generic sense of evangelical repetition. But you know, in a way, come to think of it, weren't they the same thing? Bluffing through a religious rationale for Salle's paintings, I started to feel convinced by my joke argument. (Told this to Peter, and he said, "Now you know what art critics do.")

My aim was to rise to the level of sophistication of the paintings, but I had no conviction about where that level was. (Sometimes pieces end up as pathetic souvenirs of your original ambitions.) And there's a comedy-writing inertia that's hard to keep resisting. (The "liquor courier" reference is opportunistic, and the reverse moralizing about naked women too easy.) But I was happy to be able to arrive at that one sentence about paintings I didn't understand: "David, I understand." I couldn't get there in my own voice, but I could as "Pat Robertson." When David Salle read the story, this process was all he saw—maybe because he'd never heard of Pat Robertson.

I didn't have any wider intentions, but in hindsight—here's a certain cultural situation. Here's this guy making his paintings, doing his job, and being lionized and chewed up by the art public; so he's getting millions of dollars, but if "Pat Robertson" has Christian compassion for him, why not? And the rest of us are under pressure to have an opinion about the art. The piece is just an artifact of pressure. After I wrote it, the pressure was off me, and I actually had an authentic response to the art, but what that was is irrelevant here.

A Lot in Common

On January 10, 1941, at Piedmont Hospital in Atlanta, my mother wrote in the space for my first name on my birth certificate: "Annabelle." She was from Philly, but went down South with my father when the Army assigned him to Fort McPherson, and she must have gotten carried away. When she snapped out of it, she renamed me for her younger sister Vera. My baby book, bound in pink cloth, *Our Baby's First Seven Years*, was a present from Aunt Vera, and still has her congratulations card pasted in it:

> May life bring *EVERY* joy to bless
> That tiny "dream of *HAPPINESS*!"

The book has a page for Baby's First Gifts, and my mother filled it in with her neat secretarial-school penmanship: "Bathinette—Granma. Toys—Granpa. Bunting—Aunt Vera. White wool shawl—Aunt Laura. Gold cross and chain—Ondine and Charlie O'Donnell. Baby hot water bottle—Mary Virginia Stealey. Gold heart necklace—Atlanta Q.M. Depot gang. Silver orange juice cup—Daddy. Sweater, cap, and booties—Mr. and Mrs. King (grocer). Piggie bank—Aunt Thelma." On the page for Favorite Toys, my mother wrote, "Horace the Horse" (a red stuffed horse with a white string mane). "At eleven months, Ronnie 'loved' it and sat on it." (I was nicknamed Ronnie so Aunt Vera wouldn't have to be Big Vera.)

When *Our Baby's First Seven Years* was full—when seven years' worth of physical development, food preferences, vocabulary growth, trips, and names of playmates had been duly organized, recorded, and put away—my life was on the brink of shapelessness, bereft of a unifying principle, vulnerable to any dangerous pattern that might come along and attach itself to my future in seven-year cycles of bad luck or a seventy-seven-year evil spell. But on that very day, my seventh birthday, January 10, 1948, someone I would meet thirty-five years later, a friend of mine named Donald, was born. This turn of fortune took place in a postwar New Jersey suburb, or maybe it was Brooklyn. His parents must have named him after the Hollywood song-and-dance man Donald O'Connor, who had been doing a series of low-budget Universal musicals as the juvenile lead opposite such starlets as Ann Blyth and was destined to make the Francis the Talking Mule movies.

Back in Philly, I celebrated many January 10ths with my best friend, Marie, whose parents owned a greeting-card shop. (After school, I'd help her put price tags on the cards with tiny oval clips, making fun of the verses—"May life bring *EVERY* joy to bless"—and then we'd go sit on a park bench and draw pictures of women wearing spike heels and those seamed stockings with squared-off reinforcements up the backs of the ankles.) One birthday she gave me a record album of fairy tales read by some actor; and whenever we listened to "Sleeping Beauty," as the Prince approached the briar hedge that had grown higher and higher till it covered the castle where lay the Princess in her hundred-year sleep, Marie would stop the record and intone, "He came to the edge of an impen—, an impen—, an impen—, an impenetrable forest."

On January 10, 1949, after Donald's first birthday party, a gathering of relatives at home, wherever that was, he fell asleep on the sofa; and as his mother carried him to his crib, tucked him in, and kissed his toys goodnight, he half woke to the rustling of her full-skirted cocktail dress of changeable taffeta, a popular fabric of the period, shimmering black green black green black green black in a sensuous poetry of flux which made a lifelong impression on him. I don't know how I know this, but in that moment he internalized a blissful, bamboozling mockery of his own intellectual rigor. When he turned five—January 10, 1953—his kindergarten teacher had him sent to a nearby college or university for IQ testing, a fad of the era. Little Donnie was seated in front of a board with different geometric-shaped holes in it, given a selection of geometric blocks, and told to fit each block in the correct hole. "You must be joking," he said, as with a sweep of one small hand he sent the blocks flying.

Bobby Fischer used to say things like "Crash!" and "Kaboom!" when he captured pieces. At fourteen, he won the U.S. Chess Championship—on January 7, 1958, just three days before my seventeenth birthday. He was a mysterious intimate—a peer I knew of but didn't know. A better me, out there untouchable. Hazel-eyed Bobby, however, was not the one whose passage would intersect with mine. He had been born on March 9th (or, according to one source, 12th), on a life path to Brooklyn, Cleveland, *I've Got a Secret,* Mar del

Plata, Stockholm, Cuba by telex, Zagreb, Spassky, silence. Not even close.

On January 10, 1963, Donald's fifteenth birthday, his parents gave him a Raleigh English bike. He made his preferred sandwiches (peanut butter and marshmallow fluff), lashed his collection of forty-fives to the bike rack, and left home, cycling due west through Pennsylvania. Near the Maumee River in northwest Ohio, on the outskirts of Defiance, with 714 miles on the odometer, he finally realized that being a ward of the state wasn't all it was cracked up to be, and retraced his route. (I'm sure this is right about the 714, because it was also Joe Friday's badge number.)

That year, I was just out of the University of Pennsylvania and living in New York for the first time. My younger brother, Steve, was studying bad-younger-brother behavior, hanging around the city and getting in trouble. On my birthday we went to the Five Spot and heard Roland Kirk play weird instruments he'd invented and named—stritch and manzello. I don't want to name the deep trouble my brother got into around that time; it scared me, and one night I refused to let him stay in my apartment even though it was raining. I still think about this, although he forgave me and later a psychiatrist told me science couldn't say what I should have done.

Donald spent his twentieth birthday—January 10, 1968—buying a mattress for his first New York pad. He was carrying it back from Dixie Foam, balanced on his head, when he heard rolling thunder. The hard rain that had been predicted for five years began to fall, saturating the foam and turning it into a giant, burdensome, oppressive household sponge. He became a feminist.

I don't remember much about my birthdays through the 1970s, but probably they had something to do with sex.

By Donald's twenty-sixth birthday—January 10, 1974—he had wandered out to L.A. Some girlfriend called him that afternoon and asked him to meet her in Fitting Room No. 7 in the lingerie department at Bullock's, in Westwood. When he pulled the curtain, he found her in there wearing nothing but a lacy black garter belt, mesh stockings, spike heels, and an apron, bending over a chafing dish and a lighted can of Sterno, making his favorite dessert, crêpes with Clementine orange sections and Cointreau *flambé:* mother, sister, hostess, lover. . . . Bullock's pressed charges. Neither Donald nor the girlfriend served any time, but the store's inhospitality so aroused his anti-bureaucratic temperament that he stopped feeling guilty about frittering away his life at the track.

At Santa Anita, where he went most mornings, the trainers and stablehands welcomed his presence around the stalls, for he had a way with the horses. His magic was to call them by names he made up instead of the monikers laid on them by the owners. One day, after Donald had made his usual pre-race visit to the paddock, a magnificent chestnut stallion who had not lived up to his potential (neither would I if I were on the books as Can't Get Arrested), having heard for the first time what he must have felt all along was his true name, went out smoking, sprinted clear along the inside, was in full flight at midstretch, and crossed the wire with something left—winner by six lengths in the Nature vs. Nurture Futurity. This, of course, was the famed champion henceforth known unofficially as Impenetrable.

Once a few stories like that got around, Donald's services were widely sought for consultations and christenings. Among his successes over the next decade were High IQ, the semiretired fourteen-year-old he nicknamed High Heels to inspire her stunning comeback in the 1975 Bobby Fischer Memorial Sweepstakes; 1976's Dixie Derby sensation, Marie, a big bay mare who had suffered from an aging crisis until Donald tactfully called her Philly; Changeable Taffeta (the first thoroughbred yearling he was hired to name), who in 1977 swept the Cross and Chain Handicap and the Silver Orange Juice Cup; Booties, who won in a waltz after crashing the 1979 Dragnet Invitational; Stritch and Manzello, the siblings who took win and place for a combined purse of $850,000 in the 1981 Sterno Hospital Classic; and the 40–1 long shot who captured the 1982 Piggie Bank Stakes, the amazing Just a Coincidence.

On Donald's thirty-fifth birthday—January 10, 1983—his secretary made a list, for thank-you notes, of the presents he got (and I believe these touched his heart more than the huge fees he commanded): white cashmere saddle blanket—Calumet Farm; gold ID bracelet—Mom and Dad; silk-covered hot-water bottle in black and green stripes, racing colors of Grimm Stables—Grimm brothers; silver horse-insignia roach clip—Chet (groom, Pimlico); greeting card with verse ("May life bring *EVERY* joy to bless/*Ese pequeñito sueño de FELICIDAD!*")—Angel Cordero.

January 10, 1988, was my forty-seventh birthday, Donald's fortieth. Some years ago he had wandered back east, to New York, and made his home here, and we'd met through my boyfriend, Jimmy, a photographer who had taken his picture. When we first found out we had the same birthday, we didn't make a big deal out of it, but as we became friends it seemed more and more significant. This year, we discussed offering ourselves for a new kind of study by those people in Minnesota who studied twins. Our hypothesis was that the many similarities in our lives formed a pattern; that discovering the pattern made us feel happy; and that our case might provide valuable data for investigating the phenomenon of friends reared apart. But we were afraid of being rebuffed as astrology cranks, or as frauds who had subjectively distorted the truth out of pure longing to have a lot in common. So, with a sweep of his hand and mine, we sent the scientific method flying, and threw a party.

December 1987–January 1988

> Long after the liner has been put in drydock
> The wish still steers the rudder of its will.
> They are carting away the remains of a novel
> Two people worked on for years. . . .
>
> —Howard Moss

Howard Moss had also been the *New Yorker*'s poetry editor, and his office was two doors away from mine. That fall, I'd been overjoyed to see him back after a leave of absence; a few days later he died. He used to come into my office to bum a cigarette just to hold, and then stand there praising a "gorgeous" poem he'd read—or he might say, "My dentist novel, *Night Cavities*, is almost finished." His book of biographical sketches, *Instant Lives*, was on my mind: "Where will it end, Liszt asked himself, preparing for another whirlwind tour of the musical centers of Europe: Lannion, Vaasa, and Bruges. Getting the piano up on the horses was not the least of his difficulties."

Howard had once told me that an important part of the work of writing is the time when you do nothing, take a walk, read for fun, go to the theater, etc. Here are some things I saw and read in the "spare time" around the writing of this story; it seems now that I'd never have tried it without them:

Burn This, Lanford Wilson's play. Standard premise (and-then-an-insane-guy-comes-in), but it used convention to carve out a big, strange space for the opposite. Joan Allen talked with extreme normalness, John Malkovich with extreme extravagance, and at the end they got together.

"Family," by Harold Brodkey (a Reflections piece in the *New Yorker*). All kinds of mental memorabilia about generations of Brodkey's relatives. Made a literary form out of coincidence and hearsay. About the past but not bound by the past, it had momentum and a final swan dive into conviction.

Prison-Made Tuxedos, a play by George Trow. Two parallel lives. Real-life jazz saxophonist Frank Morgan was onstage, talking and playing music; in alternate scenes, an actor played a satirized version of the author. The two characters never met, but the writing and music made other encounters between them.

"Fordham Castle," in *The Marriages*, a collection of bizarrely symmetrical stories by Henry James. A man banished by his wife as an impediment to her social ambitions is traveling in Europe under a false identity, and guesses that a woman he meets is in the same boat. The "communities in their fate."

"New Year's Eve," by rock critic Lester Bangs (written in 1979, reprinted in a collection of his work, *Psychotic Reactions and Carburetor Dung*, edited by Greil Marcus). Every New Year's Eve he could remember:

1971: I stayed home and read the Bible. No, that's a lie. What I did was go to the drive-in with my girlfriend—all hopped up (me, that is) on vodka and her mother's thyroid pills, totally unable to concentrate on the double feature of *I Drink Your Blood* (starring Rhonda Fultz, Jadine Wong, and somebody merely billed as "Bhaskar") and *I Eat Your Skin* (William Joyce, Heather Hewitt) . . . thinking all night how next morning I was gonna do like Jack Kerouac and just jump in my car eating speed with one hand while flicking the starter with the other and drive drive drive till I splashed through Blakean breakers of light on the golden prows of the Rocky Mountain Shield. Of course I didn't, woke up with a muzzy hangover instead, which is probably just as well: I coulda ended up being John Denver.

"Subconscious Mind," a dance choreographed and performed by Karole Armitage. The sound was a tape of a routine by the hipster comic Lord Buckley, the décor was a few circles and squares of color and light (including a giant square-cut "diamond" ring), and the dancer seemed pulled between the Cool and the Square.

The whole time I was writing, I denied that this story was "really about" Donald Fagen (who does have the same birthday I do). I claimed it was a cool decision to write something to get money for my half of our birthday party; that writing it about the birthday was just a handy modernist trick (make the thing about the process of making the thing, etc.); and that the "Donald" in the story was merely "a construct." *It's all right—all doctors do this.* . . . Then when I finally showed it to him and asked if I could leave his name in, I admitted it was "really about" him. It was an excuse to be romantic about our friendship.

There's nothing more fun than using your work to make a present for a friend. Much more fun than knocking things. Part of the present was giving him a collection of entirely fake memorabilia. The "You must be joking" episode with the blocks came from Nancy Cardozo and Mark Jacobson—their daughter Rae did that. The parts about me and my family, and the last section, are fact.

I'd never written so directly about myself or my family and was scared that the story was nakedly revealing and embarrassing. This isn't the detached feeling you need to fine-tune your own sentences, so I asked Harold Brodkey for help; his fiction seemed emotionally fearless, and he was always using the word "prose" around the office. He taught me to be wary of habitually writing a certain kind of sentence, with a structure he described as "Blah blah blah, *but not really.*" It's a humorist's sentence, which self-destructs—no good when you're trying to say, "Blah blah blah—fantastic though it may seem, *really.*" He also encouraged me to "hint more strongly at the idea of two common souls separated in another life, or something like that." This was the kind of suggestion that emboldens you in what you tentatively, secretly hoped to do. I'd been leafing through Joseph Campbell's *The Hero with a Thousand Faces* (looking for what he had on the Sleeping Beauty story), and had copied out these four sentences:

> Another image of indestructibility is represented in the folk idea of the spiritual "double"—an external soul not afflicted by the losses and injuries of the present body, but existing safely in some place removed.
>
> Sequences of events from the corners of the world will gradually draw together, and miracles of coincidence bring the inevitable to pass.
>
> [Sleeping Beauty] "opened her eyes, awoke, and looked at him in friendship."
>
> All existence . . . may at last be transmuted into the semblance of a lightly passing, recurrent, mere childhood dream of bliss and fright.

Liz Macklin, an editor at the office, got a friend of hers, Arnaldo Sepúlveda, to do the Spanish translation for the verse for Angel Cordero's birthday card. I'd expected anything in Spanish to look romantic, but some of the words looked normal, so I only used half of it. Later Liz said, "To my mind, two of the most beautiful words in Spanish are *brinde* and *alegría*, and you seemed to find them repellent—as if they looked like words for birth control." But then, Arnaldo thought the verse in English had "no schmaltz whatsoever."

III

New Stories
(1987–1996)

Not an Endorsement

We—that is, I and Ed (this is my boyfriend, no relation to the Mayor)—are not endorsing anyone at this time. However, we feel that no harm will be done to any of the announced Presidential candidates if we engage in some "wishful thinking" about a well-qualified man who is too little known outside our home state of New York. If this be unrealistic, perverse, useless, irrelevant, and counter-productive, so be it, though Ed is a bit more realistic than I am.

MY SCENARIO

LATE APRIL: Someone gives Matilda Cuomo a copy of *Women Who Love Too Much*, and she rebels against her subservient, nurturing role and moves out to Colorado to study poetry writing with Allen Ginsberg at the Naropa Institute for eight years—the average term that an intense lust like mine for Mario takes to play itself out. (Note: My subsequent projections do not necessarily hinge on such a dramatic turn of events; this is simply a "best case" scenario. The same result could be obtained by amnesia, a tour of the USSR gone awry, a mistaken identity or twins plot, etc.)

EARLY MAY: Out from under her shadow, Mario looks more desirable than ever. Insists he isn't "available," but men *say* all kinds of things.

MAY 14: "SUPER SATURDAY": I pretend to have a dentist's appointment in Albany, and one thing leads to another.

MAY 15: Mario panics, says I misunderstood his body language, and sends me packing. But there are frequent hangups on the answering machine—I can tell it's him.

JUNE 6: Al Gore has stopped bothering me. A good sign—he probably knows something I don't.

JUNE 7: Mario goes on *Nightline* and gives an impassioned speech asserting his loyalty to his long-standing relationship with Matilda no matter what she does. But Ted Koppel is on the ball; in masterly, tough questioning he manages to suggest that Mario's "denial syndrome" masks a deep-seated fear of change. Mario is furious, showing Koppel got to him.

END OF JUNE: Seeing a lot of Mario. Nothing has "happened" yet, technically, but I'm overwhelmed by the feeling that this thing is bigger than both of us.

JULY 1: Mario being a real tease, sensing his power now. Has taken to wearing a big, wide-brimmed hat and using it to hide his face, like Bob Dylan in *The Last Waltz*. Yet I suspect he wants me to seize control, so he won't have to feel responsible or guilty. As if part of him feels, "It's not bigger than both of us—it's just bigger than *me*."

JULY 17: Mario not thrilled about tagging along with Dukakis, Jackson, Gore, and their wives on trip to Atlanta. Hoping to get him to myself here for a whole week, I make the mistake of trying to pin him down to a definite decision. In a desperate attempt to elude my clutches, he runs away to Atlanta to hang out with his cronies. They need him more than I do, Matilda flies down for a reconciliation (I was just a pawn in their sick psychodrama), and the rest is history.

ED'S SCENARIO

LATE APRIL: Not long after the New York primary, Dukakis, Jackson, and Gore leave the state. This gets them off Governor Cuomo's back. He now has time to catch up on the newspapers, and finds that he ruled out a draft—a subtle misrepresentation of his signal. He clarifies his position as being more complex, less simplistic. Although I, Ed, am far from being a professional politico, the Governor seems to be thinking along the same lines I am—brooding yet dynamically watchful, playing a brilliantly disciplined cat-and-mouse game.

EARLY MAY: I make my move—put out feelers for a Draft Cuomo effort at our weekly tenants' meeting of West Side Glenliving Towers Independent Democrats. The response is impressive (98 percent of those whose second choice is Dukakis favor a Cuomo draft if the combined popular vote for Dukakis, Jackson, and Gore *after* the Oregon primary is not proportionate to their delegate count in the citrus states), so I take on more leadership—hardball negotiations with Elevator Bulletin Board Committee, advance trips to Coast, etc. *Somebody's* going to have to broker this thing.

MAY 14: "SUPER SATURDAY": Huge success with the guest speaker I get for our North Dakota Strategy Tea—Madame Oracula, a psychic, who predicts that Cuomo will receive the nomination when "great Birnam Wood to high Dunsinane hill shall come."

MAY 15: *Forest Hills Diary*, by Mario Cuomo, becomes the focus of our study group.

MAY 16: Still no word from Cuomo about our grassroots support. But a lot of hangups on the answering machine, which constitute indirect authorization. Extremely smart move.

JUNE 6: Dave Garth quits the Gore campaign to make antismoking commercials—so he says. Shrewd guy.

JUNE 7: Cuomo devastating on *Nightline*. Comes off as conscientious yet electable, family man yet political animal, exuding hidden depths of wise omniscience in not showing his hand. Koppel hasn't a clue.

JUNE 8: Duke and Jesse claim confidence after their respective showings in California, but they don't understand the forces of destiny at work.

JUNE 9: Aide to Dukakis releases a weird report that an owl attacked a hawk at midnight near the White House. Duke, a very superstitious man, freaks out, charges omen is a Jesse hoax. Both camps in disarray, giving Mario an excuse to delay endorsement.

JULY 10: Madame Oracula, filling in for Robert Novak on *The McLaughlin Group*, repeats the Birnam Wood prediction she made for the first time at West Side Glenliving Towers Independent Democrats. This makes us look very good with Mario's people, and we are in superb shape going into convention week.

JULY 17: I have the greatest girlfriend in the world! Somehow through her twin sister, who works for Ted Turner in Atlanta, she wangles me superdelegate-at-large credentials to the convention. So I'm right there to play a major role in the healthy, democratic brokering process, the good old-fashioned horse-trading, caucuses and smokers, shakedowns, paternity suits, heavy drinking, threats and deals. When it's all over, I wake up from a blackout in a motel with two itchy tree branches tied to my head for some reason. I can't recall exactly how it happened, but the best man won.

Man and His Watch

> *Esquire*'s promotional advertising . . . will lead off with a picture of a man . . . [in] a sports shirt open to expose a hairy chest upon which nestle nine gold chains with pendants. . . . The . . . copy . . . sets the tone for the campaign to follow: "It may surprise you to learn how few men have the taste or the means to acquire the finer things in life. In fact, fewer than 1 percent of American men spent $1,000 or more on a watch in the past year."
>
> —"Advertising" column, *New York Times*, April 11, 1988

Jack Magnuson braced his big rancher's hands on the glass display case and looked down at the rows of wristwatches. Not that looking meant he was set on buying. He could tell from the slant of sunlight on the Mobil pump across the street that it was exactly one-thirty—time to mosey on home, sit down at the old burled walnut desk in his study, and phone his commodities broker in Chicago, where it was two-thirty, as any damn fool could figure out.

The store manager, Alvin Seltz, stood behind the counter in attentive patience, for Jack Magnuson was the most prominent man in town and a favored customer at Walgreen's, which took pride in its tradition of supplying the Magnuson Ranch with the finest in dishrags, rubbing alcohol, and other sundries. From above the open neck of Jack's plaid flannel shirt, a chest hair drifted down onto the glass countertop. Alvin courteously leaned over and blew it off.

Jack was thinking that he already had Great-Grandaddy's gold pocket watch. Of course, Jack hadn't spent his own money on that; it was a reflection of somebody else's taste and means. Great-Grandaddy had bought it, so the story went, from a peddler on the Chisholm Trail for five dollars. Thirty-five cents if you discounted for inflation. The watch had some sentimental value—it had saved Grandaddy's life when a Comanche axe glanced off it, and Daddy had worn it as ambassador to the Court of St. James's. Still, the resale value wasn't but a couple of hundred dollars.

And now this morning on the telex from New York City, Jack Magnuson's investment counselor had asked him out of the blue whether he'd spent a thousand dollars or more on a watch in the past year. So Jack had got to wondering why he never had, and what it would be like if he did, and whether it was the kind of thing a man ought to do.

He tried to remember watches he'd seen on men he respected—men in a position to know and appreciate the best that life could offer. There was Judge Burleigh, a connoisseur of rare bourbons and fine-looking female civil-liberties lawyers. But the Judge had been in Washington during the New Deal, and still favored the Brain Trust fashion for a dime-store stopwatch worn around the neck on a length of yarn.

Alvin cleared his throat and said, "Any particular one catch your eye, Jack?"

"Well, now, Alvin, I don't know. They all look right nice." He thought of Jody Windermere, trustee of the Grange Hall Art Museum. Considering the impeccable cut and sheer luxuriousness of the string tie Jody had on at the champagne reception for the exhibit of all those fine-looking Minoan pendants, he surely had the wherewithal for the perfect watch. But Jody traveled a lot on museum business, and had picked up the continental curators' style of just carrying an alarm clock in a briefcase.

Alvin was looking awfully eager to oblige, so Jack said, "What is the price range on these?"

"These here are forty dollars." Jack's face fell, and Alvin added,

"These other ones go on down to ten. You can get yourself a pretty good watch for ten dollars, and I wouldn't try to tell you different."

Jack Magnuson knew he could call one of his old girlfriends in Paris and have her send somebody over to that Cartier place, but instinctively he rebelled against the notion that a man couldn't spend a grand on a watch in his own hometown, if he happened to feel like it. Jack wondered if it would count to buy twenty-five forty-dollar watches. He guessed that Coach Whitehead, his hero from his days at Trinity College, Cambridge, would have said that was cheating. Anyway, the Coach had been famous for just drawing the numbers from one to twelve on his wrist with a fountain pen and then telling time by the way the angles of his wrist hairs reacted to momentary changes in atmospheric pressure.

But what about getting a hundred ten-dollar watches? Maybe that would be eccentric enough to qualify as a costly personal statement. Like the time that little operator at Drexel Burnham Lambert had tried to get him to take over Walgreen's and liquidate its assets, and just to spite that sucker he'd gone out and bought himself 14,000 head of prize longhorns for the pure pleasure of seeing the prairie sun burnish their tawny flanks to the fine sheen of a premium motorcar's custom enamel. A hundred watches, though—Alvin would think he'd gone loco. And no way to claim they were presents for the ranch hands; it was common knowledge that all Jack's men had taken up the new Schick disposable watches, grateful that nowadays a man could spend a long hard day out on the range, mending fences till the barbed wire took on the hand-honed keenness and lustrous patina of the finest set of imported kabob-skewers, and then ride home, wash off the dust, put a pot of coffee on to perk, and throw away his watch.

As Jack stood there trying to think of a different excuse for buying a hundred watches without getting a reputation around town as a wastrel frittering away the family fortune on accessories, old Yancy Beeb came into the store for a dozen of the Anchor Hocking pilsner glasses on sale. If there was anybody in this neck of the woods who qualified as a genuine celebrity, it was Yancy, a renowned guide who had once taken Ernest Hemingway on a snipefishing trip. Jack noticed that Yancy didn't have on a watch, so he went over and said howdy, and one way and another he finally worked Yancy around to the subject of watches.

"Used to wear one," said Yancy. "That was years back. And then Papa told me—this was around the time of the snipefishing trip, you know, and he was real mad at me—he told me it was decadent to wear a watch. He said that Coop—that was Gary Cooper, you know—Coop said any real man could tell the time of day just by checking the amount of wear on his boot heels. Well, in spite of the fact that it was Papa talking, that just sounded like plain common sense. So I tried it. Never worn a watch since."

Jack speculated as to how Yancy might be having some fun with him. But to humor the old man, he lifted one foot and bent over to study the heel of his boot, which gave off a fine aroma like the subtlest master blend of calfskin-bound first editions, wet Donegal tweeds, prewar Havana Perfecto stubs, overpriced designer cologne, and burning plastic collectibles. The tiny scratches and abrasions on the heel formed a pattern he'd never noticed before—a pattern unique to that moment, which was two o'clock, three in Chicago, closing time on Wall Street, and sunset on Madison Avenue.

Summer Session

THE TIME: *July 1962.*
THE SCENE: A *screened porch, evening. Sound of crickets.*
THE CHARACTERS:
STEVE *(just graduated from high school)*
RONNIE *(his sister, home from her senior year in college)*
DAD

STEVE: Hey, Dad, didn't we use to have a couple bowling balls?
DAD: What do you want with bowling balls in this heat?
RONNIE: Maybe they're in the garage.
DAD: Don't be silly.

STEVE: Come on, Dad, where are they?

DAD: Don't go in the garage now. What do you want bowling balls for at this time of night?

STEVE: Ronnie has to bowl.

DAD: Aw, what are you talking about?

RONNIE: We're just going bowling.

DAD: What do you mean, bowling? Do you know what time it is?

STEVE: It's only nine o'clock.

DAD: Nine o'— Jesus, what's the matter with you? Your mother's already asleep.

RONNIE: Gee, then I guess we can't bowl in the house. We'll have to go to the bowling alley.

DAD: Nine o'clock at night people don't go bowling. Look at it, it's dark out.

RONNIE: I thought the car had headlights.

DAD: You don't even have bowling shoes. What are you gonna do, bowl in those? You can't bowl in sneakers, you gotta have shoes.

STEVE: Look, Dad, they rent the shoes.

DAD: *Rent?* What, you're gonna wear somebody else's shoes?

STEVE: Everybody does that. They put powder in them.

DAD: What do you know about powder? You're a powder expert now.

RONNIE: Fine, then we'll buy some shoes.

DAD: Oh, you're gonna buy a pair of shoes now for one game.

STEVE: Listen, you rent the shoes, they put powder in them, and you wear them. And you bowl with them. They have these nifty little—

DAD: "Nifty"? "Nifty"? Where the hell did you learn to talk, anyway?

RONNIE: Dad, leave him alone. This is getting to be a hassle.

STEVE: It's no hassle, Ron.

DAD: "Hassle." What is it with you two? You got a hassle, nifty, go bowling.

STEVE: Dad—

DAD: What do you want to go bowling for? All of a sudden you've got this big interest in bowling now all of a sudden.

STEVE: Dad, look—Ronnie couldn't pass her grades in college because of her phys. ed. credit, so now she has to bowl because she didn't want to go in the water and swim.

DAD: What do you mean, she didn't want to—

RONNIE: Look, Steve, just forget about it.

STEVE: Ron, are you jumping on *me* now?

DAD: How are you two going bowling? What are you gonna use for money?

STEVE: Ronnie, you have money, don't you?

RONNIE: Let's just forget it.

STEVE: No, now I'm getting interested. Come on, Dad, want to go bowling with us?

DAD: What, *now*?

RONNIE: Forget about it.

DAD: Aw, for Christ's sake, you don't go bowling at this hour.

STEVE: Come on, Dad, just bowl a few frames with us. You and Mommy used to bowl all the time, remember?

DAD: You don't know what you're talking about. Your mother doesn't bowl at midnight.

RONNIE: Come on, Steve, I can't stand here all night arguing about the proper times to bowl.

STEVE: Dad, come on. You can wolf down an order of French fries.

DAD: I'm not hungry.

RONNIE: You're sitting there with candy bars.

STEVE: So he eats candy bars—so what? Leave him alone.

RONNIE: It's not healthy.

STEVE: Yeah, Dad, come on over to the alley and work up an appetite for some fries.

DAD: Jesus Christ, do you know how much a bowling ball weighs? How is Ronnie gonna go bowling? She looks like a good meal of corned beef and cabbage would stand her on her feet.

RONNIE: Look, all I want to do is graduate from college.

STEVE: Dad, leave her alone. She's upset enough that she doesn't want to put her head under water.

DAD: What's that got to do with anything?

STEVE: You know, it's a swimming credit she couldn't get.

DAD: Swimming. You know what it is, swimming?

RONNIE: No, Dad, what is it?

DAD: Swimming—all swimming is is relaxing. In the water. That's all it is. Swimming is a relaxing. You put your head in, you relax, that's it. Otherwise you sink like a stone. Tense up in the water and you can forget about it.

RONNIE: Oh, so, Dad, wait a minute, when's the last time I saw *you* swimming? You go out there and wade.

STEVE: Come on, Ronnie, don't pick on him.

RONNIE: You *wade* in there, in your shorts—

DAD: Get out of here. You're gonna tell me about swimming! You've been in college too long, that's what your problem is. Then you come here and tell me about bowling and swimming.

RONNIE: This is just really upsetting me. If I don't fulfill this credit—Oh, forget it. Forget about it. I'm not graduating from college. Just forget about it. We're not going bowling.

DAD: Oh, you're not graduating from college now, huh? Now it's my fault you're not graduating from college because you don't have bowling shoes.

STEVE: Dad, forget the bowling shoes. They have millions of 'em in the alley.

DAD: So you know all about bowling. Where's your bowling ball?

STEVE: They have balls all over the place.

DAD: What, at this time of night?

RONNIE: They don't take the balls away just because it gets dark outside.

STEVE: Really, she has to bowl to graduate from Penn. She was supposed to pass her swimming test, but she can't swim.

DAD: Of course she can swim.

STEVE: She can't swim. She's afraid to swim.

DAD: Where in the world did you get that idea?

STEVE: Dad, look, have you ever once seen her swim?

DAD: You're crazy.

STEVE: You know how she just stands there in the shallow end and then comes out and lounges around on a towel.

DAD: She could swim fine if she wasn't too goddam hoity-toity to swim.

STEVE: Dad, I'm telling you, she had a traumatic experience in Atlantic City that time when we were kids. She got knocked down by a wave. So now she won't put her head under water.

DAD: Where the hell do you get this stuff?

RONNIE: Forget about all that. They said I could graduate without swimming. All I have to do is bowl a certain number of frames over the summer and send them the score sheets.

DAD: That's the silliest thing yet. They're gonna let you go bowling when you're supposed to swim?

RONNIE: They couldn't care less what I do. So I'm not swimming.

DAD: You better start swimming in a hurry, because you're not gonna be able to bowl. You couldn't bowl if your life depended on it.

STEVE: Dad, anybody can bowl.

DAD: And that's where you're wrong. Swimming, yes. As long as you don't tense up. But with bowling it's a horse of a different color.

STEVE: Dad, if she can't bowl I'll teach her. It's no big thing. All she has to do is keep hurling the ball down the alley and boom!—sooner or later she'll hit something.

DAD: She'll hit something, all right.

RONNIE: They didn't say I had to bowl *well*.

DAD: What, now you want to have a traumatic bowling experience? You have to prepare for these things, you can't just get up there and—

STEVE: Bowling is a Zen thing. It's all in the—not actually in the mind but in the non-mind. Like an animal, or a fish.

DAD: Fish breathe in the water.

STEVE: That's what I'm saying.

DAD: Look, people cannot breathe water. People and animals—they have lungs, not gills.

STEVE: Will you stop? Of course people don't have gills. Of course they don't. Do you think I'm stupid?

DAD: Are you calling me stupid?

RONNIE: Steve, look, leave him alone. Forget about it.

DAD: 'Cause if you're calling me stupid, you can forget about the bowling.

RONNIE: I don't care. This is upsetting me now.

DAD: *You're* upset?

RONNIE: Yes. This is just upsetting me. Forget the whole thing. Forget college. I'll go to the Sorbonne.

DAD: She'll go to the Sorbonne. Listen to this. What are you gonna study there, French water sports?

STEVE: Dad, are you coming bowling with us or not? That's all we want to know.

DAD: If you're so smart, what are you planning to do for money? You know how much it costs to go bowling?

RONNIE: It's only a couple of dollars. Just give Steve a couple of dollars and we'll go. I don't need anything.

DAD: Give *Steve* a couple of—Jesus Christ, you want me to give him money to go bowling? He's only a kid! It's dark out there. You're being silly now. You want to go bowling, first of all you need *shoes*, and then you need money. And you're gonna take this kid in the middle of the night—

RONNIE: It's not the middle of the night at nine-thirty.

DAD: You don't listen to reason. You know how hard your mother and I worked to send you to college, and now all it comes down to is bowling in the middle of the night?

RONNIE: Look, it's not—

STEVE: Ronnie, let me tell him. All you're doing is pissing him off.

RONNIE: What are you, my lawyer now?

DAD: All this happens because you don't want to put your head under water? That's what this is all about? I thought I told you about swimming.

STEVE: Dad, will you back off the swimming thing?

DAD: No, wait a minute, let me tell her about swimming. You reach down to the bottom of the pool, and you keep your head straight, and you breathe. When you're in the water, you breathe. That's it.

RONNIE: That sounds terrific on paper—

DAD: What do you mean, "on paper"? What are you talking about? Where does this kid get this from? I'm talking about swimming, she's talking about paper.

STEVE: Dad, will you—

RONNIE: Steve, no, wait a minute, I want to hear what Daddy has to say about swimming. He's telling us all about swimming now.

DAD: Look, don't get smart.

RONNIE: No, I want to hear this. I want to hear about swimming. *That's why I can't swim! Because you never taught us to swim!*

DAD: Oh, you want to hear *me* now. I thought two minutes ago you wanted to go bowling.

RONNIE: Fine. Forget it, I'm not staying here with this. I'm packing. I'll be upstairs, packing.

STEVE: Ron, look, forget about packing, we're going bowling.

DAD: Bowling, packing, swimming . . .

STEVE: Dad, stop.

DAD: All I'm telling you is, you don't fight the water. Otherwise, if you fight the water— You never fight the water. Never ever. You let the water support you, because if you're afraid to let it support you, you just go right to the bottom. The bottom will draw you like a magnet. Gravity takes you right to the bottom and you can't breathe and that's it.

STEVE: Dad, this is the same thing I'm saying about bowling. It's a gravity thing. The alley creates its own momentum, and you just go with it. It happens *for* you. And the gutters—the gutters create fear in a bowler. They're there as a fear thing. If you tense up, the ball will leap into the gutter. Whereas the pins actually draw the ball to them. It's an attraction of bodies—like planets. It's perfectly natural. If you relax, the ball goes for a strike.

RONNIE: Yeah, but only in the middle of the night, when it's really dark out. You turn on the car headlights, you breathe, keep your head down, plenty of powder, a few candy bars just to make sure you keep your strength up, and boom!—the next thing you know you're graduating from the Sorbonne with a degree in packing.

DAD: I swear I don't know where you kids learned to talk this way. (*Goes into house, slamming screen door.* STEVE *and* RONNIE *look at each other, shrug, and exit toward bowling alley.* DAD *opens screen door and calls after them.*) You want to go bowling, go bowling. But I'm telling you, they're not gonna let you wear those shoes.

My Ideal

"He was a tall, large, and muscular man who liked to take advantage of that fact. He had a great, hairy torso and a stone wall abdomen on shanks that were . . . overwrapped with sinew and his strength sometimes seemed to burst through his arms the same way his arms sometimes burst through his shirts." This homoerotic paean to a distinguished writer—regrettably abbreviated for space—is the early work of Peter Hamill (with Alfred Aronowitz) in *Ernest Hemingway: The Life and Death of a Man* (Lancer Books, out of print). It shows the young, sensitive Hamill, not the postliberal hack.

—Letter in the *Village Voice*

I feel that the author of this letter is too pessimistic. There's a tone of resignation I don't like, a so-much-for-him attitude I find presumptuous. Mr. Hamill is written off as a lost soul. But how can we know for sure that his sensitivity won't come back later, that he won't be saved in his middle or declining years? Even one moment from now—it's always possible. It's what happened to me.

Although I'm a woman, my own early years were basically just one long paean to the masculine physique. My perfect man was not a projection onto Ernest Hemingway but an abstraction, a pure construct I called My Ideal. Nonetheless, the concerns were similar: height, strength, abdominal hardness, body hair—the universals. Fortune didn't present me with an Alfred Aronowitz to collaborate in packaging my material, so all it amounted to was a series of idle handwritten *pensées*, illusory quests for embodied form. A surviving fragment:

Maybe he's a dream, and yet he might be right around the size of a marble colossus, his muscled and hairy chest straining at the confines of his little skin-tight ribbed undershirt the way a heavy boulder would if encased in fragile netting of some kind.

These early intuitions were reinforced by observations of external reality, recorded over many years in a diary I labeled "Paeans":

> Noticed a fireman (they're all gorgeous), one hand gripping axe, the other with strong sinews of wrist dangling just below sleeve of that black rubber overcoat they wear. His no doubt muscled arms invisible under sleeves, yet somehow an explosive quality came through.
>
> Male passenger sitting next to me on D train, powerful feet enwrapped by Earth shoes. Hair on backs of hands as he perused nihilist pamphlet, v. sexy.
>
> Shopping for present for [name deleted] in Barnacle Bill's [at that time a discount store, not upscale like today], saw guy, artistic loner obviously w/o a clue how staggeringly handsome he is, trying on Italian Merchant Marine mohair sommelier's jacket much too small. Bulges of his shoulders threatened to split seams of tight-fitting fabric—thought I'd die.
>
> Car trip w/ [name irrelevant], summer shower, then sun came out just as we passed a Ready-Pump station, two grease monkeys in camouflage jumpsuits soaked to the skin, like great and drenched tropical cats.
>
> Seems to be new 80s fad of men wearing wallet tucked into front of pants waistband, buccaneer-style. Creates impression of abdominal muscle on varied builds—short, medium-short, small-medium, average, biggish, husky, massive, custom, apocalyptic.

But young and sensitive isn't enough if you're ambitious. Somewhere was a high plateau to strive for, and I felt ready to enlist the help of Alfred Aronowitz. When my letter, c/o his publisher, went unanswered, the rebuff was devastating. Why I couldn't forget it and move forward I can't explain. Maybe I wanted an excuse to immobilize myself: perfection or nothing. I became obsessed with Alfred Aronowitz as the ideal and only possible partner in the grand enterprise that would now never happen.

The last refuge of the obsessed is superstition. I turned to numerology for answers, studying crank medieval screeds and primitive iconography to learn how many weeks, months, or years lay between me and my unattainable goal: two (classical symbol of balance, justice, and death), ten (complete cycle of life and death in measurement system going back to Romans), three hundred and sixty-five (random figure obtained by throwing clamshells). And then, aggression being the last refuge of the superstitious, I went into sadistic fantasies: Alfred Aronowitz totally in my power, his forearm muscles groaning against the half hitches in the hairy hemp seamen's rope. . . .

As such thoughts grew repulsive to me, the repulsion generalized to all of reality. One day I ran into an old friend in the gun store. It was fine weather, and he was in a great mood until he burst out, "You look so angry! What is all this anger about? What is your goddam problem with anger?" My problem, of course, was that my little toy dream world had shattered. Even my friend's gruff, Papa Bear charm had lost its magic. My hand accidentally brushed against his abdomen, and it was rock hard with repressed anxiety. Maybe he, too, had suddenly seen that life was no timeless Eden full of noble strength clad in some torn shreds of fur but the exact opposite.

Paean from a typical evening around that time:

> Dinner at [omitted]'s house, seated next to one of top men in city—could easily put out contract on any guest at table yet mysteriously just "happens" to never get around to it. (Misguided notion of heroism?) Every sinew in room taut w/competitiveness at knuckling under to [then-powerful hostess], who bragged abt. her affair w/some Caribbean strongman and called French champagne by euphemism "sparkling wine" to bully us all into collusion w/totalitarian fantasy that she could redefine luxury drink as casual subalcoholic working-class commodity like Champale. Not one person (incl. self) w/guts to shove her nose in facts. Her current husband, some sort of ex-bullfighter, speaks no English, spent dinner reading own passport. To her right, ghastly world-champ social climber, [——], practically busted his shirtfront coming up w/new sentences containing the word "servants." Everybody like vultures,

oohing and aahing abt. size of the fish and their "strong feelings" re some world disaster they took as private affront to sacred memory of how much hair they had in 1960s. Meanwhile, table centerpiece on closer inspection not row of coconuts but *actual shrunken heads w/the hair still on them,* which everybody pretended not to notice because nobody else saying anything or because saying something might halt flow of "sparkling wine" or diminish sense of entitlement to universe as their personal villa, salvage dump, and clinic. Hated self for sitting there like a mummy. Across table, one of those graybeard avuncular-doctor Norman Rockwell types w/ lifetime of stored-up voltage a millimeter under surface. Dropped my napkin, saw his shank kick the cat.

At the time, I didn't view myself as embittered. Unable to admit perfectly normal feelings of failure and disappointment, I dwelled on what was wrong with people. Their humanly understandable unrealistic delusions drove me to some pretty cynical theories: "Let Jack do it," "I'm all right, Frank," "Rot in Hell, Harry"—the whole panoply of middle-age malaise gallows philosophies came to me like newborn truths. I stopped being friends with women who gawked at younger men's bodies in public or described their portly husbands as Apollos. I picked a fight in a bar. Walked right up to her and for no good reason sneered, "How's your old man?" and she sloshed her Rattlesnake longneck beer at me on purpose. I guess that was when I bottomed out.

We assume that people going through these postliberal phases are enjoying themselves, but no one really likes having a crisis of lost youthful sensitivity. How did I get through it? Gardening helped. Also, it's easier for a woman, because when you collapse and harden your heart and turn on people, they can say, "Oh, she's into gardening now." It was a tough time, though. My point is, IT DOESN'T HAVE TO STAY THAT WAY. These things have a momentum, and you can ride them out.

Sure, it still crosses my mind, Maybe there's something in my mailbox today from "Alfred Aronowitz" (I've realized that he was unreal to me, an illusion or figurehead)—after all these years, a postcard from a foreign country, with an apology and an airtight excuse:

"Shipwrecked in the Straits, pirates stole my files, sand in everything." But now, thank goodness, I'm able to feel guilty about having these foolish thoughts. It's a more mature—an enlightened sensitivity.

Anyway, my ideal has changed:

> Man w/stone wall face that sometimes bursts into smile. Possible to find fault, but life so regrettably abbreviated for space.

Nowhere to Run

> DOCTOR CALLING IT QUITS TO RUN COIN LAUNDRY
> He said insurance rates drove him out of his 20-year practice.
>
> —*The Times*

Dear Doctor:

Please don't do anything until you read this.

I'm sending it c/o the AMA, so God knows how long it will take to reach you. But I consider it my duty to write, as a colleague who once shared your vision of the coin-operated laundry business as a refuge from the insurance fiends.

If only life were so simple.

A year ago, I was still practicing general medicine in my home town of Calamine, in upstate New York, administering vaccinations and checkups to patients who thought "malpractice" was a problem with the high school basketball team. That was what old Doc Williamson always said. He had been our family physician ever since I was a little girl; he helped me get into medical school and then took me on as his associate. I understood that his professional confidence in me was enhanced by my conservative management of a legacy from my maternal grandfather, a prosperous dairy farmer whose generosity enabled Doc and me to go on feeding, temporarily, those voracious actuarial parasites all too familiar to someone in your shoes, Doctor.

But Doc's nerves were shot. I sent him abroad on a therapeutic mah-jongg cruise, and the last I heard from him was a notarized picture postcard (Balinese dancers) giving me power of attorney to dispose of the office and appurtenances when my inheritance ran out. It did, but then I happened to win the New York State Lottery. That fortune, however, was swallowed up before my endorsement on the check was dry, and finally I had to throw in the towel. I sold the office, paid off the loan I'd taken in one last try at satiating the premium-bloated sharks of whom surely I need offer no further description to yourself, and rented a studio apartment in lower Manhattan, determined to change my life.

So believe me, I know how you feel. Twenty years of cliffhanging, strung out on terror and relief, relief and terror—the awful cycle of indemnifying yourself against Mrs. Smith or Mr. Jones, that grateful patient with the billion-to-one chance of blindsiding you as a subpoena-waving freak litigant—and now, freedom! How delightful the prospect!—each day a dance in the embrace of Dame Fortune (for me, Señor Fortune), a delicious creature of spontaneity and not, after all, a greedy monster whose mood swings demand to be bought off with yet another bribe ripped from a mutilated checkbook. Normal human risk—how charming and comfortable it sounds!

I guess I must have walked by that boarded-up cinder-block laundromat on Prince Street ten times before it dawned on me: Here was the helping profession of my dreams. The lowered prestige—even a degree of marginality—would be offset by a modest independent income secure from the bloodsuckers I swore I'd never think about again. Life was going to be marvelous.

The premises were hardly palatial compared to the oak-paneled office on Main Street, but the lease was cheap. I could sleep on a cot in the storeroom. The soap vendors gave credit, and their experimental products!—a fantastic pharmacopoeia of strange-hued fabric softeners and high-tech stain removers to dispense to my heart's content, even for people using alcoholic beverages while operating the machines.

Small wonder I was flying high by opening day at Mercy Memorial Wash 'n' Dri. Coin slides clicked and agitators hummed, complimentary champagne flowed for everybody trying an experimental product, and during Happy Hour I let children punch the temperature-select buttons at random, just for fun.

And it worked! A sample of the warm response:

Dear Doctor:

Just a note to let you know how grateful I am for your treatment of my laundry. I was so upset when I learned it would have to go in. I can't begin to describe the dread when I first saw the unmistakable symptoms of soil. My husband and parents were extremely concerned, and it was very kind of you to call them from the pay phone just to reassure them that everything was going smoothly.

Nothing was stolen, and your decisive intervention in an emergency, personally transferring my wash to the dryer while I was shopping, seems to have been the right thing to do. It was worth every penny of the extra fee, as was the impeccable folding. I know you must perform similar operations all the time, but I couldn't have done it better myself, ha-ha!

Much appreciated also was your lighthearted manner during the after-care period.

Well, I sure pray I won't need your services ever again, but if I do (God forbid) you have my eternal confidence.

[Name Withheld in Confidentiality]

So far, so good.

Around six o'clock this morning, a man raps on the storefront window. Suit and tie, but who knows? Maybe he's trouble, maybe he left a sock in the dryer. Isn't my new life supposed to be all about taking a chance? Surprise, surprise—it's a pitch.

"Lady—or should I say 'Doctor'?" he says. "You're on a suicide course. Destination bankruptcy. And then the inevitable retreat into an even lower-status business, in one of the redlined failure zones along the downward trajectory channels where no insurance company in its right mind would guarantee you against certain ruin, I guarantee you. Now I will explain the background, even though I don't have to.

"In recent years— O.K., in recent years the whole country has gone nuts, but we limit ourselves, and in recent years more specifically the coin-op laundry sector has been overrun by unprecedented numbers of doctors and other health-care practitioners. Similar example, the classic brain drain of the sixties, when all those academics went into the saw-sharpening business thinking it would be an attractive lifestyle—working with their hands, no more squabbles with tenure committees, dream on—and then found out that in the field of saw-sharpening, as in any other, the rules are brutally dictated by the marketplace.

"Believe me, I personally would love to buy a piece of land upstate and retire by some little blue lake, but here I am in a barrel of rotten apples, God willing.

"This is not to deny for one second that your surgeons, internists, radiologists, and the like are upping the technological sophistication at many laundry venues. And welcome aboard! *But*—and it's a big *but*—as the industry thus becomes more scientific, innovative, and humane, I say to you that so too does it pose hazards unheralded, and not just for the bags of laundry themselves but for those selfsame entrepreneurs who imagine they can waltz carefree, financially secure from protracted and devastating lawsuits at the hands of rapacious attorneys for customers increasingly perfectionistic, affluent, and educated in modern laundry management standards as reported by the mass media.

"Lest this analysis strike you as alarmist or the economic consequences inconsequential, let me share if I may a few case histories from our claims adjustment files.

"Item: Since 1988 a Minneapolis broad has had a legal vendetta going against St. Luke's Coin-o-Mat, where despite the twenty-four-hour presence of a certified anesthesiologist, a failure in the oxygen support system caused her load of heavy-duty work clothes to suffer an irreversible case of mildew.

"Item: In 1989, right here in Manhattan, the owner of Columbia Presbyterian Washaterium got clobbered with a fifty-thousand-dollar fine. Why? He recommended chlorine bleach without advising the client of the right to get a second opinion.

"Item: 1990, out in L.A.—important test case. Some movie star's fancy pillowcases were in a private Intensive Presoak Unit at Cedars of Lebanon Lying-in Laundry. While a consultation was being set up with a specialist from the Delicate Care Institute of Bethesda, the plaintiff was denied visiting privileges over a holiday weekend. Domestics Court awarded emotional damages at a hundred and thirty-five thou per diem. I ask you. Now under appeal, and don't hold your breath."

I'm not deaf to his implied threats, but I feel immune. From a position of control, I choose to go with him to his Wall Street office for what I assume will be a textbook case of high-pressure insurance solicitation. It's important for my continued personal development to confront the beast in its lair.

The office is palatial compared to a laundromat. The crowded reception salon is ebony-paneled, with a marble staircase leading to a balcony ornamented with gilt phoenixes and dragons, encircled by pillars rising from the backs of live bejeweled tortoises—more intimidating than expected, but I can't let that stand in my way now. There's an announcement from a loudspeaker: "Guilty as charged, sentenced to death by beheading!" Somebody screams.

"Erstwhile proprietor of the Good Samaritan Laundromat," my companion whispers, and pushes me up the staircase. "Just answer the riddles as best you can." At this I feel a pang of apprehension, which I embrace. And then I recall the fundamental tenet we learned in medical school—that the seeming infinities of life always converge in a few lucid biochemical structures: there's Boy Meets Girl; there's Dog Bites Man; and there's the Riddle Scene.

And it's a real thrill. I'm at the top of the staircase. The crowd below falls silent. The loudspeaker says my life will be spared if I answer three riddles, or I can go straight to the executioner's block. I take my chances.

"There is that which is wet yet at the same time is dry—how can such a thing be?"

I'm not afraid of the obvious. "A wash treated with Dewdrop Mildew Retardant," I reply, "turns the dankest basement as fungus-proof as a sunny meadow." The crowd applauds. This is intoxicating.

"Who or what is the following: freezing cold as ice to the touch but burning within like a hot flame?"

"The face of a doctor who has been contradicted by a second opinion." How I come up with this under stress I have absolutely no idea. Adrenaline is a wonderful thing.

You could hear a pin drop now.

"A wingèd demon flies over the land"—I can tell already this one won't be easy—"and it's name is what?"

Totally unfair! It could be anything! Not enough clues have been given! My face is cold but hot. I take a wild guess, blurting out the first word that enters my head: "Risk! Risk! Risk! Its name is Risk!"

Well, Doctor, I guessed right. I was free.

So I raised the stakes. I told the loudspeaker I agreed to be executed anyway if it could guess my name within twenty-four hours.

I'm writing this at midnight, cowering in a motel room in one of the failure zones. Where I'll be by morning is another riddle.

Why did I do it? I just wanted to be sure. Does the word "insurance" ring a bell? Because that's the bottom line here, Doctor, let's face it: I am a risk-insurance addict. And so are you. We can't help it. It's an illness. I don't want to be a wet blanket, but take my advice and do not follow in my footsteps. You're only deceiving yourself. You and I are incapable of handling normal human risk; we'll always find some way to escalate it into the same old roller-coaster ride driven by our love-hate dependency on the cruel whims of the very predators we claim to be running away from, and there is no running away. Not by going into the laundry business, or into telemarketing or small-engine repair. Get some help for yourself.

It's probably too late for me, but please, as a professional courtesy, do not give out my name.

Post-Euphoria

Frankfurt Stock Exchange
Frankfurt, Germany
DEAR SIRS:

Specifically speaking, how does a stock exchange work? One would require approximately how many tables and chairs? And then what?

As fledglings, we are excited to be initiating such a body! Having in readiness for our members a fifty-litre samovar, we now await merely your input on final refinements of procedure.

Gratefully,
FREE MARKET PLANNING
COMMISSARIAT

British Humane Society
London, England
LADIES AND GENTLEMEN:

Begging your advisory as per the ensuing hypothetical. Someone on my street, not me, keeps surrealist parasites in his basement as a hobby. Supposing he decided to release them from the holding pen—what would be the safest way? Should he just smash the pen open with a hammer and then run? I heard there is a danger that uninhibited specimens have a difficult transition phase and might form roving packs of killer strays. Is this true, or would they reenter the natural population?

Very truly yours,
CONCERNED SIBERIAN CITIZEN
(RET.)

Editor-in-Chief
Le Monde
Paris, France
ESTEEMED COLLEAGUE:

Our best regards to you and your enchanting wife.

By the way, how do you decide which are the news stories and which are the editorials? Is it by word count or, rather, a collective decision reached by secret ballot? Or perchance you leave this matter in the capable hands of your delightful spouse. In that case, might we consult with her now and then, purely on a professional basis?

With felicitations,
Izvestia Editorial Board

P.S.: Please forgive the ironic idiocy of the above query if yours is one of the Western press organs which have been taking their instructions from us. Someone told us to forget about all that, so we had to.

Supervisor
Cook County Board of Elections
Cook County, Illinois, U.S.A.
Dear Sir or Madam:

Knowing your reputation far and wide, we were just wondering. What if there occurred some voting machines of a highly democratic technology—for example, allowing multiple choice by means of extra slots and levers? Is there some method, in its sophistication a mystery to us, for insuring that a candidate with more votes does not obtain an unfair advantage over a candidate with not so many votes? There could be a situation where the latter is more deserving, due to family needs or health problems, etc., yet is passed aside by a hasty or whimsical electorate for a candidate they think they "want." Then idealism would cry out on its hands and knees to serve a higher justice. Is there a special device for this?

Also, do you happen to know how to get the ballots out of the machine—smash the whole thing open like a piggy bank, or what?

Sincerely,
Supreme Election Reform
Central Committee

Mr. Akio Morita, Chairman
Sony Corporation
Tokyo, Japan
Dear Mr. Morita:

This is not your problem, but in our admiration for your fantastic acumen we hope to presume upon your farseeing wisdom and top-notch business sense.

A woman named Yoko Ono has made us a firm offer of $30,000 in hard currency for eight hundred thousand hectares of state-owned pasture in the northeastern Urals. She asserts managerial skills such that over a five-year period she can transform the area into a profit-making dairy farm equipped with automated milking system, carriage barn, historically restored rustic stone walls, manor house with large deck, hardwood floors, antique lighting, Tulikivi radiant fireplace, all-electric kitchen, aluminum siding, up-to-the-minute recording studio, and much more, and will then rent it back to us on terms to be mutually deferred.

Naturally we are tempted to gobble this while her enthusiasm is still at fever pitch. But the wife of our deputy agro-industrial minister suggests we ask if you know a hard-nosed tactic to sweeten our end of the deal.

Most respectfully,
Land Development
Inspectorate

Hughes Tool Company
U.S.A.
To the Board of Directors:

No doubt it is something out of the blue, receiving a letter from an unknown woman in Russia. I have selected your company because my husband is a fan of your unique oil-drilling equipment, which he appreciates only by remote lore and word of mouth but aspires someday to purchase for his business here. Having started from a single informal kerosene drum in a shed behind our dacha on the Black Sea, he has created over the years quite a formidable oil-and-gas-pumping endeavor, and now stands in position to operate on a mammoth regional scale.

However, I am concerned that he is the victim of a fairy tale about capitalist management principles. A small cohort of men visiting from your state Utah have attained influence over him. They are causing him to discharge fond employees of loyal longevity, and to sign many papers, and now they have him in a reclusion, lying in bed with long fingernails, watching a videotape of a film, *Ocean's Eleven.* Recently he sent out to me an elaborate pencil memorandum explaining how I should open herring jars in a certain way so germs from my hair cannot tumble in. He said that titans of capital have to protect themselves from poison elements, but I believe this to be a propaganda romance, indoctrinated by the Utah men. Finally, would it be a fact that executive decision-making power is enhanced by hourly injections of the substance "codeine"? This is what they proclaim, although they themselves are fanatically abstemious when it comes to even vodka or tea.

As I am too typical of our national unfamiliarity with these parts of the free enterprise system, I pray that you can inform my perspective before it is already too late and I smash open the attic with a hammer.

DESPERATE

TO WHOM IT MAY CONCERN:
I am free. What should I do?

Salt of Life

AUSTERITY

On the Miracle Mile we're hurting, but nothing like most people. While it's true that Bill, of Bill's Pottery, has recently had to melt down surplus auto chrome for his glazes, he considers that an artistic challenge, and the proceeds from his 1991 Christmas Edition Bread Pudding Compote in pearl gray would have gone to charity if he'd sold any. Right before the holidays I had to fire Sam and Isaac, the two kids I'd hired to make deliveries for my wind store, but they were just going to use the money to buy their parents a gift, probably some silly piece of art pottery, so it wasn't a tragedy.

The worst-off retailer on the strip is my friend Maud, a former actress from L.A. who was taking home soup crackers from Musso & Frank's until she saved enough money to move here and open her own restaurant, Pane (Italian for "bread"). It's still charming, with the homemade hog-tallow candles since her gas and electric were cut off, and her husband Jean-Claude, who's from Alsace, knew how to build her a hog smoker out of an old oil tank, but there are certain breads she can't bake in that, so she comes to my apartment every day to use the oven.

PAIN

No man is an island, but there is a down side to that. For instance, near Thanksgiving I read in *USA Today* that President Bush said, "I hurt when other people are hurting. And I've got to convey that a little more to the American people."

Larry's Pharmacy carries a new over-the-counter pill for pain of that type, pain caused by the pain of others. The pill is being marketed under the brand name Beach Head, with a picture of a palm tree on the bottle. There isn't much demand for it in this neighborhood, though.

PRIDE

The Miracle Mile harks back to a dysfunctional newsboy turned petty hood named Mickey Overcast, who made a fortune during the First World War in contraband morphine. Hard hit by the post-Armistice recession of 1921, he used it as an excuse to eat inventory, and drifted into a netherworld of delusional investment schemes. The most grandiose was a plan to develop what was then a mile-long stretch of vacant shipyard into a pleasure resort. (Ivory Arches, he wanted to call it; his psychedelic-style ink sketches show present-day Main Street as Oceanus and every cross street as Sunset.) All he actually did was commission and erect a huge baroque allegorical hammered-copper public sculpture, "Morphia and Pain Wrestling for the Soul of America." The sculptor welded together three items he already had on inventory: for Morphia, some socialite of the era in a nightdress; for Pain, Lady Macbeth (the whole thing is thirty-two feet tall to the tip of her raised dagger); and, for the Soul of America, a bas-relief of George Washington. It still stands, outside the Savings & Loan, and Richie the security guard always says, "It's two broads fighting over a dollar bill." Now there's a movement to tear it down, because the junior-high kids are unnaturally fascinated by what they call "the warped legacy of Mickey Overcast," but it might draw tourism if the city Visitors' Bureau had the funds to print up a nice pamphlet.

Anyway, after Overcast went to jail, the property fell into government hands and was auctioned off to war veterans. They dubbed it the Miracle Mile and gave it the community character it retains to this day, an urban multiethnic commercial-residential mix of pastel stucco storefronts topped by middle-class apartments—a few rooms for rent but nothing seedy.

SURPRISE

When the call came from Washington, D.C., I was still asleep; I'd been at Club Marilyn after hours, on business, hoping to change her ridiculous New Year's Eve order for generic punch by giving her a free bottle of vintage Cordon Rouge.

I answered the phone while trying to get up from beneath Curtis, a fairly good Cuban trombone player who works under the name Flor Blanca, his tone said to be redolent of a white Caribbean tree orchid now prohibited.

So when the caller stated that as authorized by executive order he wanted to give me the opportunity to share my pain with the President, it was a bolt from the blue.

EMPATHY

"We've been monitoring your area," the caller went on, "and there's just a blip or a blank spot there, where we should be seeing a jagged zigzag of pain. The President needs to feel how people are hurting with pinpoint accuracy. For gosh sake, he doesn't want to be wrong on this. If you hide your hurt —Look, everything has to be entered into Presidential feedback, and it's no help when all we're getting from you is flatline."

"You're personally calling everyone in America?"

"Boy, you must be hurting deeply if you're imagining something that extreme."

There was a pause while I pointed out my white terry-cloth robe to Curtis, who went to take a shower.

"Silence," said the caller, "is a very dismissive attitude toward a program designed to target your suffering. It's your responsibility to express yourself. We can wait. This President himself is the kind of human being who would gladly wait till Doomsday if possible. But politically that's impossible, so if you aren't prepared to confide within the next few minutes, a local detachment is sent to your home and you're interviewed—stenographic transcript, tape recording, or videotape, whichever you would find most painful."

I said I'd need time to organize my ideas about domestic and foreign policy.

"No, no, no, the President is quite confident of his ideas. He has batteries of advisers telling him his ideas. He has made a decision, and the decision is to share your anguish in a direct biochemical way."

"It sounds creepy."

"Oh, now you're putting a value-laden word on what is a neutral fact of Presidential brain chemistry. The endorphin receptors . . . it's a technical thing."

"But why me?"

"Because yours is exactly the mentality we have to work hardest to change. You're viewing the President of the United States as an elected official instead of an integral component of your neurological system."

I must have made an involuntary sound. "That's good," he said. "You're beginning to realize that you hurt more than you realize. The President will feel this very keenly."

FEAR

As I told Curtis when he came out of the shower, here's what I'm comfortable with: I meet somebody, we both put our best foot forward, maybe have a glass of 1989 Yakima Valley Merlot or a *café con leche*, eventually take our clothes off, then after that's been going on for a while and the person has showed up for it punctually several times in a row, mutual trust is built and we can start agonizing. For all I know, this Administration could be gone after next year, so why should I be a laboratory mouse for their receptors and then have the rug pulled out? Curtis said it's a cultural thing. For example, he said, as a Cuban he was having an intricate response to the idea of a government coming into your home and acting like a member of the family, and therefore he intended to get dressed and run away immediately. Then we both cried.

Just as he took off, Maud came by to bake a batch of the twirly bread sticks she calls *coda di maiale* ("tail of the hog"), and I asked her to do the interview for me. She said sure—she had levels of dark and desperate torment to explore, and as an actress she never got the one big break that would have positioned her to take that risk in the supportive context of the federal government. So I did the baking while she went into the bathroom to put on my makeup and do an emotional preparation. I could hear her in there crying and having an imaginary fight about rent arrears with Jonathan, her landlord, who's threatening to seize her one possession of value, a framed 1932 editorial cartoon that hangs over the restaurant bar and shows a patient in surgery with a black anesthesia mask over his face and the caption "No Decent Speakeasy Would Have Me."

SNAFU

(The following transcript of Maud's interview was obtained with no problem under the Freedom of Information Act. Although the offer of audio- or videotape formats was a cynical public-relations frill the White House never had the funding for, the aide they sent took notes and was can-do right down to the sharp way his pinstriped pants bloused over high-top steel-toed paratrooper boots.)

White House Aide *(name deleted)*: At ease. You blew last month's pay on payday, and now you're up sorry-ass creek. Correct?

Subject *(sniffling)*: Not exactly.

AIDE: Homesick. No mail in six weeks. Wondering how to get laid.

SUBJECT: Nothing like that. I—

AIDE: Loud and clear. Any tropical dysentery, pack-humping abrasions, desert foot, shrapnel pinch, bombardment tinnitus, sandstorm mood swing, unauthorized clap, or chronic thousand-meter stare?

SUBJECT: Not that I know of. Knock on wood.

AIDE: Affirmative. *(Taps her on right elbow with government issue HM-1 hammer. Her arm jerks.)* Negative weapon-recoil dislocation. Extend your other hand, and that's an order. God damn! How long have you had that Persian sandfly bite infection?

SUBJECT: It's not. I burned myself on the hog smoker.

AIDE: KP disorientation. Outstanding. The Commander-in-Chief will be gut-grabbed when they wire this one up his heinie. *(Issues her one government issue SAL-100 plastic bag of tablets.)* One every four hours. No skivvy and no mox-nix juice.

(Subject did not request to see the chaplain.)

SALT

"I think that went well," said Maud. "Do I need these?" She opened the bag of white tablets, put one in her mouth, rolled it around, then took it out and said, "Salt." The salt receptors on the tongue, she explained, aren't only on the tip but on the middle and sides, too. Each has fifty to seventy-five cells, which die off and are replaced as often as every seven to ten days. "I think of them as tiny people," she said. "Tiny people with a tragically short life span." (She was still keyed up.) "All they want is to feel *piquant* now and then. While they last."

We considered giving away the tablets to someone hard up, but were afraid they might contain an indetectable substance that would inhibit the capacity to enjoy life on a limited budget. Besides, the good coarse kosher salt was on sale at Griswold's Grocery, three-pound box for a dollar, and even ritzy Miracle Mile Market always has specials on table salt, including the beloved brand with the deer-lick scene on the label. Harry's Health Hut carries Dr. Brody's Burpless Kelp Salt, a steal at eighty-nine cents per jar. The florist,

Lindsay, keeps a complimentary saucer of rock salt next to her cash register, like mints—a lure for anybody willing to hang around all day and shoot the breeze about gardening. Some plants that tolerate a salty atmosphere are bayberry, dusty miller, eel-grass, *Rosa rugosa*, and beach lavender. If you can't afford to eat at Dodd's Steak House, it pays to go in anyway for a free paper packet of their steak salt, which Maud thinks is a crock-aged blend of non-iodized salt, basil, coriander, fenugreek, curly parsley, *orégano dulce*, and Herba Barona (caraway-scented thyme). And if you're in the mood to navigate the rickety outside stairs next to the pool hall and deal with Miss Mitchell (for my money a soupçon of temperament is a plus for a home business), she now sells her baffling secret-recipe seasoned salt for fried chicken or a roaster cavity: fifty cents for about eight ounces, weighed by eye. Curtis knows where to get an unusual Cuban salt. You sprinkle it on your lover's food; it makes your lover perceive the taste of your rival's skin as repulsive and the taste of your skin as the crystalline tang of Mar de Lágrimas, off Isla Combo. It's probably not cheap, but, as with all salt, you only need a little.

Faculty Lounge Surveillance Tapes

(What the Education Presidency Has Been Listening To)

"Talk about right and wrong, and they'll try to mock us in newsrooms, sitcom studios and faculty lounges across America."

—Vice-President Dan Quayle

FBI FILE: FL-1

TIME: 10 A.M.
PLACE: *Ravenite Faculty Lounge, Mulberry Street, Manhattan*
PARTICIPANTS: MR. GOTTI
MR. GRAVANO
MR. LOCASCIO

MR. GOTTI: *Inaudible.*
MR. GRAVANO: *Faint, smirklike sounds.*
MR. LOCASCIO: *Snort of amusement.*
MR. GOTTI: *Cynical laugh.*
(Flicking noise commonly associated with scofflaw hand gesture.)
MR. GOTTI: *Long stream of derisive laughter.*
(Indistinct sounds of sociopathic buffoonery.)
MR. GRAVANO: *Butt-of-joke-type silence.*
MR. GOTTI: *Short bark of laughter edged with contempt.*
MR. GRAVANO and MR. LOCASCIO: *Simultaneous coughing fits laced with ridicule of Judeo-Christian values.*

FBI FILE: FL-96

TIME: 3:45 P.M.
PLACE: *VIP Faculty Lounge, O'Hare Airport, Chicago*
PARTICIPANTS: MR. PEEPERS
MR. NOVAK
MR. KOTTER
MISS BRODIE
MR. CHIPS
MISS BROOKS
SIR
PROF. KINGSFIELD

(Sounds of popping champagne corks, clinking glasses, and shifting of weight on leather upholstery.)
PUBLIC ADDRESS SYSTEM: Now boarding, Gate 17, Flight 723 nonstop to Portland, Oregon.
MR. PEEPERS: Tim-ber-r-r-r-r-rrrr!
MR. NOVAK: *Smutty laugh.*
MR. KOTTER *(snide falsetto):* Now taking off without you, Gate Number I-don't-know-because-I-never-learned-to-read-write-or-count-to-ten, Flight Number who-gives-a-flying-corncob, bound for Jerkwater, U.S.A.
MISS BRODIE and MR. CHIPS: *Patronizing titters.*

PA SYSTEM: Will Mr. Akira Ikiru please pick up the free phone at the information center. Mr. Akira Ikiru . . .

MISS BROOKS: *Sardonic jeer.*

MR. NOVAK: Will Mr. Jimenez Jimenez Jimenez please contact the nearest Coast Guard patrol for moral rearmament, a free bag of nuclear waste, and a one-way ticket to nowhere.

SIR: *Flamboyant West Indian–type laugh with provocative subtext of disrespect for white people.*

PA SYSTEM: Ready for preboarding now, Gate 22, passengers with small children or needing special assistance, Flight 926 to Jerusalem, with stopovers in Kuwait, Belgrade, and Los Angeles.

PROF. KINGSFIELD *(malicious pause):* If it's Tuesday, this must be arson.

(Jolly good laugh all round.)

FBI FILE: FL-11, 715

TIME: 2 A.M.

PLACE: *"The Faculty Lounge" lounge, Caesars Palace, Las Vegas*

PARTICIPANTS: MR. YOUNGMAN
MIXED ENSEMBLE

MR. YOUNGMAN: *(trademark staccato laugh):* So goodnight and thank you, ladies and germs.

HECKLER #1: I've had funnier Medicare forms!

MR. YOUNGMAN: And now please welcome the band with a warm round of heckling.

HECKLER #2: I'm not making enough money!

(Silence.)

FACULTY LOUNGE BRASS QUINTET: *Motley warmup blats and hoots.* TRUMPET *razz, answered by raspberry-type spit take from élitist* FLUGELHORN. *Bronx cheer from* TUBA. SLIDE TROMBONE *repeats offensive slurs underneath all this, building to crow of brazen defiance from* BUGLE.

HECKLER #3: You sound like a bunch of junkies in the pay toilet!

(Band laugh.)

(Silence.)

FACULTY LOUNGE BRASS QUINTET: *Improvisation on John Philip Sousa's "The Stars and Stripes Forever," played as a slow, urgent blues.*

The Cheese Stands Alone

Will President Clinton bog down in political debts owed to party bosses, heavy-hitter campaign contributors, labor leaders, early supporters, and prominent Democrats who didn't hold grudges against him when they could have—i.e., Governor Mario Cuomo? Not if Clinton makes good use of Michael Dukakis's most creative legacy to political discourse: the cheese tray.

Back in July 1988, the *Daily News* reported, Dukakis met with Cuomo to

> begin planning for the fall campaign in New York. Cuomo [was] asked whether he felt snubbed because he [had] not been invited to appear on the [convention] platform with Dukakis. . . .
>
> "I was sitting there with him. He offered me cheese. He offered me food. I said hello to his mother. I didn't feel snubbed," Cuomo said.

Of course not! For no one feels snubbed when cheese is offered. In the Middle Ages, it was traditional for a man to indicate that a wheel of cheddar was en route to the family of a woman he couldn't afford to rebuff; and today there is no more certain sign of eternally dangled promise than a nice hunk of fragrant Bel Paese presented on a Ritz cracker or, even better, held out on the palm of the hand. In politics, as in love—as in all human endeavors where we try to say more than we can say in words or deliver in costly and irrevocable actions—it is to cheese that we turn for the tendering of complex emotions, subtle hints, and just plain reassurance.

Dukakis has never been given full credit for the eloquence with which he spoke the language of cheese. Clinton is said privately to admire him for this skill, and during the 1992 New York primary campaign, when a certain anti-Italian slur hung ominously in the air over the State Capitol, the timely offer of an herbed chèvre gift pack, from Little Rock Fancy Fromages, allegedly turned the situation around. But now Cuomo is just one of a great many allies to whom favor is due, and it remains to be seen how well Clinton will use assorted cheeses to work the ambiguous area that lies between snub and ambassadorship.

The following document was leaked to this magazine by a member of the Clinton transition team who has resigned his position on the board of directors of the National Council of Cheese Lobbyists:

THE HIDDEN LANGUAGE OF CHEESE

SWISS: This is a nightmare.

STILTON: There's a reporter right behind you. Don't make any kind of revealing gesture—just take the cheese.

PORT DU SALUT: My wife will be doing that from now on.

CAMEMBERT ON WHEAT THIN: Any government contract you want, if you can persuade me my conscience is clear about Jesse Jackson.

GOUDA: A ceremonial spot on Robert Reich's necktie.

VELVEETA ON FLATBRØD: More figures needed from OMB on the worst-case scenario if we develop the courage to blow you off as a cynical parasite.

FETA ON PITA: That was then, and this is now.

CUBE OF LAUGHING COW ON TOOTHPICK: Sir (or Madame), does your hypocrisy know no bounds? The spectacle of you and your ilk turns even my stomach. Request denied.

PART-SKIM MOZZARELLA ON SALTINE: See that man? He's a U.S. marshal, here to arrest you for trying to bribe a federal official.

PROVOLONE: Get your snout out of the public trough!

TRIPLE-CRÈME ON CELERY STICK: Boy, if things were only different, we could be somewhere, just the two of us, the banks of a trout stream in the Dordogne, trailing our fingers in the water and talking about books and ideas till the sun goes down, then back to the inn for oysters and white wine and a serious discussion about philosophy and life—but instead you're laboring under the misapprehension that kissing my ass at a fund-raiser bought you a free ride on the back of the American taxpayer, you toadying little weasel.

SCHMIERKASE ON TOAST WEDGE: Maybe by 1994 or 1995 something will shake loose, but I'd feel like a bum making promises I can't keep.

HERBED CHÈVRE GIFT PACK: The Supreme Court.

AMERICAN: Would you like to say hello to my mother?

Prime Suspects, U.S.A.

Criminal justice, Janet Reno has said, must "put away . . . the truly violent, what I call the 'mean bads.'" But she faces administrative problems. (Viewer discretion advised: theatrical blood and some language.)

"I dislike being addressed as 'Ma'am,' 'General,' or 'Madam Attorney General.' I should have said so before. What counts is, I'm saying it now. 'Guv' is all right. So is 'Top,' 'Honcho,' or 'Hitch.' There's a violent repeat felon in Dade who says he was put away by 'Collar and Cuffs,' and that's one sobriquet I wouldn't mind earning a thousand times over. Use the imagination the Lord gave you."

She looks around the situation room. The boys stare down at their fingerprint kits and civil-rights injunctions. She knows they want to hold her at bay with professionally feigned politesse. But this isn't the damn State Department. This is public television. A woman AG has to belt her trenchcoat and go to the mat on every tiny little thing, because there's only one law her character can be 100 percent sure of: If a gun is introduced in the first act, it will go off in the third act.

The variables—misjudge those and the boys won't let you forget it. She's still being twitted with some maxim of Robert Towne's about how a splashy action-packed start causes an almost mathematically inevitable sag or lull twenty minutes into the first reel. And she learned the hard way that a sag or lull should cue the entrance of the

Special Prosecutor. (As Kenneth Tynan noted, the Special Prosecutor ranks with the Player King, the Gentleman Caller, the Fugitive, and the Man from U.N.C.L.E. as one of the terrific classic parts just tailor-made to thrill an English-speaking audience.)

Hundreds of supporting players have yet to be cast—the elite Cuban Cigar Naturalization Service Flying Squad, the Hillary Rodham Clinton Pressure Tactics Counter-Tactical Unit, all the way down the line to the White Hat sidekicks, Bad Mommy, Judge Advocate for Casting Against Type, Brechtian ensemble of wiretap electricians, and Woman Gentleman Caller. In an early episode, the AG lost a tough policy fight to political higher-ups who want open casting (a procedural nightmare). What do they think this is, public television? This is the U.S. Department of Justice. Recurring image: the AG in a darkened office, screening videotapes from all over the country. Her top priority is finding the right First Murderer. She murmurs, "Once you have your First Murderer, all else follows."

Hi, I've done some regional, a couple bits on *Vice*, was a Ski Mask Spree Killer in *JFK*, and that's about it. My scene is from *Taxi Driver*. "Are you talkin' to me? Are you talkin' to me? I'm the only one standing here. It's your move. Are you—"

I studied Judicial Temperament with Sanford Meisner and now take classes in Erratic Breathing and Torts with Michael Moriarty. *The Revenger's Tragedy*, by Cyril Tourneur, Act Three, Scene Five, Vendice speaks: "Now with thy dagger / Nail down his tongue, and mine shall keep possession / About his heart; if he but gasp, he dies; / We dread not death to quittance injuries. / Brother, if he but wink; not brooking the foul object, / Let our two other hands tear up his lids, / And make his eyes like comets shine through blood. / When the bad bleeds, then is the tragedy good."

As a member of Congress, I was in a recent non-Equity photo op at a firing range. Learned how to handle the Tec-9 assault pistol. So now I do all my own stunts: "Bang! Bang! B—"

You wanna know my experience? Zip! And I got no technique—that's bullshit. Just watch what I do here. You think Polanski was scary? I'm gonna blow your head off with this: "Hold it there, kitty-cat. You're a very nosy fella, kitty-cat, hah? You know what happens to nosy fellas? You want to guess? They lose their noses. Next time you'll lose the whole thing. I'll cut it off and feed it to my goldfish. Understand? Hah? Understand?"

Hello, I am classically trained and played Assistant DA Ben Stone on the dramatic series *Law and Order.* From *Measure for Measure:* "Condemn the fault, and not the actor of it? / Why, —"

No First Murderer in this batch. The AG is after a hardcore, third-strike type—a Baby-Faced Beastly or School of Dramatic Arts Stalker, not these Method Monsters and Moment Junkies. Their tapes will be remanded to rehab centers, inner-city sports leagues, or the police corps.

This season's scenario has the AG finally winning the boys' respect. Late one night, after a taut scene about technical violations in a warrant to search for the MacGuffin, she comes home, gets into the shower—and the phone rings. It's the situation room: The most dangerous and powerful tool in the law enforcement arsenal—the confession—has fallen into the wrong hands. Society confronts an onslaught of paid squealing, celebrity gargling, showboat plea-copping, and groveling for the marital contrition vote. Will these decadent canaries be our children's role models in the eternal drama of good and evil?

The AG zeroes in on a gang of thugs called Me, Myself, and I, who have occupied a major metropolitan newspaper. Perhaps they could be controlled by some form of bounty provision in hunting licenses. At the cliffhanger climax, she stands accused of favoring censorship. No way, she says. If there's a smoking gun in the back story, of course it must be revealed—in exposition, in dialogue crafted or improvised, in a flashback with slow-motion carnage, reaction close-ups, and iambic pentameter. Just stop the promiscuous spilling of guts.

Testing, Testing . . .

> [A national-security official] suggested that I not publish my information on the link between organized crime and Russian nuclear-weapons security. . . . [A]nother well-informed national-security analyst told me . . . "Yes, our public posture is Pollyannaish, but there is some value in not panicking the whole world."
>
> —Seymour Hersh, *Atlantic Monthly*, June 1994

Caution: You are about to take the National Security Analyst Recertification Exam. Do not bring into the examination room any classified negativity or apocalyptic scenarios.

VOCABULARYOLOGY

PUBLIC POSTURE
POLLYANNAISH
SOME VALUE
PANICKING
THE WHOLE WORLD

For each term, select the definition that will make Earth a nicer place and bring a ray of light to those whose lives would be a wee bit darker without it.

1. PUBLIC POSTURE is
   a. showing concern for Russia whenever we get too wrapped up in problems with our own plutonium inventory
   b. telling the truth to reporters who are itching to be threatened with censorship
   c. a 1931 Warner Bros. gangster movie with James Cagney
   d. the new French-designed toilet for urban spaces
2. POLLYANNAISH, the term used to reassure a layperson about the Russian mafia, describes the West's policy of
   a. Puzoisme
   b. Petrograderie

c. Struwwelpetermania
d. wondering if Boris Yeltsin's glass is half full or half empty

3. SOME VALUE is
a. news value plus 20 percent discount coupon for a Happy Meal
b. the mystique of the KGB as a force for order, now that Russia is trying something else
c. vigorish on sales of Common Market products
d. voodoo physics

4. PANICKING is
a. a capitalist luxury
b. a technical correction in the financial markets
c. the God-given opportunity to invent Halcion
d. a bipolar disorder caused by the similarity of the Russian words for "Heads will roll" and "Go to the mattresses"

5. THE WHOLE WORLD is
a. the Beltway and Ann Arbor
b. a Joan Baez song
c. a fleeting nightmare during the human soul's brief transit from heaven to hell

Is this material churning up your apprehensions or grandiose control fantasies? If so, do not proceed until you have analyzed the feelings by visualizing and naming them in alphabetical order, as per the technique recommended in the official handbook by Maurice Sendak, *Alligators All Around.*

ESSAY QUESTION: *Who Will Panic?*

Construct a model panic-projection-and-resolution program, being sure to extrapolate from the "glad child" theory and principles laid down by Eleanor Hodgman Porter in *Pollyanna* and *Pollyanna Grows Up* (U.S. Government Printing Office, 1913, 1915).

Then show how your program becomes operational when, on a given tomorrow—gloomy or even rainy in parts of the international community—word leaks out that there might be something amiss in post-Soviet Russia. Impact your outcomes on lots of statistically representative lives, including these prototypes:

Mr. McGregor is a myopic old xenophobe whose idea of a weapon of mass destruction is an iron garden rake; should he scent worldwide panic, he might use it as an excuse to loot his retirement savings, thus incurring a disadvantageous tax bite. The Red Queen is armored against her own emotional instability by the trappings of monarchy; her strategic capability notwithstanding, her secretary would keep any disturbing information from her, lest she flip out and make life miserable for everybody. Histories of trauma incline the Elephant's Child and Bambi to panic attacks, but the symptomatology suggests that these are triggered by loudspeaker announcements about the ozone layer and the rain forests. Stuart Little has ended up in a forced-labor camp, so he is pretty impervious to bad news.

Makes the Going Great

> "Every other week someone says that books are dead or dying, that . . . the obliteration of distinguished literary houses and imprints in the age of the corporate takeover [is] synonymous with the inevitable disappearance of books. The hearse followers mournfully announce that no one reads these days, can't read, won't read. . . .
>
> "The book is small, lightweight and durable, and can be stuffed in a coat pocket, read in the waiting room, on the plane. What are planes but flying reading rooms?"
>
> —E. Annie Proulx, speaking at the 1994 PEN/Faulkner Awards

As a stewardess, I am of two minds about the PEN/Faulkner Awards. PEN/Faulkner is a more frantic crush than Thanksgiving, Christmas, the Frankfurt Book Fair, Whitbread or Booker time, or even the week of the Lila Acheson Wallace–Reader's Digest Writers' Grants Reception. Peak PEN/Faulkner has me on twenty-four-hour call for added flights; although that spells overtime pay and a chance to serve the public above and beyond the routine nurturing of airborne literacy, there are moments when the phone awakens me from a nap in my uniform and I must repair my *maquillage*, hail a taxi for JFK, and be courteous to avid readers and writers whose boarding passes are printed with ink-blurs of indecipherable bibliographical data and call numbers, conflicting reservations for rare editions, expired or nonapplicable guarantees of free upgrade to Belles-Lettres Class—truly, at such moments I almost wish for a job where I might help people just by twisting open Smirnoff miniatures or dispensing headsets for a first-run feature or a program of rock oldies.

But I love being a stewardess. It is the stewardess's privilege to hand out the little magnifying glasses for the compact one-volume OED stowed above each seat in the overhead bin, and then to stand in the aisle of the main cabin and demonstrate emergency procedures for consulting that incomparably useful work if need be. The stewardess is in on the romance of flight's arcane traditions and lingo; the pilot greets her with his usual line—"Coffee, tea, or McPhee?"—and she can hear, beneath the ritual laconic tease, reference to a shared code of research standards, as well as respect for the stewardess herself, a fellow professional trusted to honor the superstition about never flying with a copy of the Scottish Play on board.

Such superstitions derive from a morbid awareness of d---h which is, I suppose, an occupational disorder and which perhaps also accounts for aircraft passengers' affinity for literature. Few, it would seem, desire to plunge to a briny or fiery d---h while reading ephemera or trash. In any case, it is part of my job to be conscious of danger. Lately, stewardesses have all been taught how to conduct a body search, for even the most elaborate security-gate technology has proved unable to detect the John Grisham novels that occasionally slip through in defiance of CAB regulations. I must also keep a trained eye on the type of passenger who restlessly changes seats; unexplained movement from genre to genre may constitute a suspicious behavior pattern, unstable dilettantism, or mere browsing.

Accidents do happen. On one occasion, a live rattlesnake being shipped to Frankfurt as a promotional stunt for the Diamondback imprint escaped in the cargo hold, causing unforeseen publicity; it was found a month later, near a warm air vent, curled up on a copy of *Robinson Crusoe*. E. Annie Proulx, the novelist and futurologist who predicts that books are here to stay, is a frequent flier; she advocates bringing your own book, but books have been known to fall out of coat pockets. There is very little that air traffic control can do about such risks.

The majority of passengers rely upon the crew to meet their needs. With advance notice, we can provide virtually any book available within the web of our destination routes, via the Detroit hub—even works written in Hebrew or vegetarian. And the regular selection of reading matter is excellent, with particular depth in Virgil, Dowson, Rimbaud, Egyptology, Plath, Forensic Pathology, Poetry of World War I, Aeschylus, Twelfth-Century Social History, and Edgar Allan Poe. On the "red-eye" between LAX and JFK, you can reserve the Norton Chair, a curtained sanctuary-like carrel forward of the Classics Section. Sadly, we have yet to find a safe way to permit reading in the bathrooms. But if you feel distracted by the pilot's Yeageresque recitations from his navigational charts, it is my pleasure to tiptoe up to the flight deck, put my finger to my lips, and go "*Shhhhhh*. . . ."

The only unpleasant aspect of my job is the stereotype of stewardesses as sexless grinds with eyeglasses and sensible shoes. In fact, we have to pass a rigorous optical examination that entails reading the footnotes to *The Waste Land* in a flight simulator under conditions of heavy turbulence. As for our white boots, their sensibleness cannot be denied: the Velcro soles are a safety feature for climbing the bulkhead library ladders during takeoff and landing. The boots, as well as our chalk-white jackets and pants, allude to the costumes designed by Hardy Amies for the air hostesses in the film *2001: A Space Odyssey*. Many men who discern that allusion find us seductive, and I suspect that the others are responding phobically, to unconscious fears stimulated by the film's theme of d---h.

I am proud of my uniform, and was never more so than at the high point of my career as a stewardess—the stewardesses' strike in support of Salman Rushdie. On February 15, 1989, the day after the Ayatollah called for Mr. Rushdie's d---h, word spread quickly on the grapevine of air terminal cocktail lounges and out-of-print bookstores. I happened to be at the Holiday Inn out at LGA, in a mandatory Poise Refresher Course, and when the announcement was made in the classroom, the book fell off my head. (If memory serves, it was a novel by Tanizaki.) Our union shop immediately voted for a wildcat work stoppage; after picketing the Pan Am Building for an hour, we won our demand that the airline replace the in-flight magazine (which everyone hated anyway) with a free copy of *The Satanic Verses* in each seatback pocket.

We wanted to do something further, though, to address the issue of Mr. Rushdie's personal safety. And one of the girls came up with the idea of putting a life-sized effigy of Mr. Rushdie on every single domestic and international flight, to confuse his enemies. (She got this idea—where else?—out of a book.) Fabricating hundreds of effigies was not a formidable task, given the exacting techniques of makeup, coiffure, and grooming that every stewardess commands. We have all grown rather fond of carrying "Mr. Rushdie."

And so, if you fly Pan Am on a regular basis, now you know the explanation for that mysteriously omnipresent figure, the one who always sits next to a stewardess, in the rear row, in the only seat whose overhead reading light is never switched on. It is not really he . . . or is it?

A Good Man Is Hard to Keep: The Correspondence of Flannery O'Connor and S. J. Perelman

These imaginary letters were read at the Authors Guild Foundation's benefit dinner, "Literary Affairs," on February 27, 1995, at the Metropolitan Club in New York. Veronica Geng wrote and played the part of Flannery O'Connor and Garrison Keillor wrote and played S. J. Perelman.

Dear Sid,

Gone and got me a new dress. Black satin and it has what I hear tell they call a "plunging neckline." The lady in the fitting room at the Milledgeville store took a good hard look and then she said, "That idn't you." I said, "It is now."

Well, I reckon I sound most highly pleased with myself and for that I do thank you very kindly. "Plunging" is the word all right and I guess that is a fact.

Were they-all a bunch of geniuses in our panel discussion or was it near on to about the dopiest panel discussion ever? What I got out of it was a vision of yr starched white shirt front, blinding white like a nice new sheet of paper. What a lousy comparison, a sheet of paper hasn't got seven pearl buttons down the middle.

My mother is skeptical on this one point of your having ordered us up the room service at that Ritz. She says there is no Ritz in Iowa City. I have been telling her the juicy details so she won't want a television.

Anyhow, I was much taken with you and figure on putting you in a story. Have one going where this family on a car trip has an accident and goes into a ditch, and I need a man who comes along in a car and what all. He has blue eyes like yrs and a clean white shirt on and he has got him a picnic hamper with champagne in it and sandwiches and a portable Victrola and some jazz records.

Yrs truly,
F.

My little Peach Cobbler,

When I was a schoolboy in Providence, I spent my Saturdays sitting dazed and feverish in the balcony of the Pantages watching Mary Pickford in *Hearts Adrift* over and over until the manager pried my shoes from the floor and sent me home, and now I am in the same fever over you, but without the licorice whips. I do remember that it was the Hilton, not the Ritz, but passion is sweet no matter what the marquee, and I can't wait to make a fool of myself again as soon as possible. You are my ideal of Southern womanhood, and you have crept into my heart like kudzu. As for you putting me in a story, O.K., but be careful not to use the terms "rapier wit" or "dark flashing eyes" lest our secret be revealed and our names dragged into the gossip columns and our love cheapened. And please let me know when I can come to Milledgeville and see you. Do you have a refrigerator, by the way?

El Sid

Dear Sid,

Oh my.

Well, I thought I best ask my mama to see will it be all right putting up a New Yorker gent in the spare room. There is a nice rug in there and all. She says she don't mind but has yet to lay eyes on a man worth getting a new refrigerator for. Can you cope with an icebox which it is pretty full up with peacock feed? Don't wear those nice shoes, we are awful muddy hereabouts.

As I recollect, the newspapers have a limited interest in my affairs and are blind dumb to boot, so if I was you I wouldn't get myself in a lather about publicity.

Now on this story. Yr character is seen from an omniscient pt of view. Not one living soul would reckanize you, human nature being suchlike that you don't even reckanize your own sef. Anyways, the details are all changed around now. The dark side of you has got to emerge and the sooner the better. He has got himsef a pearl-handled gun of some kind and is inclined to push these country people to the limit just on the pure meanness of it. I don't see fit to alter my method of working to your say-so.

Yrs truly,

F.

Mon amour,

I was stitching a plume on my chapeau, all in a flush over my upcoming trip to Georgia, when the mailman dropped your letter in my lap, and I must say it gave me a violent tic and I had to smell salts when I came to the part about the gun. Gallantry, my little chickabiddy, has its limits. First you say you are going to portray me in a story as a snappy dresser with a Victrola and blue eyes, and then I become a sullen thug who terrorizes innocent people at the point of a pistol. What do you say we segue back to the love scene, fade out on my dark side, fade in to a violent mist of perfume and ambrosia, you and me in closeup, our lips intertwined? Why not sell the mules, send your mother to a Bible camp, come north, and cohabit with me at the Plaza while we write a hit musical—you supply the colorful characters, the robust scenes of peasant life, etc., and I'll provide the verbs and prepositions—and we'll retire off the royalties to a Pre-Raphaelite snuggery in the Cotswolds and recline in a bower and adore each other? Meanwhile, could you reserve me a suite at a hotel near your farm where you and I could reconnoiter when you are done with chores?

Your Sid

Dear Sid,

Well, your plan is a real horror. To my mind the bidnis of living off of royalties is downright sinful, and I would as leave be strangled in my nightdress as do any such thing.

So I do thank you most profoundly as this is the exact feeling I was after and have been all day at the typewriter banging out the truth and getting the entire family gunned down in the woods excepting the old lady. Now she is face to face with the Misfit which is what I call him as you will surely agree is the word for him if you are able to take a good clean look into yourself. He has got the pearly-handle gun pointed right at her heart. MY HE IS AS BAD AS THEY COME. She looks into his pale blue eyes and then she says, "I'd like to kiss you but I just washed my hair."

Yrs truly,
F.

My little rosebud,

I must confess that surrealism is, to me, a powerful aphrodisiac and that I am thrilled by attractive women who say bizarre things. The dashing, sloe-eyed, silken-skinned Sid you know from the Sunday rotogravure was once a bohemian too, my sweet. Back when Edna St. Vincent Millay and I used to dip candles in her loft in the Village, I swapped symbolism with the best of them, wrote sonnets on mutability and decay, wore black silk shirts, read Rilke, drank espresso, the whole megillah, so believe me, kid, I can be as Gothic as the next guy. Kafka, let me remind you, was not a Southern Baptist, and if you enjoy spooky stories, I have a snootful—but why be obsessed with darkness when the bright lights beckon? My ticket to Georgia is purchased and sits atop the bureau, my shoes are polished, my hosiery is folded and wrapped in tissue, my white flannels are pressed, my heart is pounding like a triphammer, my palms are clammy with anticipation, but of course I won't come if I am only going to serve as the model for a psychopath. At the risk of sounding like Norman St. Vincent Peale, why not lighten up a little? If you want to wash your hair, come up to New York. We have hair dryers here.

Yours,
SID

Dear Sid,

Well, we have us a disaster here with our icebox, which is of a mind to go crazy every oncet in a while. The only one who can fix it is a convict who comes down from the Atlanta pen, so I am waiting on him and can't travel. Besides my mother says there is not a man on the face of this earth who she would allow to visit without a good supply of ice to hand.

Please give my very kindest regards to Miss Edna whoever that may be.

Yrs truly,
F.

My Dream Team

Senator Specter: Didn't it cross your mind . . . that your evidentiary position would be much stronger if you had made some notes?
Anita Hill: No it did not.
Senator Specter: Well, why not?
Anita Hill: I don't know why it didn't cross my mind.

> *Senator Specter*: Well, the law of evidence is that notes are very important. You are nodding yes. Present recollection refreshed, right?
> *Anita Hill*: Yes, indeed.
> *Senator Specter*: Prior recollection recorded, right?
> *Anita Hill*: Yes.
>
> —Clarence Thomas–Anita Hill Hearings, October 11, 1991

Inaudible. Tinny laugh. "Don't get mad, now. Maybe I'm being too childlike or idealistic but the last thing I am is manipulative. All I want to do is clear the air."

I hereby affirm that the person whose words I just wrote down while pretending to work and ignore him, and whose actions I intend to note insofar as I can see while feigning inattention and writing fast enough to keep up with his lohgh lhoggohr shit what a stupid word to pick under this kind of pressure his blabbering—I do solemnly swear and state that this person is one and the same Mr. Barry Sloat, co-worker and subject of Contemporaneous Notes Parts 1–85; and further I avow that this, Part 86, commences on October 6, 1995, 3:45 P.M., when Mr. Sloat made known his presence in my office doorway, whereupon I once again made Standard Warning Statement (as per Manual, p. 5) in conformance with EEOC Anti-Entrapment Guidelines (Attachment to Part 1) and then wrote down what he said, contemporaneously with his saying it. By the way (chance here to squeeze this in while Mr. Sloat pausing for dramatic effect enjoyed by him alone), I also attest that I am not type of woman who normally uses "shit" as expletive, but crossing it out now might look as if I have something to hide.

Mr. Sloat resumed talking few seconds ago but only telling *au pair* anecdote again (#4: see Appendix A, Full Versions of *Au Pair* Anecdotes He Tells). Heeeeere's punch line! and braying self-infatuated

Please excuse preceding intemperate digression, Your Honor or Whoever will read this. Now I missed stuff, blah blah up to "so everything I said before is a classic con, and you're smart enough to see right through it, sit there working oh so brilliantly with your brilliant uncompromising brilliance, which don't get me wrong is exactly why I respect you and not these other pathetic cheese bitches—" Not sure that can be what he actually said. Now lost more stuff, sorry, up to "outsmart yourself. Nobody's for real, right? The whole world is a fraud? And this makes you what? The perfect pigeon for another guy coming along with an emotion-based pitch you're too lonely to resist? Do you ever relax? Now let *me* ask *you* a question. Your favorite color is burgundy."

Mr. Sloat staring expectantly. I glance at my watch (3:53 P.M.), then up at him with discouraging frown (from list of Nonverbal Body-language Terminations of Interaction, p. 6 of Manual). Can feel Special Agent Victor Cortez shift position slightly in hiding place under my desk, evidently impatient for me to keep Mr. Sloat rolling without enticement, and I here acknowledge that I understand Enticement as defined in US Sup. Ct. *Snake* v. *Plissken*, and agree to abide

Mr. Sloat rolling, blabbetty-blab, old material from before, had a hard year . . . divorce . . . would I hide $100,000 in cash in my apartment . . . dislikes anti-Semitism . . . feels threatened by me because told me about secret $100,000 . . . would I cover for him if he stays home from work—oh sure, Sloat won't be in today, fell down stairs cleaning his gun—excuse me, Your Honor or Whoever, but really, although I agreed to take notes one more time, to supplement Agent Cortez's sound-recording, copying down whatever Mr. Sloat says has component of involuntary complicity that is SICKENING, and since he just repeats self I would prefer to use this time and space for higher purpose.

First, I recommend that Agent Cortez get commendation for offering to handle intractable situation and conducting self impeccably even today in position of what must surely be intense physical discomfort crouched between my legs. Although he has personal relationship with my family going back to 1968 when my brother saved his life in Laos, Agent Cortez volunteered to help me without making long-winded speeches or using U.S. Government supplies. On his own time, he coordinated our Dream Team, which will undoubtedly perform to his high standard. They too should be singled out for commendation:

- Col. Cameron R. Ryan, USMC (ret.), former Pest Control prosecutor, Parris Island. Thank you, sir!
- Mrs. Constance Kilowicz, FBI field agent on pregnancy leave. Hungry for action—and here's hoping she'll see plenty of it today!
- Father Devlin Paul Monahan, SJ, Prof. of Ethics, Notre Dame University. Initially retained as a consultant, Father showed up in such prime shape that he also became the team's fitness trainer.
- Josiah Lucien Belvedere, Minister of Defense. One hundred and ninety pounds of power and mental alertness.
- Det. Lt. Samuel Mohr, NYPD Bunco Squad. An expert in human nature, Sam recruited John Doe for us.
- John Doe, stoolie now in Witness Protection Program. Interesting guy. Back in 1987 he helped Sam on a high-profile case against bilko artist Stuart Van Cleef, who then made verbal threat to "get" Mr. Doe someday. Van Cleef is still incarcerated, but photos in which he bears a slight facial resemblance to Mr. Barry Sloat are being used to churn up and refocus Mr. Doe's paranoid impulses. We're all keeping our fingers crossed that Mr. Doe is about to achieve a therapeutic purgation.
- Jonny Forty, sound engineer. Bruce Springsteen most generously revamped his entire studio schedule so Jonny could fit us in while mixing *Tell It to the Boss* (in a workplace, Jonny reports, where women are worshiped to such an extent that

Uh-oh, my assistant, Ms. Karen Dickinson, just came to door—could wreck everything. Ms. D: "Excuse me for interrupting, but Mr. O'Gross just asked me to get him coffee when I had just gotten him coffee. Which seemed kind of weird. So I was just wondering if it seems weird to you." Now Mr. Sloat starts to tell her *au pair* anecdote—don't know which one, cut him off. Self to Ms. D: "That's in the Manual, Karen, page 17, Appropriate Intervals Between Refreshment Requests." Ms. D: "Oh." "I'm making a note of it. You make a note of it next time and O'Gross's days are numbered. But it has to be a contemporaneous note, which means right while he's talking. Like the way I'm writing what we're saying right now." Ms. D: "Well, but why would he do something like that, though?" "If you give your mind over to that metaphysical question, you'll forget to make the note, or you won't make a timely note, and then you're screwed when they ask where are your notes or why did you wait so long before going on the record." Ms. D: "Oh."

Now she's gone. Now Mr. Sloat's body language indicates he mentally reconnoitering his legal position. Meanwhile, I herewith petition Court or Whatever Body to review Manual, which I understand is pragmatic incrementalist tool for setting limits on accurate description of reality but is arbitrarily selective. Now Mr. Sloat, body language evincing empowerment by aforesaid limitations of Manual, takes one, two steps into office, slams door shut behind him, shouts "I am a very angry person!" starts sobbing violently. Sobbing scene always lasts long time. Agent Cortez has read about it in previous Notes, but firsthand experience shocking (my hearsay conclusion based on his breathy sounds, "Whew!" "Sheesh!" and "Pff!"). Also audible, faint crackle from his earphone receiver, indication Dream Team communicating re positions as they break up into assault wedge w/cuffs and net, persuasion unit, and larger backup group sealing elevator/stairwell/cafeteria exits and fanning out to secure corridor/management perimeter. Cont'd sobbing from Mr. Sloat shut up shut up. I apologize, Your Honor or Whoever, that simply popped out.

Back to Dream Team:

- Wes Buddy Clothier, de facto resolution expert, on *pro bono* furlough from Attica. To get to the point, because I don't have all day here, this man embodies the human capacity for change. A former notary public who abused that trust, he is now the prison's paralegal and toastmaster. Agent Cortez (who heard about him from a woman they had both dated under circumstances irrelevant to the events and time frame of these Notes) got him a provisional reduction of his sentence for Aggravated Menacing with a Notary Seal. In exchange, Wes would persuade my employer to deal with Mr. Sloat through corporate punishment channels, obviating the need for *ad hoc* special-ops intervention. It's no reflection on Wes's skills that he failed, at which point he was reassigned to the team as a warm body. Talk about motivated!

- Mia Farrow. My idea. Although Mia is comparatively small, she works out and is strong. And quite the tactician. A joy to have aboard.
- Richard Shigeta, criminalistics. A student at John Jay College of Criminal Justice, he is my hairdresser's brother. Evidently the Japanese have a code of fierce loyalty to their siblings' clients, a trait you see sadly little of in Occidentals. Richard has bright new ideas on fingerprinting which he's raring to test in the real world, starting with Mr. Barry Sloat.
- Skip (pseudonym), mercenary.
- My boyfriend, my brother, and a gang of my brother's friends were deemed too personally involved and overwrought to submit to command discipline, but have done valiant unofficial duty as gofers, drivers, finaglers, relief, and detailees. Their volatility has been a good reminder that the rest of us are not yet vigilante barbarians. (Some people notably absent from this support faction have families or key social or business contacts that precluded

Sorry, Your Honor or Whoever, this is now not strictly contemporaneous, but the operation went down fast. At 4:45 P.M. Mr. Sloat stopped sobbing, said clearly "I have a reputation to protect," then seized my plastic metric-measurements pencil holder and tried to use it as a voice-altering device. Agent Cortez, in whose evaluation the legal threshold had been crossed, gave the signal. The door burst open, and the room filled with gray clouds of fingerprint powder. When the air cleared, Mr. Sloat was gone.

- Security guard wounded in final scene, identity unknown as of this writing.

La Cosa Noshtra

(The missing chapter from Mario Puzo's Godfather*)*

I'll start with Connie Corleone's wedding to that despicable Carlo. Handled beautifully. Security was fantastic. And the dancing—you couldn't tell who was security and who wasn't security. My husband, Clemenza, had grown quite heavy by then, but was light on his feet. And the food—all on ice. Huge bags of ice brought in and replaced every half-hour. Invisible under the white tablecloths. The food just rested gently on these hidden beds of ice. The sun could beat down—not one single poisoning. The organization that went into it was miraculous. Some FBI came in cars, and Connie's older brother Sonny made them leave the driveway because they were blocking the union ice trucks.

Now, let me flash back here to Sicily. I'm fifteen, I'm aspiring to be an opera singer, some men come from America and talk to my parents. I listen, I hear "New York," I hear "Clemenza." So I think I'm being sent to the Metropolitan Opera to sing in *La Clemenza di Tito*. That's a work by Mozart. *La Clemenza di Tito*, it means the clemency of the Emperor Titus. He catches his wife with somebody—the story isn't so great, but it's good music. The soprano role is Vitellia, a good role. Vitellia! But no. They say I have to marry this man Peter Clemenza. I ask who he is. They say he's a *caporegime*. I think, *caporegime*—that must be the rehearsal master, or the conductor. O.K., good. But once we're married he tells me, "Never open your mouth."

It turns out *caporegime* over here means working for Vito Corleone, in the olive oil business. At first we lived in Hell's Kitchen—that means 10th Avenue. Vito, now, he was genteel. When he came to the house, he liked just a simple, honest plate of bread, salami, and olives. Never dessert, never those vulgar cream pastries—he liked just a piece of fresh fruit. So I never had those pastries in the house. Clemenza would eat them somewhere. Slip into restaurants for extra meals—a little pasta, the veal, a glass of wine, finish with an espresso and a couple of cannoli. I had aspired to be an opera singer and the one thing an opera singer will not touch is a cannoli. The cream filling—it does something to your vocal cords, it's like a drug, it thickens the voice. The one thing you'll never see is Maria Callas and Giuseppe di Stefano wolf down a box of cannoli before going on stage to sing *Tosca*.

So not long after Connie's wedding, Vito Corleone buys oranges from a street vendor and ends up in the hospital. I feel terrible, because I had foreseen something bad would happen, but no, I'm supposed to keep my mouth shut. This young man Paulie, Vito's regular chauffeur—Paulie had been coming around complaining he was sick and could Clemenza get him off work. I could see this Paulie was faking. He said he had a bad cold. He had a handkerchief up to his nose, a big white cloth he was waving around—ridiculous, it was the size of the nightgown for *La Sonnambula*. And the coughing and the sniffling—oh, please, a travesty of Mimi in Act IV of *La Bohème*. How exactly this led to Vito's eating a poison orange I didn't know, but obviously this Paulie was evil. So after it's too late, Clemenza sends for him. I'm hoping at least he'll take Paulie for a ride in the car, poison him, and good riddance.

All I did was knock on the garage and tell Clemenza, Paulie is here. There is a rumor about me—a complete myth—that as they got in the car, I called out, "Don't forget the cannoli!" I suspect Connie was behind this, spreading this lie. Not that she didn't have her own troubles. She couldn't send her own husband even for Chinese food.

You know what's in a cannoli? First, it's cream, heavy cream, and eggs. Like a custard. Wrapped in dough. Sometimes they put in ricotta. You buy those, you have them in a car, sun beating down—O.K., they're in a box, not even a real box, a flat piece of thin cardboard folded into a box shape and tied with string. First the wax paper inside, then the string so you can carry the cannoli. Then the box gets bent or crushed, the string is tied with that one loose end so if somebody pulls it the whole thing unravels, there's no refrigeration in the car, maybe security isn't so good—by the time you get home, poison. So to anyone who believes I called out "Don't forget the cannoli!" I answer this: Clemenza and I, Catholics, we go to all the trouble of getting married and not using birth control and having children—only to poison them and ourselves with cannoli?

To tell the truth, though, as Paulie backed the car out of the driveway, I was hoping he'd run over the children and kill them. But of course you can't say this for some reason. God forbid you should utter some temperamental remark.

Then Michael. Suddenly Michael gets an overwhelming desire to eat in a restaurant. I don't know what it was—a cannoli, maybe a sfogliatelle, BOOM! He has to be sent to Sicily to recover. Then Sonny—this was 1946, 1947, postwar, you don't know what's in a cannoli at this point. Meanwhile, thanks to this whole story, I miss Pippo di Stefano's debut at La Scala. 1946.

So eventually Michael came back and married Kay, the girlfriend from New England. I always liked Kay. Educated, listened to music. A little deficient in temperament. They said Connie had temperament, but she didn't. Connie's idea of a singer was this Johnny Fontane person. He was all right, popular, God-given vocal cords, but he was no Pippo. Then they all moved to Las Vegas. Suddenly Las Vegas was someplace. These people were living in a dream world. Oh, let's all move to Las Vegas, and Fredo is gonna make a lot of money with Johnny Fontane.

I was obliged to remain here with Clemenza. We moved into Vito's old house—a big place, quiet. Later I heard that Frankie Pentangeli was out in Las Vegas, telling them Clemenza died of a heart attack, like Vito, but that was far from true. Willie Cicci knew it was no heart attack, but he was poisoned in some kind of stupid gunplay.

Have you ever really looked at a cannoli? It's wrapped—the dough is wrapped across. Like an overcoat. With this filling inside. You line these up on a plate, they're lying there. Spare me the sight of these revolting—*Mi fa schifo.* That's difficult to translate. It means, "I skeev on them."

ABOUT THE AUTHOR

Veronica Geng, a writer, editor, and critic, was born in Atlanta, Georgia, in 1941. She grew up in Philadelphia and attended the University of Pennsylvania. In 1975 she joined the staff of the *New Yorker*, where she wrote and edited until 1993. Her work, including film and book reviews, also appeared in other periodicals. Two volumes of her stories were published before her death in December 1997. Veronica Geng once told the *Christian Science Monitor* that *Alice in Wonderland* "and the paperback collection of the Watergate transcripts are my two favorite books. They're not unlike each other."